THE GATOR
LEAVES NOTHING BEHIND
PART I

THE DISTURBING HISTORY SAGA

KAMI BOLEY

www.boleybooks.com

16477 Live Oak Drive

Prairieville, LA 70769

Published by Boley Books LLC

Printed in the United States of America

ISBN: 978-0-9975217-9-5

ISBN: 978-0-9975217-8-8 (ebook)

To surviving histories and building futures . . .

For my daughter Kirstie

and

My inner child (the struggle is over, rest now and dream)

Contents

Saturday
July 4, 1964

Why didn't I learn to swim?

is the first thing that pops into my head while flying through the ungraspable mid-morning air. The blow my hip sustained on the portside railing is already throbbing when the water slaps me in the face. The brackish water embraces me and pulls me close as if to apologize. Now submerged, my ears fill with the vicious buzzing of the propeller as it just misses my head. In a soundless scream, I lose the last of my air. Frantically, I scratch my way through underwater flora to follow my bubbles to their destination, barely breaching the surface before my lungs betray me. Through ragged chokes I greedily gulp the air—there may not be another chance.

Must stay calm and float,

I think, attempting to tread water. As I bob up and down in the boat's wake, everything becomes intermittently vivid and fuzzy—a feeling quite familiar to me, having passed out on several prior occasions.

Slow breaths . . . slow breaths . . .

I plead with myself, a litany to fight the ebb of consciousness. I'm surprised at my ability to stay afloat, to keep my nose just above the water line—until I feel the reason beneath my bare feet: something below, beneath the murky waters, something odd ... unyielding, covered in a layer of slime. Its assistance is surely crucial to my survival, and so I am willing to endure the sick, squishy feeling underfoot.

The panicked thumping of blood in my ears subsides enough for me to think beyond drowning and I begin to survey the situation, bouncing from my slimy springboard to get a better look, each time trusting my feet will again land in the same spot.

What the hell just happened?
A fine July fourth outing this turned out to be—my hip is killing me!
Where is he? He has to have realized that I'm not in the boat,

I think impatiently, despite the fact that the boat seems to be turning around in the distance. Out of the corner of my eye I spot my sun hat floating, sneaking away on the shallow ripples that remain from the boat's wake.

How I've always loved that bright pink hat.
It came with a matching sundress that no longer fits.

The hat is too far away, but I reach out in vain. Considering my swimming skills—or lack thereof—I decide to stay put. Perhaps the hat can be retrieved later.

Does he not see me?

I think, realizing that the boat is headed toward the hat, which has now drifted even farther away.

Maybe he saves the hat first?

My foot slips. I scramble to find my mysterious platform. Just as my nose once again breaches the surface, I see the boat speed up, raging through the water, aiming, shredding my favorite hat under its angry hull.

I blink, wide-eyed. Could this mean what it implies?

Did he . . . did he mean for me to fall out?

A brand-new kind of panic washes over me. The pounding of my heartbeat in my ears is almost deafening; so much so that it prevents me from hearing the hungry propeller return . . .

Saturday
September 6, 1958

Chop! chop! chop! the knife repeats as it splits apart the flesh of a large yellow onion. Another sacrifice for this morning's hash.

Mary has been fascinated with onions ever since she learned that ancient Egyptians worshiped them, believing they saw eternal life within the many rings. She has mastered making artful incisions into this pungent necessity, but she isn't as skilled in preventing the tears that inevitably follow. For that, she has tried everything from soaking the onions in milk first to wearing her father's reading glasses as a makeshift shield. One day, when she has some money, she plans to buy swimming goggles and test that method; for now, she has to wince and endure the pain of the onion's acrid juices.

Once this necessary torture is over, Mary smiles in relief and tosses half the bits into the heated pan, where they sizzle and hiss, forming a warm caramel-colored glaze.

Onions are a must-have in the creation of almost every recipe she knows—the total of which can be counted on just one of her overworked hands. Whoever said variety is the spice of life wasn't trying to feed ten hungry mouths on one meager income. Prepared a multitude of ways, the potato is another delicacy their poor family could not survive without. Add a few freshly laid eggs and some spices, and you can call it breakfast.

Mary's first lesson in potato preparation had been to remove their myriad eyes. At six years old, she was greatly disturbed by the idea that these defenseless vegetables were watching in horror as she performed optical surgery. It had been days before she gathered the intestinal fortitude to ask her mother, Vivian, if the spuds could actually see—that is, before their eyes were snatched away by the flicks of her tiny kitchen knife.

Splatter from fat and grease speckles the tin backsplash. Mary reduces the gas flame flicking along the sides of the well-seasoned cast iron pan. Satisfied with the deep golden hue, she gives the dish one last dash of Morton salt and a final toss before snuffing the flame altogether. She wishes for meat to add to the table, but the pig is being saved for the holidays, and the chickens already gave their contribution this morning.

The smell of breakfast in the air draws the attention of her empty-bellied brothers and sisters throughout the house, as is made evident by the stampede of bare feet slapping on the worn oak floor.

"There are biscuits on the table. Only take one each!" Mary says, barely turning to greet them while she scrapes the last of the eggs into the serving dish.

"Can I feed the twins?" Sarah asks, separating her biscuit into two even halves.

"No, they had some mush earlier," Mary says, hurriedly placing a small dish of fig preserves in front of Sarah as consolation. "I'm sure you could be a big help come lunchtime, though."

Mary touches the tip of her little sister's nose, leaving a syrupy fingerprint. Sarah appreciates the affection by wearing her mark proudly.

The kitchen soon fills with the normal chaos that eight children tend to generate in such a small space. *"Nana nana boo boo, we're gonna get you,"* taunt two of the boys, sending their younger sisters squealing around the kitchen table.

There is no worry about the noise—Mother wakes from her hibernation for no one. It's when Vivian is up that everyone cowers in silence.

Mary continues her breakfast duties, oblivious to the ruckus that surrounds her, dodging obstacles large and small. She nimbly avoids catastrophe time after time, providing her siblings with servings of aromatic sustenance. She had cared for this brood of seven younger siblings ever since she could reach the stovetop on a chair, and is now a seasoned professional.

"EEEEKK!" shrieks Jenny.

"What's the problem?" Mary asks, hoping it doesn't involve the food.

"SPIDER! He's gonna get me! KILL IT!" Jenny bellows, nervously rising up onto the nearest chair.

Mary grabs a used rag from the counter. "No, don't kill it! Give me a minute and I can put it outside."

"But he's *sick*. Look at him . . . he's *green*," Jenny says in an almost concerned tone, revealing the spider's location with a small finger.

Mary follows Jenny's rigidly frightened pointer to the culprit. It has made itself as small as possible, cowering against the baseboard. It is apparently unaware that it is no chameleon, with its bright green and orange body against the old white paint.

Mary crouches to study him further. "That's an orb-weaver . . . he's supposed to be green, so his enemies don't see him hanging out in the garden." With one adroit motion, she scoops the skinny arachnid up in the small rag.

"It's *weeeird*! Why can't we just kill it?" Jenny blurts, twisting her face up in disgust as the rag passes her at eye level.

"Because I don't think he'd hurt you any, so we'll give him the benefit of the doubt."

"Fine, but when it sneaks in and bites you, I bet you'll wish you killed it *then*."

"I'm not afraid of this little spider, and you shouldn't be either." Mary holds the rag in front of her, careful not to squish its passenger while opening the screen door with her backside. As soon as Jenny feels safe enough, she scrambles to the door to make sure Mary's task is completed without anyone falling prey to the heinous creature.

After a thorough shake, Mary adds the rag to a pile of soiled articles on the back porch. "There, now. All gone." She lightly brushes her hands together and displays them palm side up for investigation by the pint-sized sentry. "Now go eat, or I *will* find it and put it in your bed."

Jenny turns in a huff. She brushes her older brother Jason aside as she stomps back to the table, accidentally knocking the last of Jason's breakfast to the floor in the process. A chunk of biscuit is now strewn, inedible, at his feet. While cleaning it up, he mutters something only for Jenny's ears, setting her eyes ablaze.

"Am *not*! You take that back!"

Jason snickers, scraping the crumbled mess into the trash before placing his dish in the sink. Nothing further is required of him to send her into artful retaliation. Jenny's anger, even when suppressed, can offer a sting of ample poison—more so than any spider.

"Mary, can I use your dictionary to look up a word?" Jenny asks, arms folded and face configured in an advanced stage of pouting. "Jason called me a six-year-old *coo yon*, and he won't tell me what that means."

Mary cuts her eyes over to Jason, who immediately shrugs in denial at Jenny's accusation.

Mary speaks in a firm voice: "We do not call each other stupid or crazy in this house in any way, shape, or form. Is that understood?" She pauses, her eyes scanning faces for a trickling of *"Yes, ma'am"* responses. Considering Jenny has developed an awful habit of tearing pages out of books, Mary doesn't want to let her sister touch her prized dictionary, so she adds, "Besides, that's Cajun slang. Not something you'd find in the dictionary."

Mary received the dictionary as a gift from her father years ago, on her first day of school. She was unable to read it at the time, but he told her it would someday help to explain the meaning of things in the world around her. Now fifteen, Mary loves that dictionary, with its gamut of words and wisdom. It is the only book she can call her own—except a small secondhand Bible, compliments of the local Welcome Wagon.

Her father had purchased each of her brothers a dictionary, too, when they'd started school, but the boys didn't take care of theirs. Mary had suggested to her father that he should wait until Jenny matured a little before giving her one of her own.

The ordeal of breakfast has ended, and the kitchen is empty once again. Elbow-deep in sudsy water, Mary removes all evidence of the meal she's lovingly prepared for her siblings. She's done it all so many times before. But this time is different—this is the first time she wants to be somewhere else. Her mother Vivian had promised Mary that she could spend this weekend with Gayle, her best friend in the whole world.

Please let Mom come downstairs soon.

The mantra repeats in her head as she looks out the window and sees Gayle crossing the street. As usual, Vivian is still in bed. Mary frantically searches the rooms for chores left undone.

Gayle comes in through the screen door. As she looks around at the all-too-familiar scenario, disappointment spreads over her face like a dam that's just given way. Mary lowers her head, preparing for the tongue-lashing that's bound to follow.

"MARY LOU POCHE, you mean to tell me that you're stuck caring for these ankle-biters on our big day?" Gayle says, hands perched furiously on her narrow hips. "Where's the warden?"

"Shhhh!" Mary puts her finger to her lips, like they teach you in kindergarten, despite the fact that Vivian sleeps like a rock. She whispers, "Mom isn't down yet . . . and I haven't told her where we're going." She removes her cooking garb and points at Gayle's shoes, which they both know are forbidden beyond the front room.

"Why are you whispering? It's like a damn zoo in here." Gayle cocks her head, noting the obnoxious monkey impersonation coming from the next room.

"What haven't you told me, little girl?" Vivian exhales in a tone of disgust, slowly descending the stairs. The girls both look up, jolted by her sudden presence and sharp glare. The stairs moan under her substantial weight and seem to let out a sigh of relief as she reaches the bottom.

As matriarch of a large family, Vivian rules with the disconnect of a commander, rather than the warmth and compassion normally associated with the role. The children feel a drop in temperature with her arrival and the primate sounds cease.

"I was hoping it would be all right if we go to the festival that started today," Mary says tentatively, with a progressively tighter wince as her mother moves closer.

Vivian doesn't respond just yet, but her arms folding across her chest are answer enough.

Mary adds quickly, "Gayle already has her parents' permission to go."

"I guess that means I'm supposed to let you run wild like a heathen, too, huh?" Vivian growls, deflecting the parental peer pressure.

Mary just shrugs, knowing that any opposition at this point will surely end in defeat. She waits for her mother to process the information, the moment shrouded in a heavy silence and Vivian's brutal stare of intimidation. Mary deflects her gaze to the floor to make this part easier to bear. The unnatural quiet nearly causes Gayle to come unglued.

An eon passes with only the sounds of shallow breathing and the ticking clock. The younger children sit in the next room like eager newshounds outside a courtroom, all waiting for a verdict.

Eventually Vivian speaks: "Did you feed the chickens and the young 'uns?" Her eyes cut like ice and her folded arms tighten with contempt.

"I did everything you asked me to," Mary nods, adding sweetly, "I even chopped extra onions for the gumbo tonight."

Vivian continues to eye the two girls with suspicion, from their ponytails to their bobby socks.

"Oh, please let us go! We will be on our best behavior, I promise," Mary says, in desperation. She wears her best sad-puppy face, knowing her mother is not an easy woman to please and is unlikely to let her fifteen-year-old daughter loose with just a gal pal at her side. Mary glances at the clock over her mother's shoulder. She swallows hard, feeling the sensation of tears rising from her throat and gathering just behind her eyes. Preparing for disappointment, Mary takes a long, painful breath into her tightened chest.

The tension grows. Gayle chews on a nail to keep her mouth occupied.

Vivian's lip curls. She swats Gayle's hand away from her face. "You won't get any money from me," she says, "and you'll have to call from the bus station on your own dime. There and back."

"We will!" Gayle almost shrieks. She shoves Mary out the door as they grab their shoes. "THANKS A MILLION, Mrs. Vivian!" She adds in an undertone to Mary, "Let's get gone before she changes her mind."

The girls squeal with delight at their success. Gayle marvels at having convinced Mary to step out of her rigid normalcy. The high Mary experiences is a dangerous one—the exhilaration that comes from risk. Any gambler who's lost everything started with that brief tingly feeling of power over their future. Luckily, Mary only allows herself to taste it, and then lets the feeling pass without swallowing.

"Did you check out my new pedal pushers?" she asks Gayle, giving her hip a cocky upward twist as they move along the driveway, crunching oyster shells beneath them.

"They're very cute pants . . . just like Sandra Dee's," Gayle says, though her tone isn't convincing.

"They're as close as I could get, anyway," Mary says, eyeing the cheap fabric. "We made the Sears order back in July. If I'd known it would take till now to get them, I'd have made them myself. Two months! I was beginning to think I was going to have to wear one of my flour-sack dresses."

"Your homemade dresses aren't as awful as you think. I really like the one I dumped the purple ink on. It came out such a lovely shade of lavender." Gayle keeps a straight face, though her voice is full of amusement.

"Along with all my *underwear*," Mary says, her eyes slanted in accusation in Gayle's direction. "I'm lucky I do my own laundry. If my mother saw that, my hide might have turned lavender, too."

Dresses made of flour-sack and feed-sack material have been fine to get Mary through each summer—until now. Most years her father can only afford to buy the children clothes once a year, and usually during that time, they outgrow most of their wardrobe. They find clever ways of making the most out of what they have, by turning pants into shorts, handing down clothing, and such. Mary's know-how with the secondhand Singer sewing machine has come in handy many times.

Wearing homemade clothes didn't seem to matter when she was younger, playing in the red dirt back in Provencal where she grew up. People in the country didn't seem to care about what she wore. They never looked at each other the way they do here in Houma. Just the thought of wearing one of those dresses *here* makes Mary's eyes darken as if a cloud has crossed her face.

Her gaze falls to the shell road that resembles shattered crockery. It's been worn thin by travel in what seems like such a short time—it's only been two years since her family moved here. But it feels as if some part of her has been here all along.

"Penny for your thoughts," Gayle probes.

"I'm just being silly," Mary says, bumping shoulders with her pal in reassurance.

"Good, because you can't be poopie on such a beautiful day," Gayle says with a twirl, arms spread in the air ready to embrace the morning sky. She flashes a brilliant smile. "Especially when I have a surprise."

Mary lifts her head out of her rumination and gives Gayle a squinty sideways glance. "What are you up to, Miss Ma'am?"

"Remember when you helped my mom cook for the bake sale at church?" Gayle's eyebrows enunciate along with her words.

"Yeah, aaand . . . ?" Mary says, circling her hand with impatience, urging for an immediate conclusion.

"Well, I told her about us making the cheer squad . . . and she wants to pay for your uniform," Gayle explains proudly.

"Really? I was going to ask—"

"Who? Your mom? We both know your mom would tan your hide or make you quit if she knew that it was going to cost her a dime. Why is she always so sore, anyway? You make straight A's, do all your chores, volunteer, and practically raise your brothers and sisters like

they're your own kids. You can't get any more goody-goody than that."
Gayle makes an exaggerated eye roll and a quick gagging gesture.

"She's just tired, that's all," Mary says, glancing back at the house.
She loves it, despite its decay.

Gayle raises her hands in front of her like a mime trapped behind
a pane of make-believe glass. "*Please* tell me you did not just defend
her! The only thing that could make her tired is watching you all day."

"Tell your mom thanks a bunch for the uniform. She's a peach.
Make sure she knows I didn't expect anything for helping out," Mary
says, avoiding the real issue.

"She knows that, you big lug." Gayle grabs hold of her best
friend's hand, falling back into silence while Mary reflects.

Gayle's got a point . . . Why is Mom always so grumpy?
I've only ever seen her happy a handful of times.

The term *postpartum depression* has not yet been coined, but that
doesn't prevent the illness from existing. Mrs. Vivian Poche seems to
be suffering this particular affliction sevenfold. Why seven, you ask?
Because she was satisfied after having her firstborn, Mary, the one and
only child she was completely prepared for or wanted. Every one of
the seven children born thereafter has worn her thin.

At this time, birth control in South Louisiana is not readily
available to women. Men have the say in whether or not to plant a
seed. Besides, having large families is the norm due to the labor
needed to run a household. On top of this, Louisiana has always been
so steeped in Catholicism, the only state in the Union to call their

division of land a *parish* instead of a county—so even if an oral birth control were available, it still wouldn't be close to social acceptance or obtainable by a family of insufficient means.

I try so hard to be a good girl, to make my parents proud . . .
Why doesn't Mom ever notice?
It almost seems the more I do, the angrier she is.

Realizing these thoughts could erode the carefree tone of the day, Mary drifts to thoughts of a more pleasant figure in her world—her father.

The Norman Poche she knows is a hardworking good ole boy, always making sure that he has a good word for anyone and everyone. He's a man who needs very little to make him happy—a cup of coffee, the day's headlines, and a puff on a pipe after a decent meal. He often manages to make Mary feel like a princess even when the world seems against her, and his protection includes the cushioning of anything harsh her mother dishes out. She loves her father dearly, and hopes to someday marry someone just like him.

My daddy loves me to the moon and back,

she thinks, beaming. Her smile broadens as she searches her mind for the best dictionary entry to describe her father, her shiny ebony hair rocking to and fro as she walks.

Gayle can't help but notice her friend's mood shift after receiving a tap or two from Mary's whip-like ponytail. *Who could compete with that?* Gayle thinks as she admires the smiling face of the blue-eyed beauty walking beside her. *It's a damn good thing I have my sense of humor.*

Mary has matured a good bit over the summer, developing the kind of features that solicit the fascination of both male and female eyes. Of course, with her wavy chestnut hair and big brown eyes, Gayle is no ogre by any stretch. In fact, before Mary moved to town, she had been considered the prettiest girl in her class. Gayle rarely concerns herself much with how she rates in the looks department. Her wild, infectious personality is how she manages to gain favor, always onstage no matter where she happens to be.

"I bet we can hitch a ride into town with Mr. Melancon," Gayle says, hearing the familiar backfire of the milk truck as it approaches, on time as usual.

Four slender arms waving in the air, the girls flag down the unsuspecting transportation. Brakes abrasively squeak as the truck comes to a halt. The girls skip up to the door, ready to pounce upon the driver's good-willed nature.

Mary can't help but smile in the milkman's presence. Mr. Melancon always reminds her of a man-sized marshmallow—all in white, sweet as candy, and a bit on the puffy side.

"Can I help you ladies with something?" His inquiry is hesitant; it perplexes him to see his customers' offspring greet him in the middle of the street.

"We were hoping we could catch a ride to town, if it wouldn't be too much trouble," Gayle solicits, demurely pawing at the shell road with her shoe—an act he can easily see through.

"Let me think about it while I get this delivered to your folks," he says with a wink before removing his foot from the brake, letting the truck roll forward and lurching into gear.

"You think he'll do it?" Mary asks doubtfully as they continue walking to the end of the road.

"Of course he will. Didn't you catch the wink? He just wanted us to squirm a minute or two. For a smart girl, you really can be a little slow sometimes."

"I'm hip . . . I dig . . . you're a cool kitten with an angle." Mary recites from a movie, but it sounds awkward coming from her lips. She adds, "I'm just not as conniving and presumptuous as some people."

"Nice comeback. You might survive high school after all. You have to try harder this year to fit in and speak their language. Just remember—they can smell fear." Gayle had spent some time over the summer teaching Mary to stand up for herself against the tyranny of a group of girls known as the "Ettes." (Not sure why they call themselves that, but most boys know them as the Bimbettes. Seemingly, all are guilty of allowing quite a bit of base action with little conversation required.)

It isn't long before the intermittent rattle of the milk truck's engine comes creeping up behind them.

"He really needs to get the timing adjusted on that thing," Gayle mumbles, flashing Mary an *I-told-you-so* expression as the truck slows down to pick them up.

"You girls headed to the fair?" asks the milkman, already suspecting as they quickly board the truck that he has been recruited for an adventurous cause.

"Yes, sir!" the girls answer in harmony.

"I can't bring you all the way there, but I can get you close," Mr. Melancon says. He gives them a chance to get settled before finding his pedals. The cabin is cool, despite the fact it's not air conditioned. A faulty seal on the cargo area allows the scent of sweet cream butter to leak out with the draft.

"We don't want to be any trouble, Mr. Melancon. Whatever you can do will be just fine," Mary says, thankful to be regaining some lost time in such a pleasant atmosphere.

She sits watching the milkman's pudgy fingers grip the steering wheel as they make a right turn onto the only paved road into town. She studies his wedding ring and how it recesses into his finger, surely too deep to ever remove short of surgery. She tries to imagine what he must have looked like when he first put that ring on . . . a good bit thinner, younger, and no doubt more attractive to have landed a wife like his. Mrs. Melancon had been the homecoming queen the year she and her husband-to-be graduated high school. Mary had seen a picture of her once, wearing a crown, displayed proudly on a bookcase in their cozy living room. It had been taken years ago, but Mrs. Melancon still closely resembles that image, despite a few creases here and there. Mary has grown a close relationship with the Melancons over time, doing some sewing and mending for them occasionally when her father is behind on the bills.

Her family hasn't always had their milk delivered. Back in Provencal, they had Sissy, a dairy cow; but with no way to transport her safely to Houma, they were forced to sell her. Norman Poche means to purchase another cow, but for one reason or another has never gotten around to it. Her home is one of four on the route that still receive almost daily deliveries because of their old, outdated iceboxes. Gayle's family has a refrigerator, yet they still get milk and eggs delivered twice a week. As stores begin to sprout up farther and farther out of town, along with the prevalence of residential refrigeration, Mary supposes that may spark the demise of their milkman, this beloved figure in her community. Possibly Mr. Melancon will still be in business a while longer, at least in the rural areas. Luckily for him, there is an expanse of rural area in Terrebonne Parish.

Gayle can't help twisting in her seat, eyes glued to a large sign announcing new construction on behalf of the TPCG.

"What's the TPCG and what are they gonna do way out here?" Gayle inquires to no one in particular.

"It stands for the Terrebonne Parish Consolidated Government," Mr. Melancon says. He takes an excited breath, but what he says next does not answer the second half of Gayle's question. "Did you know that Terrebonne means 'good earth' in French? And did you know that Terrebonne is the largest parish in Louisiana?"

To be polite, Mary pretends this is new information. But in fact, she learned the statistical details about the area her first few months in residence. As for Gayle, she has learned and forgotten it twice already. It would need to be information she deems vital before she'd commit it to memory—like how many distinct fluids are found in an automobile, for instance.

"We're flanked in the south by the Gulf of Mexico—did you know that?" Mr. Melancon makes a noble effort to educate the girls on the short trip. He continues to spurt random facts about the area, but Mary is not listening. She is thinking more about the contradictions of the parish namesake and its French translation.

Despite the vast area that it covers, not all of that "good earth" is actually earth at all. The area consists of mostly swamps, bayous, canals, and other various forms of wetlands and waterways. Places that sometimes you can only get to by boat, some only by pirogue (pronounced *PEE-row*, so claims Mary's dictionary)—much like a canoe, except the pirogue's bottom is flat and able to float in a minute amount of water. Not very practical for open waterways, as it can take on water or flip, but there is no better solution for travel in densely overgrown marshlands. When in shallow water, you can use a push pole to propel the craft.

Mary tries to imagine what Mr. Melancon would look like delivering milk in a pirogue. She can picture him standing, pushing the boat full of ice and milk—except it morphs into something more like the pictures she has seen of the romantic gondolas of Venice, his outfit now a horizontally striped shirt, dark pants, and a hat with a ribbon flowing from the back, his robust belly hanging just beneath the edge of the shirt.

She belts out a laugh barely disguised as a cough. Fortunately, no one can tell the difference over the sound of the milk truck's erratic engine.

"Next stop, downtown Houma," Mr. Melancon says, shifting gears.

Houma is the heart of Terrebonne Parish, a municipality much larger than where Mary came from, and still growing rapidly. It is, however, still very small compared to the city of New Orleans, which is merely an hour away, yet a million miles ahead.

A nervous energy builds, filling Mary's head with fantasies of what might be waiting for her down the road.

My story's just beginning,

she thinks as they pass the bus station and decelerate a few blocks shy of the festivities.

Eager to finish the journey, Gayle bails out of the open cabin before the vehicle comes to a complete stop. "Catch you on the flip-flop, Mr. M!"

"Thank you so much—you saved the day," Mary says, carefully disembarking from the truck and turning to say goodbye.

Mr. Melancon hesitates. "Glad to be of service . . . I could use a favor in return, though," he says with a pained expression, as if he were holding in his morning movement. "My anniversary is coming up soon and I have no clue what to get my wife. She's so good to me, you know . . . do you think you could help a fellow come up with some gift ideas?" His eyes are wistful. He sinks down in the driver's seat as if the dry ice is no longer keeping him safe from the heat.

"You'll have ten by Monday, I promise." Mary smiles and crosses her heart with her finger in a solemn vow.

Mr. Melancon perks up, the burden lifted from his shoulders. "I hope you have yourself some fun. You deserve it. You girls stick together, and don't go taking any wooden nickels." He pops the clutch and lurches back into motion.

Standing on the side of the road with Mary, Gayle offers up a viable proposal. "We made such good time—your mom won't be expecting a call for almost an hour. Let's go check out the grounds for a bit and then go to the bus station."

Mary pauses to consider this before posing a semi-serious question. "Only if you know the time . . . do you know what time it is?" She adopts a comical grin.

"What time is it?" cheers Gayle, knowing full well she doesn't actually want the time.

"You know what I like," Mary says in a suggestive tone.

"It's *BIG BOPPER time!*" they shout together. They skip, arm in arm, and sing, *"Chantilly lace and a pretty face and a ponytail hanging down . . ."*

How can Mary know that the events of this day will turn on her and change the course of her life?

"Needs to be higher!" hollers one of the men. It takes four of them to drape the large banner, which announces in bold yellows and reds:

Apparently it takes two of them to hoist the sign up, and two to stand around and watch. One of the watchers is a middle-aged man with dark, recently barbered hair. He has not missed any meals lately, nor has he missed going back for seconds, and his size hinders his ability to reach around into the taut rear pocket of his creamy brown linen pants with any semblance of grace. Determined, the round man manages to wiggle free a severely white cotton handkerchief embroidered with the initials *JK* from its elusive hiding spot. Victorious, he mops first his brow, then his upper lip, and finally the back of his neck, leaving the cloth moist and wilted. It's as if the strain of telling people what to do made him perspire. He is not dressed for outdoor labor, with his light blue dress shirt ironed with meticulous creases; his face does not show any discomfort even though he seems to be melting.

The quieter and younger half of the ground crew is first to notice the girls. He touches his hat brim and nods politely, giving them a motion of safe passage beneath the banner-hanging job. Gayle recognizes him right away as the older brother of a classmate, someone who used to sit behind her in church and tug at her ponytail. She doesn't remember his name—only that it starts with a D.

"Good morning," the round, sweaty man says. "You girls get a whiff of dat roux? Don't you miss dat good gumbo, now. I plan to have Andouille sausage wit mine. Cajun tradition, ya know." As he speaks, he haphazardly tucks the dampened handkerchief halfway into his front shirt pocket.

"It might be too spicy for me, Mr. Jimmy K," Gayle tells him playfully.

"Too spicy?" he questions, his broad smile melting in disbelief. "Too spicy?" he repeats, as if to give her a chance to recant. "Is dat even possible?" He looks to his subordinates for confirmation.

The younger man whose name starts with a D smooths a newly established mustache, cleverly hiding his impish grin. "I believe she's pulling your leg, boss," he says. "I bet she drank hot sauce for breakfast this morning," he calls out after Gayle.

"No . . . but I do like it on my pancakes," Gayle says, turning around and tossing him a wink as she and Mary walk away.

For a second or so, the two men look at each other with wide eyes. A chuckle escapes Big Jimmy's lips as he wags a leery finger in Gayle's direction. "Be careful of that one there, young man! A firecracker can be an unpredictable thing."

"Don't have to warn me twice, boss. I want to keep my hands intact." Contrary to what he says, his dark blue wolf-like eyes remain transfixed in the direction of the virginal prey.

Mary can feel the heat of his gaze upon them. Timidly, she turns to look, and his face suddenly softens with unblinking, arid eyes that lower in shame.

"Who was that?" Mary asks.

"That's the mayor, ya goof."

"Not him. The other one . . . the young one."

"I think his name is Dan, or David. He used to go to our church."

"He's a little creepy . . . but very handsome," Mary says, thick with intrigue.

"Handsome—that guy? Are you serious?" Gayle stops abruptly to turn and take a better look. The longer she studies him, the more Mary flushes with embarrassment, even though they are no longer on his radar.

"Huh. I guess he *is* pretty cute, now that you mention it. Maybe we should go back and tell him so." Gayle takes a lengthy step in his direction.

Mary's eyes flare in alarm. "Don't even—"

"You only live once, Mary," Gayle says, her voice and upper body going limp with the blighted hope of turning this day into a self-made fun factory.

"You only *die* once, too," Mary reasons, gently pulling Gayle in a safer direction.

"How many times do I have to explain that flirting isn't dangerous?" Gayle asks testily, throwing up her hands in frustration.

"Not everyone who plays with alligators gets eaten. But every once in a while . . ." warns Mary teasingly, yet half serious, too. "Poke the animals on your own time, Gayle."

"Fine. Let's go over by the tree. I'm meeting someone who owes me a favor." Huffily, Gayle heads for the rear of the festival grounds next to a canvas-covered stage.

People are already marking their spots by the stage with blankets and flimsy fold-out lawn chairs, the five-and-dime kind with aluminum tube frames and plasticky fabric scantily stretched in grid-like webs that will eventually pinch and brand any sensitive flesh exposed to its so-called seat with a wicked pink-checkerboard pattern.

"Laissez les bon temps rouler!" a cheerful roadhand shouts out to the small crowd, while preparing instruments for the bands performing later in the day.

"I thought we would be the early birds." Mary marvels at the multitudes of people already assembling across the grounds, talking, joking, eating, drinking, playing games, and getting in line for rides that have yet to take passengers.

"If you haven't noticed by now, we take fun very seriously around here," Gayle says, distracted by the gathering of classmates waving to her from under a huge oak tree. It is one of the oldest live oaks in the area, with majestic sprawling arms and Spanish moss draping down like multiple delicate scarves, as if it's attending a fancy afternoon wedding.

A friendly girl's voice calls from the group beneath the live oak: "Hey, Gayle, I got you some tickets! Y'all come sit. We're just taking a break from the sun while we're waiting for the rides to start." She dusts clover lint from the front of her pleated maroon skirt as the girls join her. "It might be September, but it's still ninety degrees in the shade. No fall for us yet—just an elongation of summer."

Mary sits down, thankful for the soft grass. She is tickled to hear the thicker end of the Cajun accent appearing in conversation, with *da, der,* and *dat* being used instead of *the, there,* and *that.*

"You used to the heat yet, Mary?" another girl asks. "It's not likely to dip for another month. People round here don't seem to mind the heat when there's a good time to be had."

"It's not so much the heat, but the humidity that's so rough," Mary replies, blowing her bangs away from her forehead.

"Yeah, it's like the inside of a country club sauna sometimes," a male voice adds.

"What would you know about a country club?" Gayle says with a giggle, tossing some torn grass his way.

Suddenly the first ride springs to life with movement, lights, and noise, as if the gathering of children had willed it to do so.

"That's my cue." Jane shakes her maroon skirt. The other kids wave to Gayle and Mary as they follow her lead, skipping over to be the first in line for the carousel.

"Be there in a minute, Jane," Gayle calls out. Once they are out of earshot, Gayle says to Mary, "I'll pay for the other rides if you buy the sodas." She knows she is getting the short end of the stick, but she doesn't want her best friend to feel like she's a burden.

What she doesn't know is that Mary has brought everything she's saved since the spring and plans to repay whatever money Gayle spends today, just because she can. "Sounds like a good deal to me," says Mary, rising to her feet, dusting off her rear, and shaking out her hair. Not long after she moved here, someone mentioned that roaches live in oak trees . . . which had no effect on her until the night she was introduced to a flying version of this abhorrent creature.

"I'm going to teach you to have a good time, like it or not, young lady," Gayle says, ushering Mary to the back of the carousel line.

"What about calling home?"

"The line is short. Let's ride just once, then we'll call. I promise." Gayle flutters her lashes.

"If I get into trouble, I will never see the light of day again." Mary carefully makes sure that her sewing money is deep enough in her pocket to survive the ride; it is, after all, the most she's ever saved.

There they are, two young ladies, standing in line for the carousel, holding their childhood in one hand and reaching for the future with the other . . .

"So . . . who would you bring to the Homecoming dance?" Gayle inquires with a devilish grin.

Mary shrugs. "You mean theoretically? Like if I were in an alternate universe and we were actually allowed to go? Or do you mean if—"

Gayle sighs heavily. "Don't think, just pick."

"I don't know. I haven't been paying that much attention."

"You'd better start, or all the good ones will get snatched up."

"You make finding a date sound like an Easter egg hunt."

"At the rate you're going, you'll end up with Humpty Dumpty over there." Gayle points to a round boy with his face buried in a large cloud of pink candy.

"What are we talking about, ladies?" Jane lines up behind them for round two on the carousel. Jane is athletic. She likes to run track and play volleyball, and has a sinewy body to prove it. Mary studies Jane's bronze hue, no doubt acquired from hours at play over the summer. Mary would give up just about anything for hours to spend on herself.

"I just wanted to find out if we have the same taste in boys, but Mary won't cooperate," Gayle complains.

"Does that mean you're both free agents?" Jane asks, acting only semi-interested, watching her own foot draw a heart in a patch of dirt.

"For now," Gayle chirps.

"I might know someone who's interested," Jane mentions, while slyly studying the edges of her freshly manicured nails.

"If it's your brother, Mary thinks he's creepy," Gayle taunts in a whisper.

Mary's cheeks burn with a rush of blood. "I also said he was handsome," she blurts, compelled by an immediate self-conscious defense mechanism found in most adolescents.

Jane is unfazed by the outburst. She puts her recently inspected finger to Mary's lips. "No offense taken. Danny *is* creepy." Jane's eyes are calm and thoughtful. "Keep your eyes and ears open today, Mary. Opportunities to snag a date are bound to appear."

Mary is stunned by Jane's ease of familiarity—the girl is almost a stranger to her. She has no idea how to react. So she doesn't (other than her enlarged eyes, of course).

Gayle trumpets, "See, that's what I'm saying! Keep your eyes peeled, Mary. We're gonna snag us a cutie by the day's end."

"Who needs a roller coaster when you have *friends* to scare the pee out of you?" Mary says nervously.

Jane pokes Mary in her side. "I didn't know you were shy, Mary. Most people think you're all brainy and snobby."

"Really? That's awful," Mary says, deflating.

"Don't worry. I can smooth that out for you." Jane gives Mary a secret-hiding smile.

"All aboard!" the carnival worker interrupts. His ragged hands drop the chain and capture all the small, bright red squares of paper from the riders as they pass.

Upon boarding the carousel, Mary notices that the details of the horses are truly a sight to behold in all their painted glory. There are three rows of gallantly posed stallions, each with striking expressions and vivid colors. The last time Mary rode a carousel, it had exotic types of animals, a menagerie of sorts, and each time she rode a different animal, dreaming of adventures in lands far away. She likes this carousel no less, but can see that it doesn't hold the same fantastical nature. It reminds her that she is losing the ability to get lost in the imaginary journey. *Growing up*, she believes it is called.

The horse beneath her gently begins to rise and fall as she hums along with the cheerful waltz ascending from the Wurlitzer. The rotation creates a welcome breeze, a refreshing gift as her magical steed reaches a full gallop. She closes her eyes to feel the tickle in her tummy, the same one she used to get when her dad threw her in the air when she was pocket-sized.

She reopens her eyes and catches her reflection in the mirrors adorning the ride's center panels. Seeing herself with an expression of joy is like catching a glimpse of a stranger. A stranger she wants so much to know. A small shadow of guilt begins to creep into her thoughts—a guilt that seems to plague generations of females, compelling them to question what they do and do not deserve in life.

Do I deserve to have fun when others suffer?
Do I deserve a better life than those who came before me?
Am I good enough? How do I prove to myself that I am worthy?

Just then, she eyes the brass ring on its holder and dares herself to make a grab for it. Stretching, she touches it with the tips of her fingers, but it passes so fast that she is unable to get a firm grip. Before she has a chance to go completely around for another go, the momentum begins to wane.

Better luck next time,

she tells herself, not wanting to give in to such a small defeat.

I'll prove it to myself some other way.

The ride is over and it is time to make good on the promise she made to her mother.

As Mary and Gayle cross close to the midway, passing at the rear of the tents where the games stand, a sinister bony hand reaches out from between the tents and both Mary and Gayle let out shrieks of fright as if they have encountered a large, flying roach. Delighted squeals from the children at play nearby keep the resonance of their screams from drawing any attention. This turns out to be very amusing to the beautiful, light-skinned Negro woman with the bony hand; she gives a soft laugh at the commotion she has caused.

"You never see a Creole before, child?" she says, studying the horrified expressions of the two girls. She is clothed in a way neither girl has seen before, adorned in a long and colorful wrap-style dress with a headdress made of matching material. "Come now, little ones . . . Mambo Beulah give you no harm. Wouldn't even hurt a fly." Her tone, quite opposite of that ghostly hand, is soothing. "With closed eyes, I reach for hope and I catch me a beautiful ting." She giggles. "Can Beulah give a free reading to ease da fright I cause?"

The girls exchange a look of confusion. "A . . . reading?" Mary asks.

"Sha, I can tell you the future—an much more. Jest come into my tent an let me consult de cards."

"I apologize, Miss Beulah," Mary says, "but we need to be going. We're expected by someone shortly." She feels uneasy, like an animal before a natural disaster.

"Dis won't take long. Your phone call can wait, child . . . unlike your fate." Mambo Beulah's voice holds a weight of urgency.

"I think we should hear what she has to say," Gayle whispers, baffled by how this woman knows that they were going to make a phone call.

The girls enter her tent. Inside sits a small round table with a black, velveteen tablecloth and three small wooden stools. Behind the table looms a chest of drawers; atop the chest several candles burn, each a different height. An unidentifiable substance burns in a small dish on the grassy floor of the enclosure, filling the air with a strange, spicy scent. Curiosity draws the girls to the table where Beulah is now shuffling an odd deck of cards.

"Clear your mind and listen close to everyting I say. Cut the deck any way you want, den spread dem out across the table. Careful to choose ten cards now, and slide dem to me." She places the deck in the center of the table.

Mary does as Beulah says, slow and deliberate in every card choice.

The old woman flips over each card, placing them in a pattern. The arrangement of the cards and the disturbing images they display make no sense—except, of course, to Beulah. She touches each one as if to absorb the story they tell. "Hmmm . . ." is all she utters for what seems like an eternity to the girls. After the long pause, Beulah scoops up the collection of cards and sets them aside. "I need more information, child. Place your hands in mine, palms up," she says, her hands on the table, open and ready to receive additional messages from beyond.

Mary is frozen—she is not terribly sure if she wants to proceed with an enterprise that may be antithetical to her religious upbringing. Gayle, however, nudges Mary impatiently. She has no such hindrances.

Mary searches Beulah's kind features for reassurance until the woman's face seems to morph into the unblemished radiance she most assuredly possessed some years ago. As Mary hesitantly places her hands in Beulah's, a wave of peace comes over her like a blanket. Her flesh tingles as the woman traces the creases in both her hands.

Gayle has to hold back a giggle—it makes her think of her mother's dinnertime hand-washing inspections.

Beulah lets go of Mary's hands and leans back in her chair. She reaches for one of the shorter candles and places it on the table. After taking a cleansing breath, she begins her analysis in a trance-like state, her eyes riveted on the flame.

"Listen close. You have a good head, child . . . you de smartest one around . . . not de bravest, though. You fraid of everyting . . . even what mean you no harm. You no stranger to hard work . . . dis will help get you tru hard times. Da future full of possibility . . ."

Mary winces as Beulah's talons suddenly wrap around her wrists, encasing the tender flesh. She tries to pull away, only to have Beulah's grip tighten, her voice growing louder and more urgent as she continues.

"Two males to enter your life soon . . . one a good man tru and tru . . . de other wit a dark center he keeps hidden from de world. One will try to cage you, an de other will set you free. Choose de right one an you will know peace and success . . . choose de wrong one an you will suffer in bondage many a year. When de water comes, stay calm and float, child, or you will surely drown. A fallen bird shall protect you. Take de money you got wit you now an place it in de red sock . . . someday it will buy a ticket and shelter you from de storm. Your steps will lead smaller feet, so walk a careful line." Beulah exhales hard, her breath blowing out the candle, and lets go of Mary's hands.

For a moment the tent falls silent as Mary rubs her irritated skin, attempting to digest the bizarre revelations.

"Wow, that was far out! It was just like the beginning of a scary movie!" Gayle blurts with spontaneous applause. She stops just as abruptly as she began, realizing she is alone in her enthusiasm.

"Thank you, Miss Mambo . . . I mean Beulah. We really must be going now," Mary says, in haste to leave the tent. She no longer feels she can inhale. Scrambling uneasily, she tugs at Gayle's arm. Mary yanks her friend outside to escape the fear pulsing from her inability to breathe.

Gayle bellows, "Oww, that hurts!"

Mary stops and doubles over, gasping as if she has just finished a marathon at high altitude.

"Are you all right? Should I get help?" Gayle hovers over Mary, unsure of what to do—she once saw a boy turn blue choking on a jawbreaker at a parade.

Mary waves her hand in an "A-OK" sign to ease Gayle's mind, allowing her to concentrate a moment longer on how a lungful of air can make all the difference in the world.

"What happened?" Gayle asks as Mary rights herself, her face vivid with color.

"I'm . . . not sure. All of a sudden, I just couldn't breathe," Mary says, swiftly recovering from the affliction that plagued her only moments before.

"Maybe you were allergic to the perfume in there, or the heavy vibe she was putting down."

"Yeah ... maybe." Mary looks down at her hands, still itching along the palm lines, like wounds that are starting to heal. She rubs them together, hoping to hasten the process. "I wonder what all of that meant."

As she and Gayle pass the banner under which they'd walked earlier—although that already feels so far away—Mary notices a French phrase printed on the back, which she can't read in the shadows. Truth be told, she would not have been able to understand it if she *could* see the words; there is a movement in the schools to discontinue teaching any form of Cajun French, thinking it obsolete (only to reintroduce it a decade later, thinking it the height of class).

"I wonder how much Beulah charges," Gayle says. "I want to have my own reading done. She might give more jingle for some jangle."

Annoyed with herself for having bought in momentarily to such cheap theatrics, Mary declares, "Don't waste your money. It's a bunch of nonsense! You don't really believe that she has any way of knowing who we are or what we'll experience in the future, do you? If anything, her vague announcements will plant themselves into our subconscious, and we'll make them somehow relevant. Self-fulfilling prophecy and all that."

"You've been reading books about psychiatry from the library again, haven't you?" Gayle asks, poking fun at Mary's love for information. "Her vision may have been figurative, meant to make you pay attention to the world around you."

Mary turns her frustration onto Gayle for not letting the subject go. "What's the point if it's not literal? What if she were to do a reading on *you* and you were never able to figure out what it means? How is that supposed to help? You're better off with education and prayer to guide you. Stop being so gullible."

"*I'm* gullible? You're one to talk! So everything has to be literal and make perfect sense? For someone who always has to have proof that something exists, I don't see how you can go to church on Sundays and not question that!" Gayle spits, gathering up her feelings after having them tread upon.

She has no idea that her comment will send Mary grasping for a new hold on her faith in all things intangible. From that moment on, Mary will critique every verse in her Bible until it no longer makes sense. Before this, she has always relied on the adults around her to already have made sure that what they were spouting in church was the *God's honest truth.*

Mary considers Gayle's words.

> *How many things could be added to that list: God, love,*
> *hope, dreams, perception itself.*
> *Too deep. Maybe Gayle is right and it is figurative.*
> *This is the water . . . and I need to stay calm and float, or*
> *I'll drown.*

Mary feels her head begin to swim, not sure if it's the thoughts making her dizzy, or the heat.

"It's too hot to be angry," she announces. "Truce?"

Gayle remains silent to choose her words (and to let Mary sweat a little). "I wasn't mad that you didn't want me to get a reading, just disappointed. You overthink stuff, Mary. I thought it was entertaining. I guess things are a little different for those of us who don't have the rest of our lives all planned out. Nothing exciting will ever happen to you if you never let it."

"You're right. Partly, anyway."

"I am?" Gayle asks, confused. She hadn't expected Mary to concede so quickly. "Which part?"

"I *do* overthink things. What Beulah said was a little scary to me, and I don't know what to do with the things she told me. I mean, how am I supposed to put my money in a red sock if I'm about to spend it on snacks?"

"Don't even think that some fortune-teller lady is going to get you out of that deal!" Gayle says, looking both ways before crossing the street. "Do you even *own* a red sock?"

Near the festival grounds is the hub of all social activity in Houma: a small diner located within the Greyhound bus station. It is a meeting place for young and old, local and wanderer alike. The best thing about it is the air conditioning, which is considered a luxury; most homes here don't have it yet, and very few businesses either. Mary and Gayle look forward to that frill today, a much-needed respite from the heat. Their steps grow faster, spurred on by that cool breeze and coke waiting for them just one block away.

Outside the bus station, Chick steps out of his new Impala and pats her on the side of her hardtop. "My baby . . . tropical turquoise, fresh off the lot. She's an eight-cylinder sport coupe," he brags to a guy who whistled with interest when he saw the car pull into the parking area. Chick just bought the Impala on a whim. It's one of the reasons his friend Vinny has agreed to ride the bus down from New Orleans to visit. Vinny isn't big on bus travel, but he does rely on it when he is in-between vehicles. Unfortunately, Vinny is often in-between vehicles. His last car drowned in a canal in some undisclosed location.

Chick walks from the lot to the front of the bus depot, where an employee has just finished cleaning a large pane of glass covering a Coca Cola advertisement featuring a cute brunette.

Chick pulls a comb from his pocket and says to the worker, "Nice work. I'd pay for any drink *she* ordered."

Meanwhile, on a Greyhound bus traveling to Houma from New Orleans, a budding teenage girl continues to disturb a fellow passenger with her curiosity. "Is a friend supposed to meet you here?" she asks, her shrill voice piercing the nap of the young man sitting in the window seat next to her. Her unremarkable face is surrounded by fine strings of straight, mousy brown hair.

The young man's enchanting dark brown eyes are hiding, tucked behind tired lids. Without stirring, he answers her in a slow, sexy, half-asleep way that makes her want to keep him talking. "Yeah, you can't miss him," he says. "Just beyond six-foot, could use a pound or two."

"What was his name again?"

"I only know him as Chick."

"You say this guy is a good friend of yours and you don't even know his Christian name?"

"I know all I need to know. He's a guy I can trust. No name in the world can tell you that much." As the bus rocks and groans into its destination, a stream of sunlight rudely crosses the young man's exotic Italian-looking features, demanding his eyes to open.

The teenage girl quickly looks away so as not to be caught staring. Through the bus window, she spots a tall young man standing outside the bus station, combing his pomade-saturated hair, passing time in his reflection.

"I think I see him," she says. "Not bad. He's a tall drink of water, but not nearly as handsome as you."

"You think I'm handsome?"

"Handsome enough."

"Enough for what?"

"An invitation," she says, rising up into the aisle to stretch. She hands him a business card. The bus doors sigh open and passengers begin to unload.

Still seated, he examines the card and raises his eyebrows in interest. "The Babin Inn? Hey, look—you're a little too peach to be handing out calling cards like these, don't you think?"

At first, she appears irritated by his reaction, gathering up her purse and sweater. Then she smiles politely. "My family owns that inn, and I thought you might need a place to stay while you're in town."

He wipes the shame from his face with his hand. "Oh, wow . . . I feel lousy about what I said. Look—"

"Don't worry. I'm partly at fault for poking my nose into your business for the last hour or so. I hope I wasn't a terrible pest."

"You were buzzin, all right, but I never swatted, did I?"

"Thanks for that," she says, extending her hand. "Friends?"

He takes her hand. "In order to be friends, I have to trust you," he says. "Can you be trusted?"

"Trust is a two-way street, pal. I'm willing to take a ride—the question is, are you?" She winks and walks away, leaving him standing alone in the aisle with the card in his hand. He flips it over to reveal a message scrawled on the back in girlish loops: *Room service at no additional cost.*

He shakes his head, not quite sure whether to even put the card in his pocket. But he does, and joins Chick, who's been patiently waiting outside.

"Hey, Vinny! Long time, no see. I knew you'd change your mind and come to work with me!" Chick says heartily, towering over Vinny and landing a firm slap on his friend's back.

Vinny flashes a harsh glare, visibly blanching Chick. The height difference between the two men seems to level out for a second or two.

In his excitement, Chick has momentarily forgotten all the unspoken rules of this particular friendship. Remembering that Vinny has the warmth of a tea-light, Chick backs off and waits for him to initiate conversation, watching him retrieve a black leather duffel from the Greyhound's luggage compartment.

Chick has no need to look in Vinny's bag to know that whatever is packed inside is clean, meticulously placed, and premeditated.

"I'm just here for a visit to check out this new car of yours," Vinny says. "Besides, I heard about the festival this weekend. You know a bash can't start without me." He smirks.

Chick catches Vinny exchanging looks with a girl from the bus; she's getting into a car.

"Who's that?" Chick asks.

"Trouble . . . with a capital T," Vinny tells him coolly. He shoves a Parliament in his mouth, lighting it up with a talented flick of his Zippo.

"A sure thing?"

"Sure enough to put me back on the farm," Vinny says, exhaling a cloud of tobacco.

"Step lightly, then."

Vinny looks to Chick with a minacious grin. "Don't worry, my friend. I don't leave prints . . . of *any* kind." He adds, "Besides, she's not my type. Not pretty enough."

"Ready to meet the new woman in *my* life? She's a looker! I paid almost three thousand—and worth every penny. She's parked on the other side." Chick rubs his large hands together.

"Can I get a burger first? I'm starving."

"Sure thing, big daddy," Chick says, trying not to show his disappointment as they go inside the depot.

A red-headed waitress is behind the counter wiping down some menus. She could pass for Maureen O'Hara if she dropped twenty or so pounds. Seeing them, she says, "Seat yourself, boys. I'll be right with you."

They choose a table in the corner and Vinny sits facing the door. The waitress maneuvers her curves across the room, pulling an order pad from her apron pocket. "What can I get you growing boys to drink?" she asks, handing them each a damp menu.

"Water for me, and I'm ready to order, if that's all right," Vinny says, his finger on the specials.

The waitress fishes a pencil from her red hair. "Sure, hon. Shoot."

Chick aims and fires an imaginary gun at Vinny, who ignores him. "I'll have a burger, well done, with fries and a cup of chili."

"And for you?" she asks, turning to Chick.

"I'll just have a coke. Does that come with a brunette, like in the picture outside?"

"Will another color do, sugar? I get off in twenty," she says playfully.

"Uhhh . . ." Chick mumbles, searching for a response.

The waitress gives an obnoxious laugh. "Sorry I scared you like that, hon. I knew you were just like the chili—full of beans."

"I hope that chili is as spicy as you are," Vinny says with raised eyebrows, handing her the menu.

"You betcha. I'll be right back with those drinks to cool you down," she says, returning the pad and pencil to their respective places. The two men watch her every movement until her wiggle is out of sight behind the counter.

"So when you going to stay put and get a real job?" Chick asks. "I just got a foreman gig and I need someone I can trust to take my old position."

"When you going to give up trying to tie me to the ground? I can't imagine working offshore, stinking like a grease monkey all day," Vinny says. "I like the feel of a well-tailored suit too much to give it up for some step-in zip bag—and if I ever do, you might as well get me fitted for a strait jacket, too, while you're at it."

"All righty, then . . . now tell me what you really think," Chick says snidely. He pokes a straw in the soda that the waitress has just set in front of him, giving her a customary thank-you nod, then leans in to make a final plea to Vinny. "Look, I just think it's a good opportunity for us to make a lot of money is all. After Audrey slammed the coast last year, there's been steady work for welders on- and offshore. Between that and working with my cousin in construction, I make a killing on the up-and-up. Not bad for a delinquent high school dropout, huh?" He takes a sip of soda.

"You still working a seven-and-seven shift?" Vinny asks.

Chick's eyes cloud with confusion. "Yeah. Why?"

Vinny's voice lowers, almost a whisper now. "The way I figure is, I get more time off, I make way more money than you, and my job is recession-proof." What Vinny does for a living is off the books, dangerous, and extremely covert; even Chick, a true friend, is not privy to that information.

Just like a magic trick, Vinny makes his food disappear only minutes after the plate hits the table, without a trace on his face or his shirt and nothing left on the plate—not even a crumb.

By the Greyhound station parking lot, Gayle stops in her tracks, her mouth open in pure amazement. "Geeze Louise! Would you cast an eyeball at that mean machine!" she exclaims. "She must belong to someone from out of town. I don't know anyone here who has the taste for a new Impala." Gayle darts toward the car.

To Mary she sounds and acts like a sugar-fed lunatic. "Please get away from there, spaz, before you get us into trouble!"

Mary just doesn't understand. Even before Gayle could read, she pored over the pictures in every issue of *Motor Trend* magazine she could get her hands on, either down at the library or at the market when she went with her mother for groceries. When she did finally learn to read, Gayle wrote a heartfelt letter to Santa requesting a subscription of her very own. Each issue of *Motor Trend* is as precious to Gayle as that dictionary is to Mary. To witness one of the cars she has studied within those pages, in showroom condition, sends her into orbit.

"Look, it has tri-colored seats! You don't get it—I have to meet the person who owns this car!" Gayle says, running a hand delicately over the Impala's smooth hide.

Mary quickly stands in front of her, blocking her path toward the bus station. "Cool your jets! I know you have this obsession with cars, but *please* don't embarrass me today." Gayle is very much an extrovert, and has on many occasions embarrassed her very reserved best friend. Mary is afraid that everyone—especially those of the male persuasion—will think she is as kooky as Gayle. "We are going to go in there, call my mother, and have a coke," Mary orders, impressed by the level of confidence in her own voice. "If you can stay calm, you can ask about the owner of this car. Otherwise, I will have to crawl under a rock and *die*. I'll go first so you can compose yourself." Mary turns the corner of the bus depot and waits for her friend to come to her senses.

"Fine. You win," Gayle says, pouting, reluctantly following Mary's lead. On her way inside the station, Gayle is briefly distracted by an advertisement in the window: a brunette with a Coca Cola whom she imagines looks like an older version of herself.

Mary then takes the last few steps she will make as the girl she knows herself to be.

Mary opens the door to the soda shop and walks in, instantly bombarded with the stench of old grease commingled with the sweet aroma of soft-serve ice cream.

Both Chick and Vinny are instantly enamored with her; their conversation abruptly halts. The hum of the Electro-freeze machine gives off just enough noise to mask the sudden silence.

"Now *that's* my type," Vinny says as he and Chick stare brazenly at Mary, not even noticing Gayle walking in not far behind her.

The trouble with Mary is that, with all her preoccupations, she is completely unaware of her budding beauty. She has the kind of beauty that young boys such as her fellow fifteen-year-olds avoid for fear of rejection. Bearing a striking resemblance to a young Elizabeth Taylor does, however, draw attention from the older, braver members of the opposite sex.

Mary brushes aside loose wisps of her dark hair as she crosses the room toward the wall where the Crosley rotary payphone is set up. A stool sits below next to a silent jukebox. She inserts a dime in the center slot to make her promised phone call. Gayle follows, plopping on the phone's stool. She can finally feel the air conditioning blow cool upon her face.

Chick and Vinny return to their conversation, eyes still on Mary. Gayle is studying the two unusually well-dressed young men and realizes they are fixated in their direction. Judging by Vinny's fancy, short-sleeved silk shirt and designer slacks, she figures he isn't homegrown. The young men Gayle knows don't even dress that nice for church.

"I think those guys are looking at us," Gayle whispers, leaning in to Mary.

Still on the phone with her mother, Mary turns to look. Blood rushes to her cheeks as she locks eyes with Vinny. All of her life, people around Mary have argued about the exact color of her eyes so often that she has to look in a mirror when asked, just to feel she is not lying. Depending on the lighting or what she's wearing, her eyes can take on hues of blue, green, sometimes gray. It is rumored that Elizabeth Taylor's eyes are violet-blue; looking at Vinny, right then, for the first time, Mary's eyes are that exact shade.

That is the most beautiful man I have ever seen . . . and he is looking back at me.

To Mary, seeing Vinny is like spotting a famous movie star. She admires his dark hair, his chiseled jaw, the healthy glow of his skin. Feeling the heat of his stare, she has to look away—or she might melt into a puddle on the floor. She focuses on Gayle instead, wrapping up her phone call.

"Yes, ma'am, I understand," she says in a tight voice, and gently replaces the handset back in its cradle as if it were made of glass.

Meanwhile, Gayle has been straining desperately to listen to the young men's conversation.

"I think the cute guy is from New Orleans. He must own the car outside," Gayle says, her previous excitement returning. "He's dreamy like Sal Mineo in *Giant*, except his face isn't all pudgy. *And* he has honest-to-goodness muscles." She giggles softly. "The other one looks really tall, like a jolly giant with a DA hairdo."

"Don't even think about it! They're too old for us." Mary being Mary, she quickly dismisses any romantic delusions of grandeur.

"Don't be a wet rag! I just want a coast in that cruiser." Gayle shrugs. "Anyway, what'd your mom say?"

"She said I have to come home in time to help with supper dishes," Mary says, her spirit visibly deflating. "I'm real sorry, but she sounds so overwhelmed."

"I can't believe you fall for her tricks!" Gayle screeches, her voice elevating in frustration. "That woman never gives you any slack! It means we have to leave that much earlier to walk home."

To get a better vantage point, Vinny has ambled over to the jukebox and is pretending to give the selection panel a once-over. He overhears the girls' last bit of conversation and decides to intercede, having already devised his plan to procure a role as knight in tailored armor. Vinny signals Chick, who closely follows his lead—albeit less gracefully—getting his long legs tangled in the chairs before successfully navigating his way across the soda shop at an impressive and rather conspicuous clip.

"I hope I'm not intruding, ladies," Vinny says earnestly. "We would like to be of assistance to you if needed. It sounds to me like you are having some sort of transportation difficulty." He wears a veil of concern on his face.

The girls are stunned into silence. They just stand there, blinking first at Vinny, then at each other.

Then Gayle cocks an eyebrow. "So . . . you have a car?"

Chick fires back, "Depends. You have a need for speed?"

Mary is suddenly thrust into tension-relieving laughter, the kind of belly laughter that is contagious, and soon all four are doubled over and in tears. It is quite cathartic for Mary to release all the emotion of the day thus far, and it takes a few solid minutes to rein herself back in.

Finally, through ragged giggles, she says, wiping the corners of her eyes, "I'm not sure there is anything you can do."

Playing the ever-diligent Boy Scout, Vinny sees a perfect opportunity to get to speak with her further. And he takes it. "How about joining us at our table for a soda while we figure this out?" he says, as smooth as his silk shirt.

"That sounds like a keen scene to me. Can you make it a float?" Gayle pipes up, receiving a sharp glare from Mary. Gayle mouths, *What?* as they make their way to the chrome-edged dinette set.

The gentlemen hold out two of the scarlet-red vinyl chairs for the girls to be seated with their backs to the door.

When nervous, yank out your etiquette, so you don't look like a dumb kid!

Mary's inner voice advises. "Let's start with a proper introduction. No nicknames, please," she says. Mary harbors a pet-peevish dislike for both nicknames and being in daring situations such as these.

"Oh, and ages—don't forget ages! It's almost my birthday. I'm Gayle Marie Gautreau, almost sixteen!" Gayle trumpets this fact proudly. She is both juiced up that she is in a daring situation and trying to impress whomever the car belongs to.

"I'm Ch– Ahem . . . Clarence Bourgeois, twenty-one," Chick says reluctantly. He is in no way, shape, or form fond of his given name.

"Vincent Carlino. Just turned twenty," Vinny says, trying to soften the age difference. He is impatient to hear exactly how big that difference is.

"My name is Mary—"

"Jane, or like the virgin, hee hee?" Chick interrupts. He likes to think himself a bona fide comedian, but the looks he gets around the table suggest otherwise.

Vinny coolly reaches over and pulls Chick toward him, says something in his ear, then gently puts him back where he found him. The blood visibly drains from Chick's face. Guarded, he stands to get the coke floats the girls have asked for.

The girls exchange a look of bewilderment.

"I humbly apologize for my friend's ignorant comment," Vinny says, searching deep into Mary's eyes in pursuit of her leniency.

Apprehensively, she continues, eyes narrowed. She is still leery of these strangers. "My name is Mary Lou Poche and I'm fifteen. I'd like to add that I don't think my parents would approve of me being here like this . . . unchaperoned."

Gayle immediately sinks in her chair and looks to the heavens for assistance. "And you think *I'm* embarrassing," she whispers to herself.

Seemingly recovered, Chick returns with the treats. Mary is explaining about her mother's new orders for them to return home early, cutting their day short. Vinny is quietly pondering how to win her over as he pops a stick of Doublemint gum in his mouth—when an idea hits him like a lightning bolt from above.

"Would you mind if I speak with your mother?" he asks, snapping his fingers in tandem and trapping the idea inside a closed fist, as if he has just captured a tiny treasure.

Mary's mouth falls open, but the words do not come; she is unaccustomed to being speechless. Then to her own surprise, she rattles off the phone number and her mother's name. Vinny is off in a flash to the phone. Mary is left dazed, holding her lip as if it had come unbuttoned. What just happened? She is snapped back to reality by Gayle's reaction.

"Now you've gone and done it! Your mother is going to tear your hide and talk mine into doing the same. Not to mention the fact that we won't get to leave the house ever again," Gayle says, overly dramatic as usual.

Chick comforts the girls by explaining how Vinny's charm is well-accepted by females of all ages.

"Not her mother! *Nooo* way, *nooo* how," Gayle says. Then, with an astonishing redirection, her brain switches gears. "Is his car the new one outside with the super-cool fins?"

"No, indeed. She's mine, paid in full." Chick shines his knuckles on his shirt, thrilled to finally be able to brag to someone who can truly appreciate it.

"Is she totally cherry?" Gayle's admiring grin is cut short by her need to hide the arrival of a proliferous amount of drool.

"As cherry as you are, pretty kitten," Chick oozes, thinking he is paying her a sweet compliment.

Gayle smiles, completely unfazed by his answer. They appear to share a strong common interest, and continue to connect in a way that worries Mary—though she's not sure for which one of them.

"She's just my cruisin' vehicle. My other one is a souped-up 1950 Rocket 88. That's the one I run at the dragway. *She's* a real screamer."

"What color is she?" Gayle asks, trying to get a mental picture.

"Flint gray. Wanna see?" Chick pulls out his wallet to show her a newspaper picture he saved, featuring him in front of the gray Oldsmobile holding a trophy. "Even though it's a black-and-white picture, she came out the right shade. Go figure."

"How do you keep your cars so shiny?"

Chick begins a detailed explanation of the steps it takes to properly wash and wax such a possession. Gayle is intensely hanging on every word, as if he were reciting love poems to her. All Mary can do is feign interest while nervously shifting her gaze to Vinny, still on the phone with her mother.

> *Is he . . . laughing? My mother never says anything*
> *remotely funny!*
> *Is this some alternate universe that I have entered? This is*
> *just so surreal.*

Disturbed, she gives herself a pinch to make sure this isn't all some dream that is getting out of control.

Vinny hangs up the phone, but picks it back up and dials again, as if he forgot to ask Mary's mother something. He raises his arm to look at his watch, hangs up again, and crosses the room with a swagger and a mischievous gleam in his eye.

Mary is starting to think someone is playing a strange practical joke on her.

"Am I in a lot of trouble?" she asks, praying for a merciful answer.

"You are if you don't start answering all of my questions—since I *am* your guardian for the rest of the day," Vinny says coolly. He tactfully exhales on his pinky ring, buffs it on his shirt, then briefly holds it out for inspection.

"What?" the others respond in bewildered unison.

"I'll explain everything as soon as my new friend here starts spilling the beans," Vinny says, playfully smacking his gum.

"Go ahead and ask your silly questions. If I don't find out what's going on very soon, I am going to go berserk," Mary says, flustered.

Vinny grabs a chair from the next table, swings it around, and sits on it backwards. He begins his interrogation by pulling her chair almost between his knees so that the two of them are face-to-face.

"Are you jacketed?" he asks, his breath sweet and minty.

"No. I'm not allowed to date until I turn sixteen," Mary says, her cheeks red-hot with worry that her breath may not be as fresh.

"Do you like me?"

"I guess."

"Do you *trust* me?"

"I don't *know* you."

"If you were allowed, would you go on a date with me?"

"My mother would never—"

"I'll ask again," he says, rattling her chair a bit. "Would you go on a date with me?"

"Yes, I suppose I would let you take me out. If my parents allowed."

"Good—then it's a date!" he says, satisfied.

"What just happened?" Mary blurts. "Am I on that *Candid Camera* show or something?"

"This is no joke," Vinny says. "I wanted to get to know you. I did whatever was necessary to get that chance." He turns to Chick. "By the way, remind me I need a favor later today. Now, ladies," he says, turning back to the girls, "we will escort you back to the festival, while I enlighten you with a new and improved plan for your day."

The girls comply, shaking their heads in disbelief as they walk out to the car. Gayle starts to jump up and down when she remembers she is getting her opportunity to cruise in style. Not the usual commute in her mother's family-friendly automobile, a 1948 Meadow Green Ford Woodie (not a bad car, mind you—it just wasn't appreciated by this particular car enthusiast).

Chick opens the front passenger's side door for Gayle. She slides in, so elated that all she can do is sit in awe and molest the interior.

Vinny opens the back driver's side for Mary. She gives him a look; she has never been in the back seat of a car with an adult male before, not even her father. He feels her apprehension, and it only makes him like her more.

When they embark on their very short journey to the festival, it is agreed that they stay in the car until everyone is privy to how these new arrangements manifested. Vinny begins to explain how he made everything come to pass within the course of one phone call to a woman named Vivian.

"How did you get the old bag to go along with your shenanigans?" asks Gayle, full of impatience.

"First of all, you shouldn't talk about your friend's mother that way," Vinny chides.

"You're right," Gayle admits, lowering her head in shame.

Mary had never heard anyone but herself and her father defend her mother before. This young man Vinny was beginning to leave quite the impression. "I appreciate your manners, but please tell us what happened," she pleads. She feels ill from the suspense.

"There isn't a lot to tell. I just introduced myself to her, and explained basically how we met. We had a nice conversation about her feelings and concerns about you. I let her know that I understand those feelings. I told her that it was important for you as a young lady to have time away from the pressures of school, chores, and such. I appealed to her frustrations, reminding her that you will soon have your own life and responsibilities with no experiences worth looking back on. I let her know how important it was to me to have the chance to spend time with you." Vinny adds, deceptively offhand, "Oh, and I offered to buy her a television set so she could occupy the children."

Mary's only response is wide-eyed disbelief.

"I *knew* there had to be a catch!" bursts Gayle, then immediately admonishes herself and tries again. "That's wonderful, Mary! You've never had a TV before."

"Wonderful? It doesn't *feel* wonderful. It feels like I've been sold at market, bought and paid for." She asks Vinny scathingly, "How could you do this?"

"I'm so very sorry," he says, and to Mary he sounds sincere. "I thought I was helping. I didn't think it would make you angry with me. Please understand that it was the only way I could take you out this evening for a date. She said you usually help with the kids in the evening. It was the only thing that came to mind to remedy your not being there. I won't do any of it, if it hurts you," The depth of remorse and compassion in his voice take everyone aback—even Chick.

Mary begins to feel bad for venting on Vinny, when it's actually her mother who has hurt her. "I don't know why I am getting so upset. Please don't think me ungrateful. It's such an extravagant gesture. I am positive my brothers and sisters will be thrilled, and that thought makes me happy. I don't want to deprive my siblings of that kindness."

"I understand that this has all been so unexpected—for both of us. Take some time today to think about it. If by this evening you don't want to go with me, then I'll take you home, no obligation whatsoever. Do we have a deal?"

"I suppose that sounds fair," she says, feeling heard and respected—something she has never felt with her mother.

"Can we put this behind us for now, so I can show you a good time?" Vinny says, relief showing in his voice.

Meanwhile, it's vehicular brain-slaughter in the front seat, as Chick and Gayle try to impress each other with their abounding knowledge of cars.

"They only made the glass top on the Skyliner for two years. I have the article at home," Gayle says, challenging a comment from Chick.

"Would you like to see one? My cousin knows a guy," Chick replies.

"Is your chassis classy? Of *course* I want to see it!"

Chick finds a place to park in the field, and the group walks proudly hand in hand with their new crushes. The festival is in full swing, with the stage now occupied by one of the local bands, performing a heavily syncopated number highlighting the use of an accordion. Influenced by the newer generation, the band has a few more instruments than traditional Cajun music calls for. Older folks are dancing a quick, intricate two-step, showing up many of the younger crowd's attempts. The rhythm is so infectious that even the people just walking around still bounce to the beat. Blankets and folding chairs are plentiful enough now to create a natural barrier between the makeshift dance floor and the gaming area where the group is headed. The first attraction to summon them is the tall, vertical tower of the High Striker, with its silent bell suspended at the very top.

"*Step* riiight up! Show the girls your brute strength! Only ten cents a pop," calls a carnival worker with a homemade eyepatch. He's pointing at the game with the wooden handle of a rubber mallet. "Hit the bell and win the top prize! Win a cuddle bear for your sweetheart!"

"I bet you could hit that bell with one arm tied behind your back," Gayle says, nudging Chick, her eyes glued to a periwinkle teddy bear dangling by its golden rickrack loop on a pole beside the tower.

Unable to pass up the chance to flaunt his machismo, Chick takes the mallet in hand, lightly tossing it about in a showy evaluation of its bell-ringing potential.

The carny's foot suspiciously travels to the platform, housing the device. After a brief examination of the rig, Vinny frowns in disapproval.

"All I have to do is hit the bell and she gets the bear?" Chick asks the carny, who is nervously observing Vinny with his good eye.

"Sure, champ. Give her a go. I'll step back and give you some room," the carny says, and cautiously steps away, giving Chick a wide berth.

Chick positions himself for maximum impact, and looks again to Vinny for approval. Vinny gives him a satisfactory nod. Chick carefully takes aim with a few slow-motion passes before putting his weight behind it. The mallet makes contact with a deep *thump* followed by a triumphant *ding!* of the bell.

The carny relinquishes the prize to Gayle, who hugs and adores the feel of her new teddy bear's velour-like fur.

"Be more careful in the future, my friend, or you may need a dog and a cane," Vinny says to the carny. He takes the mallet from Chick and, with little effort, repeats the manly feat.

Vinny tosses the guy a dollar, which floats to the ground like a fallen leaf. While the carny is busy collecting the take, Vinny lifts a duplicate bear off the rack and presents it to Mary. She takes it with an uneasy smile, leaving the man. She looks back at the carny, reassuring herself that he seems content with the margin.

"The only other place with this much activity is Mary's house in the morning," Gayle quips. They walk the midway. Ringing, buzzing, snapping, and clicking sounds bombard them from every direction. The clumsy concerto is accompanied by blinking lights and barkers beckoning them with their clever come-hither taglines.

They consider game booths with names like The Peach Basket, Milk Bottle Toss, Tip-a-Troll, Football Toss, and, Vinny's favorite, The Shooting Gallery. Despite all the carnies' tricks to taint the score of each shooter who dares, Vinny still finds victory a simple task. He easily wins several beautiful pieces of carnival glass for Mary. One piece in particular is a fancy vase—Mary imagines it one day gracing her own dining room table or mantel.

At the end of the row is the Lucky Ducky booth, where everyone's a winner. The girls selectively pick floating ducks out of a trough full of water, turning them over to reveal a number. Unfortunately, the prize for most of the numbers is a small celluloid Kewpie doll. Kewpie dolls have been around long enough that for most girls, they have lost all charm.

Frustration sets in as the games show every sign of being rigged in one way or another. With arms full of prizes (and wallets drained of cash spent to attain them), they decide to call it quits at the game booths.

"A ride on the Ferris wheel sounds more romantic, anyway," Gayle says, fluttering her lashes at Chick. He is holding various chalk-ware figurines, glassware, and a doll to keep Gayle's teddy bear company in the car.

Vinny hands Mary a five-dollar bill. "Why don't you girls take this and go get yourselves a snack while we put these away for safekeeping."

"But the line is so long," Mary says, holding the bill with both hands as if it would try to get away.

"Don't worry, it will move fast. We'll be back in two shakes of a lamb's tail," Vinny says, shifting his load of tchotchkes and turning to leave.

Gayle vibrates as she holds onto Mary. The second the males are out of earshot, she whispers, "Have you ever had so much fun in your life? I could just *burst* . . . like an overblown balloon!"

"I can't imagine having a better day than this one, I can tell you that much. Even the weather is cooperating," Mary says, looking up at puffy clouds floating in the peaceful afternoon sky.

Both girls are silent for several minutes, basking in the smells coming from the concession stand: fragrant scents of salted popcorn, soft pretzels, candied apples, caramel, and, of course, cotton candy, all wafting past. They inhale deeply and sigh.

"What happens tomorrow, or at *midnight* for that matter? Will everything be as boring and dull as it was before?" Gayle asks dreamily, twirling cotton candy around her finger and inserting it into her mouth all the way to her knuckle. Removing her finger, she adds, "I've never felt this way before. I don't want it to end. *Please* say you will go tonight! My mom will only let me go if you do. I will do *anything* you want. I can help you with your chores. Anything!" Gayle pleads with desperation. "Don't you like him?"

"Yes, I think he is a nice person. It's just that I have aspirations. Look where I am coming from. It's important that I keep my wits about me to reach those goals. I feel like he will only be a distraction, you know? Besides, don't you think it's strange that he's acting this way? He barely knows me!" Mary stuffs a wad of pink fluff into her mouth, leaving her with an unnaturally red set of lips.

"It's just a *date*, Mary. It really doesn't have to be more than that. I guess it is a little weird, but he did say 'no obligations.' I think you might be looking a gift horse in the mouth . . . isn't that something your dad always says?"

"Yes, that sounds like his advice," Mary agrees.

"You need to give the guy a break. One day you're gonna have to let someone through that coat of armor you're always wearing. Why not today?" Gayle spots the fortune-teller tent they visited earlier. "Let's go ask Beulah!" she demands, tugging Mary by the arm.

Mary decides to let Gayle have her fun, and follows willingly. Turning the corner of the tent, they see a haggard Caucasian woman wearing a dingy gypsy outfit at the entrance.

"Would you like to know your future, my dear?" the woman asks. She is missing a front tooth.

"We were looking for Mambo Beulah," Gayle says, peering into the tent; everything is the same inside, minus the prognosticative Creole woman.

The haggard woman's jaw drops, revealing more missing teeth. "How you know Beulah?" she probes, her eyes narrowing.

"I had a reading done with her earlier today, and I just needed some more advice," Mary says. This woman frightens Mary, particularly as she cackles like she has just been released from an insane asylum.

"Someone has played a nasty trick on you, little one!" she hollers after the girls as they dart away. They run until they can no longer hear her eerie laughter.

"I told you all of that is hokey-pokey nonsense! That woman is crazy!" Mary says, falling to the ground to catch her breath and mindlessly ripping out blades of grass.

"You should have seen your face when she started to laugh! I thought you were going to pee your pants," Gayle says, giggling wildly.

"It was because of her breath. Did you see those teeth? Talk about needing a toothbrush." Mary tosses grass confetti into Gayle's face and hair. "No more fortune-tellers."

"I'll agree to that on one condition. You have to keep cool and have fun the rest of the day." Gayle helps Mary to her feet and dusts her off.

"All right, all right. I will go and try to relax enough to enjoy myself."

"What's that—you're . . . *enjoying* yourself? I knew you could do it," Vinny says, returning from the car. He is smoking a cigarette.

"Ewww, you guys smell *icky*," Gayle says with disgust. "I don't like smokes."

"You see, Vinny? I told you these ladies were trouble. It's only been a couple hours and they're already trying to change us," Chick says, hooking his arm around Gayle. She pinches her nose shut and stares at him pointedly until he puts the cigarette out on the bottom of his shoe.

"Sure did take your sweet time. If I didn't know better, I would have thought you took off," Gayle says, releasing her nose.

As they walk over to the rides, a group of football players happen by and stop to congratulate the girls on making the freshman cheer squad. One young man in particular seems ready to ask Mary something, but as Vinny puts his arm around her, he leaves abruptly—like a deer at the sound of a cocking gun.

"So you're a paper-shaker?" Vinny asks Mary in disbelief, waiting in line for the Ferris wheel.

Before she can respond, Gayle butts in. "This girl is on the stick. She's not your ordinary ditsy cheerleader like me. She was valedictorian of our eighth grade class."

"So you're a regular Einstein, huh?" Chick says to Mary, impressed.

"Not *Einstein*, but I did test at a second-year college level. I'm only on the squad so I can have an extracurricular activity. Colleges tend to favor only well-rounded female students." As she speaks, Mary absently plays with the bag of leftover cotton candy.

From behind her, Vinny says for her ears only, "You look like you're well-rounded from where I'm standing." He's close enough for her to catch a whiff of his subtle cologne, a delectable combination of wood and citrus.

Her brow furrows at her inability to be offended by his forward comment. Betrayed by the smile tugging at the sides of her mouth, she draws her lips in and bites down on them in retribution.

Gayle continues where Mary left off. "Mrs. Tisdale is from up north and says that Mary could be an Ivy Leaguer—with a scholarship, no less."

Vinny seems a touch disquieted by this revelation. He gazes upon Mary admiringly.

Chick walks beside Vinny and whispers, "I'm glad you ended up with the smart one." Vinny just gives him a look that makes Chick step back.

"The line went quicker than I thought it would," Mary says almost somberly, as if she needs more time to prepare to sit so close to him. And, in fact, she did.

Slowly they ascend in the Ferris wheel, the full aerial view of the fairground developing and revealing to Mary an evolving kaleidoscope of the pedestrians and dancers below.

Is this what God sees when he looks down on us from
time to time?

she thinks, as the warts of the immediate surroundings quickly lose focus.

"Is it just me, or does the world seem less complicated and more beautiful from above?" Mary says, inspecting patterns created by people and tents.

"It sure is beautiful from where I'm sitting," Vinny says, making eye contact.

Turning her eyes back to the ground, Mary says bashfully, "You seemed different after we talked about school. Does it bother you that I want to go to college?" She is holding her belly, which is wildly fluttering from the ride picking up speed—or perhaps from his intoxicating stare.

He picks up on the apprehension in her voice and decides to drop his pursuit long enough to be candid. "Not as much as it bothers me that you might look at *me* differently if you knew that I didn't— I didn't even get as far as you have already." He distracts himself with the chipping paint on the safety bar with his thumb.

"I would never look down on anyone for their education, or lack thereof. It's character that makes a person large in my eyes. To think otherwise would be the ultimate ignorance," she says, and adds, "I would have easily thought that you were a high school graduate if you hadn't said anything. Your financial success is a testament to your innate social intelligence."

"I needed to make sure you wouldn't think I was some lame duck," he says, open and vulnerable.

Instead of using words, she reaches for his hand and slides a little closer to him.

He studies her face a moment before posing a question. "Has anyone ever told you that you look like Maggie the Cat?"

"No. Who's Maggie the Cat?"

"Never mind," he says, developing a naughty grin and adding, "Look who else is getting better acquainted." He points out their counterparts, who are sitting a little too close in the next seat.

For the few minutes the ticket allows, it is bliss.

Just as they regain their footing on the grassy ground, a new craze band arrives onstage, playing a fusion of the old and the new, striking a chord that tugs Gayle by her boogie bone.

"Let's go dance! I *love* this song," she says, pulling Chick toward the dance floor, and he turns to Vinny and Mary for help.

"*See you later, alligator! After a while, crocodile!*" they all chime into the chorus.

"Way to shake a leg, man," Vinny says, giving Chick a sliver of encouragement on his feeble attempt at dancing. As the song begins to wane, Vinny catches a glimpse of the insistent face of his wristwatch. "It's getting late, and I promised to have you girls home by five-thirty." He herds them forward, fumbling through the crowd, with the girls emitting grumbles of disappointment as they rush to the car. "We have to hurry! Get you back to help your mother and get ready for the flick."

Much attention is drawn to the sudden traction of rubber once it finds the pavement. The tires' high squeal is loud enough to drown out the one made by Gayle. Chick welcomes the admiration he receives from his new number-one fan, as well as the squeeze she gives him for the thrill. The expression of contentment on her face lessens only slightly as "Tequila" fades off of the radio. An overly enthusiastic barker introduces a standard commercial reel of local vendors droning on about their space-age this or that before returning with the girls' new favorite DJ.

"This is Stew in the afternoon taking your phone call requests, and today we have a question from Sue—go ahead with your question, dahlin."

"Well, I just wanted to know if you know what time it is, Stew?"

"Turn it up—I love this bit," Gayle says, looking at Mary.

"Do I know what time it is? Why, yes, I do," Stew announces. *"For all you teeny boppers out there who want to bop till you drop—what time is it? It's Big Bopper time!"* Stew introduces the girls' favorite tune of the week, followed by the jovial voice of the Big Bopper transmitting over the airwaves, *"Hellooo, baaaby!"*

They are having the time of their lives, within the small space where most make the fondest of memories, in the pocket between childhood glee and adult responsibilities.

Upon reaching familiar landmarks close to home, Mary instinctively squirms with guilt for having such a good day.

The construction sign. Five minutes . . .

The old cemetery. Three minutes . . .

The rusty mailbox on the corner. One minute . . .

All the while dreading the possible wrath of her mother—that is, until she spies the delivery truck in her driveway.

"How in the world?" she asks, playfully shoving Vinny.

"Well, I got the address from your mother while I was on the phone with her. I also called Chick's cousin, Lester. He met us at the bus station to pick up the money, left to pick the TV out, and marked it for immediate delivery."

"You went back to the bus station?" the girls ask simultaneously, looking at each other in wonder.

"Skills, ladies," says Vinny, "skills. Remember when Gayle asked us what took us so long? It really only took a few minutes to go there and back. Besides, Gayle knew all along. She was to ensure a stall if needed."

"You *traitor*!" Mary shouts, blissfully aware of how much Gayle cares about her.

"Don't worry. Maybe one day you can return the favor."

"Just you wait," Mary threatens with a joking shake of her small fist.

Chick pulls in the grass alongside the delivery truck, and they all get out of the car.

"I think I'll wait out here a while," Chick says, lighting up a cigarette.

"Yeah, I think we'll wait out here," Gayle says, taking the cigarette from Chick, dropping it to the ground, and squashing it with her penny loafer.

Before she is able to get all the way inside the house, Mary's mother ambushes her with a loving embrace. Mary stiffens in shock. She has no prior experience of this nature, in public or in private. It bewilders her, but not as much as the sight of the 24-inch, black-and-white Magnavox console television casting a glow on the faces of her seven siblings, all gathered around it. All that is on the screen is static, yet not one of the children even notices she is home.

A sweaty man in blue-on-blue pinstriped overalls rises from behind the TV, tucks a tool back in his pouch, and shimmies his way through the children. He clears his throat and pulls a pad and pen out of his breast pocket. After Vivian releases her anaconda grip and turns her attention to him, Mary can feel blood rush back into her feet.

"The antenna will only take a few more minutes, and you'll be in business," he says, holding the pad out to Vivian.

Her demeanor changes to one that looks way more familiar to Mary. "What do you want me to do with *that?*" she scowls, low and indignant.

The man is unaffected by her tone. Surely he has dealt with this reaction before. "The bill has already been paid in full, ma'am. I just need a signature for warranty purposes." His voice is smooth, in a *Just-doing-my-job* sort of way.

Vivian brightens. Faster than a schizophrenic, she reverts to her former demeanor. "Why didn't you say so, silly?" Her autograph is easy enough and she is happy to give it, along with a little flair, ending with a hard pop of an *i,* dotted like you would expect from a much more famous pen. She hands it back to the unimpressed man and he heads outside to finish the installation.

Before she has a chance to switch again, Mary takes advantage of her mother's good mood to reveal their benefactor. "Mom, this is Vincent Carlino, with whom you spoke earlier," she announces, stepping out of Vivian's way before she gets mowed down.

"You just don't know what this means to me and my family!" Vivian gushes, wrapping both of her hands around Vinny's. "I thank you so much."

"Delighted to meet you in person, Vivian," he says, reading her and the surrounding room as if for research.

"Now get your things and go get ready at Gayle's so you can dress in peace," Vivian says, shooing Mary away.

"But the dishes—I thought . . ." she says, confused.

"Don't you worry about that. I have it under control. Now go on," Vivian says softly. She jerks her head in the direction of Mary's room.

"First I need to get my prizes."

"Prizes?" Vivian looks to Vinny, as if she should have held out for a better payout.

"Just some trinkets I won for her at the fair." Vinny excuses himself to walk with Mary back to the car.

Out front, they find Gayle giggling as Chick chases her around the yard, trying to rescue his pack of cigarettes from her clutches.

"You and Gayle need to get moving," Vinny tells Mary. "Don't worry about me and Chick—we'll stay here. I'm going to talk with your parents. We'll make sure the guy installs the antenna and everything's working. Then we'll get gas and freshen up. The movie starts at eight." He hands Mary the vase.

He follows her with an armful of stuffed trinkets, narrowly avoiding Chick and Gayle's horseplay on his way to the house.

"This vase is my favorite. Isn't it pretty?" Mary shows it to her mother on her way inside.

"It's lovely, dear." Vivian's nice tone still weirds Mary out. It's as if she were in some off-Broadway stage production. Mary stops long enough to look at her mother with a scrunched-up face. She has no memory of the last time Vivian said *lovely* or *dear* to her or anyone else.

She also pauses and takes a good long look at the television.

So that's what people are selling their firstborn for these days,

she speculates on the way to her room.

Mary walks into her bedroom a different person than she last left it. Something has awakened deep within her that she never realized existed.

She places the vase on her dresser; it catches a ray of the setting sun in iridescent facets, holding the light there like the small flame of a candle. She reaches into her pocket and retrieves her money—she'd spent only the dime it took to call home. Even though it seems silly, she stuffs the cash into a small sock trimmed in lace that she has kept from when she was a baby. The sock isn't red, but it will have to do.

She grabs some essentials and is on her way. Outside, Gayle rattles in her ear about what they should or shouldn't do on a first date according to the latest issue of *Teen* magazine. They walk down the road laughing and reflecting on their amazing day so far, anticipating some grand finale.

Gayle's house isn't very far from where Mary lives; in fact, it sits on the same land. When Gayle was small, her grandfather lived in the old farmhouse where Mary's family now resides. After his death from pneumonia in 1948, the family felt it was time to make a few changes. It seems that Gayle's father James has done well recently with some clever investments and another piece of land in the swamp, which is now leased to an oil company, and has enabled him to build a new house and subdivide farmland once used for sugar cane. It has turned out to be more profitable this way, considering he can collect rent and no longer has to maintain all the properties himself.

James never thought himself much of a farmer, but he held out that illusion for his father's sake, until the old man passed. When James decided the farmhouse needed to have indoor plumbing, he sought out highly skilled hands for the job—and that is how he came to know Mary's father, Norman.

Norman was in Houma doing some contract work for a company based in Natchitoches, near his hometown of Provencal. James met him on the job and offered to pay him top dollar to take on the farmhouse plumbing project. When they became good friends, James convinced him to move his family here to Houma and rent the old house on an "as-is" basis, which simply meant it was stuck in a time gone by. Gayle's father has offered to owner-finance the purchase of the property, but Norman has yet to make that commitment, due to an increase in monthly expenses.

At Gayle's house, the girls tell Mrs. Gautreau everything surrounding the chance meeting with Vinny and Chick. Well, perhaps not everything.

"Boy, that's a lot of excitement for just one day," Gayle's mother says.

Gayle gives her the hard sell. "Mom, can I go? They will be here soon and I need to know!"

Shirley mulls it over. "Well, I suppose. If Mary is going, at least you will be well looked after." She knows what a good influence Mary has been, and is ever grateful for her friendship with her daughter. "But I'll have a better answer after your father and I have a chance to speak with them."

It isn't the firm answer they would have liked, but the girls wash up and put on their clean duds just in case.

"It just seems too plain for such a milestone," Mary says, standing pitifully in front of the mirror, disappointed in her colorless ensemble.

He could have anyone. How could he want me?

"You're being silly. But if you'd like, put this scarf on, and this top with your beige skirt." Gayle grabs items from her closet and tosses them to Mary.

"That might work . . ." Mary holds the baby blue top up for assessment in the mirror. Quickly she removes her plain white shirt, tossing it aside, and replaces it with the livelier one.

"Now—does that make you feel better?" Gayle stands behind her with her hands on Mary's shoulders, both of them looking in the mirror.

"Only if you help me with the scarf," Mary says, lifting her ponytail.

Gayle smiles knowingly. "I swear you sound like you *like* him or something."

Meanwhile, at Mary's house, her exhausted father arrives home from his long day at work—to the surprise of a new TV and an unusually happy wife.

Vivian explains the events of the day as he eats his supper. Then they leave the second oldest, Charlie, age thirteen, in charge of the rest of the children, while they walk over to have a chat with Gayle's parents and await the arrival of the young men who want to whisk their daughters away till all hours of the night.

In the front room, at the Gautreaus', Mary and Gayle present a compelling argument to all four of the adults who hold sway over whether or not they can leave in the car—now heard pulling into the driveway. Vivian, already sold on the idea, rushes to open the front door. The young and virile male energy that comes through the door turns her into a younger, giddier version of herself.

"Vincent, Clarence, this is my husband Norman. And these are Gayle's parents, James and Shirley Gautreau," Vivian says with a flirtatious smile, smoothing her lazy attempt at a trendy up-do.

There is a hurried exchange of pleasantries, enough to put minds at ease before the parents hug their little girls as if they are going off to war. Norman reaches out to give each of the suitors a handshake that displays the strength of a much younger man.

"You two better mind yourselves and remain gentlemen, or there will be hell to pay." Not a hint of warmth can be found in Norman's voice.

"Have you ever seen your folks look so worried about somethin so silly before?" Gayle asks Mary, still waving at her parents as they drive away.

Mary nods, tugging at the shirt that suddenly feels too revealing and tight. "It must be hard to watch something that you've nurtured all its life suddenly become somewhat independent of you."

Chick stage-whispers to Gayle, "Does she always talk like that?"

"You'll get used to it. Sometimes I feel like I need a reference book just to have a conversation with her," Gayle says, checking out Mary's comical pout.

"Oh, come on," Chick says, "we're just goofin on ya." He reaches back to tickle her.

"Both hands on the wheel there, buddy," Mary says, pushing his hand away. She notices Vinny sitting silently. Most likely reveling in the fact that everyone is getting along so well and all his plans have fallen into place perfectly. "You really think you have it all figured out, don't you?"

"I know who I am and I know what I want. Can you blame me for taking a chance?" He is looking at her in a way that she doesn't recognize and that usually would make her uncomfortable; but his eyes are so electric and fixed on hers that she is unable to pull away. No words, no blinking—just an energy flowing between them.

That is, until Gayle breaks the moment, in true Gayle fashion. "What are we going to see, anyway?"

"We are going to see Mary's look-alike in *Cat on a Hot Tin Roof.* I want to introduce her to Maggie the 'Cat,' " Vinny says, smirking.

The front-seaters shrug—it must be an inside joke.

Mary folds her arms. "Am I supposed to be impressed? You really think you're something special, don't you?"

He sighs and shakes his head, a little defeated.

"Well, I'm starting to think so, too," she says. She unfolds her arms, touches his soft, wavy hair. He completely melts into her fingers, relinquishing his control, now unsure who is to be puppeteer for the rest of the evening.

When Chick pulls up to the ticket booth at the drive-in, the attendant hands him the tickets with his change. Surprised at the amount, he counts it again. "You gave me too much change—we have four people," Chick says, confused. The attendant takes another look in the car at his passengers.

"No, sir, that's correct. Mary gets in free for life. Enjoy the show."

Mary, too embarrassed to face them, is focusing on a bug crawling outside the window.

"Now how in the world did you manage that?" Vinny asks, surprised that she has such an unusual arrangement.

"I did someone a favor, that's all," she says modestly.

"It must have been some favor!"

Unable to resist, Gayle spills the story as Chick finds them a good parking spot. "Okay, so the guy that owns both the theaters in town has twin boys. They were both failing math and science. Mary tutored them for free, and it was the only reason either one of them passed the sixth grade. He offered to pay her, but she wouldn't take it. So he gave her a free pass instead."

"For life? Here I thought I was treating you to something you didn't normally get to do." Vinny's voice was amused and irritated at the same time.

"It's not like I go see a movie every day just because I can. I'm no freeloader," Mary says, crossing her arms again and softly throwing herself against the seat.

He cradles her face in his hands. "You are so adorable when you get defensive. How's a guy supposed to impress a girl so impressive all on her own?"

"Aw, that's so sweet," Gayle says, breaking the sentiment. "Now impress me and go get us some food. I'm starving."

The girls watch their dates intensely as they walk toward the concession building.

"Aren't they just the *most?* There go two of the dreamiest dreamboats I could have ever imagined for us! God really does listen, Mary—you were right. It's like we ordered them straight out of the Sears catalog. It's like Christmas came early this year!" Gayle hops up and down in her seat.

"You really need to calm down. You're going to scare them away. Don't you know that men hate crazy, high-strung women?"

"I'm just having the most fun I could ever imagine and I am trying to share that with my best friend . . . ex*cuuuse* me! No need to pee in my Cocoa Puffs."

"Forgive me. I don't know what is wrong with me," Mary says, bowing her head in contrition as if she were part of another culture. (Gayle, of course, rolls her eyes at this.) "I am not used to this attention or this freedom. I am feeling as if I am falling and I have nothing to brace myself."

"Falling . . . like you're falling in *love* . . . hmm?"

"You are so lucky I love you, or I would clobber you to death," Mary says, laughing.

"You're the one always making it difficult with your rules and your morals. It's a good thing you have me to save you from all your seriousness. Guys don't like that either! They don't go around like, 'Check out the virtue on that one.' "

Mary pays careful attention to the traffic to and from the concession building until she recognizes some familiar Italian silk. "Thank goodness. My throat feels like gravel," she says, her mouth too dry to salivate at the many choices in store for them.

The guys are balancing two trays filled with popcorn, burgers, corndogs, fries, and candy. Despite her growling tummy, Mary would give up all the food if it meant a huge swig of any beverage. Her eyes scan the contents of the trays, disappointed at the absence of any item to end her torturous thirst. That is, until she spies a young boy following them with a tray of sweaty Dixie cups balanced precariously in his tiny hands.

"That is just too cute." Mary hops out and snatches the tray from him before he has a chance to drop it. She says, "Thank you very much, little man," and bends to kiss his cheek.

"Yes, ma'am," the boy says. Vincent gives him a quarter for his trouble, and he bolts off with his shiny reward.

"I didn't get a kiss, and I carried the heaviest tray," Vinny says, pretending hurt at being overlooked.

"It depends on how well you behave during the movie," Mary says playfully, raising her eyebrows and placing the tray of drinks in his hands. She picks up one of the cokes and quickly applies a straw before inhaling nearly half its contents.

"*Let's all go to the lobby . . . and get ourselves a treat,*" Gayle sings along with the commercial—until she realizes they have no ketchup.

"I'm sorry. I'll go get some," Chick says, opening the car door.

"That's all right. I'll be right back. They'll let me take a whole bottle if I go." Gayle sprints to fetch her beloved condiment.

Once she returns, it doesn't take long to wolf down half the food and settle in for the duration of the picture. The guys position themselves with their backs against opposite doors, providing the girls with an open invitation to lean against them.

Gayle is the only one brave enough to cozy up.

There is no funny business on this date, though—nothing to blemish the girls' integrity or reputation. The guys keep their word and return the girls to Gayle's house safe, sound, and unspoiled.

"At least it had a decent ending," Gayle says, hopping out of the car and onto the hood before Chick has a chance to be gentlemanly.

"I think the husband was a moron," Vinny says. "How could he have been so blind to her needs?" He stops half in, half out of the car in the Gautreaus' driveway, as if he has forgotten what he is doing.

Mary decides to artfully dodge the sexual aspects of the film. "I think he was confused about his desires. People have their issues and defenses. It's hard to see the source of pain. They build a wall."

Vinny travels around the car to Mary's side. "I'd climb any wall to take a gander at *my* Maggie the Cat. She's a knockout," he says, offering a hand to Mary after opening her car door. She gives him a grin that mirrors his own.

Gayle stabs an elbow in Chick's side.

"You're too fast for me to keep up with," Chick says, rubbing his wound.

"And don't you forget it, buddy," Gayle says. She slaps his cheek with her puckered lips as she slides off the hood, her hip coming into contact with his, grabbing his full attention as she leans on the car.

She is facing her house, where no doubt her parents are peering out at the couples.

Vinny pulls Mary aside a moment so they can say goodnight in semi-privacy.

"I had a nice time today," Mary says, staring at his freshly shined leather shoes. "It's hard to believe it's only been one day."

It's a good sign when a man takes care of his shoes.

Vinny touches her chin and lifts it gently until her eyes meet his.

"It was the best day of my life so far, and that's no lie." A slight tug sounds at the back of his throat, like the words are slicing him on their way out.

Mary's nervous fingers seek out her earlobe, as if holding on to it will keep her voice steady. "I don't know what to say . . . we barely know each other."

"With all your education and all your wisdom, I know it's hard for you to believe in love at first sight. Hell, I didn't believe it myself until this morning." He shoves his hands deep in his pockets. "Can I see you tomorrow?"

"Yes. I mean, I have church in the morning—but you could come after, I suppose."

"Good, then. It's a date." Vinny points at his cheek for a peck, worried that kissing her on the mouth would scare her off, as inexperienced as she is. After letting go of her irritated ear flesh, she leans in for a brief kiss.

Gayle has no such timidity: she throws her arms around Chick and plants a smooch on him while he is in the middle of explaining how he paid extra to have the new level air suspension in his car.

The porch light comes on and James emerges to announce that Shirley has just finished making lemonade, signaling the end of the date.

"Tell her we appreciate the offer, sir, but it's getting late and the girls need to get rested for church," Vinny says with a wave, walking to the car.

James scratches his head, a little dumbfounded that he didn't have to end up running them off with a stick.

"See you later, alligator," Gayle says to Chick, imitating his awkward dance moves.

"After a while, crocodile," he replies, his lips still wet from her kiss.

The girls barrel inside to spill their guts to Shirley over lemonade. The prospect of spending the night apart is so unbearable that Mary obtains permission to stay at Gayle's.

Not that either of them gets much sleep before needing to rise the next morning for church.

Sunday
September 7, 1958

Everyone in the Gautreau household is rushing around, trying to be on time for church.

"Now you know, that is my very favorite dress on you, Mary," says Gayle's mother Shirley. It is the one she bought Mary for Easter earlier this year. "Oh, how I adore you in pink! Be sure to grab a sweater for your shoulders, and that darling matching hat." Shirley's voice brims with a motherly affection. "And here are a pair of gloves for such a demure young lady," she adds with a wink.

Suddenly mindful of her daughter's rebellious nature, Shirley turns on her. "Gayle, I hope you have brushed your teeth this morning—and run a comb through your hair!"

Gayle grabs a piece of bacon. "Yuck, Mom! Bacon and toothpaste don't mix well. I never did understand why we have to brush before coming downstairs."

"If you ever caught a whiff of your morning breath, you would know why," Mary says, and they blow raspberries at one another. "I've got to go help Mom with the kids. I'll see you at church." After a quick hug with Gayle, Mary rushes out the door and down the porch steps, trotting down the shell road.

Why do I feel so different? I feel like dancing or singing
or something.
I hope I am not turning into one of those dopey girls I'm
always surrounded by at school. This feels like I've been
exposed to some sort of virus going around.

She shakes her head, grimacing at herself and trying to dispel thoughts of Vinny.

Get a hold of yourself, girl!
Don't let some silly crush take away your good sense.

Mary has always been a clever girl, a solid decision maker. She recognizes that any misstep at this point in her life could change everything. The thing she hasn't counted on is that her heart and her body are beginning to voice their own opinion.

She enters her home and sees, to her dismay, that her mother is up and breakfast has been consumed.

Surprisingly, Vivian is smiling. Seeing Mary enter, she announces, "Charlie must have been taking notes all this time. He took up right where you left off."

"It's the least I could do for all you have done for us," Charlie whispers to Mary as he clears the dishes, not wanting to dispel his mother's new mood.

She doesn't know whether it is her brother's words, her mother acting so cheerful, or the lack of sleep, but her vision begins to blur as the tears well up; she fights them back tooth-and-nail.

Who knew a man with a cocky smile and a television
could fix all that ailed this family—when I couldn't seem
to?

At that thought, Mary can no longer contain her emotions and cries unfettered.

Her mother rushes to Mary's side, wiping her hands on a rarely used apron. "What's wrong? Did that boy hurt you?"

Her genuine concern makes Mary cry harder.

"I'm getting your father—NORMAN!"

Mary grabs Vivian's arm, and the children gather to witness the episode as if it is the evening news. "No, Mom. He was a perfect gentleman. I'm crying because I'm happy," she sniffs.

"I think she's got the menses, Pa!" her little sister Jenny explains to Norman as he bursts into the room, nostrils flared, ready to defend the homestead.

"Would someone please tell me what was important enough to catch me a heart attack?" he says, still confused. Nevertheless, he steps in to comfort Mary.

"It was a misunderstanding, Pa," Mary says, enjoying the hug.

"Hmmm . . . there's been many of those in my day. Ita work itself out." Norman rubs her back and lets her go. "Now, tell me more about this gentleman caller—"

Vivian turns to shift about; clumsily she applies wrong-sized hand-me-down shoes onto little squirmy feet, pretending not to hear.

"I'm not sure, but I could have sworn we had agreed no dating till your sixteenth birthday." He says these last words in Vivian's direction.

"I'm sorry, Pa," Mary says, trying to protect her mother yet again. "But the circumstance presented itself out of the blue and caught us by surprise."

Vivian gives up on the mismatched shoes and stands to face her husband. Strangely, she is still smiling, in this inexplicable good mood, but a familiar glint has entered her eyes. "Now, Norman, I told you he seemed like a right decent young man. You met him yourself. I made sure he understood about what's expected and all. You get to talk to him yourself this afternoon. Shirley and I asked them to come to lunch after church. You're going to listen to what that young man has to say, or I am going to tell the story of how you—"

"All right, Ma," he says quickly, cutting her off. "I'll hear the boy out."

All the kids turn in Norman's direction, wide-eyed and wondering what dirt their mother has on him. Jenny says what all the others do not dare. "Tell us the story, Mama!"

Vivian glares around at the little ones. "Your ears are too little. Now get your hide in the truck—all of you!"

They scatter reluctantly. Jenny walks away rubbing her ears, and she turns to Jason. "You have big ears. Why couldn't she tell *you* the story?"

"She meant you're too *young*, dufus."

"What's a dufus?" she asks, perching to tattle.

Sensing himself in hot water, Jason explains, "It's the Latin word for *sister.*"

Surprisingly, Jenny accepts his fib as the truth.

Mary follows the little ones outside. Sarah, walking beside her, asks, "What's that song, Mary?"

"What song?"

"The one you were humming." Sarah gives her a knowing look, on the verge of a giggle.

"I don't know ... I didn't realize I was humming," Mary says, mortified.

> *Oh man, I'm like one of those lovesick girls you see in*
> *the movies.*

Attempting to maintain her dignity, she piles the children into the open bed of the truck, humming the tune to "Stupid Cupid."

Norman and Vivian climb into the cab. Jenny starts a singsong chant of *"Mary's got a boyfriend, Mary's got a boyfriend!"* that lasts until they pull onto the main road—no one wants to sing when there is the possibility of swallowing bugs. That happened once to Jenny, so she is the first to stop.

Mary welcomes the taunting, letting them relish it.

> *You have to take joy where you can find it,*

she reasons. She puts her gloved hand out of the window and lets the wind flow through her fingers as she ponders the universe.

Norman parks the truck near their house of worship, with its ornate stonework skin in various shades of tan and taupe, and large, colorful stained glass windows, surrounded by neatly manicured greenery. The well-cared-for compound stands in sharp contrast to the houses that inhabit the same street. A castle in the midst of a village.

Mary ushers the little ones to their respective Sunday school classes. So as not to lose her favorite hat, she only half-runs to her own class, Bible in hand—the only parishioner who brings one.

Gayle has already taken her seat in the class, anxious to see her friend again (even though they just parted an hour or so ago) like they share some secret world where no one else has been.

Mary takes the seat that Gayle so patiently saved for her, keeping it from Veronica Babin. Veronica is a snobbish girl who has wanted to be friends with Gayle ever since the Gautreaus entered a higher earning bracket. She has no idea why Gayle would want to associate herself with a poor person such as Mary.

Without disturbing the rest of the class, Mary relays highlights to Gayle from the conversation she had with her parents about the guys coming for lunch. She is acutely aware that Veronica is attempting to eavesdrop from across the table.

Having been unsuccessful, Veronica decides that retaliation is in order. "I see someone has taken pity on you, Mary, and provided you with a new pair of gloves," she says scathingly. "They go so well with that dress that was generously given to you, no doubt."

"Damn you, Veronica Babin!" Gayle comes at her across the table, Mary barely able to hold her back.

Veronica moves toward the door, terrified, but before Gayle can get at her the teacher enters the room. "Ladies, not in the Lord's house," she admonishes. "Take your seats. I don't want to hear another word." As the teacher fiddles with her papers, Gayle is still threatening Veronica by pounding one gloved hand into the other. Veronica recovers her composure and pretends to be unaffected.

Hoping to placate her best bud, Mary whispers, "Don't let her upset you so much. We don't need any trouble. She isn't worth it."

After class, Veronica calmly rises to leave the room with Gayle still burning a hole into her skull with glaring eyes. Before Mary can stop her, Gayle gets up and breaks into a run after her—long enough to make Veronica run all the way to the main chapel. After Mary catches up with her and they share a good laugh at Veronica's expense and airily stroll the rest of the way. In the last pew, settled next to an engrossed Mary, Gayle finds herself sitting with tainted memories, unable to pay much attention to the sermon on forgiveness.

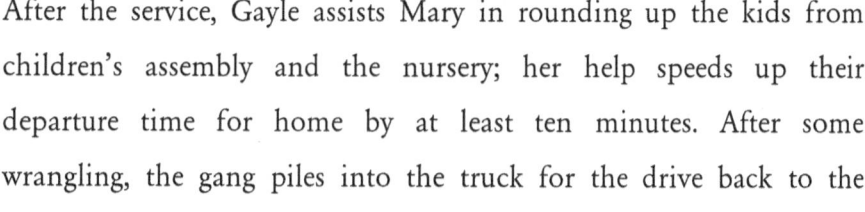

After the service, Gayle assists Mary in rounding up the kids from children's assembly and the nursery; her help speeds up their departure time for home by at least ten minutes. After some wrangling, the gang piles into the truck for the drive back to the Poche house. Jenny refuses to sit in the back of the truck, so Mary rides home with Gayle and her parents.

"I sure am glad I'm an only child," Gayle says, exhausted from the ordeal.

"Try doing that every day of your life!" Mary says. "They were actually kind of cooperative today."

So begins a heated discussion about why or why not to have children when each of them marries, entertaining Gayle's parents all the way home.

The girls light up when they see Chick's Impala parked on the road, and the Gautreaus and Poches part ways to host their gentlemen callers separately.

Even after seeing Vinny's fancy shirt and slacks, Mary opts for shedding her Sunday clothes for a less formal outfit, seeing as she hardly ever makes it through a meal without wearing some of her or someone else's food. She chooses dungarees and a red-and-white seersucker button-up tied in a square knot at the waist. This leaves her underdressed compared to Vinny—she is painfully aware that if she sees him just a few more times, he will have witnessed every decent piece of clothing she currently owns.

Jambalaya is on the menu today—relatively cheap to make for a large gathering since it is mostly rice with just enough sausage to add flavor. Vivian adds a bit of chicken to the mix today because of the current company.

After lunch, Vinny and Norman sit on the porch to get to know each other better, while Mary is told to return to her normal kitchen duties. But cleaning dishes feels like torture at the moment.

I wish I knew what they were discussing out there.
What if Dad is telling him he has to wait until I turn
sixteen in February?

"I can't wait that long to see him again," she says aloud, before looking around to see if anyone notices she is talking to herself.

When the men finish sniffing each other out, Norman calls Mary to the porch. She is practically jumping out of her skin with nerves, but relief floods her body as her dad sends the couple on their way with his blessing.

As they walk toward Gayle's house, where Chick's Impala is parked, Mary asks Vinny, "Can you tell me what you talked about?"

Vinny smiles, strolling nonchalantly. "Like any other father, he just wants to make sure that you are to remain as pristine as I found you, and that you are to be respected, taken care of, and allowed to pursue your dreams, whatever they may be. All the usual dad stuff."

Mary frowns. She is bothered by his casual tone—it suggests he has heard that spiel a hundred times.

Vinny picks up on her unease. "Hey, now . . . *I* want all those things for you, too," he soothes. "I was in agreement with everything he said—and then some."

She tries to shake it off, forcing a smile back on her face. She waves to Chick, Gayle, and her parents on the porch next door.

"We'll be right here!" Mary calls out to them. She climbs into her designated seat in the back of Chick's car, and Vinny takes his usual spot as well. She leaves the doors open, letting the breeze keep them cool. "This is so wild to me," she says. "I hardly know anything about you. I have so many unanswered questions."

"Shoot," Vinny says, his arms wide and vulnerable.

"Where do you live?"

"In a hotel in the French Quarter of New Orleans."

"You live in a hotel?" she asks in curious amazement.

"Yes, I'm a good friend of the owners. I have to travel a lot for my job, and they are always able to accommodate me."

"What do you do for a living?"

He draws closer to her and lowers his voice, as if someone else might overhear. "What I am about to tell you has to be kept between you and me. Can I trust you?"

"Yes, of course. Cross my heart and hope to die," she says, drawing an invisible X on her chest with her finger, honored to become his confidant.

"I'm a personal assistant of sorts. A cleaner for a pest control company. When there is a big mess, it's my job to go in and fix it. No one wants people to know when things are dirty, so it's kept secret."

Mary blinks, not exactly sure what that means. Her intellectual gears begin to turn. "Like when visitors pop over unexpectedly?" she asks naïvely. "That can be embarrassing."

"Yeah. Women don't like that too much, do they?" Vinny says, studying Mary's long, shiny hair and beautiful profile.

She nods. "Wow, I never knew that line of work could be so lucrative. Which company is it?"

He coughs into his hand. "Miller the Killer," he says weakly.

" *'We kill them all!'* " she sings to the tune of the familiar jingle. "That one?"

He bursts into hearty laughter. "You nailed it! Yeah, that's the one."

Mary has enough siblings to know when she might be hearing something close to a lie. It is not so much in what is said, but in the way they dodge and weave with the words. Apprehensively, she begins to scan his features for honesty. Perhaps he is just amused by her lack of tonality when she sings.

Vinny, noticing Mary's scrutiny, can see that this one will be a bit harder to seduce than the others. "I'm laughing because you are so darn cute . . . and I can't believe how lucky I am to have met you."

She swallows this thin commentary and moves warily onto the next question. "Where do your parents live?"

A silence falls—a silence so sudden, it is as if the air has emptied into a vacuous void, all his lighthearted laughter vanquished over such a benign reach into his background. Mary sits in this new quiet, afraid that she has stirred something wrong, something previously stagnant, and turned it rancid. Unsure how to proceed, she tries not to move or breathe, awaiting some sort of outside guidance.

Finally, after what seems like an hour to Mary, he says in a slightly forced voice, "They passed away. They are buried in New Orleans."

She reaches for his arm with a gentle touch of sympathy. She wears a somber expression, believing she has pried open his painful scab. "I am so sorry."

He recoils from her advance. "It's okay. It was an accident. A long time ago."

He dismisses her concern abruptly as the others climb into the car, doors slamming shut. Chick shoves a key in the ignition, bringing the engine to life, stale air blasting out of every vent. They are ready to roll.

"Clarence here made a wonderful impression on my parents," Gayle says proudly of her new beau. Chick visibly shudders at hearing his real name, as if she has written it on a chalkboard with her nails.

Gayle's fingers reach to stroke his hair but pull back in disgust. "You really need to take it easy on the hair goo, buddy!" She wipes her hand on his pants, then pets his neck instead. "Where are we going, anyway?"

"Why, into town to buy new dresses for our favorite girls, of course," Chick says, trying to be debonair. He adds, "And to pick up some supplies for my cousin Lester."

"The stores aren't open today. It's Sunday. There is a blue law or something," Mary informs them, heavy with disappointment.

Chick's face breaks into a sly sideways grin. "There are ways around the law, Mary," he says to her reflection in the rear-view mirror. "People have to make a living. You just have to make it worth their time. Green is a powerful color."

Despite being unsettled by her last exchange with Vinny, Mary's jaw tightens in deliberate effort not to preach the necessities of law in society—knowing her words would probably be lost on everyone present.

Gayle, unaware of her best friend's unease, faces the back seat and squeals. "This is so cool! Hey, Vinny, can we get more than one outfit for Mary? She so deserves it, and I know exactly which ones she should have."

"Sure, whatever she wants," Vinny answers, putting his arm around Mary as if nothing happened just minutes before.

First she is surprised, but this is soon followed by the release of her coiled muscles. "Please don't go out of your way," Mary says, embarrassed by Gayle's insolence.

"It's going to be fine, Mary. You'll see," Gayle says.

"Yes, Mary," Vinny says, "what else would you expect from your Steady Freddy?"

Suddenly, everyone is curious, yet too afraid to ask. A heavy silence settles over the car, only broken by the crunch of gravel beneath tires.

"What . . . do you mean?" Mary asks. The word *steady* doesn't seem to fit in her ear.

"What I am trying to say is, I want to be your one and only. I'm asking you to be my girl," Vinny pleads, his voice like fresh velvet. "So . . . will you?" Knowing she is going to be a hard sell, he ups the ante by adding, "Your father already said it was okay."

Her mind flies into a litany of excuses and reasons why this is a bad idea and she is unable to speak, or breathe for that matter.

Too fast! Is he the right one? The wrong one? This could
be a cage.
But . . . surely my dad would know the difference.

She takes a long, cleansing breath and looks at Gayle, who has wide eyes and is practically biting the top of the seat in suspense.

Mary can hear her friend's words from yesterday as if Gayle is sending them telepathically:

Nothing exciting will ever happen to you if you never let it.

After an anxious moment of deliberation, she sighs and gives him her answer. "I . . . I guess so, Vinny. I'll go steady with you." Mary feels as if she has just jumped off the high dive at the public pool for the first time. She has never been on the high dive—too afraid of the diving board, and the water—never even been in water deeper than the bathtub. Her main concern now is to make sure that Vinny understands nothing can disturb her studies. Already, her mind whirrs with images of daily planners and deadlines—she will have to stay on top of her work during the week to continue achieving her lofty educational goals.

Mary is snapped out of her thoughts when Gayle suddenly smacks Chick on the shoulder. "I hope you're taking notes, buster, because I want you to know I'm a hot commodity on the freshman market," she says, arms folded and reeking of jealousy.

"It looks like a ghost town here. Huh—I guess all the law-abiding citizens are back at the fair today. Some blue law!" Chick says, pulling into town after seeing a beer tent in the fairgrounds parking lot that was twice as full as it was the day before.

Unlike the fair, Main Street is quiet as the grave, lined with an orderly succession of squatty storefronts. The pavement in front of them is deserted except for a tired blue pick-up truck sitting near the hardware store. Mary half-expects to see a lonely tumbleweed hopping in the breeze alongside the car as they roll down the street.

"This looks as good a spot as any," Chick says, parking in a space right in front of the barbershop that happens to sit midway between the dress shop and the hardware store.

Vinny walks the girls over to the dress shop. Mary never even knew the shop existed, either because she hardly ever comes into town, or because even if she did, she never would have peeked inside—to avoid the dangling carrots with the unattainable price tags.

Vinny knocks gently on the door. From out of the shadowy depths of the shop, a middle-aged, smartly dressed woman with angular cheeks appears. Nervously, the woman unlocks the door and ushers the two girls across the threshold. The girls, enthralled by the store's wares, miss her caution, the way she looks from side to side to see if anyone is around to notice. Vinny passes an envelope and whispers something to the woman, and her face brightens like that of a child who has been promised a prize for being on her best behavior.

"They will be in good hands. Give us about an hour," the woman says softly, giving him a warm smile before locking the door behind him.

She doesn't turn on the lights, and is a bit fidgety when the girls want to check out the window display. It takes a moment for Mary's eyes to adjust to the low lighting, while her nose receives an unexpected treat: the store's air smells faintly of lavender perfume (which Mary's mother would no doubt refer to as the smell of a French whore). Perhaps it is emitting from one of the many artsy glass decanters on the shelves behind the counter. Some have bulb atomizers glamorized with fringe, and others are quiet in their beauty. All are tantalizing.

I wonder which one contains that particular scent.
Lavender . . . I wonder if that's something Vinny would
find alluring . . .

"What am I doing?" she says out loud.

"We're shopping! Isn't it fun?" Gayle squeals from her spot in hanger heaven. Shopping is her second-best subject, right after cars. Too bad they don't give grades for such talents, or she might make the honor roll. Gayle is voraciously scraping metal hooks along several of the racks.

Mary timidly peruses the first rack she comes to, preoccupied by feelings of guilt for imposing upon this poor shop owner on what is likely to be her only day off. The woman eyes Mary up and down, calculating her dimensions before plucking a petticoat slip from among many others and checking the tag for the size.

"Girls, I have picked out some of our best selections and put them on a stand in the changing area. Go ahead and get started. Call me if you need help. I need to grab a few more things, and I will join you shortly," she calls, flitting from rack to rack like a hummingbird in a garden full of bee balm.

"Try this blue one on first, Mary," Gayle urges, handing her a calf-length cotton shirtdress from a rack near the front of the store. "It will make your eyes more vivid."

Mary blushes, and together they turn and head for the changing room.

"You're going to need this slip with that dress, dear," the woman says, rushing over to deposit the silky slip in Mary's arms before she has the chance to commit some sort of fashion faux pas. "My name is Mrs. Picou, by the way. I will be right here if either of you need any assistance." The girls close the curtains to their individual dressing rooms and Mrs. Picou flits away once more, to hover nearby.

Prior to this trip, Mary never had the opportunity to shop in a bona fide dress shop—she relied mostly on the grainy pictures in catalogues to make her selections. She is not prepared for this jolt to her senses. Overcome with awe, she stands for a moment, lost in the glorious texture of fabrics she has never before had the privilege of wearing. Hearing Gayle speak to the saleslady snaps her back to the moment, and she hurriedly begins to undress. They only have an hour, and Mary plans to enjoy every minute.

"I am not as well-endowed as Mary," complains Gayle. A hint of shame has crept into her voice. "None of the tops of these dresses fit right . . . Can they be taken in?"

"Let me see how it looks," Mrs. Picou beckons. Gayle emerges from the fitting room, arms crossed beneath her small bosom, with enough clearance to plainly see her A-cup brassiere.

"Oh, that just won't do. I have a better idea. I'll be right back." And away goes Mrs. Picou, a woman on a mission.

Gayle is left to wallow in a pool of self-pity until the shop owner returns momentarily with a fresh armload of appropriate cuts for the girl's slim figure. Gingham checks, polka dots, and floral dresses with boat necklines are all it takes to put her right again.

"How are we doing in there? Can I help fasten anything?" Mrs. Picou calls to Mary, as if afraid somehow Mary has fallen through the floor and into an abyss.

"I . . . I'll be out in a second," she says, while indulgently allowing her fingers to skim over the sateen cotton of the dress Gayle wanted her to try on. For the first time, she sees what everyone else has been seeing all along: a beautiful girl. She keeps repositioning herself, as if it must be one of those funhouse mirrors where what you see is all a distorted illusion. Eventually, she passes through the curtain to get a second opinion.

"My goodness—you're an angel!" Mrs. Picou gasps, her hands on her chest as if to keep her heart from falling out.

"Wow, you look sassy!" Gayle says, poking her head out of the curtain, half-dressed.

Mary blushes madly, sheepishly caressing the expert stitching on the fitted bodice. "I think I'll take this one."

"I should say so! I don't know that I have any other day dresses that can do you any more justice," Mrs. Picou says, now rummaging through the selections she had previously placed in the dressing room. "This pink halter dress will look fabulous on you. It would be perfect for an evening event."

"I couldn't. This one will be plenty," Mary says, not wanting to be swayed from her choice.

"Silly girl. That young man said that you were to have as many as you could fit into."

"I don't want to take advantage of his generosity. We only just met . . . and he has done so much already." Mary reluctantly steps back in the dressing room to disrobe.

"He gave me enough money for five of my most expensive dresses. I am to keep the money whether you get them or not, so I suggest you get his money's worth out of the transaction—otherwise, *I'll* be the one taking advantage," Mrs. Picou discloses pointedly, hoping Mary will take the bait.

Mary sighs in utter disbelief, shaking her head at her fortune. "I'd better get crackin, then . . ." She pulls on another dress.

"I love this one!" Gayle says, exiting the changing room and twirling in a dress covered in bright-red cherries.

"That says 'Gayle' all over," Mary giggles, taking a peek at her friend's favorite pick.

"I have enough school clothes. I need something flirty and fun! This will do just fine," Gayle says with a satisfied grin.

Four doors down at the hardware store, Chick is preparing to load up all the supplies his cousin Lester has paid for.

"Thanks for letting me pick this up on a Sunday," Chick says to the clerk as he thumbs through a thick catalogue of special order items on the counter.

"No problem. All this stuff was on backorder, and I know Lester has been needing these roofing nails for a week. I wanted him to have them at sunrise," says the clerk, looking over the list and gathering all of the assorted items. "Your cousin is one of our best customers. Always pays his tab on time." He begins to cheerfully bag Lester's items. "Need any help back there?" he calls to Vinny, who is drawn to a gun display at the back of the store.

"Just looking," he says, eyeing a .22 caliber pistol. It sits in a glass case on the wall filled with various sporting firearms.

"You looking to hunt big or small game?" says the clerk.

"Depends on the offense and the offended," Vinny says under his breath, void of emotion as he turns to acknowledge the clerk. "Just passing time." He forces a smile, but it doesn't quite reach the eyes, as if he were posing for an unwanted photograph. He lifts one of the bags and heads out to Chick's car.

The clerk shrugs and continues to load the final bag. "I didn't mean to disturb him. I just thought he might like to hold one."

"Don't mind him any. He's just nervous about impressing a new girl he just met," Chick says matter-of-factly, without looking up from the catalog.

"Would I know her?"

"Mary Poche . . . you know her?"

"Ahh, Mary Lou. Norman's daughter. That girl is becoming quite a dish, isn't she? Wouldn't mind a taste myself," the clerk replies. Apparently he has been keeping his eye on her. He writes out a receipt and rips it from the pad.

"I'd keep comments like that to myself, if you value your health," Chick warns, taking the slip of paper. "Thanks again, pal." He scoops up the last sack and walks out to the open trunk of his car, passing Vinny, who is finishing a cigarette he lit after leaving the store.

Vinny inhales the last drag, then flicks it into a nearby drain. "I had to leave. Nosy people rub me the wrong way." He spits, leaning against the car like a runner stretching before a race.

"He's a nice guy. He just doesn't know when to shut up," Chick says, amused, closing the trunk with a heavy *thud*. "You think they're almost done?" He shades his eyes pointedly from the hot afternoon sun.

"Let's give them fifteen more minutes." Vinny looks at his watch as he sits on the bench under the barber shop awning. He leans forward, elbows on his knees, too vain to risk wrinkling the back of his shirt. Chick joins him on the bench, seeking a position where a nap can find him.

Amazingly enough, it only takes the girls a few more minutes to try on the rest of the garments. Mary makes good use of Vinny's investment by finding four sensible daytime dresses, plus a less demure pink one that makes her feel like Marilyn Monroe. Gayle only finds two dresses that she feels comfortable in, fitting her quirky sense of style.

Mrs. Picou gathers all the duds, packaging them in large zippered garment bags. Mary has to leave behind two dresses that require slight alterations. While the girls are putting themselves back together, Mrs. Picou places the garment bags on a tall hanging rack near the cash register. She notices that Vinny is pacing back and forth in front of her establishment. "I think someone is getting antsy," Mrs. Picou says to herself as they acknowledge one another with a nod.

In an attempt to expedite the process, she unlocks the door and allows him to enter. Chick has fallen asleep on the bench, but when Vinny whistles to him, he pops up like a jack-in-the-box and joins his friend in the store.

"Would you like to see how your money was spent?" Mrs. Picou announces like the MC of a fashion show.

"I trust that we will see them soon enough," Vinny says, offering her an extra folded bill between two fingers, like he was tipping a valet attendant.

"That won't be necessary. Mary kept herself abreast of the cost of all her merchandise. Most of her choices were on the conservative end. There was plenty left over to make it worth my while," she says, pushing buttons on her register. Mrs. Picou clears her throat as she hands an invoice over to Chick. "Gayle, however, is of a different mind . . . a girl after my own heart."

Upon seeing the figures, Chick gets a little taste of sticker shock. "Well, I guess that isn't bad for a week's worth of dresses," he says, pulling money from his wallet and handing it to Mrs. Picou. She holds up two fingers in a V. "Only . . . *two* dresses?" Chick asks, surprised at the whopping grand total all over again.

"I appreciate you letting us do this today," Vinny says. "Tell the girls to meet us in the car when they come out." He takes the garment bags and drapes them on his shoulder.

"Mary has a dress or two to be altered. They can be picked up in a week."

"Will do." Vinny looks back at her from the doorway with a wink.

What I wouldn't do for a piece of that pie, Mrs. Picou thinks. It has been a long time since anyone that young has winked at her and made her feel like a red-blooded female again. Over the last few years, her husband has stopped visiting her side of the bed. When a woman goes long enough without a man's touch, she no longer feels movement in her veins; the heart becomes quiet and still, as if it is practicing to cease its rhythmic beat. It is at the very moment of Vinny's wink that she resolves to end her loveless marriage and seek out someone who can breathe life into her, while she still has something to offer. With renewed spring in her step, she goes to check on the girls, melodiously calling to them, "What's the hold-up, ladies? Your admirers are waiting patiently in the car."

"We wanted to help pick up, Mrs. P," Gayle says, proudly standing in the pristine dressing area.

To the shop owner's surprise, the girls have put every dress back as they found them. With a distant husband and a clientele comprised mostly of rude, pompous debutantes, no one in recent memory has said or done anything remotely as endearing. She is moved to tears, cementing the need for a change in her life. The girls give her parting hugs at the door, not knowing what gift that afternoon's visit has bestowed upon her.

Outside, the changing wind is spinning little dead-leaf tornados along the sidewalk, making Mary glad she did not wear one of the dresses home. She would just die of shame if the wind blew the skirt up over her head.

"I am in the mood for a banana split. Would you girls care to join me?" Chick invites from the driver's seat, revving the peppy engine just to get a rise out of the females.

It does the trick. Gayle squeals with delight, hopping in for a ride to the place where they first met.

"*I scream, you scream, we all scream for ice cream!*" Gayle sings. "Could you put her flat out?" she dares Chick.

"Goose it. I don't see any heat around," Vinny says, wrapping Mary in his arms for protection.

Chick punches his foot down on the accelerator; the sudden change in momentum presses them deep into the seats. Sleepy bayou side scenery blurs by the window where Mary wraps her fingers over the edge of the seat, knuckles white with fear.

"*I scream, you scream, we all scream . . .*"

Bam, the car door slams.

"We're here," Vinny whispers in her ear.

Mary's eyes pop open, surprised to be alive. "Just order me a regular split, however it comes. I need to visit the ladies' room," she says, relieved not to have left a puddle in Chick's new ride.

In the diner, Gayle orders her ice cream last so she can hear what everyone else wants—just in case she changes her mind. She adds to the waitress, "No whipped cream, and extra cherries."

When Mary joins them at the table, Gayle whines, "I can't believe our first day of school is *tomorrow*," pulling a napkin from the chrome holder and slowly shredding it into tiny pieces.

"I can—and I'm dreading it for a whole different reason," Mary commiserates. "I wish I could have found a dress in that store that would make me invisible."

The guys sit quietly, not knowing how to console them, since neither one ever took their own education very seriously. Spoons quickly in hand, they are all thankful for the arrival of the frozen treats, so that they can forget about tomorrow a few moments longer.

"Mmmm . . . they always use fresh bananas," Gayle says, catching a dribble of chocolate on her chin with a sliver of the shredded napkin.

The table becomes a concert of slurps and giggles as they tease each other about table manners (or lack thereof).

"You gonna eat all those cherries?" Chick says, reaching over to save one of the maraschinos from drowning in the pool of Gayle's melted ice cream. She blocks him with her spoon and growls at him like a junkyard dog protecting its scraps. He backs off, getting a kick out of her animated antics.

"Here, Chick." Mary tosses one of hers into his bowl.

"I didn't really want it. She just cracks me up," he says, holding the cherry up for Gayle to catch it with her mouth.

Mary wonders if Chick sees Gayle as a new pet rather than a girlfriend.

"It's getting late," Vinny announces. He waits not-so-patiently for Gayle to finish her cherries before adding, "We have to get the girls home before we make the folks worry. It is a school night, after all."

As the girls approach the car hand-in-hand with their escorts, Veronica Babin walks by, and the look on her face is acerbic. Gayle stops long enough to give her an unladylike gesture before happily jumping into the front seat.

"Who's that?" Chick says, ready to defend Gayle's honor.

"She's a big fat nobody is what she is. She makes me so angry, I could spit. She's always looking for a reason to be cruel to Mary and I'm sick and tired of it!" Gayle says, her voice escalating in a burst of anger.

Chick decides to kiss Gayle full on the lips to deflect her rage. Ensured that he won't be on the receiving end of her wrath, he takes her speechless reaction as the opportunity to ask her to go steady.

Her rage is quickly replaced with blissful admiration. "You're like a muscle car," she tells him, "only *better.*"

Chick sighs, filled with the same feeling—for them both, this is the strongest form of flattery.

The guys bring the girls home, exchange contact information, and leave a couple of harmless kisses on the cheek.

"Thank you so much for the clothes," Mary says to Vinny, "and a wonderful weekend. It was the most fun I've ever had—honest."

"Yeah, me too," Gayle says. "Thanks for the threads, my little hot-rodder! You'd better catch me on the horn to make plans for next weekend." She mimes holding a phone with a wink and a smack of her gum.

"I'm sorry, Gaylie baby," says Chick, "but I have to work until Monday of next week. I'll write you a letter for every day that I'm gone."

"So that will be like A through G, then," she says, miffed.

Chick shrugs. "I have to make some more lettuce to keep you in gifts and whatnot."

Vinny and Mary flash a look of amusement at this alien courting exchange.

The boys retreat to the car and blow kisses as they drive away. Because it is still partially daylight, the girls know their parents are probably watching this entire interlude.

"There they go—Romeo in duplicate," Mary says with a mournful sigh. "Who knew the last weekend of freedom before school would yield such a prize for us both?"

"Ditto, I guess. I swear—sometimes I don't understand how you talk," Gayle says, ruining the sentiment.

"Ditto," Mary laughs.

Gayle heads for her house, leaving Mary dazedly watching the dust lingering from the car's departure, particles still hanging in the air—proof that she hasn't been dreaming.

Gayle calls out to her, "See ya later, alligator!"

With sincere reverence, Mary answers, "After 'while, crocodile," then turns to go toward the place she calls home. Somehow, she knows, just like that dust still hanging in the air, her universe has shifted.

When she goes into the house, everyone is in the front room watching the evening news.

"They are still talking about Elvis's mother," Vivian announces. She shakes her head. "Died almost a month ago. That poor boy. The Army took him away from his mother, and she died of grief."

"She had hepatitis," Jason corrected.

"They buried her up in the Forest Hill Cemetery, near that mansion he bought in Memphis," she says, as if she is talking about extended family. "You know—whatchamadoogle."

"Graceland, Mama. The name of his place is Graceland," Jason says, rolling his eyes.

Utilizing leftover meat, vegetables, and a few clever skills picked up from his big sister, Charlie prepares homemade pot-pies for dinner. Vivian allows everyone to eat in front of the television to watch *The Ed Sullivan Show*, which may be a mistake, considering the excitement about Georgia Gibbs performing so close to bedtime.

After all the little ones are finally tucked away, Mary seeks out her father, who is on the front porch in the rocking chair, enjoying his pipe. Normally she doesn't like smoking, but there is something about the smell of his pipe that makes her feel safe.

"Hello there, little Mary," he says, the same way he did when she was as tall as his knee. "You sure have had some big changes a happenin all a sudden. You look like you feelin it, too."

Mary studies her father's curious diction, different from the usual flat accent of the area, until she realizes he is waiting for her to join the conversation.

"To tell the truth, Pa, I don't know what I'm feeling," she says, searching for words to describe her desperate uncertainty.

"Well now, that's a part a being a young'un. You're not supposed to know bout those things . . . until you do." He waits for his eldest to process this.

"I'm not sure I know what you mean," Mary admits.

"Figure out how you feelin about this young feller. Then an only then should you be thinkin and decidin on it. Right now's when you should be enjoyin the ride before you're grown. Remember that you are drivin your own vehicle. Don't go lettin a feller or no one tell you to turn, iffin you don't want to. You're right smart. Don't go ignorant on account of pleasin the world," Norman says, rocking and chewing on the end of his pipe, which is no longer lit.

Unlike her mother, who can stay up all night arguing her point of view until you are converted, once her father says his piece, he is done. You either get it or you don't.

Am I worrying about nothing?
Should I just enjoy being young and save all the serious

stuff until I'm sure who I am and I know what I want . . .

to avoid making stupid mistakes before I even get started?

"Thank you for setting me straight. I sure do love you. You're the wisest man I know," Mary says, kissing him sweetly on his tired forehead. "Goodnight, Pa."

"Sweet dreams, baby girl," he says softly, eyes at half-mast.

Her mind is set at ease, allowing her to climb into bed and relax in her room, admiring the vase that Vinny won for her just the day before. Girlish fantasies dance around her, visions of someday placing that beautifully crafted piece of glass in a place she can call her own.

Monday
September 8, 1958

The first day of her freshman year and Mary barely makes it to the bus. She has lost track of time while making a list of anniversary gift ideas for Mr. Melancon to give his wife (for which she comes up with ten frivolous suggestions, ten affordable ones, and ten that won't cost the milkman anything at all). Hurriedly, Mary stuffs the list in an envelope with the week's payment, depositing it on the porch as she runs past, thankful to Gayle for holding the bus.

"Whew! That was close. My dad already left for work. Thanks for the stall."

"I see. *Now* you thank me for stalling," Gayle jokes, referring to her part in the TV plot. "I swear high school would be more fun if we didn't have to get up so dang early in the morning." She yawns with puffy, sleep-deprived eyes.

"Amen," the school bus driver agrees.

"By the way, you look great in that blue dress. It brings out your eyes perfectly," Gayle says, in an *I-told-you-so* kind of way.

"You have such good taste. You get that from your mother," Mary says. "You should be a shopper for movie sets. For all the stars!"

"I vill only work for you vhen you become a famous vhatever, darlink," Gayle says, doing her best Gábor impression. "Too bad you're going steady. That dress is sure to drum up a date for Homecoming."

"Don't forget we are in this together, sister. You are going steady, too! I guess you'll have to do more studying and less flirting. Your grades might benefit from it." Mary hopes this might turn the subject away from boys or dances; she wants Gayle to set her goals higher than just becoming someone's housewife.

Arriving at Terrebonne High School is every bit as intimidating as Mary imagined, even though she is familiar with the layout, having attended cheer squad practice there. The campus was more inviting over the summer than it is now; something about it being filled with activity changes it somehow. It has morphed into a peculiar city of sorts, filled with venomous, judgmental inhabitants. If only it could be the serene shell it had been just days before.

Everything is suddenly strange and foreign—new school, new people, new clothes, new attention . . . curious classmates bombarding her with questions and commenting on how pretty she's become. Mary just wants to be left alone—or at least find some middle ground. She's used to the normal teases for being poor, smart, or a fashion disgrace, but *this?* Now she is receiving too much attention over a dress, a boyfriend, and the whispers of racy behavior no doubt started by Veronica (whose vicious laughter can't be ignored). Both ends of the spectrum feel equally as cruel; popularity in any form is not something Mary longs for.

On the outside, she maintains a cool appearance, seemingly unaffected by the teenaged sea of amateur correspondents. On the inside, she just wants to run until she finds sunlight and stillness. She closes in on the class roster posted on a wall inside the main entrance. Cool on the outside but burning on the inside, her head houses the tirade of a much too sensitive version of herself:

> *Just leave me alone. I just want to learn, for*
> *Pete's sake!*
> *Why does that have to be so complicated by all these silly*
> *people with their fashion,*
> *their cliques, and their hidden agendas?*

"It's none of their business," she hisses at the whirl of activity around her, the thin skin of her finger scanning the homeroom roster for her name. "Mrs. Prejean, Room 109."

"They aren't teasing, Mary," Gayle says. "Just too nosy for their own good. Let's just find our class and skip past this crowd." Gayle yelps after her toe is smushed by someone's rogue shoe. "What homeroom am I in?"

Mary locates the page with the G's and finds it right away. "Mrs. Tisdale, Room 112."

"Well, at least it's in the same hall," Gayle says, limping away from the traffic. "Stuffing your head with information will make you feel better. It always does."

They travel through a thick pine scent in the recently mopped corridor. A quick hug meaning to soothe each other's anxieties is given in front of Room 109, where Mary is determined to calm her temper and re-fluff her dignity, despite the echo of Veronica's cruel laughter still in her ears.

"It won't be the same without you," Mary says, mirroring Gayle's pouty face. "It will be the first time on my own since we met."

Reluctantly, Gayle keeps moving with the sea of students and Mary slips into the classroom. The desks are all lined up in their familiar rows, like squatty soldiers awaiting inspection. A trickle of new and old faces enters; students drop notebooks, staking claim to their preferred empty seats.

Mary has found early on that the best way to stay out of trouble in class is to not engage, to instead sit like the desks—stiff and still—facing a large black expanse of board behind the teacher's desk; the chalkboard stares back at her, unblemished and full of promise. Avoiding eye contact with the natives is easy when there is so much to envision.

"Good morning, class," Mrs. Prejean sings, shutting the door only seconds prior to the bell sounding. Her ample hips sway in the aisle as she calls roll, passing out schedules to her eager pupils. In middle school, the students had only switched between three classrooms, just to get them used to moving around; high school is going to be a far less comfortable experience. Mary's schedule consists of mostly honors courses, which brings joy to her face—until she remembers Gayle's schedule does not.

As the students rise to recite the Pledge of Allegiance, Mary notices that some of them revert to saying it without the "under God," which was added a few years back. She begins to wonder if this is merely an oversight, an act of adolescent defiance, or out of some sort of protest she isn't privy to. She normally isn't very curious about what other students are up to, but this is different from the mindless drivel she prefers to avoid. As she matures, she is more and more aware of the religious and political undercurrents of the world around her that never seemed to grab her scrutiny before.

When the bell announces first period, the students stream out of homeroom, filling the hall once again with a noisy rush. Mary feels strange staying put in her seat for Civics, waiting to learn how to be a good citizen, when to her surprise, Gayle enters the room.

"Well, hello, stranger! Looks like they couldn't keep us apart after all," Gayle says, landing in a seat across from Mary.

"If only . . ." she replies, avoiding eye contact.

Gayle grabs Mary's schedule to compare it with her own, in disbelief. "I guess I won't see you again till lunch." Gayle hands the schedule back, irritated by the injustice. "Meet me in front of the cafeteria."

"Can you believe this stuff they try to pass off as food nowadays?" Gayle says above the loud cafeteria chatter, shoving Mary's leftover yeast roll into her face and dumping her tray into the trash.

"You can't live on French fries alone. I don't mind it. I like food I didn't have to cook," Mary says close behind her. As she goes to empty her tray, a young man helpfully takes it from her hands.

Preoccupied, she releases the tray and follows Gayle into the sunlight without even her usual polite thank-you.

A lone empty table sits off to the side of a concrete path, away from several others meant for outside study and dining. Mary finds it inviting. "We should eat out here tomorrow."

"Yeah, it feels good out here. We could sit over there with Jane," Gayle suggests.

Mary purses her lips in disapproval of the idea, but says nothing. She cannot come up with a reason why sitting with Jane isn't a good idea—only that she prefers to be on the outside looking in. She knows Gayle's extrovert ego won't understand.

The gym coach, a stout woman with a pug nose, starts class by delivering her "I'm going to make winners out of you" sermon.

With her athletic shoes squeaking on the shiny, varnished hardwood floor, the coach calls attendance and sends packaged Phys Ed uniforms flying carelessly through the air as if she is on a float in the middle of a Mardi Gras parade.

"I hope this fits," Mary says, holding up a shapeless step-in suit that seals with a row of snaps along the front and gathers with elastic mid-thigh. It looks more like a onesie suit for a perpetual toddler than a uniform for a high schooler.

Some names are called again; this time, the coach starts handing out items in boxes.

"Over here!" Gayle says, grabbing her box. Mary and Gayle sit and spill out the contents onto the gym floor like small children with boxes of toys. Lying between their widespread legs is a crimson, gold, and white cheer squad uniform, complete with pompoms. The sweater has a picture of a megaphone transposed over a large *T*. The skirt is solid crimson, pleated, and long enough to reach just below the knee—which signals a northward trend from the original calf-length styles of yesteryears.

"Ladies, listen up!" the coach barks. "Locker assignments and combinations are posted on the wall. Try on all uniforms and make sure they fit. I need all reorder forms filled out by the end of the week."

The girls retreat to the inner room to change. To protect her new so-so fitting uniform and her street clothes from pranksters, Mary reassures herself by opening and closing her locker door, testing the combination on her lock a few times. Satisfied, she gingerly places her new dress inside.

"I can't believe how bad it smells in here," Gayle says, cupping her nose with her hand.

"That's your upper lip, Gautreau!" a voice calls from the bowels of the echoey sweat-house.

"Let it go," Mary pleads from the bench, gripping the top band of Gayle's underwear and recreating the famous Coppertone ad.

Ignoring Mary, Gayle shouts, "I dare you to come say it to my upper lip, you village bicycle!" She guesses it is one of the Ettes trying to stir the pot. Poised to fight, she waits for a comeback, but there is none that she can hear. "That's what I thought," she grumbles, backing down slowly and onto the bench next to Mary.

"We still have practice to get through after this. Can't let them under your skin, G. We are going to be surrounded by them for the duration."

Jane pops her head from around the corner. "Don't worry, guys—we have your back."

"See, we have reinforcements. Jane has pull. Her brother is a lawman," Gayle says, proverbial hackles rising. "I dare them to try something!"

Friday

September 12, 1958

G ayle plops in the worn padded seat of the school bus. "Whew! Thank God it's Friday . . . and no cheer practice!" Seeing a young man attempt to sit next to her, she thwarts his efforts by thumbing to the rear of the bus. "Git along, little doggie."

From behind him, Mary reaffirms, "Scoot!" She is carrying a heavy load of information both in her arms and in her head. With a great sigh, she slumps down into the seat beside her friend.

"So what did you get called out of PE for?" Gayle asks, digging in her purse for lip balm as the bus pulls away from the school.

"I somehow got nominated for a spot on the Homecoming court, so the principal gave me this paper," Mary says. She opens her Algebra book and hands over the evidence. "I don't want it. The whole thing is silly, really."

"Have you lost your marbles? You could become so popular! And you *know* colleges like that kind of stuff."

"I don't need to be involved in things that I am completely against to get into a good school. It would be in denial of what I believe. Women have been objectified for far too long because we have allowed it by participating in such nonsense. When they nominate me to be on an academic court or debate team along with the boys, I will gladly accept." Mary turns her attention back to her Algebra book.

Gayle throws herself against the back of the seat, pouting. "Sometimes I wish you were less smart and more fun. At least I have the weekend to bring you to your senses. Maybe Vinny could convince you. Is he coming to pick you up tonight?"

"I have been so consumed with school, I really don't know," Mary says, preoccupied. "I need to finish these last two math problems before my weekend can officially begin." Grumbling, she returns to her notebook.

"Oh no! You'll never get into college *now*," Gayle says sarcastically, looking out of the window at everything passing. "You know, you really should pay more attention to the world around you. I happen to know that a certain star football player is quite keen on you and can't seem to get you to notice him."

"What are you talking about?" Mary says with irritation—but she is half-listening, scribbling variables in her notebook.

"Haven't you noticed?" Gayle steals Mary's pencil, forcing her to listen. "Bobby Vicknair is a handsome junior with college practically in the bag. He has been following you around, picking up papers you drop, holding doors open for you. He has even tried to start conversations—and you barely acknowledge him! *I* thought you were ignoring him because of Vinny."

"No," Mary says truthfully, stealing back her pencil, having solved for *x.* "How do you know all of this?"

"Jane says that he has been crushing on you since cheerleader tryouts last April," Gayle reveals, wondering if this is how teachers feel when students don't quite get the point of the lesson. "The boy *likes* you, Mary!"

"Why would he be interested in me?" Mary asks in disbelief. "I think you're reading too much into this."

Gayle scoffs. "For a smart girl, you sure are dumb."

The bus slows as it approaches their stop and the girls rise from their seats. Gayle steps off the bus behind Mary, who is trying to read and walk, and guides her along the side of the road so she does not wander in front of the bus as it continues its afternoon journey. Amused, she continues to herd Mary down the road, passing the Poche house.

When Gayle hears the sound of an engine approaching from behind, she spins around, hungry-eyed at the unfamiliar purr. "Here comes a square bird—a 1958 Ford T-bird!" She takes off running for the car.

Mary finally snaps into the moment.

> *I swear, if that girl knew as much about science or math*
> *as she does about cars,*
> *she could be a university professor.*
> *If only she could harness that power for good instead of*
> *silly.*

Mary laughs out loud until she hears Gayle yell, "It's Vinny!" and she too begins to jog toward the car—after setting down her precious books on the side of the road, of course.

On her way to him, she sees Gayle leaning into the car and then running into her house waving some loose-leaf.

Unsure of the significance, Mary picks up the pace. Vinny leaps from the Thunderbird and heads toward her. When he picks her up and spins her around, she feels herself loosen, all the strictness falling aside and returning her to the girl she'd become in his arms last weekend.

"Is everything all right?" she asks, glancing back in Gayle's direction.

"Everything is right as rain," Vinny says, admiring her like some rare flower.

"What are the papers about?"

"A letter from Chick. He wrote it Sunday night before he left. I promised him that I would watch out for her. I invited her to go to the movies with us tonight—I hope that's all right with you."

"Of course it's all right. I think it might keep you on your best behavior," she says, noticing the way he is looking at her.

"You better go get ready while I visit with your family. Hop in and I'll give you a lift." He cordially opens the passenger door for her. She jumps in, happy to oblige him—even if it is only for a few yards to her driveway.

"Is this your car?" she asks, trying to remember if he has mentioned having a car.

"It is for now . . . You see, my boss is peculiar and doesn't like me to have the same car for very long. Whenever I travel, he provides one for me."

"Wow! You must be great at your job. Do you ever have assistants to help you?"

"No. I really do a better job on my own," he answers, enjoying her innocence.

"I hate working in groups, too. It's so annoying," she says, thinking of school projects gone wrong. "By the way, what's playing at the drive-in? Do I have time to finish my homework?" Opening the car door, she suddenly remembers to retrieve her books from the roadside.

"*The Long Hot Summer* starts at eight o'clock. You have plenty of time to finish. I called ahead for your mother to make out a grocery list. Go get it for me, so I can be back in time to sit with your parents before we go," he says in a *do-me-a-favor* sort of way.

"You really shouldn't try so hard to make her like you."

"Who said I was trying to make *her* like me?" he asks foxily. "Please let me do this. It's important to me that you're eating well."

Hugging the books, Mary nods in solemn agreement and heads into the house. A few minutes later, she comes back with a long list, handing it to Vinny, wearing shame upon her face.

He pockets the grocery list, tenderly bringing her dainty hand to his lips. He kisses her knuckles softly. "All I want to do is take care of you. All you have to do is let me," he says, looking in her eyes as they fill with tears. "I'll be back as soon as I can. It looks like I'm going appliance shopping again."

He winks and blows a kiss before he drives away.

Mary stands there a moment, thinking that this man is the first person she has ever known to even come close to filling her father's shoes. She turns slowly, watching him leave, and then hurries to her room, determined to complete all assignments so she can get pretty for her date.

"Oh, my heavens! Here it comes!" Vivian calls out from the porch, like a game show contestant awaiting her prize delivery.

Everyone in the house emerges to see what the commotion is about. Vinny is pulling up, his car stuffed with groceries. A delivery truck follows close behind him, hauling an ostentatious replacement for their small, antiquated icebox.

"He has bought an honest-to-goodness *refrigerator* . . . and enough groceries to fill it up!" Vivian squeals. She rushes outside to greet Vinny as he climbs out of his car. "You are a good boy! I hope your mama's lookin down on what a good boy you are!" She marvels over her new treasure as the deliverymen unload it from the truck. "This way, boys . . . I have a spot all cleared out for it!" She directs them to the kitchen, and then gives Vinny a hug that makes his eyes bulge.

"I figure you guys grow most of your vegetables, Mrs. Viv, so I wanted to give you something to put next to them on the plate," he says, soaking up her gratitude. "Let me tell you about the features. You will have ice in no time now."

Unable to concentrate over the noise of excited children, Vivian drops her good mood. "All you monkeys are getting in the way! Go out and play till your supper's ready!"

The screen door opens and shuts several times with a quick succession of *thwacks!* before Vinny feels safe to continue his instructional tour. "I think I have it from here. I love all the nooks and crannies," Vivian sings, putting all her groceries away.

"Pa's coming!" a child's voice calls from the porch to the sound of an engine growing and then cutting to silence. Vinny, eager to speak with Norman, greets him in the driveway with a hearty handshake.

"What's all the hubbub?" Norman asks kindly, sensing he has missed some kind of event.

Vinny knows he needs to tread carefully. "Just trying to lighten your load, Mr. Poche."

Jenny appears and tugs on her father's overalls, shouting, "He brought bloody cow meat, Pa!"

"Did he now?" Norman scoops her up and kisses her cheek.

"How about we discuss it over a glass of sweet tea? Let me chew on your ear for a few moments in private," Vinny says, watching Norman scratch the back of his weary head with his cap.

Norman sits very still as they converse on the back porch, watching Vinny pace a little. It is a good while before Norman is free to settle with the children in the front room, and Vinny, satisfied with the exchange, returns to the kitchen to help cube meat for Vivian.

Mary enters the kitchen, watching her mother add newly cooked beef to the soup. "I hope I get as much attention as that refrigerator did," she says to Vinny jokingly.

"You look wonderful," he says, attempting to be genteel while small children hang from him like ornaments.

"You need to get off the poor man before he takes back his TV," Mary scolds.

With squeals of delight and mock horror, the children scatter to the front room to watch and guard their treasured boob tube.

"You kids should go on and have a good time," Vivian says as she stirs the savory morsels in her largest pot.

"It smells good, Mama," Mary says, and kisses her mother's cheek goodbye.

"Don't worry. I'll save you some," Vivian says, proud of her tasty creation.

In the front room, Mary leans over to kiss her dozing father. "Love you, Pa."

Startled, he replies sleepily, "You be careful, sweet girl."

When they drive up, Gayle is standing outside the Gautreaus' house, rereading her letter from Chick. Gayle's parents are sitting on the porch swing, enjoying the last bit of day; Vinny hops out of the car to go fill them in on the agenda for the evening.

Gayle climbs into the back seat, clutching the letter to her chest. "Chick is such a sweetie, Mary. I hadn't realized how thoughtful he is until I read his letter. He says—" She clears her throat as if she is about to deliver an oration. "He has 'yearned for the day he would find something he wanted more than cars, but he just didn't know that something would be me.' He likes me more than cars! Yearns, even! Oh, I'm in love!" She throws herself against the seat, the back of her hand pressed against her forehead, as if she's got a raging fever. Mary can't help but giggle at her ridiculous antics.

Vinny hops in the driver's seat and turns on the radio, only to catch the first lines of an advertisement for cigarettes. He turns the volume down.

"So, Vinny, I really like this car. Can I see under her dress when we park and she's cool?" Gayle asks. "Did you know that this is the first one of these to have a backseat?"

He laughs. "Yes, you can get under the hood—but it will have to be right before we leave the drive-in after the movie. I don't want you burning your fingers. Tell you what—you and Chick are a match made in Detroit. You are the only two people I know who get hot and bothered discussing car specs." Vinny looks for her reaction in the rear-view mirror. "Does anyone know who stars in *Touch of Evil?* It's playing at the Bijou."

"I think Charlton Heston and Janet Leigh . . ." Gayle says, absentmindedly fidgeting with the car interior. "But I have no idea what it's about."

"I guess that means there aren't any cars in it," Mary says, lightly slapping her knee in parody.

Gayle narrows her eyes. "Hardy har-har."

"I won't go to the Bijou unless it's raining," Mary announces.

Gayle shrugs. "Who would pick Charlton Heston over Paul Newman anyway?"

"Sorry," says Vinny. "I just talked to a guy at the gas station who said it was edgy, that's all."

Gayle chuckles.

"What's so funny?"

"Imagining Mary doing or watching anything described as *edgy*."

"Keep it up—you're cruisin for a bruisin!"

"*Ooo*! You're scaring me with your edginess!"

"If you can stop hounding each other for five minutes, I will tell you about the surprise I have for you ladies," Vinny says, his head high, his chin jutted forward.

"It's a done deal," Gayle consents. Mary zips her mouth, tosses the invisible key to show her obedience, and waits for him to continue.

He sits with a straight face and lets the silence linger long enough for Gayle to begin squirming out of her skin. A good-natured grin softens his lips as he playfully taps his fingers on the steering wheel.

"Uncle! *Uncle* already! You are killing me," Gayle says, writhing in her seat.

"I was just enjoying the peace and quiet. It's only been two minutes," Vinny laughs. "Oh, all right, I guess I've left you in suspense long enough. I have asked for permission to take you both on a day trip to the city, and your parents all said yes."

This indeed is a big deal. The girls gape at each other, wide-eyed. Neither has ever been to the city before.

"No way! When do we go?" Gayle asks, bouncing around elated in her seat.

Mary pokes him in the side. "Come on, when?"

"Tomorrow," Vinny says, bracing himself for the noise to follow.

The girls look at each other before reveling at a pitch possibly high enough to disturb all animals within a five-mile radius (well, maybe not—but it does leave Vinny unable to hear out of his right ear for nearly an hour).

"We are going to New Orleans! Turn up the tunes! *Yakety yak, don't talk back!*"

They continue the spontaneous party all the way until pulling into a decent parking spot in the center of the drive-in theater. Vinny takes the top down (Gayle doesn't usually like a soft top, but finds herself interested in the mechanism). No one is really hungry, so the girls get some money for sodas from Vinny, who stays behind with the car to smoke a Parliament while they walk to the refreshment stand.

When the girls return with a large bucket of popcorn, Vinny says, "I thought you weren't hungry."

"I figured we could share," Mary says, feeling guilty for changing her mind, and hands him the change.

"No problem, doll. There's more where this came from." He gently tugs on her chin, dropping the change into his pocket.

Vinny lets Gayle sit in the driver's seat, which suits her just fine. This way he can sit in the back seat with Mary without feeling like they are under heavy scrutiny. As soon as the movie starts, Paul Newman appears onscreen, captivating everyone with his steely blue eyes. Mary's stomach drops when his character, Ben Quick, jumps off a barge into the water fully clothed. Not one of them speaks; the only sounds are the munching of popcorn, an occasional gasp, or the *swat!* of an overly friendly mosquito.

During the movie, Mary feels Vinny's hand on her thigh, and it sets her aflame like the barn on the screen. He does not seem to be trying any funny business; she does not understand why just the weight of his hand could be such an enjoyable distraction. After a while, she begins to wonder why he isn't trying to fondle her further; it's strange and surprising to her that she would want him to.

I am turning into one of those bad girls
you hear about.
My thoughts are becoming impure.
He is being such a gentleman, and it turns out I am the
one I have to worry about.
How could I have let this happen?

As the credits roll on the movie screen, Mary feels like her body is firing on all cylinders, although she attempts to hide that fact. Each time Vinny makes any physical contact with her, no matter how slight, she blushes.

"You okay, Mary? You look flushed," Gayle says, getting out of the car to stretch her legs in the plethora of headlights exiting the drive-in.

"I might be coming down with something," Mary replies, trying not to blush more from embarrassment.

"Take some medicine. You'd better not get sick tonight! Even if you do, you will just have to go to New Orleans tomorrow anyway. Maybe we can get out of going to church on Sunday to sleep in and recuperate?"

"We are definitely going to church Sunday morning, young lady, and we are going to pay attention," Mary says in defiance of her new feelings.

Gayle looks at Vinny. "What's gotten into her?"

He shrugs, not knowing, but having an idea.

"Wasn't Joanne Woodward just lovely?" Mary mentions dreamily.

"She's no Maggie," Vinny counters.

Mary adds, "Paul and Joanne looked like they were really gone for each other."

"It's called *acting*, Mary," Gayle says haughtily.

"So, half-pint," Vinny says to Gayle, "she oughta be good and cool by now, if you want to take a look."

"Goody gumdrops!" she exclaims, clapping her hands, ready for her treat.

Vinny pops the hood, then gets out of Gayle's way. He walks directly over to Mary, who is leaning up against the car. He presses into her until she can feel his breath on her neck.

He is going to be the death of me.
I don't know how much more of this I can take.
Heaven help me, for I am weak.

He continues to stand there like that for several minutes, with Mary melting, while they listen to Gayle rattle off information.

"You know, I didn't know this year's model came in a convertible. Man, oh man—she is a three-speed cruise-o-matic!" Gayle is in utter ecstasy. She makes an abrupt start for the trunk. "I read that the trunk is huge. They redesigned it to make more room."

With reflexes like a jungle cat, Vinny leaps from Mary to take position in front of Gayle. "You can't go in the trunk. I just returned from a meeting with a colleague of mine, and I have been entrusted with a present to deliver for my boss. It's a secret surprise," he says, remembering his loathsome chore.

"It's okay. I know how to keep a secret. Come on, I just want to peek," Gayle pleads, attempting to erode his barricade.

"I'm serious. You can't go in there. I will get in big trouble. I can attest to the size of the trunk. It's really big," Vinny says, hastily wiping away a single bead of sweat from the side of his face.

Gayle smells an opportunity. "Can I drive, then?"

"Will you behave if I let you drive around the parking lot?"

With her hands together in prayer, she swears, "I'll be an angel!"

"Selling your soul to that devil in disguise," Mary says, shaking her head as she gets into the back seat alone, yet thankful for small mercies.

Vinny gives instructions from the passenger's seat as Gayle slowly snakes around the parking lot three times. Finally, Mary says, "Are you done yet? We need our rest for tomorrow."

"Oh all right, mother hen. You really know how to kill a party," Gayle grumbles. She reluctantly puts the car in park and returns to the back seat, where she folds her arms and snorts her disappointment.

"Come back up front with me, my little cupcake," Vinny tells Mary, sliding into the driver's nook. He quickly makes all the necessary adjustments to return the seat and mirror to their former positions.

Mary normally despises the condescending nature behind men and the pet names they give to women. But tonight, she chooses not to make an issue out of it. In fact, for the first time she doesn't quite take it as an insult. For whatever reason, it is almost endearing . . . almost.

With the top down, pulling slowly onto West Main and enjoying the breeze beginning to whip all around them, Mary welcomes the cool, damp air as they coast along the road listening to Elvis croon "I Beg of You." Her head is tilted back, looking up at the inky star-filled sky passing, giving the pleasant sensation of floating.

Just when Mary feels completely recuperated from her hormone-induced torment, Peggy Lee snaps her way onto the airwaves with "Fever" and it all comes flooding back to her with a tenacious grip. To make things worse, she senses the weight of Vinny's right hand resting on her thigh, slightly higher than before. She cannot move or speak for fear of betraying herself by showing any sign of enjoyment.

Almost home, almost home . . . just a few more minutes
and I'll sit in a cold tub.

"Vinny, can you tell Chick how good I did, so he will let me drive the Impala?" Gayle sounds sleepy, like a small child, as the tires hit gravel.

"I will put in a good word for you—as long as you remember to return the favor someday."

"You got it," she replies with a yawn.

In an abrupt state of panic, Mary asks Vinny, "Where are *you* going to sleep?"

"Don't worry. I already arranged a room at the Babin Inn."

Gayle solemnly puts her hand on his shoulder. "Say it ain't so, Joe. You're in bed with the enemy."

Vinny pulls the car to a stop in front of Gayle's home and turns to Mary. "What is she talking about?"

"Remember that girl Gayle wanted to clobber the other day? That was Veronica. Her family owns and operates the Babin Inn."

"I'm sorry. I won't make that mistake again. It's just that it's the closest motel I could find. If it's that big a deal, I could sleep in the car."

"Don't be silly. There is no reason for you to be uncomfortable just because some little girl has a mean streak—is there, Gayle?"

"I guess I can overlook it—for someone who lets me drive his car and takes me to New Orleans," she says, conceding Mary's point as she slips from the back seat.

"Don't forget to wear your favorite dress tomorrow—in case we take pictures for Chick!" Mary calls after her.

"Bye! Don't do anything I would do," Gayle sings as she walks away.

Fear grips Mary.

Oh no, we are alone. I hadn't thought of that! What to do, what to say?

Vinny rolls the car to the house, idles alongside Norman's truck, then kills the engine. Mary expects quiet, since most of the inhabitants of the house are already asleep. Loudly chirping crickets can barely compete with the sound of her heart beating like a hammer. Vinny turns to her and she is visibly jumpy, like those pesky little bouncy spiders around the house; when you make one move toward them, they relocate. Vinny's eyes slowly caress her shape in the moonlight for a moment, hoping she will relax.

"I don't bite," Vinny says sweetly as he sneaks a little closer.

She stiffens. "I know, it's just—"

He places a finger over her lips to silence her. He picks up her hand and flips it over to reveal her palm. He slowly traces the lines that palm readers so often pull information from and then brings it to his mouth. First he exhales his sultry breath upon her palm, like he did on her neck earlier, and gingerly runs his tongue along the path his finger took, ending with a long, lippy kiss near her wrist. She has lost all her stiffness as he gains his.

"I'm not going to hurt you, Mary . . . I promised your father you would be safe." He kisses farther up her arm, sending chills everywhere.

She sits silently except for her panting breath, in awe of what he is doing to her.

"I just want to kiss you . . ." he whispers. He reaches her ear. "Only if you want me to."

Her head slowly nods yes, though she hasn't willed it to do so, moving completely on autopilot.

He cradles the back of her head in his large hand, covering her face in slow, tender kisses until he makes contact with her parted lips. He patiently waits for her to respond. She pulls him closer, letting her mouth fall open to accept his eager tongue, their mouths melding together.

Vinny pulls away abruptly. He twists around to recline his head on her lap, and looks up at Mary's lovely face surrounded by stars, gazing as if she were the original Virgin Mary. She covers her embarrassed face with her hands, stewing in the fact that he is the level head, while she is the one left wanting. Wanting . . . *more.*

Vinny lightly tugs for her to remove her barricade, until she decides to bring it down. "I don't think I could stop if we continue," he says. "I don't want to take advantage of the situation. I need to prove to you that I truly respect you. I want you, but I can wait as long as you need me to. I've never been a person known for demonstrating weakness, yet here I am . . . belly exposed." He has the soft eyes of a man under Cupid's spell.

Mary is conquered by his words, filled with such integrity. "Vinny . . . I am afraid I just might fall in love with you," she says, kissing him on the forehead as her eyes well up with tears.

"Don't be afraid . . . You won't be alone. I'm already there." He sits himself upright and kisses the back of her hand.

"Thank you for being so completely wonderful." Love drunk, she stands and raises her arms, feeling like she could fly. She steps over the side of the car and hops to the ground—to Vinny's dismay.

"You bring that out in me," Vinny replies. He rubs the back of his neck as he shuts the car door behind him.

"Tonight I feel like I could go soaring into outer space and visit the stars." She inhales the night. "Think I should be an astronaut?"

"No, I think you should come here and give me another smooch." He picks her up and spins her around like before, kissing her lips and setting her down on the dewy lawn. "I want to marry you," he says, losing himself in the moment, and bracing for her inevitable reaction.

"Me . . . *marry* me?" she says, searching for lucidity and a more stable patch of ground.

He follows her meandering path in the yard. "I understand we don't know each other yet . . . but we will. I will wait until then to ask you again. I know you might think I'm crazy. I just wanted you to know my intentions. I explained that to your father just this afternoon."

"What did he say?" she asks, apprehension entering her voice, spinning around to face him.

"He wants me to settle down first and make sure it's what I want before I ask you."

"What about me and what *I* want? What about school . . . about college!" She speaks in an enraged whisper-scream so as not to wake anyone, crossing her arms in defiance.

"Calm down. I had no idea this would upset you so much. We will discuss everything later. We will work it all out. Besides, your dad already said that you were to finish high school no matter what. He said it was important, that you'd be the first in the family to complete their high-school education. I want whatever you want. I want to be whatever you need me to be." He falls to his knees at her feet, completely at her mercy.

She shakes her head, pleading, "This is happening too fast! I need you to slow down. I don't want to have to make any decisions, and I don't want you to either. I don't even know who I am yet. How can you want to marry someone who is incomplete?" She searches his face for an iota of comprehension.

"I want to get to know you as you're making your journey. I know that I'm older and have more experience of the world. It is my experience that I base the decision on. I told you last weekend, I know who I am . . . and I know that I want you." Vinny lays his hand on his chest. "Now, how I see it—I'm the one taking the chance that someday you will reach the same conclusion. I already told you, no obligations. What do you have to lose?" He raises his eyebrows with bright optimism.

"You won't pressure me into doing anything before I am ready? You won't make me give anything up?" Mary fires at him in rapid succession.

"I've sworn to your father, now I am swearing to you—you call the shots." Still on his knees, he reaches up, holding her waist and waiting for her to bring his heart relief.

Mary takes a few beats to assess. "All right then," she says, taking charge. "If I am calling the shots, then I say you'd better get up from there before you ruin those fancy pants of yours. I need to get some sleep if you don't want me to be cranky tomorrow."

"Yes, dear, anything you say," Vinny says, desperately wanting to appease her. He stands up and looks at his green, wet knees, instantly aware that the pants will go to the needy. They share one more kiss before he lets her go inside, staying long enough to see her dark, slight shadow pass in front of the window.

Mary washes up before bed with lukewarm water, reliving the evening with every unbelievably juicy detail. This night is the first night she dreams of Vinny, waking with the feel of him still on her skin . . .

Saturday
September 13, 1958

"**Y**ou were moaning. You sick?" Jenny asks, holding an overloved rag doll. "Mama! Mary's moaning like she's got a tummy ache!" she shouts, without budging from her spot in the doorway.

Mary, fully awake now, jumps into action, paying Jenny no mind. There is no time to lose—she needs to get ready for her trip.

"You best take you some castor oil and get back in bed. You don't want to be traveling with a bad stomach," Vivian says, coming down the hall.

"I'm fine, Mama. I was just having a dream," Mary calls out, glaring pointedly at Jenny, who sticks out her tongue and runs away. "I'm sorry I slept late. I'll be down to help shortly. You must be starving," she adds, putting on her robe.

"We had a meeting last night whilst you were gallivanting, and it's been decided that most of your chores will be divided amongst Charlie, Jason, and Sarah," Vivian says, handing down her new decree in Mary's doorway.

"But Sarah's barely eight years old!"

"She's got the lightest of the chore list. You been doing these chores since you was knee-high to a frog, and you think two strappin boys can't handle em split? I'm just sorry it wasn't sooner. There was no reason they couldn't have helped before."

"They would have, if I had asked. Or you would have made them, if I had complained," Mary says. She puts a hand to her mother's shoulder as she squeezes past. Mary knows how hard it is for her mother to apologize, as if it were admitting some degree of defeat or weakness.

Vivian quickly wipes an errant tear away with the bottom of her dress, as the sound of a troop of off-key voices rises up the stairs. "For the love of Mike, what is that terrible racket?" Vivian grumbles, hiding her brief sappy moment.

"It's the *Howdy Doody* song," Mary says, amused, before realizing the hour. "I need to get in gear and brush my teeth." Picking up her toothbrush, she wonders if her mother is regretting that television right about now.

Seeing herself in the mirror, she laughs—she looks like a mad dog with white foam dripping from her mouth. She catches a reflection other than her own in the mirror and finds Sarah, smiling and leaning against the door. Mary smiles back, transforming her sister's smile into laughter.

"I miss you, Mary," she says, looking at her feet.

Mary swishes and spits, then gives her sister a troubled look. "I'm sorry I have been gone so much lately. I miss you, too. Come talk with me while I get ready." She takes Sarah by the hand. "Are you okay with having to help out when I'm not here?"

"I mostly just have to help with the twins. I take care of them like you took care of me. I don't mind, except . . . it's *different* around here without you."

"What do you mean, different? If someone is getting hurt, you have to let me know, okay?"

"Okay," she says unconvincingly. "I just miss you is all."

"Oh, Sarah Bell! I love you—you know that—and I always will." Mary slips into the same outfit she wore to the fair. Much like a zealot fan on game day, she decides to wear this particular cloth as if it manifests good luck.

"Sit down and I will tie a bow for you," Sarah says, patting Mary's bed, ribbon in hand, as Mary yanks her hair into place with an elastic loop. Happily, Mary complies with Sarah's wishes to bestow such care upon her, applied with the reverence of a coronation. "All done," Sarah announces, proud at how evenly the ribbon edges lay.

"You are my sunshine." Mary turns to wrap her arms around her little sister. "I love you very much."

"Well, then I love you muchlier," Sarah manages before Mary tickles her sides.

"Let's check on the others before I go." Mary offers a piggy back ride to the stairs.

Downstairs in the front room, all the faces of the little ones Mary has spent so much time nurturing now sit quiet and motionless in front of a box, worshiping the glowing deity. Sarah joins them, placing Barbara, the smallest of the bunch, in front of her. She waves a meek and solemn goodbye to Mary, the only person who has ever cherished her.

The all-too-bright light of morning catches Mary's face by surprise as she steps from the porch, setting off a series of sneezes. "Wa*choo!* Wa*choo!* Wa*choo!*"

"Goodness! Bless you already," Vinny says. He is putting the top down on the car. "You all right?"

"She does that all the time. Can't do just one," Gayle says, coming up the driveway on foot.

"Hey, Gayle, the trunk is all yours if you want to ride in there," Vinny says, poking fun at her. "I made a delivery after I left last night and it's empty."

"I'm over it." Gayle hops into the back seat.

"Hello there, my queen." Vinny opens the door for Mary and she enters the car with a flair of regality. She flashes a *get-a-load-of-this* look at Gayle.

"Well, la-tee-*da*," Gayle says, thoroughly impressed by the chivalry.

Vinny pauses. His jaw tenses, recognizing her outfit. "Why didn't you wear any of the clothes I bought you?" he asks with a tight, manufactured smile. "I had hoped to see you in them."

"Is it a problem? I can go change. I just didn't want to get them all wrinkled, sitting in the car for such a long time."

"I guess not," he says stiffly. He gets in and turns the engine. "How hungry are you ladies?" He waves at Gayle's parents as they pass by her house.

"Well, someone kept me up late, and I slept through breakfast," Mary replies, not quite answering the question.

"Me, too." He flashes her a knowing smile.

"I could eat my left arm," Gayle says, even though she had a bowl of Alpha-Bits less than an hour ago.

"There's this place I know on the way—it has the best food and a guest cook who makes tamales that are out of this world. Sound good?" Vinny asks. He hopes the girls don't object, considering he has planned ahead.

"If you think it's good, I'll give it a try," Mary says, cautious yet interested.

Gayle is ready for adventure. "As long as it ain't moving, I'll try it. If I have ketchup, I can eat anything. How do you think I'm able to eat my Brussels sprouts?"

"I believe he has ketchup. But you won't need it," Vinny says assuredly.

The car flies along Highway 90. Gayle nails every word to a block of songs blaring on the radio. When the annoying commercials interrupt, Vinny reaches over to silence them. He has glanced at Mary several times by now, like he wants to say something.

Finally, Mary can't handle it anymore. She just wants him to stop acting anxious. "What's on your mind, Vinny?" she asks.

After a pause, he says, "I arranged for you girls to go to see a friend of mine. Her name is Camille. She works in the hotel. You can visit with her while I go see my boss."

"You mean to babysit us while you're at work," Mary replies, feeling leery and misguided.

"I'll be done before you know it, and I thought you might enjoy that sort of thing. You know, meeting my friends."

"He's just trying to be nice, Mary. It'll be a blast, you'll see," Gayle says, with a hand on Mary's shoulder, giving her a little nudge. "I think it's a fine idea, Vinny. I appreciate your kindness."

"I don't mean to be suspicious or seem ungrateful," Mary adds. "I guess I'm not used to all of these new things." Suddenly she feels like a burden. "It bothers me that you are spending so much money on me and my family, Vinny. I don't want to get acquainted with things I couldn't possibly afford on my own. I don't want you to think I expect these things of you."

"Mary, I have been working since I was tiny, and I too know what it's like to be poor," Vinny says candidly. "I have street smarts, and I use them to make myself a very padded existence. What's the point of all this money if I can't use it to give the people I care about a better life?"

Gayle nudges her again, this time harder, more like a jab. Mary is stunned and ashamed at her own behavior. "I'm so very sorry for giving you such a hard time," she says. "I really don't know where this is coming from. Please accept my apology, and I will try to be more gracious in the future."

"You're my girl. I accept you, warts and all," he says, hoping to elevate the mood.

"Warts? Ouch." She glances at the back seat, where Gayle is physically holding back her own comedic comments.

Vinny pulls into the parking area of what at first glance doesn't seem much more than a small roadhouse in the middle of nowhere. "A good friend of mine is temporarily working here," he says. "His name is 'Two Man' Pizzallatto."

"That's his name?" Mary asks, and is immediately embarrassed by her judgmental tone.

"They call him that because he is the size of two men. He got that big from eating his own cookin. I don't even think I know his real name. He's no scholar, but he sure can cook. He's from up north, but he has been down here studying our local cuisine. I'm just going to go check if he's around, and I'll come back to get you."

As Vinny enters the building, Mary studies the no-frills sign:

MOSCA'S, EST. 1946

Only minutes pass before Vinny reappears and opens the passenger door. "Here we go, ladies," he says, ushering them toward the front door of the small restaurant.

Mary suddenly thinks it odd that there are no other cars in the parking lot. A panic grabs her gut, making her afraid to breach the threshold of the restaurant door Vinny is so kindly holding open for her. She can see that the inside is under-lit, too dim to dine.

Vinny smells her fear. "They do not normally serve lunch here. This is a favor to me," he says.

This makes sense—the only table set is theirs and the place is otherwise deserted—but Mary dares not move just yet. She feels like she has read several fairy tales over the years that warn of such things.

"I'm so hungry," Gayle says, passing Mary to sit at the table, where she reaches into a basket of hot twisted sesame rolls.

A boy not much older than the girls enters the room with a pitcher of iced tea. "Welcome, all. Please sit. The food is being prepared," he says, pouring out three large glasses.

Mary finally finds her feet and passes through the entrance to take her seat. She watches the boy light a candle placed in the center of the table. Deftly, he hands out three small plates like a dealer at a Vegas card table.

"My name is Johnny. Please let me know if you would prefer a different beverage, or if you need anything else before your entree."

"No, thank you. This will be fine. We appreciate you letting us impose," Mary says, now feeling silly about her apprehension.

"No bother at all. Mr. Vinny here is a longtime friend of my family. Can I get you more rolls?" He smiles, seeing that Gayle has devoured almost two of the small portion he had set out earlier.

"Sorry," she says with a cheek full of appetizer.

"I'll get it. Be right back," Vinny says, following Johnny into the back through a pair of swinging doors with small, squarish windows.

Gayle places one of the rolls in front of Mary, who takes a bite, still soaking in the room. Her eyes caress framed photos displayed thoughtfully across pale butterscotch walls, a parade of faces floating above cozy beadboard wainscoting. Across the room, a thickly varnished mixologist's bar of dark wood polished to a high shine hosts rows of decadent elixirs.

"This bread is really good. I wonder how it was made." Mary holds it out for a closer inspection of its beauty.

"Fancy, isn't it?" Gayle says, stopping to take a gander at her half-eaten specimen as well.

"Doesn't look like my drop biscuits, that's for sure." Mary takes another bite, relishing the taste.

The door swings open, revealing Vinny with a toothy smile and a tray. "I sure hope you have room," he says. "Looks like there is a sample of his favorites coming your way. This is the side salad . . . the rest will be coming out shortly." He places the salads before them and sets the tray on the next table. "Our cook seems a little nervous—wanting to make a good impression." Vinny seats himself, rubbing his hands together before tearing into one of the rolls.

"If the meal is even half as good as the bread, consider me Two Man's biggest fan," Gayle says, pointing at the empty bread plate with her fork.

"This is a special treat," Vinny brags. "You won't find most of this stuff on the usual menu."

Mary pokes at a circular food item sitting alongside the crisp lettuce. Without knowing what it is, she bravely slices it with her fork and places it in her mouth. The taste of warm crab and spicy herbs makes her eyes sparkle. "Mmmm! What is this stuff? It is *sooo* good."

"You've never had a crab cake before?" Vinny asks, amused.

"*I* have, but it didn't taste this good," Gayle says, and helps herself to the pitcher of tea.

Out from the kitchen appears a rather large Italian man, wearing an apron with both old and new sauce stains on it. He holds a platter of food. The man barely makes it to the table before refusing introductions. "Not until the meal is over," he insists. "I must get the rest of the food out before it gets cold."

In all, Two Man brings out an herbed chicken dish, alligator sauce piquant, three large meatballs on top of pasta swimming in chunky marinara, and three large tamales made with venison—enough to fill them all twice over.

"I can't believe I like alligator. Who knew?" Mary says to her own delight. "I'm so full I could pop."

"This food is boss!" Gayle says. There is nothing but sauce residue on her plate. "How did you find this place? If you blink, you miss it."

"Like Johnny said, I've known the family a long time." Vinny leans back in his chair and finishes his tea.

The swinging doors to the kitchen open to reveal Two Man dressed in a suit. He is tall—taller than he looked before—and wide, but not in an unattractive way. More like a tank with a protective layer.

"Here is the man of the hour! Congratulations on a job well done," Vinny says, giving Two Man a firm handshake and a pat on the back. "The infamous Mr. P."

"Thanks for the grub, Bub," says Gayle, extending one hand and holding her glass in the other.

He takes her hand and leans forward in a shallow bow.

Hoping Gayle didn't offend him, Mary adds, "Your dishes are amazing. I never expected such an array of exquisite choices." She adds with a tinge of jealousy, thinking of her own cooking, "Wherever did you learn to cook like that?"

"Here and there. And if you haven't noticed, I enjoy food." Two Man pats his ample waistline. "I could show you some recipes."

"That would be great," Mary says. "So how did you wind up working here?"

Two Man laughs, looking at Vinny, who seems blindsided by the question, and pats his young friend on the back in reassurance. "Vinny and I are like family; we share a similar circle of friends. He made sure I had somewhere to go when I needed to get out of town. Sometimes you need a little extra help getting an extended vacation. I enjoy the cooking just as much as the eating—and the sharing even more. Since I've been away from home, I have had plenty of time to learn all sorts of food preparations from all over the place. It is a pleasure to meet you. I'm so glad you enjoyed the food," he says, grateful for the adoration. The large man goes on to artfully explain to Mary the important roles that quality tools and fresh ingredients play in his creations. Vinny and Gayle struggle not to appear bored. Finally, Vinny looks at his old friend and discreetly taps his watch. "It has been a lovely time, ladies, but I don't want to keep you from your plans," Two Man says, walking them to the door.

"Thank you again for the meal," Mary says. "I hope to visit again soon!"

They hit the road. For a little while in the car, all you can hear is overstuffed moans and a few burps that go unexcused. Gayle becomes restless in the back seat as they approach a bridge.

"I really need to use the restroom," she says with a squirm of discomfort. "Too much iced tea."

"We are getting close. Can you wait?" Vinny asks.

"Yeah, I guess . . ." She notices the other side of the river revealing itself. "Look, Mary—the city!" she exclaims as they ascend the Huey P. Long Bridge.

This particular bridge was not originally built with the size of newfangled cars in mind, so it is ultra-tight fitting, with no shoulder to speak of. It is also unusual in that the cars share this bridge with train tracks, which allows both to pass simultaneously—when this happens, the bridge tends to undulate or sway. Vinny sees that this is going to be the scenario today, and worries that the girls might be frightened; but, caught up in their excitement, they have not seemed to notice. Smiling as they gaze over the skyline of New Orleans, the girls squeal at each other in anticipation. They descend the city side of the bridge and meander their way through city streets. Along the way they sound as if they are watching fireworks, with their alternating *"Ooohs!"* and *"Aaahs!"* This is the first time that either of the girls has had the chance to see buildings of much height up close and personal. As they turn off Canal Street and into the French Quarter, the sounds of jazz and merry-making fill the air. Nearing the Hotel

Monteleone, the streets suddenly became narrow, much like the bridge.

Seeing the crowds, Gayle says, "I thought Mardi Gras was in February." She wonders if she will catch a glimpse of Bourbon Street.

"Correct. The sound that you hear is the continuous party that is the charm of the city," Vinny says. "The day you no longer hear the sounds of music and laughter within these few blocks will be a day the whole world will mourn. I believe that day will never come."

They arrive at the front of this white, ornate, palatial building—the Hotel Monteleone—where a tall pitch-dark-skinned man in uniform is standing in front of a large panel of glass doors. The man seems to immediately recognize the car and greets them with a large smile. He shakes Vinny's hand, greeting him as if Vinny owns the place. The doorman then assists Vinny in putting the top up, whistling for a second man to park the car. Vinny reaches into his pocket and peels a couple bills off of a thick roll of cash to discreetly hand to the men. He and the doorman both open large glass doors for the girls to enter the lobby of this historic landmark hotel.

Gingerly they walk up the carpeted entry steps and onto a checkerboard marble floor. Venturing farther into the heart of the lobby, they pass a double-sided velvet couch with a massive flower arrangement perched upon the upholstered top. There are several columns, one of which is the resting place of an enormous antique pendulum clock.

Mary knows the existence of such things in the world, but to experience this in person makes her feel like she could burst. "Wow, this place is magnificent! I've never set foot in anything so wonderful!" Unable to keep her usual decorum, she blushes, noticing that some of the staff are getting a kick out of her exuberance.

"Yeah, real swell. Point me to the restroom please," Gayle says, searching the lobby. She feels as though she could also burst, but for different, more literal reasons.

Vinny obliges, directing them to the facilities. He receives a brief kiss on each cheek before his young fans make a dash for it.

"Can you get over this place?" Mary asks, washing her hands in the cleanest public bathroom she could have imagined.

So this is what a bathroom would look like when you don't have to share with nine other people.

"I can't believe Vinny can afford to stay here. Chick told me he's an exterminator or something, like for a pest control company. Is that right?" Gayle dries her hands on a cloth towel from a recirculating roll on the wall.

"Yeah, something like that." Mary takes one last look at the immaculate bathroom as they leave.

"Well, I didn't see any bugs," Gayle says, grinning.

"And it sure is clean!" Mary is amazed at how well the bathroom is kept, thinking that someday her own place might compare.

"This way, ladies. Time is ticking, and I have a surprise." Vinny draws their attention and guides them like a border collie, avoiding all the various distractions between them and the destination that resides at the top of a marble staircase.

"It's a salon. She works in a *beauty* salon!" Gayle says, recognizing products from her magazines.

Vinny laughs. "Nothing gets by you."

A sophisticated woman with a dark-blond up-do moves toward them, working her pencil skirt. Her face brightens as she comes closer. "You must be Mary and Gayle. Simply adorable!" she says, sizing them up and reaching for Vinny's hand. He takes her hand and holds it at his side.

"This is Camille Richard. She will see that you get anything you need. I won't be long, and you will be in good hands."

With her free hand, Camille snaps her fingers, and two eager assistants spring into action. "How long can I have them for, Vinny?"

"I'll only be a half hour or so." He releases her hand and winks at Mary, who is now feeling uncomfortable with what she has witnessed. She stands there feeling ill, but not sure why.

Gayle knows why. She takes her friend's hand, whispering, "He chose you, Mary."

"We have to hurry, girls. We have a lot to do, and not a lot of time," Camille instructs.

The manicurists get them seated at identical stations, placing the girls' hands on a towel next to small bowls of sudsy water. They proceed to make the girls privy to all the beauty secrets they could possibly need to know, as they shape, soak, scrub, and moisturize. Gayle makes faces, hating the feel of the emery board scraping across the edge of her bitten, uneven nails—but she endures it, if only for the promise of the image on a nearby advertisement.

"He's expecting you ... go right on in," the busty secretary says, looking up from her work as Vinny walks past her desk to the main office.

Vinny opens the door. As he enters the office, an older man behind a desk stands up to greet him. There is a young man in a chair, not much younger than Vinny, facing the desk with a vacant stare. The boss man shakes Vinny's hand, then pats his short wavy hair as if his feathers were ruffled. Vinny looks from the young man back to the boss, running his tongue along the edge of his teeth as if to sharpen them, but says nothing.

The boss strokes his cleft chin and considers the situation. "It's okay. He's family," he tells Vinny, waving it off.

Vinny, not completely unguarded, decides to finish what he came to do. "I took care of that problem in Chalmette," he says, tossing a key on the desk.

The boss man's face floods with relief. He grabs both sides of the desk and bows his head for a second before snatching the key and placing it in his breast pocket.

"Is there anything else you have for me, Carlos?" Vinny asks. "Because I met this girl, and she's waiting for me downstairs."

"That's no surprise to me. You always have a girl," Carlos laughs. He pats his treasure-filled pocket, glancing at the young man in the chair receiving an education.

"This one's different. I want to keep this one," Vinny says, smiling. He rocks from one foot to the other like a fighter practicing balance skills.

"Say it ain't so, Gator . . . say it ain't so," Carlos says, dismayed, pitching himself forward, having rarely witnessed a genuine smile on Vinny's face. "How you gonna explain that you have no heart to steal?"

"I have one. I just don't keep it with me all the time." Vinny grins, tapping his knuckle on the desk.

"Well, don't let me keep you. See the bartender before you leave." Carlos rises to grip Vinny's shoulder and follows him out the door. "Thanks for another job well done."

"Is that to be my replacement?" Vinny jokes, thumbing back toward the office.

Carlos chuckles. "There is no replacement for you." He lowers his voice. "A friend sent his kin to me. We're going to use him as a scout. I'm trying out a training method taught to me by a very special lady I once knew. If anyone asks, you did not see him."

"Boss, if anyone ever asks, he was in the South China Sea, for all I know."

"Good. Now go get your drink. You deserve it."

Vinny heads for the carousel bar, where there will be a Vieux Carré on the rocks and a package waiting for him.

Carlos goes back to the office, where the young man is waiting in a silent trance, and closes the door. He picks up a dog whistle and gives it a quick blow, immediately thawing the young man's body.

"You could learn so much from that guy," Carlos says, wagging his finger at the closed office door.

"Why did you call him 'Gator'?" the young man asks.

"Because to me, that is exactly what he is. You see, boy, a gator leaves nothing behind. In the wild, a gator will eat everything in its path, leaving no evidence it has ever been there. It carries the trouble away, deep in its belly, never to be seen or heard from again."

"Will I be just like him?" the young man asks.

"No. There is only one gator—born from nature, out of pure will to survive, forged in the fires of passion and circumstance," Carlos says with fond memory. "You, Ozzie my friend—you are a rabbit."

"A rabbit?"

"You are good at silently detecting predators, and you are safer underground." Carlos hands Oswald a beginner's guide to Russian grammar.

"I never thought becoming a woman was going to be so much work," Mary says, thinking about all the care and maintenance of hair, skin, and nails. "There should be a whole semester given on this stuff."

"I guess it's just one more subject we have to study." Gayle rolls her eyes as the manicurist applies the final coat of Cutex nail polish, the fumes of which are enough to make her lightheaded.

"Ladies, please don't touch or bump your nails until they are fully dry," Camille warns. "Be careful and follow me." She walks close to Mary, directing her to the drying station, and says in a low voice,

"Mary, you are one lucky girl. Vinny is the nicest guy I know. Every girl in this place would give anything just to catch his eye. I have known him since we were kids, and you are the first girl I have ever seen him take serious interest in. Don't tell him I told you that he's gone soft—he wants to keep his tough-guy image intact, especially in front of the guys. It will be just one of the secrets we share today." She gives Mary a wink, then resumes at a more inclusive volume. "All we have left is to dry the polish and our work will be done." She checks her wristwatch, then places all twenty nails beneath a set of curing lights.

Mary snickers, having seen a similar light used to hatch baby chicks at the feed store.

Vinny appears and snaps a couple of candid photos of the girls getting pampered.

"Hey, I wasn't ready," Gayle whines. She holds her glossy nails up next to her face for a classic fake surprise pin-up pose while he takes another.

"That color is a little bright, don't you think, Camille?" Vinny says, closing one eye to seemingly reduce the glare.

"I'll have you know that is a new color," she informs him with an air of pomposity. "It's called Hot Strawberry, and it happens to be very popular."

Vinny snorts with laughter. "Thanks for taking good care of my darlings for me." He hands her a small envelope.

Mary finds it odd that Camille does not bother to look inside at the envelope's contents—a level of trust she has never before witnessed at a cash register.

"It was my pleasure! We are all good friends now, aren't we, ladies?" Camille asks, like they have just concluded a girls-only club meeting. "Secrets in the beauty shop *stay* in the beauty shop," she adds, glancing at Mary.

Mary wants to smile as big as Gayle, but it comes off half-hearted. She's not quite sure how to feel about her time spent with Camille.

"I have an action-packed afternoon, and we had better hurry, my pretties," Vinny says. He rushes them into the street, where a car is waiting to take them to the heart of the French Quarter.

Mary figures the ride must be to shave time, noting that it isn't too far to walk, merely blocks away from the hotel. Certain areas of the Quarter allow no cars to pass, perhaps in preservation of a few beloved cobblestone streets, so the car drops them off near Jackson Square, where a line of horse- and mule-drawn carriages wilts in the sun. Vinny, it seems, has commissioned the nearest one to escort them to points of interest.

"Where are we going?" Mary says, tickled as Vinny walks toward the carriage with a large RESERVED sign across the seat and the driver standing alongside.

Vinny, still acting with the enthusiasm of paid personnel giving a private tour, announces, "We are taking a tour to teach you ladies a little about the history of The Big Easy. Later we are taking a dinner cruise on a big paddle steamer on the Mississippi."

"You went to so much trouble. I really feel bad for the way I acted earlier, in the car," Mary says with remorse.

"That, my dear, has been long forgotten," he responds. "So no more worries. Just enjoy the moment."

Before leaving on their route, he points out the beautiful architecture of the surrounding buildings and asks the carriage driver to photograph them with the St. Louis Cathedral backdrop. He then offers the girls assistance into the buggy.

Gayle eyes the vehicle. "It's no hot rod, but it'll do." She takes his hand and steps up.

Mary follows, and Vinny takes a seat between the ladies—after snapping a picture of the horse per Mary's instruction. The driver clicks one last photo of them in the carriage before pulling out of the line.

As the horse travels with them in tow, the girls begin to see all the local artisans in their gathering spots. Vinny disseminates that you can find both genius and novice often within yards of each other—only the personal opinion of the onlooker separates the two. They move from location to location, drinking in the ambiance that is uniquely coveted by the city's inhabitants.

The driver pulls back on the reins in front of a three-story building. "Here we have an example of Spanish architecture. Notice the wrought-iron balconies rich with charm and nostalgia. There are many styles to enjoy around here, folks, but this is my favorite."

Mary tries to imagine the tales these walls could tell. "I have studied some New Orleans history, but even the pictures don't do it justice. I wasn't expecting all the wonderful food smells . . . and the sounds," she says, hearing the rich melodies that haunt each street. "Can we please stop, so I can take a quick picture?" she asks, unable to pass up the chance to snap off a few souvenir photographs to help her convey all of this atmosphere to her father.

Vinny tries his best to give the girls tidbits of colorful information in addition to the driver's, although slightly less historical. Finding herself more relaxed as the tour ends, Mary begins to see Vinny the way she sees her father—a gentle soul with only her best interest at heart. She makes a pact with herself not to question this man's motives anymore.

"The boarding area on the boat dock isn't that far. It would be a little silly to get a ride. I think we have time to hoof it if we don't dilly-dally," Vinny says, setting each girl down gently onto Decatur Street.

Their feet carry them swiftly down the sidewalk, despite the beckoning smell of fresh beignets coming from Café Du Monde, in the opposite direction.

"It's a good thing there is food on this cruise," Gayle says, inhaling the scents of warm chicory and powdered sugar treats. "My lunch is wearing off."

"I don't think you have to be hungry to be lured by those delectables," Mary says with a devilish smirk. "All my Tuesdays would be fat if I lived here."

Approaching the pier, they can see a magnificently maintained old-fashioned steamboat with a bright red paddlewheel.

"Is that the boat we will be on today?" Gayle asks. Without waiting for an answer, she runs ahead to take a closer look.

Vinny jogs to the booth to buy their tickets, and Mary waits for him, staring at the steamboat apprehensively. He concludes the transaction and grabs a few brochures. Approaching the boat with Vinny, Mary stiffens and comes to a complete halt.

"Vinny . . . I have never in my life set foot on a boat. I have to tell you I am very afraid." Mary feels herself on the edge of a panic attack.

"What is it that you're afraid of?" Vinny asks, concerned.

Mary takes a deep breath and discloses a secret long kept. "I can't swim. I have never really had a reason to learn. I thought I could do this, but . . . I don't think I can."

"It's a big boat, and I'm a great swimmer. You'll be safe with me, I promise. I won't let anything happen to you." He lifts her chin and she looks him in the eyes, seeing his fidelity.

This man has been so good to me. I have to do this. Be
brave.

She clears her throat, swallows hard, takes a deep breath, and begins her journey to the boarding plank. Vinny holds her hand and issues constant words of encouragement. "That's it. You can do it. I got you." She begins to find her backbone again. Vinny gives her a light squeeze of praise, recognizing that she is overcoming a childhood phobia.

Gayle has been talking to a deck hand about the boat's engine and how fast she can go when she spots Vinny holding Mary, who looks greenishly ill. She sprints like a cheetah to Mary's side. "What's wrong? What happened?" she probes, suddenly uncharacteristically maternal.

"I'm all right now. Please don't fuss over me—I've embarrassed myself enough. I just neglected to tell anyone that I'm afraid of the water because I can't swim," Mary says, mortified, knowing she has created a scene.

Gayle loses her show of concern. "Is that all? You had me worried you were going to toss your tamale or somethin," Gayle says. "You know I took a junior life guard course at the recreation center this past summer, remember? Besides, most of the seating is inside the cabin."

Mary nods, pushing her fears further away. "I know I was being irrational, but I couldn't seem to explain that to my body. I'm much calmer now. Let's find a good table."

They walk into a beautifully decorated dining hall.

"What a majestic vessel," Mary says.

"No one talks like that," Gayle laughs.

"*I* do. Get a vocabulary." Mary frowns with a furrowed brow and resumes studying the room's fancy tiled ceiling, chandeliers suspended above plush garnet-red carpeting, and tables covered with bright white tablecloths lined up along the windows so you can get the best views possible.

Preoccupied with her ordeal, Mary hadn't noticed a calliope being played somewhere on the boat. Now she hears the lively sound permeating the entire cabin area. Large groups of fellow sightseers begin to board and settle in for the two-hour cruise. Fancy silverware wrapped in red cloth napkins lies in wait for the food, which arrives on fine china.

"*Mmm!* Yummy for my tummy," Gayle says, then blows gently on a spoonful of gumbo.

The waiter sets a steaming bowl down in front of Mary and she asks, "What kind of gumbo is this?"

"It has shrimp, okra, rice, and andouille sausage—the best in town," he says, setting an identical bowl in front of Vinny. "Is there anything I can bring to you before the next course?"

He receives a nonverbal no from all three diners, their speech obstructed by busy mouths.

Upon his return, the waiter nods at Mary, knowing he has a curious diner on his hands. "These are stuffed mirlitons," he says, serving what look like two amply filled peppers to Gayle.

"What's a mirliton?" Gayle whispers to Mary as the waiter walks away.

Mary shrugs, turning to Vinny for help.

"Don't look at me," he says, amused. "I thought it was a bell pepper."

Outside, the scenery quickly changes as they float along the mighty river.

"Well, whatever that was, I *loved* it," Gayle says to her empty plate.

"I hope you saved room for dessert," the waiter says as he clears the dinner dishes.

Gayle sits up, at attention. "What's for dessert?"

"Bread pudding drizzled with a pecan rum sauce," he says on his way to fetch the finale. When he returns, the three of them dig in, audibly groaning in delight with every bite.

First to admit defeat, Mary sits back after only a bite or two of sugary heaven. "I just can't finish this." She pats her lips with the cloth napkin. "I think I would like to watch the sunset from the observation deck."

Vinny, impressed with her pluckiness, stands up ready to escort her before she loses her nerve.

"I'm full as a tick! I don't know if I can get up," Gayle moans, overly satiated yet still holding her spoon. Not wanting to be at the table alone, she licks her spoon one last time before reluctantly leaving the dessert behind and following them up to the deck. "What a spectacular view! Can I take a picture?" Gayle asks. "I want Chick to see."

Mary leans back on the bench after posing for several group pictures taken by a fellow passenger. A leery Vinny eyes the stranger until the camera is returned.

"The only way that meal could have been any better is if Two Man prepared it," Mary says, enjoying the evening breeze.

"We should tell him to add stuffed mirliton to his menu next time we see him," Gayle says. "B-*uuurp*."

"Excuse you!" Mary says, mortified. She glances around the deck, hoping no one heard. "We are in public." Vinny grabs Mary's hand and kisses the back of it, and suddenly she no longer cares about fussing. "I sure am glad I didn't chicken out on you guys," she says in retrospection. "It would have been a crying shame if I had missed this."

"Yeah. I woulda had to rub your nose in that for a while and tell you how much you missed," Gayle snickers.

"Thanks for understanding!" Mary says, pretending her feelings are hurt. "I can't believe you would have gone without me. Some friend you are!"

Gayle digs her figurative grave deeper. "It's okay. I would have taken pictures of everything for you."

"You sure are thoughtful—I'll grant you that." Mary laughs, enjoying the playful banter.

Vinny shakes his head at the two. "Sometimes I can't tell whether you two are friends or enemies."

"You are a fine one to talk! Aren't guys the ones who hassle each other constantly?" Mary asks. "Furthermore, I heard that when a guy picks on you, that means he likes you. Is that true?"

"That might be true if the guy is too immature to expose how he feels about a girl. And as for males joshing one another, that is just plain fun. That's how we bond."

"That's exactly what *we* are doing, and you find it strange?" Gayle says, crossing her arms in triumph at her logic.

"I want to concede before you start preaching about pots and kettles and geese and ganders! Have mercy! It's two against one. Where's Chick when you need him?" says Vinny to sidestep the quicksand. "I learned long ago not to contradict a woman. It could be detrimental to one's health."

Gayle pokes his side. "We also hate to be patronized, Mr. Man."

"Uncle! I call a truce. Mary, call her off, please!"

Laughing along with them, Mary says, "All right, children, that's enough."

Gayle stands up. "Hey, I saw a gift shop earlier. Can we take a look?" She's bouncing from foot to foot now, no doubt under the influence of sugar.

When they arrive, the gift shop clerk behind the counter eyes Mary's interest in the assortment of kites. "Tomorrow should be a good kite-flying day," he says. "Got those on special this weekend only."

Vinny sneaks up behind Mary to take a look, standing close enough to whisper in her ear. "You should pick out a few. We could take the little ones outside tomorrow after church," he suggests.

"Could we really?" she asks, as if she needs permission to like the idea. Before he can answer, she loses her footing and grabs onto Vinny for stability.

"The boat is docking," the clerk announces matter-of-factly, or perhaps in a "hurry up and get out of here, I want to go home" sort of way.

"I don't want the day to be over," Mary says, placing the kites on the counter.

The day becomes evening and a brisk wind causes the girls to huddle in close as the voyage comes full circle. Everyone begins to disembark and vacate the premises. Somehow Vinny's car is parked nearby, gassed up and ready to go.

"How do you do what you do?" Gayle asks him, climbing in the back seat.

Giving her a half-shrug and a grin, Vinny opens the passenger door for Mary. "It's all in the planning, my dear. Details are important for things to go smoothly."

"Well, you got the *smooth* part covered," Gayle says with a yawn.

Not long after crossing the Huey Long Bridge, both girls are fast asleep, and it is a quiet ride home for Vinny. Approaching West Main, he tries to wake them by turning up the radio and singing along to "Wake Up, Little Suzie."

"Oh Mom, five more minutes," Gayle murmurs. She rubs her eyes and sits upright, her hair stuck to her face on the side where she laid.

"You'll be in bed shortly," Vinny yawns.

Mary rights herself in the seat, rubbing the crick in her neck. "How rude of me—I can't believe I slept the whole way! You must have been so bored."

"It's okay. You needed your rest—church tomorrow, you know."

"Yuck! I don't want to go to church. I want to sleep," Gayle says as Vinny pulls up to her house. "Thanks, Vinny, for everything. Goodnight, Mary!" She runs inside, where her folks are most likely waiting to hear about the trip.

Mary stretches her back. "It truly was an experience. You certainly know how to plan an outing."

"I'm just glad that you two were able to go and enjoy yourselves. Now it's late, and I don't want your parents to get mad at me for having you out past your curfew," he says, looking at his watch and seeing they have missed it by two minutes. He leans over and kisses her on the cheek.

She reluctantly gets out of the car.

"Don't look so sad, I'll come by after church. Sweet dreams, my Maggie," he says, blowing her another goodnight kiss.

She pauses on the porch long enough to blow a kiss back before disappearing into the house.

How on earth did I get so lucky to find this man?

Sunday
September 14, 1958

Vivian decides to stay home from church and make a picnic lunch for the children so she can take the rest of the day to relax and do nothing. Norman braves the church trip alone, so the kids take it easy on him and, in a rare moment of cooperation, travel in a reverent and orderly fashion. Arriving at church, Mary sets eyes on Gayle, who is peering around a corner with her back to Mary.

Mary walks up behind her. "What's up?" she whispers, startling Gayle.

"Veronica's telling that group of girls that she has met 'the boy of her dreams'—and his name is *Vincent.* I tell you, she's up to no good," Gayle says in a low growl.

Mary leans in so she can hear Veronica's words, which are thick with syrup and spite: "If we were to get married, our initials would be the same, isn't that *sweet?*"

Gayle, having had enough, emerges to debunk Veronica's attempt to grab attention. "It would be," she taunts, "except you are *ugly* and he's *taken.*"

Mary sees where this is going; she steps out to pull Gayle to class, circumnavigating the small gathering.

"As far as I know, there have been no vows made," Veronica calls out, poking back at Gayle.

"You know good and well that Vinny is seeing Mary, you *cow!*" Gayle snaps.

Mary yanks her away. Mary doesn't understand the extent of Gayle's hatred. It's like holding back a rabid dog. Once they're away from the others, she says, "If she isn't bothering me, why do you let her get under your skin?"

"I can't wait until the day that girl gets what she deserves—a kick in the teeth!" Gayle says scathingly.

All the other girls begin to file into the classroom, taking their seats, still giggling at whatever information was passed amongst them. Veronica is pulling up the rear, looking like a cat that ate all the Friskies. Through the rest of Bible class, she and Gayle fight a silent shooting match of dagger-filled eyes.

This ugliness between Gayle and Veronica started a long time ago, before Mary moved to Houma. The war began when Gayle was just turning twelve. Veronica had been held back in school, so that made her thirteen already. Around the time when Gayle's father started to do well financially, Veronica began paying a whole lot more attention to Gayle. Gayle went along with it, even though she thought it odd that Veronica wanted to be her best friend all of a sudden, and not knowing that Veronica had a curious eye on her before that. In fact, their friendship was not unlike what Gayle and Mary have now—until one event that changed both girls forever.

It was a Friday night. Veronica was sleeping over at Gayle's house. They had stayed up late discussing boys and such until they fell asleep. Gayle, for the first time, was having an illicit dream. Pulled from her slumber by the intensity of her arousal, Gayle realized that Veronica was kissing her along her inner thigh, and she froze, not knowing what to do. She was both frightened and on fire at the same time, so she did and said nothing, but her excited breath continued. Veronica took this as permission to finish what she had started.

And Gayle has never forgiven her for that.

When it was over, Gayle felt guilty and ashamed of what took place. Veronica told Gayle that her enjoyment of the act meant that she was partially at fault—even accused her of participation. At this, Gayle grabbed Veronica by the throat. It was the first time she'd ever threatened anyone. She said, "If you tell anyone about what happened here tonight, I will kill you."

Veronica agreed to keep quiet, not because of Gayle's threat, but because she feared reprisal from her parents, the kids in school, everyone. Veronica never considered herself homosexual; in fact, she loved boys and their boyish parts. But she had this strangely strong attraction to Gayle—an attraction that has never dissipated—so it kills her to see Gayle with Mary. Thus, an ongoing battle has ensued. To Gayle, it's a way of venting her anger and frustration about what happened. For Veronica, it's a form of foreplay, a way to keep Gayle engaged as long as she will take the bait. Veronica is willing to subject herself to blows to keep the sick game going.

After being endowed with their weekly dose of guilt and delusive redemption, the girls help Norman round up his crew. Once this is done, Mary anxiously scans the rest of the church goers' vehicles. And then she sees him: Vinny, waiting patiently by his car in the parking lot.

He smiles. "Can I give you girls a lift?"

"Just get me out of here!" Gayle commands, looking back at Veronica, who is staring a hole into her.

Seeing this exchange, and noticing Veronica's malicious wave in his direction, he asks, "Is there a problem?"

"Don't ask," Mary says, fully aware of the existence of a slippery slope in any answer she would give.

"I'm glad you have this open field so close to your house," Vinny says. "I don't think everyone would have fit in the car." He takes a seat on an edge of the large picnic blanket after helping Jenny launch a kite.

Gayle lies on her stomach, feet in the air as she intermittently wets a finger to flip through a magazine filled with car porn. "You could have fit a couple of em in the trunk."

Vinny ignores her jab. "I guess that salesman really knew his stuff—about the wind, I mean."

"He sure did," Mary agrees, pausing to lend instruction to her siblings. "Now run and let the wind take it," she calls out to the children. After the last of the colorful wind-catchers launches successfully, Mary grabs a spot on the blanket.

The breeze cooperates, allowing the sky to embrace the colorful diamond shapes with minimal effort. Mary can remember days with a homemade kite—she would run up and down the yard with it, but to no avail. She can also recall the feeling, on another occasion, when her kite first took flight and it rose to kiss the sky, wind tugging so strong she could hardly reel it in. A memory no one should be without, but she knows Vinny has no such memories or nostalgic nuances to tap into.

"Be careful not to go near the power lines," Mary calls out to the children as they retreat, letting the cardboard spools unroll. "Thank you for this," she says to Vinny. "It's so nice to see them have some fun." The sweet autumn breeze lifts her hair and dances through it. "I don't think they've spent a day outside since you brought that talking box into the house."

"You . . . I . . ." Vinny's words trail away like the kites in the sky; he forgets what it was that he wanted to say, now hypnotized by her beauty.

"Are you okay?" Mary reaches over to feel his forehead to check for a temperature.

"Just lost my train of thought is all." He stretches out alongside her so he can stare at her while she enjoys the children at play.

Mary inhales and sighs—she knows that this moment, this blissful afternoon, is creating a memory she will be able call upon if ever she needs to remember what happiness feels like.

As the sun sinks lower into the calm sky, the light begins to dim, signaling the bloodsuckers to come and get their meal. Vinny and Mary shake out the Gautreaus' blanket.

Gayle suddenly remembers it's Sunday. "I don't want to go to school in the morning. It's such a drag." She rolls her magazine to use as a weapon against the mosquitoes.

"Just think—when you get home from school tomorrow, Chick will be here," Vinny says with encouragement. "I'm picking him up in the morning. He will be in-shore until next Sunday."

"My dreamboat's coming ashore," Gayle sings, gliding through the yard on her way home, like a trailer for some second-rate musical.

"Speaking of . . ." Vinny says, "I need to go get some sleep if I'm going to pick Chick up at five in the morning. I'll come by sometime tomorrow. Till then, I'll be dreaming of you." He brushes the back of his hand along Mary's cheek before leaning in for a kiss.

A part of her is sad to see him go without making more of an effort—but the other half would rather get squared away for school in the morning.

Time passes her by. Soon everyone else is in bed except for her and Norman, in the kitchen, marinating in a radio discussion on the civil rights movement and an imminent Martin Luther King Jr. book launch.

Mary strikes a match and lights the gas burner, then places a small saucepan over the flickering blue flame to warm some milk for her and Norman. She sits silently for a while, listening to opposing debate on the desegregation of schools. The commentators cite the showdown in Virginia, the turmoil in Little Rock, and the fallout across the South.

"Why does it all have to be so difficult, Pa? I don't understand why we can't find a way to get along." She hands her father a mug of warm milk.

"Looks like hard heads, I reckon . . . some folks havin trouble with new ideas," he says, enjoying his milk and her company.

"You'd think all these people, with all their education, would be making more sense than they do," Mary says. "What do you think about all this nonsense?"

"That's a good question, my dear. I say we should all have the right to pull ourselves upright. I think this Martin feller's got a good message and some right ideas, but I think some of his supporters are twistin it up. That's gonna make it hard for the small-minded to swallow. Without good educatin, how do they expect those young'uns to even have a chance? They're fightin so hard to keep em out—then, down the road, they'll blame em for the empty tool chest." He taps the side of his head. "I think it's a damn shame. They need to give people a chance to be somethin worth a damn, or we'll end up a nation of nobodies. Got no one to blame but themselves and their damn hard heads," he concludes, shaking his fist in the air.

Mary's head jerks back, impressed with the lather her father has worked up. "Now tell me how you *really* feel!" She takes a sip of her hot milk. "There seems to be so much unrest all over the place," she adds, defeated.

Norman nods. "I worry these politickers are gonna end up killin us all in an ignorant war over ignorant reasons. Sometimes it seems the whole world is just one big unruly schoolyard and no one 'cept the bullies get to make the rules. Some people so busy hatin and shovin each other and nothin gettin done."

"Pa, maybe there are more people in the world who feel the way you do and think it's wrong to hate for no good reason," Mary says, not yet spoiled by the limitations set by society. "You should run for office!"

Norman slaps his knee, chuckling at the thought. "They don't listen to people that don't have all them educated letters after their names. That is why it is so important for you to get them letters—so you can go tell em they're being idiots. It's a whole lot easier to change your world and the world of others when you get them letters. Now you'd better be off to bed, or the only letter you'll be gettin is a tardy note for sleepin late."

Mary, now more than ever, sees the long hours that her father keeps as the sacrifice he is willing to make for his children to have a chance to become whatever they choose to be. It makes her hurt for people in the world who aren't given that chance. A few minutes later, as she snuggles into bed and closes her eyes, she wonders what it would be like if the world cared as much for *all* its children as her father does. She feels inspired enough to take on the world as sleep envelops her.

Monday
September 15, 1958

T he occasional sniffle or clink of utensils is the music playing at the Poche kitchen table this morning, all participants either lost in thought or barely awake—or both.

"So how was it?" asks Vivian, entering the kitchen last, as usual.

Mary grins, wiping the remnants of freshly made biscuit from the counter. "How was what?"

"New Orleans, silly. You haven't spoken a word about it."

Mary reveals the better details of her day of adventure. Norman silently listens to her careful recollection, trying to imagine all those descriptive words coming to life in his head, before kissing Mary's forehead and leaving for work.

"We took loads of pictures. You can see for yourself when we get them developed." Mary picks up the butter dish and returns it to the fridge, the instinct to clean so engrained she barely notices what she's doing.

"Sure sounds like you had a real nice time," Vivian says.

The more Mary talks, the more she neatens, first cleaning up the breakfast dishes, then putting them away. Finally, she gathers her school items and says, "I gotta go, Mama, but Vinny said he might come by later with Chick. Bye!" She flies through the door, books in hand.

Mary gets on the bus and bounces into the seat next to Gayle.

"How can you be so chipper in the morning?" Gayle mumbles.

"Didn't you sleep well?" Mary says, concerned.

"I'm never chipper in the morning, no matter how I slept." Gayle assumes a napping position and grumbles, "Wake me when we get there."

The bus ride to school today gives Mary a chance to gather herself and get her mind back into a more studious modality. While the majority of the teens leave the bus with all the enthusiasm of heading to a dentist appointment, Mary confidently strides forward with the knowledge that Mrs. Tisdale is waiting for her. Apart from being the best Algebra teacher this school has ever known, Mrs. Tisdale has appointed herself as honorary guidance counselor to anyone wanting to attend college, and she has taken special interest in her newest protégée. While Mary pauses to speak with the teacher, Gayle sits on a nearby bench to wait for her.

"Mary!" Mrs. Tisdale says with a Duchenne smile. "I have been so impressed looking at your scores this weekend. I was curious why you haven't considered moving up a grade level, even two?"

Over the teacher's shoulder, Mary can see Gayle making monkeyshines in her general direction. Mrs. Tisdale, catching Mary's gaze, turns to look. Gayle gazes upward and whistles, playing the innocent.

"Oh, I *see*," Mrs. Tisdale says, giving this some thought. "You two are close, huh?" She bites her lip. "Is she interested in going to college, too?"

"I am trying to have a positive influence on her," Mary says optimistically.

Mrs. Tisdale nods approvingly. "I have some forms here that I need you to fill out for the spring SAT. I can give a set of forms to your friend if she would like to participate. I also would like to suggest adding one more extracurricular if we could—maybe art, or an instrument of some sort. We can discuss that later, but just give it some thought. Remember, I can find funding if necessary. I'll see you in fourth period," Mrs. Tisdale trails off, making a beeline for the building.

Mary is left standing with a small booklet of newly copied papers. Gayle snatches the papers away. "You know how much I love to sniff fresh ditto copies," she says, taking a long whiff of the fresh purple ink. "Does that lady spin like a top, or what? I get exhausted just watching her. What was that all about, anyway?"

"Getting us into college," Mary answers sneakily, and they start off to class.

"I don't want all that extra work. It gets in the way of my daydreams," Gayle whines, not wanting to hear the *Importance of Higher Education* speech Mary has given once or twice. "You have my support," she says, but adds defiantly, "but I'm not interested in going to old Fufu U."

"I just want you to keep your options open," Mary says, not wanting to push the issue too hard.

"I'm not the only one who needs to remember options—here comes one now. You've met this boy at least three times before and I will clobber you if you force him to introduce himself again!" Gayle coyly stops at the water fountain to have a drink.

Mary looks up. Heading toward her is none other than Bobby Vicknair in all his letterman glory. "Good morning, Mary. May I help you with your books or something?" he asks awkwardly.

"I think I'll be okay. But thanks for the offer," Mary says, fully aware of Bobby for the first time. Gayle coughs her disapproval behind them. "Well, maybe . . . okay," she says suddenly, and dumps her books into his arms before Gayle makes a scene.

"I saw you talking to Mrs. Tisdale by the buses," he says. "Isn't she great? She gave me a study guide for the testing sessions this spring. I could share." Having done some reconnaissance, he hopes this will entice her.

A little impressed, Mary asks, "So you're preparing to attend college?"

"It's a lock. All there is now are the formalities." Bobby sounds confident now, slowly walking her to class. "My dad even made me learn the violin and the piano to make sure I have something artistic to brag about."

"Sounds like a smart man that cares about his son's future," Mary says sweetly, attempting to make up for slighting him before.

"He does care. But I don't know if he cares about *me*, or just about me joining the family practice one day. I'm not absolutely sure about becoming a doctor. I might not be good enough to make him proud."

He says this in such a vulnerable way that Mary can't help but to touch his shoulder. "I'm sure he is already proud," she says. "He probably just hopes to keep you close to home."

"I don't know why I just told you that. You must think I'm a real sap," Bobby says, covering his eyes with his hand, his cheeks bright crimson.

"I am the last person you ever need to worry about judging you," Mary says, thinking of her own fears and flaws. "Besides, I'm a nobody freshman! You shouldn't even care what I think."

"I do care. And you're not a nobody," he says, taking a sober tone. He hands back her books and Mary just stands there, not knowing how to respond.

The bell rings.

"Can we continue at lunch? I need to ask you something," he says, but he leaves without even waiting for her response.

Suddenly, shame fills her gut like a swarm of moths—Mary neglected to mention having a steady boyfriend. Hurting Bobby's feelings is not acceptable, so she makes herself a promise to tell him at lunch.

Gayle enters at the bell for first period, after being waylaid by a gossipy snitchling in the hall, and gives Mary her standard *So what happened?* look. Mary just mouths, *Tell you later.*

Mary manages to lose herself in the lesson; Gayle, however, prays for the bell to end her agony, and when it finally does ring, she pounces on Mary, wanting answers. She tries her best to explain, but can't remember what was said verbatim.

"You're right—you have to tell him about Vinny," Gayle says, slightly bemused by the new stimulus. "I knew he had a thing for you, but it might be worse than I originally thought."

It seems like an eternity for their lunch period to arrive, but when it finally does, the girls head outside to the table where they routinely sit, to allow the inevitable drama to unfold. Gayle ordinarily brings her lunch, while Mary buys a plate from the cafeteria at a reduced rate. Occasionally they trade, since Gayle often likes the gruel the cafeteria mass produces. Today's treat du jour is Sloppy Joes, green beans, and mixed fruit. Mary is glad to partake of the ham sandwich and apple packed for Gayle. Shirley makes the best fully dressed ham sandwiches (minus the mayonnaise). Eating quickly, they can free up the rest of their lunchtime for socializing, studying, or, in Gayle's case, front-row seats to watch your best friend squirm. With no time to spare, they spot Bobby heading toward their table, inexplicably wearing his gym uniform, and when he stops across from Mary, many people take notice—including Veronica.

"Hope you enjoyed your lunches. I tried to give you enough time to finish before interrupting," he says, blocking the noonish sun with his hand.

"Please sit, Bobby. You're no bother . . . but there is something I didn't get to tell you this morning." Mary turns to Gayle for guidance. Gayle gives a nod of reassurance.

"I was hoping that I could ask you to go to the Homecoming dance with me before I lose my nerve," he blurts, seemingly not hearing her over his own internal dialogue.

Mary blushes, and she can see Gayle's mouth gape open in her peripheral vision. "I am so sorry, but I can't go with you," Mary says clumsily, "because I have a boyfriend and I agreed to go steady with him. I was trying to tell you when you first sat down." She does not know what it is to bruise someone this way. It nearly breaks her heart to see his reaction, reminding her of a movie she watched recently about a loyal dog who is shot at the end.

In the awkward silence, Bobby's anguished eyes dart around, sizing up a possible opponent. "Is it someone here at school?"

"No, it is someone I met from New Orleans. It's all been rather sudden," she says, in a way that is surprisingly sad to her own ears.

"It's my fault for not coming to you sooner. I've been wanting to ask you out since summer practice. I even sent Jane to ask if you were seeing anyone, and at the time you weren't. I'm the one who is sorry. I hope this doesn't mean we can't be friends."

"Why would it mean that? I mean, I don't foresee an issue. Do you?"

Bobby swallows, gauging how to proceed. "I know several guys who have steady girlfriends and won't even let them speak to other guys, let alone spend any time together."

"I'm sure that he trusts me enough to make my own decisions," Mary says, believing that Vinny is certainly more mature and understanding than a high school boy.

"Good . . . because there is one more thing I wanted to ask. During my last conversation with Mrs. Tisdale, she mentioned that a certain college candidate may need my services and asked if I would broach the subject with said student. In other words—would you be interested in learning to play a musical instrument, such as the piano? I don't live far from school. We could practice once or twice a week during lunch."

"I might have to give that some thought . . ." Mary replies, troubled by this new option.

Bobby grins at her lack of excitement. "Mrs. Tisdale told me that would be your reaction."

She folds her arms. "Am I truly that easy to read? Everyone seems to be reading my thoughts lately. What exactly is it that you suppose I am thinking, Sir Grins-a-lot?"

His grin only grows. "She said you don't like people fussing over you and don't enjoy feeling indebted to anyone for anything—and that you might become a little defensive, but you are smart enough to listen to reason."

Realizing that she is pegged, Mary immediately unfolds her arms and shakes it off. "I guess that is somewhat true at times."

"That's you in a nutshell!" Gayle suddenly injects her two cents.

Mary flashes a glare that shuts Gayle down, then turns back to Bobby. "I'm going to be frank with you. I can't afford to pay you, I can't afford a piano, and I don't know that I can afford the extra time needed to learn such an instrument."

"The violin it is," he says, not wanting to give up so easily.

"I told you, I will think about it." She smiles in spite of herself, shaking her head at his persistence.

"All I want is for you to consider me—uh, I mean, *it*—for your future," he says. "I have to go see the coach now, but I hope to see you later. Don't worry, I won't be looking for your answer until you have time to discuss it with your parents—and the lucky scoundrel that beat me to the punch."

The girls admire Bobby's sun-kissed muscles as he walks away. Neither of them can help but to sigh in appreciation for such art in the world.

Mary pulls her eyes away and playfully pinches Gayle. "Okay, that's enough."

"Boy, I sure wouldn't blame you if you replaced me with him as your new best friend. He's a real hunk," Gayle says languidly, her eyes still upon him. "Nothing against Vinny, but this guy is more your type—*and* closer to your age. Too bad you couldn't have gone to Homecoming together. That would have been super dreamy."

Mary sighs. "I think I know what growing pains are now. All these thoughts swirling around in my head . . . it hurts!" She grabs the sides of her head. "What am I supposed to do with all this new information?"

"Now you know what class is like for the rest of us," Gayle snarks.

Mary raises her head out of her hands to bug her eyes out at Gayle, warning her to cooperate.

"Okay, okay, let's see," Gayle says. "You want to get into a fancy college . . . aaand Mrs. Tisdale seems to think music lessons would help . . . which would also allow you to get to know Bobby better without messing up things with Vinny. I don't see the harm in giving it a whirl."

"Do you think I need to tell Vinny that Bobby has a crush on me?" Mary asks, feeling deceptive.

Perhaps this is a lie by omission?

"Only if you're wanting trouble where there isn't any! First of all, Vinny isn't here during the week. And it's not like you'd be going over to Bobby's house to play backseat bingo—but if you do, I want every torrid detail," Gayle only half-jokes. She gathers the remnants from lunch to toss in a nearby receptacle. "Wasn't it your dad that told you never to look a gift horse in the mouth?" She has used this technique more than once with Mary, with positive results.

"That was him, all right," Mary says, realizing it might be ungrateful, and possibly stupid, to pass up an opportunity she might not get otherwise.

This is not just any old nag . . . this is a handsome
stallion.

"Bobby said you don't have to answer right away. Let's find out what your dad thinks. For now, just let it be." Gayle waves to someone she knows at the table across the way.

"By the by, no one could ever replace you as my best friend," Mary says, knowing how much she relies on Gayle's whimsy to keep her balanced.

"I'll have to remind you of that in the future, I'm sure."

When a fellow schoolmate lures Gayle away from the table, offering up a homemade brownie, Veronica, sniffing opportunity in the air, charges over to Mary, boldly empties out a bottle of soda at her feet, and walks away. Mary, unfazed by Veronica, watches as the river of red cream soda fast approaches a nearby ant. She decides to sit passively and watch, seeing the creature is in danger yet doing nothing to prevent it. The ant scurries away in vain from what is becoming an inevitable demise.

Am I an innocent bystander, or indifferent and cruel?

A voice from the loudspeaker pulls her attention away, announcing, "We are living in an atomic age and we need to plan for our survival. There will be a forum this evening in the gym to discuss what to do when emergencies occur. Tell your parents the meeting is tonight at seven o'clock. We have flyers available in the office. Please come by and pick one up. Our future is at stake."

When Mary's attention returns to the ant, she cannot find it. She chooses to believe it escaped somehow—never to truly know its fate.

"Gaylie baby!" Chick calls.

Still sitting at the foot of Veronica's soda stream, Mary is wakened from her reverie. She looks up to see Chick walking up the sidewalk with Vinny. She and Gayle run across the neatly mowed schoolyard to greet the unexpected guests.

Gayle flies into Chick's arms and pecks at his face with kisses. "I missed you so much!"

Chick gives her a small bundle of letters he has written to her over the week and Gayle cradles the envelopes to her chest, beaming. Mary's reception of Vinny is more controlled but not any less heartfelt, her hand finding his a comfortable fit.

This small gathering pulls the unwanted attention of an overzealous duty teacher, Mrs. Buttinsky, who requires Chick to explain his presence.

"I will be working construction all week," he tells her politely, "and I want to get a pass to have lunch with my friends while I'm in town."

After agreeing to show the young men to the office, the teacher supervises their stiff, platonic goodbyes as the bell rings, sending the girls back to artificially lit classrooms for the duration of the pleasantly warm afternoon.

As the bus pulls onto the road, they see that Chick's car is sitting in front of Gayle's house. There is an unfamiliar work truck in front of Mary's house, parked next to her father's. This causes Mary's brow to furrow—her dad is never home this early.

Stepping off the bus, the girls find Chick leaning on the unfamiliar truck, dragging on his cigarette.

"What's happening?" Mary asks, more than a little anxious. "Whose truck is that?"

"Oh, my cousin Lester and your dad got off early to meet the inspector for a walk through the house, see what repairs needed to be made."

Relief floods through Mary. She is so proud to see the men in her life working together to take care of the family home.

"Vinny talked your dad into getting help, got him ta sign a purchase agreement with James—knocking the cost of repairs offa the asking price, of course." Chick flicks his cigarette butt into the yard. "James must really like your dad, because he's willing to put most of the rent he's already paid toward the price."

Mary walks over to retrieve the butt and tosses it into the bed of Lester's truck.

***

Mary finds an out-of-the-way spot on the porch to do her homework. Everyone else is preoccupied, including Gayle, who is currently engrossed in watching Chick move the lumber and other supplies with his shirt off. They all stay elbow-deep in their various projects until the lack of light forces the outdoor activity to shut down for the evening. Luckily, Mary has just completed her homework on the porch. She hears the children rushing around to wash up for supper.

"You coming in soon?" little Sarah calls from the door to Mary. "Mama's waitin on ya to help serve the company."

My, what a big girl you are.

"Only if you come over here and give me a big hug," Mary says, with thoughts of how fast time passes.

Sarah happily jumps into her lap, as she has done so often in the past. "I hope you remember moments like these and know that I love you. Even when I get too wrapped up to show you how much," she says, with the prescience that life will become more challenging from here on. With one last squeeze, they both follow the sounds of silverware clanging as the table is finished being set.

"There you are," Vivian says, filling plates with red beans and rice. "Wash your hands and let's feed these hard-workin men at my table."

"Only if they promise to keep their shirts on," Mary says, goofing on Chick as she follows her mother's orders.

Chick stands up. "No offense, Mary . . . I'm going to run over to Gayle's for supper. I promised." He pushes the chair back where he found it. "Thanks for the offer, Mrs. Viv. Lester and I will be back in the morning."

"I'll make you some fresh biscuits and coffee then," Vivian calls as Chick goes out the door. Her eyes then turn on her daughter, glaring, as if Mary has run Chick off. It is the first time Vinny sees the cruelty that lies beneath Vivian's cheerful veneer.

Mary and Vinny exchange several alluring glances as she tends to all the children, until she finally claims her spot next to him in the chair left vacant by Chick. During dinner, a discussion transpires of possible nuclear threat scenarios following the announcements of ongoing nuclear testing in the USSR. Mary is amused by how much information her family is able to regurgitate from watching David Brinkley or whomever on the evening news—the topper being how easily Vivian brazenly spouts the opinions of commentators, passing them off as her own intellectual insights. Mary sends the smaller children to watch *Father Knows Best* as the adults finish eating, hoping not to alarm them with the subject matter. Norman begins his nightly ritual of reading the morning newspaper that he can never seem to finish before work.

All this talk of nuclear testing has Mary feeling rather cynical. "I don't know why they bother having bomb drills in school. From the way they talk about the devastating effects of these bombs, cowering beneath a desk isn't going to protect us. I guess it's just to keep us calm before we die."

This prompts a chuckle from Norman, who is following the conversation despite his lack of participation in it. Mary envies his multisensory ability to absorb information. Norman often points out that you learn more from silence than you can from the sound of your own voice; she just has to work on getting the silence part down.

Vinny, sensing Mary's mood shift, tries to gloss over the Cold War propaganda. "I guess it's better to be calm than in utter chaos, just in case it's a false alarm. Besides, I doubt that any serious strategy will have small-town high schools on the list of targets."

"I hear people up north are building bomb shelters. Too bad our ground is too mushy to even have a cellar," Vivian complains.

Vinny leans back for a stretch, lacing his hands behind his head. "Enough of this doom and gloom. Let's talk about the house."

Vivian nods, smiling in sincere appreciation. "Norman and I just want to thank you again for getting Lester and his crew out to help with the repairs."

"Mr. Norman has already thanked me plenty," says Vinny. "It's actually his reputation around town that convinced Lester to add the job to his already full docket. You should be proud to be married to such a stand-up kinda guy," he adds fondly, inspiring Vivian to hug Norman around the neck—much to his dismay and delight.

Vinny clears his throat. "I'm going to stick around tomorrow long enough to make sure that Lester is aware of all the work to be done. Hopefully he can have it all finished before the year's end. Which brings me to some bad news . . . I am needed out of town for work, and I don't expect to be back before Christmas." He attempts to say this with an innocent air, hoping in vain that his news will be overshadowed by the global topics they've been discussing.

The whole family is hushed. Even the forks are still and silent. Mary's expression contorts to one of shock, almost tortured in its appearance. Her parents exchange a look, still not clear on what

Vinny actually does for a living, and together they wonder what special job would take him nearly three months to complete.

Vinny cradles Mary's distraught face in his strong, uncallused hands. "Don't give me that look. It's going to be hard enough as it is. It's a big job, and I'm sorry I wasn't able to provide you with more notice than this. When I am summoned out of town, I have to be prepared to move fast. I will call and write as often as I can. It's only a few months, and you have your studies to keep you busy. And I'll be thinking of you every day with that look if you don't stop." He swallows. He is unprepared for his own anguish at seeing her this way.

"I'm sorry, Vinny," she says mournfully. "I knew this might happen … it's just not something I had considered happening so soon. I don't even know you well enough to pick out a Christmas present for you."

"I don't want a present. But I'm sure you'll think of something to force on me," he says, hoping to make her laugh.

After dinner, Vivian shoos Mary and Vinny onto the porch so they can spend a little time alone before he has to leave for the night. They sit side by side, holding hands in near silence except for the occasional inspiration of thought, and study each other as if they will forget what the other looks like during their abrupt separation.

At bedtime, Norman appears in the doorway, gently coughing to alert the young lovers that the time has slipped away. Vinny and Mary spend another fifteen or so minutes saying goodbye. Their final parting kiss does not make either of them feel any better, but at that point Norman and Vivian come out onto the porch.

To help the young couple say goodnight and ensure a faster conclusion, Norman announces, "Everyone has an early start in the morning."

"I'll try to be here before the bus," Vinny says softly to Mary. He waves to them as he gets into the car to leave.

Before her parents have a chance to light a fire under her, Mary rips through her bedtime routine. She throws herself into her bed, begging sleep to take her quickly before this unfamiliar twist of insecurity can crush and possess her thoughts, her eyes, her cavernous interior, all the places that a love could grow.

Tuesday
September 16, 1958

I n the dewy morning, Vinny arrives just in time to say goodbye to Norman as he climbs into his work-bound truck.

"We'll be missin ya at our Thanksgivin, son. We hope to see ya at our Christmas table safe and sound," Norman says with a firm yet affable handshake. "And don't you worry about little Mary. Once she starts all them tests, she won't be looking up till about that time, anyway."

"Yes, sir. I'm just glad to know she is in such good hands."

Inside the house, Mary wipes down the twins with a damp rag after their breakfast, wondering how they could be nourished when so much of the food ends up in places other than their mouths. Just when she thinks she is going to have to leave for school without seeing Vinny, he walks in through the screen door, whistling a tune. Casually, he pulls a shiny trinket out of his pocket and twirls her away to wrap the gold around her neck. She sees a tiny cat charm dangle on the chain.

"Morning, my Maggie. Just a little something to remind you of the day we met," he says with a wink.

The cocky way he says it makes her wish even more that he wasn't leaving, a feat she would have sworn impossible. They embrace only momentarily before hearing the ominous roar of the loud bus engine advancing down her street. Reluctantly, Mary gives in to the Pavlovian trigger to grab her books. Taking hesitant steps to the door, she faces Vinny with a pain-filled gaze.

Vinny's smile wavers. "It's okay . . . you can go. I will follow."

Mary's stomach clinches as she turns to leave, afraid that if she looks back she'll become handicapped by the sadness washing over her.

Just as Mary steps onto the bus, Vinny, who has followed as promised, asks, "What's your favorite flower?"

She hesitates. "I don't think I have one," she answers lamely, mad at herself for not coming up with the perfect bloom.

"No biggie," he says. He kisses her on the hand so as not to give the bus driver anything more to frown at him for.

The bus kicks into motion, and an answer comes too late. Seized by an idea, Mary runs to the nearest seat and sticks her head out the open window. "Purple ones!" she calls.

Vinny blows a single kiss in her direction, then stands motionless until she is out of sight.

Mary sits next to Gayle. "He called me Maggie, like in the movie. No one except my father has ever had a pet name for me. It was sweet." She shows Gayle the cat pendant Vinny put on her only minutes earlier.

Gayle is in her usual morning funk, despite the unusual circumstances. "I thought you hated nicknames. And you act like you're never going to see him again."

"He is going out of town for work. Won't be back until the end of December," Mary explains, holding her pendant for comfort.

"Oh, I'm sorry . . . I had no idea," Gayle says, grabbing her hand. "I feel like a jerk."

With her free hand, Mary inspects and plays with the chain he bought her. "I didn't find out until last night during supper. He said it was an important assignment and they need him right away."

"Does this mean you can go to the dance?" Gayle asks, searching for the silver lining. "He wouldn't even have to know."

Mary pulls away, appalled. "Of course not! I can't believe the way your mind works sometimes. He hasn't even left yet and you already have me sneaking around behind his back! I don't want to be that kind of girl."

Gayle shrugs. "Just trying to find the up-side is all. At least now you have the extra time to practice a new instrument."

"Oh, no!" Mary smacks herself square on the forehead. "With all that happened last night, I completely forgot about it. I didn't even get to ask my parents."

"I don't see why you would need to ask," Gayle says, to sway her in the right direction. "You know your father would want you to do whatever it takes to boost the chances of going to a good college. Come on, Mary. You could at least look at Bobby's instruments"– Gayle smirks with innuendo–"to see if you're interested."

"I guess I could just test the waters," Mary says, in an attempt to convince herself it would do no harm.

"You could go during lunch today. I'm telling you, it's meant to be!" Gayle spreads her hands in the air as if she can read stars aligning.

"You just might be right. I'll tell Bobby this morning if I see him. I am probably just overanalyzing anyway," she says with less apprehension.

Gayle chuckles. "How could you miss him? He practically stands on his head every morning to get your attention." She nudges Mary out of the seat just after the bus comes to a complete stop, eager to see what happens next.

Right on cue, Bobby saunters into the hall as the girls make their way to their lockers. Mary looks at Gayle with bulging eyes, launching Gayle into laughter. "All I need now is a crystal ball and I'm in business," she says, and makes herself scarce.

Bobby instantly brightens at seeing Mary unoccupied and looking in his direction. His relaxed gait becomes a trot as he closes in on her. She can't help but feel very flattered by the unfettered attention this handsome young man gives her . . . but seeing the way he smiles at her, she knows she is playing with fire.

Am I setting us both up for a world of hurt?

She closes her eyes and draws a deep breath, preparing to accept his offer of tutelage. She feels like she is on some unseen precipice. "I have been thinking about taking you up on the suggestion you made yesterday. But I was wondering if it could be on a trial basis only. I don't want you to hate me if I decide it isn't working out," she says, protecting herself with an escape clause.

"You never have to worry about that, or anything for that matter," he answers and, without breathing, adds, "We will have so much fun at the dance."

"The dance?" Mary asks, confused. "I was talking about the instruments."

"Oh." Bobby scratches his neck. "Of course you were. Sure, um . . . I could take you over at lunch and let you get a feel for the instruments." He looks at his feet. "But if you decide to start, we really have to begin with reading music. I'll make it as painless as possible. You have to crawl first, so to speak." He wants to crawl away himself. "Meet me by the gym as soon as you finish eating and we can walk over to my house."

"All right, as long as you really don't think it will be any trouble. You may end up losing your patience with me," Mary says, hoping that letting him know she can be a handful will ease his disappointment.

"It's not my patience I'm afraid of losing," he says almost inaudibly.

"I'm sorry? I didn't quite catch the last thing you said."

The bell rings for homeroom, saving him from having to explain. "It's nothing, really. So I'll see you at lunch, then?"

"Yes," she answers, still pondering the feasibility of keeping this situation from getting messy. The chronology of homeroom is just enough time to stir up a mind tornado.

Mary robotically taps her pencil in Civics class, beginning to have buyer's remorse. She ponders over every word uttered in the short exchange, imagining the possible content of his careless slip at the end.

"Well?" Gayle asks, wriggling in her seat.

"I will check it out at lunch," Mary says, annoyed with all the distractions keeping her from thinking straight. "But I have a project due on Friday, and I don't know how I am going to find the time to work on it."

"Is that going to be your excuse? Whatever! I give up." Gayle lifts her textbook, pretending to be suddenly interested in the three branches of government.

When the girls exit the building for lunch, Chick is already in the school yard waiting for Gayle. He gives her a puzzled look as Mary heads in another direction. She has decided she is too nervous to eat and walks straight to her appointment with Bobby. "Where's Mary going?" Chick asks, handing Gayle a soda bottle he has just opened for her.

"She has a new music coach she has to go meet," Gayle says, trying not to lie to her new beau.

"I didn't know she played an instrument," Chick says with a shrug.

"She doesn't *yet*, silly. This is her first day. Plus, this gives *us* a chance to get to know each other." She moves her eyebrows like a prankish Groucho Marx, sending Chick into a slight panic at the thought of having a conversation with her about something other than cars.

When Mary turns the corner of the building, she spies Bobby: he is already waiting for her, supporting the wall like a buttress, and appears to be having a conversation with the notebook on the ground at his feet. Since she often does the same thing and would be mortified if anyone caught her talking to herself, she slowly begins to retreat back behind the wall so as not to rattle him.

"See you guys later!" she shouts over her shoulder, to prepare him for her arrival.

This time he is alert and holds the voiceless notebook in front of his heart like a shield. "Hi! I wasn't expecting you so soon."

"I can come back later if you'd like," she says, mildly amused by his awkwardness.

He flashes a quirky grin of embarrassment. "No, now is fine."

"How far is your house?"

"Not far—past the tree line on the corner of Andoue Street. It's the one with green shutters and a magnolia tree," he says as they walk through the grass and away from campus.

"That's *your* house?" she says, recalling its impressive and regal countenance. "I've admired that one many times. I never imagined that it housed one of our school's star athletes."

"Don't forget that I am also musically gifted," he says with a playful swagger.

"As long as you don't forget that I'm not!"

"You don't know that for sure."

"I guess we will find out soon enough, won't we?" Mary says, surprising herself with her optimism.

The Vicknairs' front door is a sight to behold, both in its size and the elegance of its etched glass panels. As they go inside, Mary tries not to appear too interested, at the same time devouring all its detail before combing her eyes across the foyer, where a lovely round table holds a grand flower arrangement.

Mary has only seen such a display in a hotel, never a home. "Are those real?" she asks.

"I had them delivered fresh this morning." A well-dressed woman appears, carrying a silver platter, topped with two glasses of lemonade and egg salad sandwiches with the crusts removed, as if she is expecting company. She sets the tray down and fusses with the flowers. "I hope the flower shop kept some for themselves! Do you think it's too much? I was afraid it might be a bit garish."

"No, ma'am, the flowers are magnificent," Mary says, wondering how much something like that costs.

The woman breaks off a small tea rosebud and slides it into Mary's hair just above her ear, briefly touching her cheek. Her hand is warm and loving, in stark contrast with the home's starchy façade. Her scarlet multi-strand beaded necklace, the plaid print of her dress, even her rosy complexion, seem to be meticulously planned to coordinate with the fiery colors of the décor. "Allow me to introduce myself properly. I'm Brenda Vicknair, Bobby's mother. And you must be the Mary we have been hearing so much about."

Behind Mary, Bobby waves frantically at his mom to shut her down before she has a chance to say too much—Mary can feel the breeze. She smiles and takes Brenda's outstretched hands. "It is nice to meet you. Thank you for having me."

"We are so pleased to have you in our home. If you need anything, I'll be around," she says cordially. Bobby shoos her back toward the kitchen minus the platter of goodies.

"How did she . . . ?" Mary says, as she gratefully takes a sandwich wedge and a glass from the tray.

They both enjoy the snack as he rambles through an explanation. "I mentioned you once or twice before . . . and we kind of had dinner with Mrs. Tisdale last night and mentioned yesterday's offer. My mom and Mrs. Tisdale made fast friends after she moved here. She and my mom are involved in just about every committee in the area. Mrs. Tisdale thinks very highly of you, and wasn't afraid to share that with my folks. As for the refreshments—my mother is a Southern belle at heart. She seems to be prepared to entertain company day or night. Sometimes I wonder if she wasn't born with a platter of hors d'oeuvres in her hand—although I'm sure they are extras for the book club meeting she is having later this afternoon."

"She seems really nice," Mary says. Brenda Vicknair eclipses her own mother in so many ways that she is suddenly uncomfortable with the obvious class difference. "Maybe this isn't such a good idea. I don't want to be some kind of community service project." She returns her glass to the tray, feeling pangs of self-disgust for being momentarily ashamed of her heritage. She knows that if she pursues her educational aspirations, she will always have to defend her humble beginnings from people not nearly as kind or understanding as these.

Bobby slams his foot down so hard that he could have damaged the intricate parquet floor. "You really need to own the fact that you are young, bright, and full of potential! Stop trying to sabotage the efforts of those who wish only to help you. I am not giving you anything, least of all *pity*. Music is something you're going to have to want and work hard for. The only thing I can do is point you in the right direction," Bobby says, so harshly that he realizes he may have scared her.

Because of her home life, Mary is desensitized to such immature displays of aggression. Focusing on his words, she feels a whole new respect for this articulate admirer. "I guess I do throw up defensive roadblocks," she admits, "like Mrs. Tisdale said, huh? And I guess you aren't going to college solely for football."

"I'm no meat head," he says, trying to regain his composure.

"Thanks for calling me on it. Before now, Gayle has been the only one to give me a good kick in the pants. I guess those are the kinds of friends you really need in life. If everyone just agreed with me, I'd probably just run myself in a self-destructive circle, never getting anywhere."

Bobby silently hands her another sandwich.

Mary takes a quick bite, swallows, and continues. "You see, I'm always anticipating that people with money will treat me the way Veronica does—either openly ridicule me or snicker behind my back. I was just protecting myself in case this was some sort of farce."

"Whew ... for a minute there I was afraid I sounded way too much like my father and I was going to send you running out in tears. I really didn't mean to tear into you like that. I have no idea where that came from. And please don't ever lump me in with Vicious Veronica for any reason whatsoever," he says. He is thankful for her ability to look past the zeal and on to the point he was trying to make.

"Now over here, we have our piano," he says, and crosses the foyer into the adjacent music room. He tinkles the keys on a perfectly polished ebony Steinway in an attempt to lift the tension. "It's a baby grand. It's been in our family since the twenties and everyone has been forced to learn to play it. Over here is my fiddle ... this one I learned by choice." He carefully opens the case to a Scherl & Roth violin. "It's not a family heirloom or anything, but it makes a wonderful sound when you get the amount of rosin just right. I enjoy this one so much that I have turned down offers of an upgrade." He removes the violin from its case and places it gently in her arms as if it were a newborn baby.

Mary holds it up to her chin and he hands her the bow. She makes contact with the strings and nothing happens. She looks at him as if she broke it. He immediately begins to dig in the case for what seems to be a small brown square of substance encased in wood.

"I forgot—that is a spankin new bow," Bobby says. "My grandfather sat on the old one by accident. I have to put a good coat of rosin on it before it will grip the strings properly." He tightens the hair with a screw at the end of the bow clockwise, careful only to touch the stick, showing her how the brown block of sticky stuff is to be applied, then hands it back to her for another go.

Mary hesitantly slides the prepped bow across the strings, creating a high, squawky sound. She tries once more—at an angle this time—and succeeds in making a clear note.

"See, you're a natural!" he says excitedly.

Mary hands the delicate apparatus back to its owner, fearful of becoming attached too quickly without having compared it to the feel of the piano. Alighting upon the upholstered piano bench, Mary gingerly depresses several keys in tandem, performing this action for several minutes, rolling the options back and forth in her mind as her fingers move back and forth over the keys. The sound is both somber and beautiful on the part of Steinway & Sons and jumbled and muddy on the part of her untrained fingers. She abruptly stops and faces him with a decision.

"I like both instruments equally. However, I do not see any way for me to purchase or possess a piano such as this one in the next few years of my life. I will have to save that for a post-college era. Therefore, I choose the violin."

"When the time comes, I will be honored to teach you the piano, too," Bobby says. He hands her several beginner music books. "Look these over before our first lesson, they'll give you a head start."

Mary admires his muscular arm, then notices his wristwatch. "Oh, the time!" she cries in a panic. "We have to go back right now or we will be late for class!"

"Don't worry. You have Mrs. Tisdale fourth hour, don't you?" he asks. "She won't mark you tardy, and neither will my teacher—he likes me too much. Besides," he adds, opening the door for her, "I think we'll make it."

The first bell rings as they cross back through the tree line where they must part ways. Mary turns to look at Bobby; it is the first time since she met Vinny that she wishes for the freedom to follow her every whim, which right now would be to lay a big smooch on this particular young man. Instead it remains just a longing, an exchange of smiles before breaking into a full run to beat the second bell.

Mrs. Tisdale pretends not to notice that Mary is a minute or two late for class as she slides into her seat at the front of the room. Continuing to talk to the class, Mrs. Tisdale writes a note and walks over to place it firmly on Mary's desk. *See me after class* is all it says— and now Mary regrets having let Bobby convince her she could get away with being late. The hour-long lesson feels like days, and she dreads the consequences all the while.

When the bell rings, she approaches Mrs. Tisdale with her head low in search of mercy.

As soon as the last student has left the room, Mrs. Tisdale brightens. "So, did you go to Bobby's house? Did you decide on which instrument to play?" To Mary's surprise, her teacher sounds a lot like Gayle.

"You're not mad that I was late?"

"You are one student I do not have to worry about keeping up with the lessons. Even if you have to miss, I could send the work home with you. We will work all of that out as we go. As long as you keep your grades up, the principal will give us the green light," she says, her voice light and bubbly. "Now, tell me—"

"I chose the violin." Mary doesn't quite understand all the special attention being shown to her.

"Oh, good! It's his favorite." Mrs. Tisdale clasps her hands to her chest. "I hope you don't find it too hard to practice at home with all your other responsibilities."

Practice at home? I hadn't thought that far.

"This is on a trial basis," she reasserts, more to herself than to Mrs. Tisdale. Feeling frazzled, she adds, "If I can't find a way to work it into my life, I will have to rethink whether or not it's worth the effort. I just don't need the added pressure of letting down so many people if I can't do this."

Mrs. Tisdale tilts her head, giving her the look she gets when she wants to give her students some perspective. "We are here to support you, not to force you," she says. "Please remember that it's supposed to be a fun and interesting addition. We have no preconceived expectation of you becoming a concert violinist."

"I don't mean to be rude, but why do all of you care about this so much? About me and my future? I keep trying to figure out the angle, the catch. I don't see every student getting this kind of assistance. I can't help but think it's because I am at a financial disadvantage."

The tardy bell rings.

Mary starts to leave and Mrs. Tisdale steps in her path.

"Oh, no, you don't get off that easy." She sounds more perturbed than Mary has ever heard her to be. "This is my free period and I can give you a note for your next class. Take a seat, and I want you to hear every word I'm about to say."

Mrs. Tisdale's movements become those of a professor in a lecture hall, full of hand gestures and pacing. "Honestly, Mary, you really need to lose this hang-up you have. The only one who seems to be carrying on about it is you! The sooner you figure that out, the better—otherwise, you will continue to use it as an excuse for anything bad that ever happens. You are who you decide to be—not where you came from or who others say you are. Keep your focus on where you are going.

"The reasons we are rallying around you are simple. You have the grades and the desire to get a top-notch education. It is our responsibility as adults in our community to see that any child who wants it, *gets* it. You are quite self-absorbed and presumptuous to think that it is just *your* future we are concerned with! Don't you see that without a new generation of bright, young, well-educated people, there will be no kind of future for any of us? This is a matter of self-preservation for everyone—not just you! Every student we are able to help stand on their own two feet and think for themselves is one less student lost to poverty, corruption, and moral decay. I hope I never live to see a day when we let our young people down by forcing them to navigate their way to adulthood without a map. That's when we have all sealed our fate and deserve to suffer the fallout of our own ignorance."

Mrs. Tisdale speaks with such fervor, her words leave them both misty-eyed.

She takes a breath and continues. "That is why I am an advocate for equality of education, for all our children. After all, children will only learn what we teach them. If we are to teach a child that they are less, then that's all they will become—less than they could have been, or should have been—which in turn would make all of our futures less than we all deserve."

A brand-new piece of chalk snaps in half in her hand, startling them both.

She concludes, "Do you need a better explanation than that?"

"I talked about the desegregation issue with my dad not too long ago and he had very similar views," Mary says, newly inspired. "Why can't everyone spend more time caring about this, rather than starting wars, conquering space, and dividing everyone into groups? Picking each other up rather than knocking each other to the ground?"

"You see! The questions you have, *those* are the kinds of questions we need everyone to be asking of each other, the world over. This is the reason for making sure that students like you grow up to find your voice, so you can ask those questions and demand answers, from governments and citizens alike. We need to be able to hear the voices of reason over all the nonsense, to bring us hope with the possibility of change. The only trouble is there are many people who will want to silence you, to keep things the way they are. That's why you need us to support your efforts. Sometimes the person trying to keep you down lives in here," says Mrs. Tisdale, lightly tapping the side of Mary's head.

"Okay, okay, I get it—I'm stubborn as a mule," Mary says in resignation.

"But as bright as the sun. Now get to class before you miss some pivotal bit of information."

Mrs. Tisdale hands her an excusal slip for her next teacher. Mary gives her favorite teacher a big hug before she bolts out of the room to her next class.

The rest of the day Mary feels as though she can make a difference in the world, the way we all do at some point in our lives—at least when we still believe that good conquers evil and heroes don't die.

During PE, Mary tells Gayle everything that happened with Bobby and the enlightening conversation—well, Mary admits, *lecture*—with Mrs. Tisdale. Gayle loses interest as soon as she finds out Mary didn't lay that kiss on him and that nothing scandalous took place. She has absolutely no interest in anything other than the immediate world around her and whatever wonderful drama is played out within that realm.

"Chick is taking me out for an ice cream after supper. You want to come?"

"No, thanks. I'm going to look over the music books tonight after I finish my homework. I'm glad that you have someone to hang out with, since I am really going to have to hit the books pretty hard this week . . . I have a report due. You go and have a good time with Chick, and don't worry about me." Mary would never admit it, but she is somewhat relieved to not have to keep Gayle occupied for the time being.

After sharing their plans, each girl is left thinking that the other's evening will be boring and trivial.

Arriving home, Mary finds a small crew replacing exterior siding over an open gash where some termite-infested planks had been. Retreating to the only peaceable alcove—her room—Mary immerses herself in systematically completing each school subject that requires her attention.

Until, that is, Jenny comes to carry out a task of her own.

"Mama said you're gonna be a boney-maroney cuz you didn't come down for supper! Everybody else is already finished and she's gonna make you starve!" Jenny declares in a threatening tone. She stands in the doorway with her hands on her hips, tapping her toe, happy to be bossing someone around and disrupt the natural pecking order for a change.

"I'm on my way right now, squirt," Mary says, trying not to laugh at the mischievous rascality of her little sister, who seems to take this errand way too seriously. Jenny snorts and turns to leave full of prissy indignation.

Norman is the only one left at the table. He looks like he has already been served his after-dinner cup of joe and is now lost in the day's headlines. She sees a plate of lukewarm rump roast with potatoes and carrots waiting for her on the counter. It is Charlie who's cleaning up the remnants of the meal—Vivian is lounging in the front room, enjoying a program with the rest of the kids.

Mary crosses the kitchen and tousles her brother's hair while he is full of suds and vulnerable to a sister's affection.

"Hey!" he says at the surprise attack. "See if I worry about saving you any supper next time you miss."

"You know I love you for that," she says, and kisses Charlie's cheek.

He wipes at his face with a soapy hand, pretending he didn't enjoy the attention, before unplugging the sink and running clear water over the foam-covered dishes. "You could thank me by mentioning to Vinny that a dishwasher would be nice."

That draws an ugly look from both Mary and Norman, who bends a corner of his paper down to do so.

"It was just a suggestion," Charlie says sheepishly, shrinking from their unified glower. "You did it this way for years. I guess it's only fair that I do it this way, too."

"That's right, and don't go forgetting it," Mary says. "He's going to start thinking twice about dating me if we start hitting him up for something every time he comes here." She is still disappointed with her brother's snarky comment, but she joins him in the dishwashing.

"I was only kidding, Mary. I didn't mean to upset you." He places the last dish on the drying rack.

"I know, and I'm not mad—I just want to make sure you know it's not all right to take advantage of people just because they're kind and generous," she replies, sounding very parental. "Just to show no hard feelings, I'll do the dishes for you tomorrow night so you can watch TV with everyone else."

"You're my new favorite sister!" he says, drying his hands before joining the others in the front room.

Mary eats her dinner in relative silence while reading the classified section on the outside of her father's paper. As she clears and washes her plate, her mind wanders, comparing Vinny and Bobby very much like she did the musical instruments, starting out liking them equally, but able to see that one is more practical. It just so happens that one isn't an option at this point. If only Bobby had approached her earlier, she would be preparing for Homecoming instead of having to worry about someone ready for marriage. On autopilot, Mary sits back and taps her fingers on the table, lost in her thoughts.

"Are you going to tell me what's rattlin in dat head or am I supposed to guess tonight?" her father says from behind his paper, expecting her to start some weighty conversation, as she so often does.

Mary blinks. "Have you been on another job down in Montegut?"

"Close . . . Bourg. Why?" A little smile touches the corners of his mouth.

"Because somehow you pick up a little Cajun accent when you do."

Ever more curious, Norman puts his paper down to give her his full attention. "Just spit it out and stop steering around it, Mary Lou." With one callused hand, he reaches across to still her brooding fingers, leaving behind a dark streak of newsprint.

"I have been given an opportunity to learn to play an instrument. My guidance counselor suggested I do it for my college application. A boy at school is going to give me lessons at lunch, when we can, or possibly after school. He is offering to do so at no cost to me. Is that all right with you?"

"Sounds all right, if it'll help you. You know I trust your ability to make your own calls. There mus' be more to it, though, for you to ask knowin what I'd say."

"Well . . . I may need a ride home if we practice after school, and I won't know ahead of time when that might be." She decides not to mention the fact that this boy could cause some possible complications other than practice times.

"That's an easy fix. I usually pass that way to come home. You can tie a ribbon on the stop sign by the school and I'll know to wait for you."

"I can do that, or just be waiting there for you when you pass," she says. "The issue is that I won't be at school. He lives across the street from the school, and . . . we would be practicing at his house." Mary knows this may be a deal breaker.

Norman's arms instantly cross. Mary frowns at his freshly folded arms requesting more information.

"He's a junior, on the football team . . . and college-bound, same as me. I haven't known him very long, but he and his family seem really nice. His dad is Dr. Harold Vicknair and his mom's name is Brenda. I will make sure that one or both of them will be around when I'm there, just so there's no question of impropriety." She hasn't made sure of that last part yet, but now that she has said it, she knows she needs to ask Bobby about it tomorrow.

"Will it cause trouble with the cheerin and such?" Norman's arms relax with the other concerns put to rest.

"Not likely, since we keep the same schedule as the football team. Gayle's mom is going to be taking care of all the transportation where that is concerned."

"Can't argue with that—unless you tryin to get me to. Is there a reason for not doin' it?" he asks, intuitively knowing there must be more for her to be so apprehensive.

Mary hesitates, then charges on. "Bobby isn't just any boy, Pa. He's a very good-looking boy who wanted to take me to the Homecoming dance. The biggest problem with that is . . . if it weren't for Vinny, I would have been happy to accept his invitation." She suddenly realizes her reluctance to admit this even to herself.

Norman rubs his head like a magic lamp that will produce a perfect solution. "I was worried about this 'zact problem when Vinny asked about gettin attached to you. I figured on you not bein' ready. I never thought you'd agree to it, with you preparin for college and all. You slipped that one by me. You can either remind yourself every day that you have made a promise to Vinny, or you have to tell Vinny that yer not ready to be on a one-and-only basis. If he's serious 'bout gettin hitched, he should still want to continue seein you."

"Or he will think different of me for even wanting to test the waters! He may think I'm some kind of tramp. He thinks so highly of me right now—I would hate to tarnish that by asking for the freedom to date boys who may not even be good enough to shine his shoes. Vinny has been so good to me and this family. I don't think it would be right to hurt him just because I'm young and foolish. What I need to do is be mature enough to honor my commitments, both to myself and to others." She reaffirms this with a random strike to her leg in self-punishment for having been weakened in her resolve by a pretty football player.

Her dad just sits and nods at her argument, knowing it's best to let her work it out. "This won't be the last temptin you will know in life, little Mary. Each of those times, you will find yerself with a hard decision to be made. Yer gonna have to choose a stretch of road to travel, even when you can't see around the corner of that road to know for sure yer goin' the right way. If you ever find yerself on a bad stretch, I want you to remember this—you may not be able to undo the damage to yer vehicle, but you can turn around, or find the next place to turn off of that road. I love you, and don't ever forget that no one else should make those choices for you—not even me. I'm just here to help with the process, mostly just reflecting the sound of yer voice so you can hear it clear." He knows that he isn't a spring chicken, and the thought makes his gut twist and ache, but it's nonetheless true. He knows it's better to take these opportunities to pass along some wisdom, rather than to be in denial of it.

Mary's world seems less tilted after their goodnight hug. Preparing for bed, she remembers to look over the beginner's guide to music.

This is going to be like learning another language entirely.

Music might be the first subject she will ever truly struggle with. Intrigued by the challenge, she is determined to at least learn to play the first song in the book, which happens to be "Mary Had a Little Lamb."

Eventually, she falls into a deep, fitful sleep. Within her dreamscape, Mary wears a wedding gown and a smile as she walks through a mist. Large shapes loom until they become musical notes and chase her down a hall. At the end of the hall she finds herself at a school dance surrounded by a crowd of faceless students. The students begin to grope her body and tear at her dress. She screams. Suddenly, Vinny appears, pushing through the crowd to protect her, and lifts her away to safety.

She awakes in the morning feeling ever more convinced that she is making the right decision, sticking by the promise she made to Vinny.

Wednesday
September 17, 1958

Mary knows well the dream where you show up to school and walk the halls naked. That is almost how strange and exposed she feels when she arrives at school without Gayle this morning.

Must have been the late ice cream run with Chick . . .
She just overslept and missed the bus, is all. Or . . .

With strange yet impeccable timing, Bobby appears beside her like a magic trick. At first Mary is startled, but then, before they even have time to exchange any kind of pleasantry, she remembers to ask, "Do you think your mom is going to be there every time we go over for practice?"

"Are you trying to get me alone, you vixen?" he teases.

She gasps, covering her mouth to hide her horrified expression.

"I'm kidding! Yes," he answers more seriously, "I'm sure she will be present, as she is most of the time."

"That wasn't funny! Don't you know how important it is for a girl to have a good reputation if she is to go to a good school or find a good husband? I have witnessed girls' reputations ruined by the rumor mill alone, no proof needed! If we are to be friends, I need you to know that I have some concerns about what people might say or think, knowing that I have a boyfriend." Mary looks around, paranoid that someone may be eavesdropping on the conversation. "I guess it will be all right as long as your mother is there to supervise," she adds, pointedly using her books as a physical barrier between her and Bobby.

"You really are cute when you're up there on your high horse." He takes a deep breath and shakes his head. "Every day is going to be like starting all over with you, isn't it?"

"What do you mean?" she says, taken aback by his offish attitude.

"I mean, just when I think we are getting comfortable with each other, you revert back to this formal and aloof version of yourself. I thought you would know by now that I would never allow any danger to your person or your reputation. Are you always going to be so serious and overanalyze everything? You're going to completely miss what it's like to just be young and carefree. We have the rest of our lives to be dull and calculating," he says. "I want to go back to how we were yesterday."

Mary audibly exhales, as if she were holding her breath to hear him clearly. "It's hard for me. I do want us to be good friends. I will try to relax more," she says, the color returning to her face.

"You, my dear, are a curious creature," Bobby says, lightly touching the tip of her angelic nose, his smile crooked and mischievous. He quickly changes the subject before he gets another speech. "Don't you have practice today?"

"I . . . uh . . . yes," Mary answers, her eyebrows squished together, trying to make the correlation.

The bell rings and he winks at her, leaving her speechless and confused. He disappears as magically as he appeared, just as Gayle arrives beside her, flushed from her mad dash.

"Did I miss anything?" she asks, short-winded.

"No, but I think I did," Mary says. She is frustrated at how Bobby seems to find a way to slip little nuggets of mystification into their visits. Gayle just gives her an odd look, like a puppy does when you talk to it and it cocks its head to the side, struggling with the language barrier.

At lunch, Gayle is happy to see Chick waiting with the food she forgot on the counter this morning. Mary doesn't pay them any mind, previewing passages from the next lesson in her Algebra book.

"I have never seen anyone actually read a math book before," Chick says in amazement.

"You never will again, I bet, because I think she is the only one who has," Gayle says.

Mary, who is not easily offended at being talked about as if she weren't there, pays them no mind.

"Let me know when you're finished with that chapter so you can read this . . . I was told to wait until today to give it to you," Chick says, passing Mary a sealed envelope.

That's all Mary needs to abandon the Algebra book. Anxiously, she tears the envelope open to see words written for her eyes alone:

To My Darling Maggie,

I am leaving to go on the road, and every mile that passes will bring me pain knowing I am farther away from you. I hate having to be away so long, but it is for our future. I just wanted you to know that you are always on my mind and in my heart. I will write again as soon as I get settled.

Love and Kisses,
Vinny

Mary suddenly realizes that she doesn't have a clue about where Vinny is or where he is going.

How could I have let him go without finding out where he would be?

"Hey, Chick ... do you have any idea where Vinny will be working?" Mary asks, frightened by her lack of information.

"He never tells anyone where he is going. It's safer that way," Chick answers unhelpfully. Seeing this isn't alleviating Mary of her fears, he adds, "Wherever he is, I know for sure he is going to miss you plenty. All he ever talks about these days is you. Don't worry—he will find ways to keep in touch by phone or in letters."

"Is it that you don't know," Mary asks, "or that you refuse to tell me?" She feels as if she is being tricked somehow.

"His job is very competitive and his boss is very particular. He has to do as he is instructed or he could lose his position. You wouldn't want that, would you? I don't know where he is, and that's the way he works." Chick shrugs, hoping this is enough to explain away the strange circumstances surrounding Vinny's occupation.

"This is all way too mysterious. What's going on, and why won't you tell me? Should I be worried?" she asks, rapidly working herself into a tizzy.

"Mary, sometimes you just need to trust him," Chick says, taking a stab at the heart of her neurosis, out of the desperate need to throw her off the hunt.

Mary's natural curiosity and intuition begin to feel like a burden to her. "Sorry about the inquisition," she tells Chick. "Some say ignorance is bliss, but the not-knowing kills me. Many times just this week I have been told that I have trust issues! I know Vinny would never do anything to hurt me." She lets the subject drop, trying to convince herself that she is being ridiculous . . . even though the issue stays with her like an itch you're never fully able to scratch.

At practice that afternoon, the necklace Vinny placed around her begins to feel noose-like, as heavy as her thoughts; her mind is preoccupied with running scenarios where she might need to reach Vinny and wouldn't be able to. She is unable to fully pay attention to the new cheer sequence they are learning for the big Homecoming game. It is a bit more risqué than the other ones in their repertoire, so they had to get approval from the principal and the football coach before being allowed to perform it in public.

Luckily, Gayle is the only one who seems to notice Mary's distraction. "What's wrong?" she mouths, knowing that her friend usually gives a more energetic performance, even in practice. The easiest thing for Mary to do is to shrug and put her head back in the present where it belongs.

After a few more run-throughs, the team captain is finally satisfied that they will master the moves before Friday's pep rally.

The football team is still on the field as Mary and Gayle climb into Mrs. Shirley's car for the drive home. The girls are hungry, tired, and smell like musty earth.

"I hope the coach doesn't overdo it on those poor boys! They won't have anything left to give by game day," says Mrs. Shirley.

"Yeah, those poor boys," Gayle snarks, wondering where the sympathy is for the cheer squad.

When Mary arrives home, she finds a telegram waiting for her from Vinny. He includes his mail box address at the Monteleone and an emergency phone number for a man named Big Al, adding that his mail will be forwarded to him. She is elated that Vinny cares enough to settle her mind—he does know what a worry-wart she is. Thanks to his telegram, she pulls out of her self-imposed panic, granting her nerves much-needed relief.

During dinner, the heavens rumble, announcing the approach of an angry, growling, spark-torn sky and demanding the attention of everyone at the table. They listen to the inevitable torrent of earth-cleansing water brewing and churning.

"I sure am glad those boys work fast! They just finished the roof repairs this very afternoon," Vivian says in anticipation of the approaching deluge. "It sounds like the sky's gonna put their work to the test. If it holds, it'll be the first rain that I won't have to put any pots out."

"We should all pay more attention to things like that, now that we are to be homeowners instead of renters," Mary announces to the children. "If anyone finds a leak or repair that is needed, tell Ma or Pa right away."

When the rain finally falls, it sounds like the too-loud static that the television displays after midnight sign-off. By the time Mary is able to settle, the storm only magnifies the exhaustion she feels from school and practice. She falls asleep as soon as her head hits the pillow, to the lullaby of fitful skies colliding overhead.

Thursday
September 18, 1958

The rain has subsided by morning, but the sky is neither clear nor sunny. Instead it has a gloomy cast, the kind of gloom Mary imagined in the moors of England when she was reading *Wuthering Heights*—the kind of weather that makes everyone sleepy and depressed. A brisk wind that arrived with the storm has lingered, bringing a northern chill straight through to the bone.

"It's so weird having a cool front this early in the season," Jane says to Mary and Gayle as they step off the bus and head for the school building.

"Everyone is worried that the rain isn't over and the field will be too wet for the game," says another cheerleader.

"*I* heard a rumor that the weather isn't the extent of the controversy surrounding this game," Jane says, taking a last look at the sky while holding the door open. Mary walks inside and refrains from asking Jane what she means.

"I sure hope the sun comes out soon! If it doesn't, all of our uniforms will get muddy," Gayle whines.

Bobby approaches them in the hall, stifling a jaw-cracking yawn. "Mud is the least of our worries. The coach kept us so late last night because he found out we're playing Istrouma tomorrow instead of

Thibodaux. If we lose this game, the coach will have our hides for sure. No excuses. We are going to have practice again today, rain or shine. But he should let us out earlier so we can rest up for tomorrow. I sure need it after last night. I'm exhausted."

"How can they change who we are playing this close to game day? It just doesn't seem right," Mary blurts in frustration.

"From what the coach said," Bobby explains, "it's some political stance over another team agreeing to integrate their football team. In forcing them out of the loop, it changes the entire season's schedule." The bell rings for class. He aims a finger gun at Mary before he turns to leave. "I'll see you at lunch."

"Why do they call it a game when they take all the fun out of it?" Gayle raises her hands in defeat. "Politics, shmolitics."

Mary silently observes how attentive Chick is to Gayle as he unpacks a brown grocery bag of her favorite snacks at lunch. At first she imagines that perhaps she feels a pang of jealousy because Vinny is unavailable to lavish the same attention. Then she looks upon Chick and Gayle tenderly, like she does her siblings. She realizes she is experiencing a rare contentment, pleased to be witnessing the beginnings of a real kind of love—not a fairytale romance, mind you, but love that could last a lifetime if nurtured and protected enough to do so.

I hope I find that kind of love someday . . .
I wonder if Vinny is the one for me.
Am I too stubborn to let it blossom?
Could we be so lucky? Could it be that simple?

She is so lost in her thoughts that she hasn't even noticed Bobby is now sitting beside her, talking about bar lines and measures as if she were actually listening.

"Who is that boy talking to Mary?" Chick asks Gayle. He is full of concern, having been left in charge of her safekeeping while Vinny is away.

"Oh, that is her new music coach, the one I told you about," Gayle answers, nervously shoveling a handful of French fries into her mouth.

"You didn't tell me her music coach was a *boy*—or even that he was a student," Chick says, getting more suspicious.

Sensing danger, Gayle swallows and blurts, "There isn't anything to be worried about because he is as queer as a three-dollar bill."

"You're kidding!" he says, loud enough to command the attention of everyone within earshot—including Mary, who has finally tuned in to Bobby's lecture on music theory.

"Shhhh!" Gayle pulls Chick away, not wanting to draw any more attention. "He's a friend of ours. We wouldn't want anyone to hurt him." Desperate to isolate the lie, Gayle adds, "You have to keep this between us! You know how awful people would treat him if everyone knew."

"But how do you know for sure?"

"Well, let's see . . ." Gayle gives Chick her best *Duh!* look. "He's a football player who makes good grades, wants to go to college, and doesn't have a steady girlfriend."

"That doesn't mean he's a punk," Chick replies, not yet convinced.

"He plays the piano and the violin, for heaven's sake!" Gayle says, hoping that this bologna is thick enough for Chick to sink his teeth into.

"You're right. That does sound pretty queer," Chick says, rubbing his chin. He accepts her explanation after looking over at Bobby, who is showing Mary how to follow a tempo by twirling his hands in the air like a conductor.

Like a slick politician Gayle appears forthright, tugging at Chick's shirt, acting like she will get to the bottom of this. "Follow me," she says, to cloak her gerrymandering. In her classically overdramatized style, she calls out to Bobby and Mary, "I can't believe you two can sit there and discuss music when we are clearly in a crisis situation! Not only might our uniforms get muddy, but so may our hopes of winning our Homecoming game!"

"I swear, Gayle—Bette Davis is going to have to work real hard to keep up with you!" Mary says, trying to keep her friend from affecting Bobby's spirit. "We're just trying to keep calm by thinking of other things. We will be doomed for sure if we let ourselves get all lathered up about it."

"It's going to be all right," Bobby says. "We know the plays and we looked good at practice. It's just a matter of getting out there and getting it done." He pounds his fist in his hand, impersonating Coach Grabert.

"I'm lost. Can someone fill me in on what is going on?" Chick asks, confused about the subject matter and at Bobby's ability to sound like a typical heterosexual football player.

When Bobby reaches out to shake hands, Chick gives him an imitation of Vinny's cold and demoralizing stare—but it comes off more like the large eyes of Don Knotts, and he grips Bobby's outstretched hand. To Mary, they look like Red Riding Hood and the Big Bad Wolf. *"My, what big eyes you have, Chick." "The better to see you with, my Bobby."*

Barely passing the male sniff test, Bobby tells Chick all the sordid details of football politics and the impact they're having on their season—when to everyone's surprise, the clouds begin to disperse, and a warm beam of sunlight floods the school yard. The lunch crowd welcomes the sun with spontaneous applause. Then the bell rings and the applause turns to moans and groans about having to return to the bland fluorescent lights of their classrooms—just one of many pleasure sacrifices to be made in the pursuit of the conventional, as they participate and adhere to the path of future taxpayers.

"Oh, word from the bird," says Chick. "The moms said I could pick you two up from practice. I could take you out for burgers after, if you want."

"That would razz my berries, daddy-o," Gayle replies, snapping her beatnik fingers with excitement.

"You can invite your square if you want. He seems nice enough," Chick tells Mary, trying to be accommodating. Gayle hops up to give him a big kiss in appreciation before rushing off to class, hoping to beat the tardy bell.

"Coach feels good about our chances of winning," Bobby says, rubbing his sweaty head after removing his football helmet.

"That's great!" Gayle says as they walk to the parking lot. "Hey, you want to grab a burger with us after you change?"

Bobby looks around, disappointed he doesn't see Mary anywhere. "Nah, I think I'll go home and get some rest for tomorrow. Thanks, though."

As he turns to go, the slap of shoes on concrete announces Mary's arrival as she jogs to the car with her books. "Thanks for waiting," she says, adding as she passes the receiver, "Bye, Bobby. See you tomorrow!" She piles into the car with Gayle.

Bobby sulks off, slapping the shell of his helmet like he just fumbled a play.

Chick chuckles after hearing that Bobby declined the invitation. "I guess he needed his beauty sleep."

In the short walk from the car to the bus stop diner, Mary feels the eerie tingle of being watched. She looks around, discovering a police cruiser parked nearby on the shoulder of the road, but it's just far enough to make it hard to see anyone inside. She is so engrossed in the idea of being under surveillance that she runs smack into the door Chick is holding open for her.

"Somebody's blood sugar's low! Get this woman a menu, stat!" Chick calls to the waitress, laughing. Walking over to the table to order the food, Mary rubs her forehead, which is less damaged than her pride.

"Oh, man, I am *so* hungry," Gayle says, watching the waitress carry her freshly grilled quarter-pound of beef to their table.

"Me, too! I could eat a horse," says Mary, picking up her burger and taking a big bite.

"How do you know you're not?" Gayle teases, meaty juice running down her chin.

Mary pauses in her chewing and opens her mouth for Gayle to see the contents of the bite she just took.

"Nice," Gayle says, surprised and genuinely impressed.

"Don't dish it out if you can't take it," Chick says in amusement.

Leaving the diner, Mary's forehead reminds her to look for the cruiser. It's still there, but now its engine is running, and as Mary watches the police car pulls onto the road. Danny Naquin tips his hat to Mary from the driver's seat as he passes.

There was a time when Mary thought that policemen existed to lock up bad guys and help little old ladies cross the street. Considering what is happening in the news lately and the queasy feeling in the pit of her stomach, she now wonders if they may have another agenda.

"Thanks so much, Chick. That really hit the spot," Mary says on the ride home.

"No problem. Hey, you guys want to see a movie Saturday night, since we won't be going to the Homecoming dance? You could invite the Bobster."

"I really don't think that's a good idea," Mary says, surprised that he would suggest something clearly in violation of his friendship with Vinny.

Chick meets her eyes in the rear-view. "I just want you to know that I'm an open-minded person and I'm cool with it."

"She, uh, probably needs time to think about it. Don't ya, Mary?" says Gayle, turning toward Mary in the back seat while emphatically nodding her head *yes* to get her to play along.

"Uh, yeah, I'm too tired to think about it tonight. Thank you for wanting to include us, though. I'll let you know tomorrow." Mary speaks slowly, watching Gayle's face to gauge if her response is adequate.

"No pressure," Chick says, unaware of the subtle signals being exchanged between the girls.

When they arrive at Gayle's, Chick immediately follows the scent of freshly baked cookies wafting from inside the house, leaving Gayle and Mary to linger behind.

"What in the world was that all about?" Mary says. The frustration is clear in her voice—she just knows Gayle has gone and done something ridiculous.

Gayle gives her an apologetic look, her face all twisted out of shame. "I sort of told Chick that Bobby is light in the loafers. It was the only way to preserve your lessons and your friendship with Bobby. You don't want him giving Vinny a report of some young football player sniffing around, do you? Now you don't have to worry about what Vinny is gonna think about your lessons. I was only trying to help," Gayle explains, hoping Mary will see her logic. Her face twists up even more, desperately waiting for her friend's response.

"Are you insane?" Mary cries, starting to come unglued. "The more time I spend with Bobby, the more I *like* him! You have removed my safety net. I figured as long as I could limit my time with him to school and in public, I could insulate us from a compromising situation. And now you want to put me in the dark with him in the back seat of a car? I'm scared of doing anything to jeopardize or sabotage me and Vinny." She is angry, yet mindful of her volume—Chick could still be in hearing distance. "Not only that, but what if Chick finds out you lied to him? That's not only going to put a rift between you two, but it'll make me look like I have been hiding more than just some innocent music lessons! And what are you going to do if your lie about Bobby gets out? It will crush him!"

"I didn't think . . ." Gayle starts, hesitating.

"No, you didn't think!" Mary says harshly. "And because of that, I will probably spend the whole night awake, trying to find a way out of this mess—when I should be resting up for a long day tomorrow!"

She has hit a nerve in Gayle. Tears drip from her friend's chin. "Please don't hate me!" Gayle whimpers. "I thought I was protecting you."

Mary pauses, seeing that her friend is truly in pain over her miscalculation, then says, "I know. I am sorry if I overreacted. I don't hate you, silly. I could never hate you. I'm tired . . . it just hit me the wrong way. Let's get some sleep and we'll figure this out later. But try not to tell any more lies. It will only make things worse!" Mary hugs her meddlesome best friend, hoping to alleviate some of the pain she has inflicted with her acrid response to Gayle's news. She lovingly wipes a tear from Gayle's face. "I'm sorry I yelled, Gayle. But you need to pull it together before you go inside, or he will want to know why you're so upset."

"I'll just tell him it's a girl thing. That always shuts them up," Gayle replies, reestablishing her composure with a little laugh.

"That'll do it, all right. Are you going to be okay?"

"If you promise to let me fix this," Gayle pleads, grabbing Mary's hands.

"The best thing we can do right now is to get some rest and put this on the back burner until after the game." Mary feels the weight of the day catching up with her. "I'll see you in the morning." She squeezes Gayle's hands gently before releasing them to leave. Gayle stands there, repentant, until Mary shoos her inside.

Rest this night is fitful and broken for both girls. Anxiety builds over the imminent game day—dawn will come whether they have rested or not.

Friday
September 19, 1958

Houma **rises to** a glorious morning. No rain in sight, no expectation of it in the forecast. The sunny blue skies and crisp cool temperatures are the recipe for perfect football weather.

The excitement of both students and faculty shows via crimson and gold displays of Tiger pride. Banners are placed strategically throughout the campus by the Spirit Club and alumni supporters, headed by Brenda Vicknair. Judging by the high quality of the signage, she clearly used her wiles to procure them with funds from local business contributions.

A significantly large section of the marching band gathers at the flagpole in the front yard for an impromptu performance of the school's alma mater, followed by the fight song. This location is a place of honor: at the flagpole's base stands a monument to local men who perished in World War I and World War II.

Once the fight song begins, random students are drawn into the singing, adding lyrics to the effort and gaining volume as they percolate.

> *"And for the football team I yell, yell, yell:*
> *We're gonna fight, fight, fight for every yard.*

We're gonna hit that line and hit it hard.

We're gonna roll those Indians on the side, on the side,

Terrebonne High!"

The bell rings and the rambunctious crowd quickly disperses, still full of song as they file into the building.

On her tiptoes, Gayle searches the sea of boisterous faces in the hall, using Mary's shoulders for balance and leverage. "I can't believe Bobby is missing this! Where is he? He'd better be there to watch us perform at lunch."

"I saw the coach giving his pre-game interview with a reporter. The team is probably stuck giving statements for the nosy newspapers," Mary says with a wince as her stomach clenches into a tight ball.

Gayle frowns. "Like there isn't enough tongue wagging going on around here."

"I am so nervous! I think I'm going to be sick," Mary says, holding her midsection. "I don't know how you talked me into embarrassing myself in front of the whole school."

"You did fine at practice. You just have stage fright," Gayle replies—just before Mary's stomach makes a churning sound that is loud enough to be heard over the noise in the hall. Gayle's eyes grow wide. "Whoa! I hope you work that out before lunch."

"Me, too." Mary queasily veers into her classroom, praying the stomach thunder is an isolated event.

Clever teachers incorporate football into their lesson plans, knowing that to do otherwise means forfeiting the entire student body's interest for the day. It is the only way to keep students quiet and on task. Mary is both amused and impressed with the lengths that some teachers are willing to go to educate groups of rowdy, distracted adolescents.

After lunch, it doesn't take long for the crowd to begin gathering in the circle. The circle is a driveway area for bus and commuter traffic, with a lush grassy patch marking the round center. Even the kids who don't normally care about football show up at the outdoor pep rally to lend support for their team.

"What if I forget the moves to the new cheer?" Mary worries aloud. She spots Veronica with a set of villainous harpies setting up camp right smack in the front row of the raucous assemblage.

"Don't let them get to you, Mary," says Gayle in an effort to quell Mary's stage fright.

Just then, the football players show up in fresh, pad-less jerseys to ignite the ceremony.

Bobby struts right in front of the girls. "Game faces, ladies," he says, just loud enough for them to hear.

Mary and Gayle join the squad as they line up into cheer formation. The crowd instinctively hush to hear the girls' new spirited war cry barked out in style as they shake their decorative tufts of paper strings; male members of the audience also ogle their youthful bodies agilely moving in tandem synchronicity.

"Ready? Okay!
Rah rah ree, kick em in the knee!

Rah rah rass, kick em in the other knee!

Get tough . . . attack!

Make them shake in those knees!

We're the mighty Tigers and we score as we please!"

Saddle shoes rising in the air for Herkie jumps and toe touches spark heavy clapping and whistles of approval. This in turn draws a larger crowd, gathering to see the source of excitement. The squad captain signals a participation cheer to include the crowd. The girls drop their pompoms and start clapping their hands sharply and in synced rhythm.

The captain cries out to the crowd, *"Give me a big 'tiger'!"* and the crowd roars back: *"TIGER!"*

The captain instructs them, *"Give me a big 'win'!"* and the crowd obliges: *"WIN!"*

The entire squad calls out, still clapping their rhythm:

"Don't give me no words, no words.

Don't give me no phrase, no phrase.

Just give me that beat, that Tiger beat."

All together, the cheerleaders on the grass and the electric crowd chant:

"Go . . . fight . . . win!

Go . . . fight . . . WIN!"

Unfortunately, the sound of the bell interrupts the fun. Back to class they go, spectators so jazzed that they continue to chant even after entering the building, filling the halls with loud discord.

The squad captain claps, proud of their strong performance. "We nailed it!" she announces through her cupped hands. Mary is just thankful she survived the rally without incident and Veronica and her cronies have no new ammunition to use against her. On the way to class, she sees the kids' faces light up as she walks through the hall, and for the first time since she put on her crimson, white, and gold uniform, she feels school pride searing through her. Not because of a silly football game, but because she now knows what it must feel like to bring hope to people who may have given up dreaming or hoping for a win.

"I'll never understand why they have us stir the pot in the middle of the day!" Gayle shouts to Mary over the roar in the hall. "The teachers will have to use every ounce of patience with these animals, for sure! I don't think there is any chance of reining them back in now."

"On the bright side, at least they won't fall asleep on their desks," Mary says before splitting off to her Algebra class.

"This day is going faster than a hot rod on a drag strip," Gayle says on the short walk to the Tigers' stadium, located directly behind the school. Mary stays quiet and focused, holding on to her pompoms for comfort.

A single groundskeeper is putting the finishing touches on the chalk outlines of the field as the kids arrive. Mary is pleased to see that the field seems dry enough to provide both teams with sure footing. She evaluates the size of the fairly new stadium, knowing that in just a matter of minutes, it will be filled to the brim with football zealots wanting something to root for.

She had attended one Tiger game here last year, sitting in these stands with Gayle and her parents, so she is very much aware of the intensity of their home crowd. Houma's fervor could be used as an intimidation tactic against most visiting teams—but not the Istrouma Indians. The team from Baton Rouge has been the hardest to beat in the district for nearly a decade.

Coach Grabert is steadily pacing, poring over a playbook that is tattered and frayed from constant handling. From time to time he can be seen glancing up, waiting for the visitors' bus carrying this week's nemesis: a team of teenage boys suited up in burgundy and gray.

The Istrouma football team, boasting the toughest defensive linemen in the state, arrives on a charter bus much like the ones that pull in and out of the local bus station. The smell of popcorn and corndogs lures early spectators; while they gather unhealthy goodies from the concession stand, they hope to catch the teenagers sizing each other up. The players oblige, comparing brawn and assessing the level of damage that will ensue shortly. The girls mainly admire each other's uniforms, strutting like peacock plumes on display.

The stadium now nears capacity, fans anxiously awaiting a formidable fight to the finish. The game begins promptly at seven o'clock. Following the National Anthem, ably played by the homegrown marching band, team captains take the field for the coin toss. Istrouma wins the toss and elects to kick off. After a short return by the Tigers, the teams settle into a rather uneventful first quarter. Cheerleaders from both sides try to rally their troops and hold up morale—both in the seats and on the field. The Tigers manage to hold off the Istrouma assault, but gradually begin to show signs of tiring. Meanwhile, each offensive attempt by the Tigers is met by Istrouma's stronger defensive line that simply cannot be penetrated. *"Hold that line!"* is the impassioned cry from the stands, sparking the band to play the fight song in earnest support of the home team's efforts. By halftime, the first and only score is a field goal by Istrouma late in the second quarter.

Sure to face the ire of their coaches for lackluster performance, the sullied players reluctantly break for the locker rooms. The Crimson Pride band and all of the auxiliary members take the field for a well-rehearsed halftime performance, giving fans and many proud parents a show worthy of all the extra time, money, and effort it took to bring to fruition.

The second half starts with a reenergized Istrouma offense. By the end of the third quarter, the Indians have increased their lead by a touchdown, to make the score 10-0. After a time-out to change players, some Tiger fans cheer frantically to rouse their offense into action, while others fall silent, feeling the chance of victory slipping away.

With ten minutes left in the game, the Istrouma offense is once again threatening to score. As their running back breaks through the Tigers' defense, only one Tiger remains between him and the goal line. In a miraculous effort, the defensive tackle knocks the Indian's feet from under him with a blow that jars the ball loose. The Tiger defense in pursuit is quick to recover the ball. The home-team fans roar with excitement loud enough to be heard outside the stadium. Sensing a changing of the tide, the Tigers capitalize on the turnover with a huge offensive strike, making the score 10-7. On the next drive, the Tigers stop Istrouma's offense dead in its tracks, and with two minutes left in the game, they have one last chance to score. Slowly and steadily, the Tigers make their way down the field, and in the final seconds, the coach signals for a long forward pass. The Tiger quarterback, dodging two defensive linemen, releases the ball into the air just as he is pummeled to the ground. He manages to look up just in time to make out Bobby Vicknair twisting through the air over the back of his defender to bring in the ball, clasping it between his hand and his helmet as he lands in the end zone.

"We did it!" The Tiger fans are on their feet roaring in celebration. Final score: Terrebonne 14, Istrouma 10. As the crowd goes wild, the teams line up on the field to touch hands in a show of respect and good sportsmanship—easier for the Tigers than the Indians after this game. The fans flood the field to congratulate the players. Bobby is hoisted up onto his teammates' shoulders and paraded off the field.

He should be basking in his moment of glory; instead, his eyes are searching for Mary's approving face in the crowd. Her adulation alone is what he craves.

"Bobby, Bobby, he's our man! If he can't do it, no one can!" shout Mary and Gayle from behind him, fiercely shaking their pompoms.

"I'll see you at the bonfire!" he calls back to them from atop his makeshift throne. He has no choice but to surrender to the celebrating mob as they carry him off the field. Once in the locker room, Bobby quickly showers and throws on clean clothes; then he boards the bus waiting to transport the winning team and their new hero to the festivities.

Chick is sitting on the road's shoulder in his chariot, revving the engine, across the street from the stadium. Gayle is grateful for a more exciting mode of transport as she and Mary hop into Chick's shiny ride. "To the fairgrounds, and step on it!" she says, slapping the hide of the passenger-side door.

The car pulls onto the fairgrounds, a democratically chosen spot for the post-game party, far enough away from houses that neither the noise nor the bonfire will be a nuisance. The car lightly bounces across the uneven grass-covered field to park. Within minutes, students of all ages begin to congregate and socialize in close proximity to the woodpile. Once they are parked and headed toward the growing crowd, Mary and Chick stumble with giggles trying to keep up with Gayle, who plans to mingle in the thick of this shindig.

"Wow, the booster club has outdone themselves," Mary says, impressed with the well-planned activity and community support.

"Let's get this show started," Gayle says to Mary, then she rallies the spirit of her comrades by shouting, *"We are the Tigers, couldn't be prouder! If you can't hear us, we'll shout a little louder!"* Voices all around join in the repeated chant, reaching a crescendo as they ignite the woodpile using a papier-mâché shield painted to look like Istrouma's crest. A few drummers from the marching band speed up the chant's cadence as the leaping flames grow higher and higher.

Not interested in school spirit, Chick lights up a cigarette and leaves Mary and Gayle to their celebrations. Wandering around the fairgrounds, he sees a small boy in a Cub Scout uniform carrying a bowl of blackberry dumplings. "Hey, kid, where did you get that?"

"There's a food truck parked over there," the skinny kid replies, pointing to the end of a line that ultimately will take Chick to either the food truck or a portable toilet on the other side—he can't tell. He stands in the line, figuring it won't be bad either way.

An older woman walks up to him and says, "Son, you are going to have to put that thing out. This is considered a school function and you still have to follow the rules."

Chick automatically obeys, stepping on his cigarette, before he remembers he is a grown man and is not bound to any school formalities. But before he can explain, the woman is off confiscating a bottle of beer that has somehow fallen into the hands of a group of freshmen boys.

On his way back to Gayle with the dumplings, Chick spies a boy in possession of an unopened Schlitz.

"Hey, you!" he shouts, startling the boy. "You're going to have to hand that over." The boy lowers his head and hands Chick the sweaty bottle. "Tsk, tsk—you should know better. Now beat it!" Chick admonishes. He works his way back toward the action, careful not to get knocked around.

Gayle spots Chick approaching, towering over most of the student body. "Where have you been?" she asks.

"I brought you a treat," he says, handing over the bowl of blackberry dumplings. Then he pops the top off the contraband to take a swig.

"My favorite!" Gayle says, digging into the berries. "You're missing it! They were announcing the Homecoming Court, and Bobby was nominated for the Junior Class Homecoming King."

Chick snorts and beer shoots out of his nostrils. "Your school sure has a bunch of dopes! He has the whole lot of them fooled. If they were hip, they would have made him their *Queen*." He chuckles softly in self-amusement and takes a fresh sip of Schlitz.

Gayle gives him a sharp elbow to the ribs to warn him to keep his comments to himself when they are in public.

The announcements finished, Bobby weaves his way over to Mary and pulls her to the side. "Chick invited me to the movies tomorrow," he says, "but now I *have* to go to the Homecoming dance. Please say you'll go with me. We could just go as friends. I can't bear the thought of going with anyone else. You wouldn't want me to go alone, would you?" Bobby adds, conjuring all his powers of manipulation.

Mary frowns and sits down on the thick grass. "I can't go with you, Bobby. I'm sorry. I made a promise to someone, and I aim to do my best to honor that promise. I'm sure that if I had made any commitment to you, you would be mighty upset if I went to a dance with someone else while your back was turned—even under the best of circumstances." She rubs her kitty charm between her fingers as if it gives her strength. "I'm sure you will get a date with anyone you ask."

Bobby sits down beside her. "Except the one I really want," he says, sounding defeated. He reaches over and tucks her charm inside her shirt, so he doesn't have to look at it. Mary flinches at the brush of his hand, her cheeks warm with insecurity. Undeterred, Bobby continues. "I guess I'll skip the dance and go to the movies with you, then."

"And miss out on being a big shot? Please don't make me feel bad. I'm not even going to the movies. I just need a night to myself," she says, flustered.

"Even if I told you it's my birthday and my wish is to spend time with you?" he says as a last-ditch effort, but the frustrated look on her face gives Bobby his answer. "I'll leave you alone about it if you promise me something." He pauses to take a long breath, placing his hand over his heart. "Promise me that if you ever part with Vinny, for any reason whatsoever, you'll give me a chance to win your heart." Bailing out at the last second, he disguises the tender sincerity of his words in a farcical delivery.

"If that will put an end to your relentless pursuit, it's a deal," Mary says, relieved to be off the hook for tomorrow night. She never thought she would be so excited at the prospect of being alone on a Saturday night.

"I won't have any fun, and I'll be thinking of you the whole night," Bobby says with a protruding lip, adding another layer of guilt.

"You're sure to be elected King because you're such a royal pain in the butt," Mary replies, as if she is talking with Gayle.

He smiles at her. "Finally, the real Mary emerges! I was getting tired of Miss Mary Manners."

Gayle spots them sitting together and calls out, "Come on, you two! You should grab some food before we leave. I'm going to get more blackberries . . . *yum!*"

"It's too chilly now," Mary says, ignoring the stir of her belly. "I don't want to leave the fire. And I left my jacket in the car."

Bobby wiggles out of his jacket and drapes it across Mary's shoulders, feeling like an idiot for not seeing her goosebumps sooner.

"Suit yourself." Gayle places the plastic spoon inside her cheek like a lollipop and turns to leave.

"I could go and get you something to eat," Bobby offers. "Or I could get your jacket."

Mary considers this for a second, but shakes her head. "I want to enjoy this before it is gone. Let's just sit here a while longer."

The crowd seems to disappear as they sit and bask in the warm glow of the dancing flames. Bobby wants nothing more than to stop time and stay in this moment with her always. The fire begins to die after an hour or so of merriment has gone by. A small crew of off-duty men from the volunteer fire department stand by, drinking what could be water, coffee, or cheap wine from Styrofoam cups, waiting to completely snuff out the tinder once everyone leaves. Bobby follows Mary away from the embers, knowing that the flame he holds for her, unlike this fire, is inextinguishable.

"We can drop you at home, Bobby. I'm sure it's no trouble," Gayle says as she skips by him, full of sugary energy and a few sips of a second confiscated beer.

Bobby glances at Chick, who says, "Easy-peasy, no trouble at all," then, casting a worried look after Gayle, hops into a jog to beat her to the car.

Veronica calls out to Bobby from a friend's car as they drive by. "Happy birthday, champ!"

Mary grabs his arm. "Wait—is it *really* your birthday?" She feels like a horrible friend for not knowing this information, and like a heel for not believing him earlier.

"Yeah, it is. I really didn't want to make a big deal out of it this year. I'm seventeen now, and that's too old to expect anything. I figured tonight was busy enough. No need to create any hoopla over it," Bobby says, trying to downplay the fact that he had kept it a secret from her and whipped it out as a last-minute attempt to find a loophole in her code of conduct.

"I wish I would have known! I might have . . ." She trails off, not knowing where her thought was headed.

Bobby interrupts her. "I'm glad you didn't know. It might have made you do something you shouldn't have. You have your reasons and they are honorable ones. I am the cad in this scenario. I will try harder to respect your answers the first time you give them. No means no. I got it." He is suddenly desperate not to subject himself to this hurtful conversation anymore.

"I'm so sorry," Mary says softly, sensing the pain in his voice.

The ride to Bobby's is rather quiet, everyone drooping from exhaustion. Bobby reaches for Mary's hand in the dark, and she allows him the comfort of holding it. From the way he stares at her with craving eyes, she can feel how much he wants to hold more of her.

Why does this have to be so difficult?

Grateful to see their intended destination, Mary taps Chick on the shoulder. "It's just up here, after the school on the right."

The car eases to a stop. Bobby reluctantly removes himself from Mary's side and takes a few steps up the street. He turns to wave goodbye in the bright stream of the headlights.

"I've never seen a guy win a big game like that and still look so sad. They don't call em queer for nothin," Chick says, putting the car in Reverse.

Mary angrily kicks the back of Gayle's seat out of disgust, but it goes unnoticed because her friend is fast asleep, her belly full of blackberries.

For the remainder of the ride home, Mary sits stewing in the fact that she can't do anything to defend Bobby's honor. She has to remind herself that it's not Chick she takes issue with—it's Gayle who created this dilemma. She knows Chick's views are no doubt a product of his upbringing, relying more on the opinions of those around him rather than any personal experience. Bigotry is a subject Mary has never understood; it is so nonsensical in her eyes, serving no purpose whatsoever, whether it is against homosexuals, Negros, Jews, or purple aliens from outer space.

> *People should be viewed by their character and their*
> *deeds, nothing else.*
> *Society limits the amount of happiness we can all achieve*
> *by placing people in some boxed-up category. Hiding*
> *behind the We's and They's of the world and allowing*
> *atrocities to happen is shameful. Hate is shameful.*

Hot, angry tears spring to Mary's eyes and blur her vision. Not in any mood to explain, she wipes them away with the heel of her hand before Chick can spot them, grateful for the cloak of night.

> *If this is part of some hormonal fluctuation, no wonder*
> *guys think we are dopey and make fun of us. God must*
> *be a man to have inflicted us with puberty.*
> *Only a man could think that wild emotions and bodily*
> *mishaps are amusing.*

Tickled by her new line of thinking, she nearly smiles as Chick pulls the car onto the grass and parks in Gayle's front yard.

"I guess I'll see you tomorrow," he says to Mary. He walks over to Gayle's side of the car and slowly reaches in with his long arms to peel her away from the seat.

"I appreciate the offer, but I'm not going," Mary says politely. She shakes the blood back into her legs from being seated and notices a creepy bank of fog has formed over the neighborhood—it looms, rolling in like some scene in a horror flick. "I want to spend some time with my family. You and Gayle could use some time alone, I'm sure."

Chick pops upright with Gayle cradled in his arms, his face panic-stricken.

Mary looks at Chick and shivers with only one arm in her jacket. "What's wrong?"

"You *have* to go!" His eyes bulge insistently. "I promised Vinny I would keep an eye on you. Not only that, but I don't know if Gayle's parents will allow us to go without you."

Mary waves off his concern and shoves her other arm inside the cozy sleeve of her jacket. "Don't worry about Vinny. I promise to stay home. If her parents don't feel comfortable with you guys being alone, you should invite them to tag along. I bet they haven't been to the movies in a while. It could be like a double date."

Chick wrinkles his nose at the thought for a second, then his expression morphs into a look of possibility. "If you wait a minute while I put her inside, I will walk you home," he says, holding Gayle as if she were a feather.

"No need to be gallant. I can get there on my own," Mary says, laughing at Gayle's blackberry-stained face.

"You sure? On a night like this, the Rougarou might get you," he says teasingly.

Mary looks out into the spooky night; the short hairs of her nape and arms lift to attention, making her want to hurry inside. But she laughs it off. "I'm too old to be afraid of swamp monster fairytale nonsense. Goodnight, kind sir, and thanks for the carriage." She gives him a Shakespearean bow, then bravely turns into the darkness for home.

"If you say so. Hope to see you when I get back from offshore—if you survive!"

Chick heads inside with his precious bundle. Mary just flings her hand up over her head in acknowledgment.

Walking slowly, feeling the shell road softly crunching beneath her steps, it seems surprising that she can hear a noise beyond the sounds of the insects that surround her and her loud, crunchy footsteps—but she does hear something coming from the cypress trees lining the back of the property, sending a chill up her spine. Probably just an owl or other harmless native creature of some sort, but unnerving all the same. She reinforces her grip on the jacket and picks up her pace, but feels a bit silly for doing so.

Reaching the perceived safety of her home, Mary stands on her front porch, looking in the window at her family: their faces bathed in the soft, stuttered glow of the demigod that now resides in the front room, this place that just a few weeks before was filled with activity, interaction, and conversations of vibrant youth. Now all sit very still, entranced with more reverence than she has ever witnessed from them in church. Troubling is the thought that something seemingly so innocent could possibly be the undoing of all they held dear as a family—the thing that just recently seemed like the answer to what ailed them.

Mary wonders about the future.

How will they learn about each other? How will they bond?

Her only comfort is that at least they must detach from it when it signs off—or they might sit there all night.

She quietly enters, scaring the bejeezus out of everyone and sparking a domino of screams.

"We're watching *Creature from the Black Gagoon*, Mary!" yells Margene, jumping up from her seat.

"I told you, it's *La-*, Margie! *Lagoon!*" Jenny shouts, being the boss that she is.

"My name is Mar*gene*, not Margie!" she bellows, followed by a snort and a protruding tongue.

"Mary, could we make some E-Z Pop during the commercials?" asks Sarah. "I like to watch the container get all puffy."

"Sure, if we have some." Mary goes to look in the pantry, tailed by three of her sisters.

"Mrs. Shirley gave us one from her trip to the store because Sarah helped her put the bags inside," Jenny says, as if to tattle. "It's already on the counter. Mama said we had to wait."

"Wait for what?" Mary asks. Sarah shrugs. "Ohhh, I see . . . wait until someone else volunteers to supervise."

"My supper is in my toes," Margene says, in the loud way that small children speak, as if they are hard of hearing or inebriated.

"Please be quiet! The movie's back on!" calls Jason from the front room, followed by the thumping of feet as Jenny and Margene return to their places amongst the horror fans.

"Why don't you go watch the movie and I'll bring the popcorn to you when it's ready," Mary says sweetly, rubbing Sarah's back, waiting for the gas stove to heat up the aluminum disk.

"I don't like popcorn very much. I just like to watch it pop," Sarah says, her eyes glued to the shiny pan. "Can I shake it?"

To allow her this small joy, Mary grabs a stool, transferring it to the foot of the stove, like she once did for herself when she was about Sarah's age.

It doesn't take long before the rattling foil pan starts to rise and fill with the explosive snack. Once fully expanded, the silver pan looks similar to the new attic turbines just installed on their new ventilated roof.

Mary opens it carefully to let the steam out. The scent of popcorn travels to the front room. Naturally, all the children start asking for a warm, delectable handful, which is the largest serving that can be distributed considering the size of the container. Mary's only rule is that they have to ask Sarah for the privilege, since she was the one who earned it.

Mary sees so much of herself in Sarah that she feels the need to protect this little sister's delicate spirit. Even compared to Mary, Sarah is the most reserved and obedient child in the bunch. All of the other children spend time jockeying for their place as the center of attention; Sarah, in her passiveness, is often ignored or forgotten in the mix.

Mary takes a seat on the front room floor with her back to the couch and pulls Sarah onto her lap to watch the rest of the creature feature. Sarah is very happy to be in her oldest sister's care, and by the end of the movie, she is almost asleep in Mary's lap. During an attempt to rise, Sarah musters a half-conscious plea to join Mary in her bed. Unable to deny her sweet request, Mary half-carries her up the stairs and into the bed; she slips into the bathroom before one of the boys can occupy it.

Upon retiring to her pillow, Mary discovers that someone has left an envelope for her to find; luckily, Sarah hasn't buried it in her jostles for a comfortable sleeping position. Ripping a line in the top by feel, fumbling for the small flashlight she keeps in her nightstand for when the electricity goes out, sliding the plastic switch—Mary is startled to see Sarah sitting up in the bed, surprised that she is awake; both are still jumpy from the movie.

"It came this afternoon. I guess we all forgot about it," says Sarah, rubbing her tired eyes. "Is it too private to read out loud?" she asks, thinking it could make an interesting bedtime story.

"Let me scan it first and we'll see," Mary says, biting her lip as her eyes search for anything tawdry. But there doesn't seem to be. "Can I trust you to keep this between us? I don't want the rest of the family to know my business." When Sarah nods her head in earnest agreement, Mary allows her sister to witness her first real love letter.

They snuggle into a comfortable position, allowing the letter to bathe in the narrow beam of the pocket torch.

I am sitting here trying to figure out how you snuck your way into my life, into my heart. I don't know how, but I'm awful glad you did. I am going crazy without you. I miss everything about you, your smile, your touch, your smell. You are in my every thought. I must sound like a real loon to you, if you only knew how sincere I am trying to be. My life has been a hard one and it has left me with an inability to trust. You make me want to try. There was a time I thought I would just go through life all alone, now I can't imagine spending it without you. Revealing all this to you has left me feeling naked. Please don't take advantage of that. If you don't feel the same, it's okay. Just give me some time to earn your love, that is all I ask of you. I'm not a learned man of many words, so my letters won't be pages and pages. What I do know is how I feel when I am with you and I will do my best to help you feel that way too.

Love,
Vinny

P.S. Keep me up to date with what you and your family are up to so I won't feel so far away.

Reading his words nearly brings Mary to tears. Her heart fills with delight—in her hands she holds proof that he is out there in the world thinking about her, wanting nothing more than to be with her . . . and *naked* to boot.

"What do you think about that, little Sarah?" Mary says, holding the letter to her chest in wonderment. When there is no reply, she looks down to see her sister has finally fallen into a peaceful slumber. She refolds the letter, puts it under her pillow, and burrows in for the night. The sound of Sarah's slow, rhythmic breathing puts Mary into a trance, allowing her thoughts to evanesce, Vinny's words still singing her to sleep.

Saturday
September 20, 1958

By the time Sarah wakes, Mary is already on the back porch, working on her first load of laundry and a second draft of a reply letter to Vinny—stopping only occasionally to kick the washing machine back into submission. Every time she reads aloud what she has written, it sounds too mushy-gushy. She finds herself questioning whether her words sound girlish and silly. After all, he is a man, not some boy who would be impressed by any old prose that she dares to pour on the page.

She begins to approach the project as if it were an assignment given by a teacher. Even with this strategy, none of her results satisfy her expectations. Her present draft comes across as dry, distant, verging on cold ... still, she would much prefer it this way, full of composure, than to ooze of desperation and immaturity.

Especially today, of all days. Today she has entered a new state of being, a rite of passage if you will. This day has been planned for ever since she was forced to watch the film *Molly Grows Up* in Health class when she was thirteen. Armed with her sanitary belt and napkins, Mary has stepped forward into the messy world commonly referred to as "the curse." "The curse" is exactly that, to every woman the world over; it is simply an ache in the rear—literally—with the cramping, bloating, and so on. The only time it truly deserves her current level of reverence is the very first time, *this* time. It's the moment when you no longer see yourself as a kid. Suddenly Mary feels herself a woman with lofty goals and pursuits, and none of them to be taken lightly . . . including this letter.

Mary folds the letter and places it in an envelope, which she seals— but changes her mind yet again, sits down, and starts yet another draft. Just in case, she tells herself, because doubt can be unrelenting.

The new draft reads:

Dear Vinny,

Your words have touched me deeply. I miss you too. I am sorry that I am more hesitant than you in the feelings department. It's not that I don't feel the same way that you do, it's just that this is still all so new to me. I am making straight A's in English and it has not helped me put what I feel into words. I want you to know that I <u>do</u> have strong feelings for you that if given time may blossom into something long lasting. I am proud of you for being so steady in your convictions. I wish I were more stable in mine. It's so hard to know which end is up at this point in my life. I will do my best to avoid anything that might disappoint you. School is keeping me very busy and the time is passing quicker than I thought it would. Christmas will be here before you know it! The past week was action-packed. We had our

Homecoming game against Istrouma—and we won! I started music lessons this week; I am going to attempt to play the violin. I don't know that I will be any good at it, but it was strongly suggested to boost my admissions application for college. I would love to know more about where you are and what you're doing. I hope you are well and will write again soon.

Your friend,
Mary

"Why can't I do this!" she cries, ripping the letter to shreds, flustered with her inability to articulate her feelings without coming across like a fifteen year old trying too hard.

"What are you up to back here?" Gayle asks, joining her by the rumbling washing machine. She picks up bits of the letter that landed on the porch.

"Trying to write a letter to Vinny." Mary lets her breath all the way out, throwing her chewed pencil onto a pile of dirty laundry.

"Looks more like littering to me." Gayle steps into the cool shadow of the awning to get a closer gander at Mary, who looks like she has not bathed or run a brush through her hair since the day before. "Whoa," she exclaims, "it's not like you to skip the rituals."

"I didn't get enough sleep. I started early this morning . . . now I'm miserable, crampy, and—"

"And whiny. Wait . . . what do you mean, 'started'? Like *started*, started?"

"Wearing my belt as we speak."

"Why on earth would you want to wear a belt? I'll go home and get you some plugs."

"Please don't," Mary begged.

"Give me a break, Mary! It's nothing to be scared of. You just stick it in your hoo-ha and call it a day."

"Would I still be a . . . a virgin?"

"It isn't going to *make love* to you, Mary," Gayle quips. "It's just going to keep blood from running down your leg without feeling like a diaper, silly."

"You should not make fun of the infirm," Mary says, hiding behind her messy hair.

"Welcome to the party, my flowing friend. If you need something for the pain, I have some pills Mom picked up at the pharmacy my last go-'round." Gayle keeps her distance as she talks, like Mary's menstrual distress might be contagious. "Anyway, I came over to see if you want to hang out with me and Chick. He has to go to work on Monday, so we are taking it easy until the movie later."

"I don't feel like going out in public," Mary says, shifting uncomfortably in the chair. "I'm going to work on my project and rest up for school. You can have him all to yourself this weekend. Are you guys going to bring your folks to the movie?"

"I should have known that was your idea," Gayle gripes. "No, Mom and Dad aren't going. They said they need to stay home to get the wax buildup off the linoleum again!" She shakes her head, furrowing her brow. "Remind me not to have linoleum in my house. Too much maintenance."

Mary shakes her head at the clumsy explanation. "I could have sworn those were no-wax floors," she says.

"Anyway, let me know if you change your mind about joining the outside world—or the tampons. Both could do you a load of good," Gayle says, stepping back into the sunlight.

Mary feels downright cantankerous with the frequent trips to the bathroom, the iron stench of blood, and that annoying *click, click, click* of the television dial as it endlessly makes the rounds. She is utterly relieved when bedtime finally rolls around for the younger crowd.

After several more attempts at completing her school assignments, Mary falls asleep on the couch and wakes to the National Anthem being played, heralding the static void of the wee hours. Sleep-drunk, she stumbles to the television set and switches it off, leaving the room black as pitch, to which her eyes refuse to adjust. After wounding her foot on a small toy left out on the floor, she feels her way up the stairs and finds that one of the children has forgotten to turn the light off in the upstairs bathroom. She flips it off—then right back on, not knowing what may lurk on the floor between there and her room.

Once she finds a suitable position to rest her limbs, sleep takes Mary down hard and fast.

Monday
September 22, 1958

S truggling to force air into her lungs, Gayle ambushes Mary in the hall at her locker. "Man, oh, man," she exhales, and takes a moment to swallow. "I just heard in the bathroom that Bobby . . . got drunk at the dance and slapped a girl in the student parking lot"—another swallow, another breath—"for not letting him . . . you know." Gayle adopts a look of shock and adds, "In the back of Roy Fontenot's car!"

Mary doesn't share in Gayle's shock. "He wouldn't do that. Don't believe everything you hear in the girls' bathroom." She spots Bobby en route, looking as if he has been mauled by a restless night. "The horse's mouth approacheth."

"Horse's *ass*, maybe," Gayle says. She leans on the lockers to await his side of the story, her expression dubious.

"I hope you had a more exciting weekend than mine," Bobby says to Mary, rubbing his forehead.

"Trust me, I didn't," Mary says, then presses her lips together to allow him to speak.

"You should have gone to the dance with me. It was awful without you there. I was surrounded by all that Terrebonne's elite has to offer, but none of them held my interest." Bobby avoids Mary's penetrating gaze, intently thumbing the flaking paint on one of the lockers.

"That's not what they're saying in the girls' bathroom," Gayle sneers, folding her arms as if arming herself for a verbal battle should he choose to deny the allegations.

He looks at Gayle sharply. "Oh, that—I can explain exactly what happened." Leaning forward, he lightly punches the paint-peeling locker.

"So it's true?" Mary says, immediately bruised and incensed.

"I don't know what version you have heard," Bobby says evasively, reeking of self-reproach, "but—"

"There are versions?" Mary asks, taking a step back to make room for her disappointment, just before the bell rings.

Bobby backs away at the sound of the bell, his hand patting his chest with an open hand. "Meet me at lunch. Don't form an opinion until you hear me out."

Mary's narrowed eyes follow his advantageous retreat down the hall.

A murmur spreads through the student body as Bobby travels across the patio to where Mary is eating her lunch. "Now, please—let me explain," he says, plopping down on the bench. He's out of air, placing his hands palms up on the table as if to beg for clemency and a minute to catch his breath.

Gayle leaves Jane mid-sentence when she sees Bobby has come to confess, walking over and sitting beside Mary in solidarity.

"All right . . . explain," Mary says with her nose in the air, pushing away the remnants of her lunch. She drags her tongue across her teeth, ready to hand him over to the morality police.

Bobby takes a deep breath. "I was very depressed that you turned me down," he began, "after I had planned the night out in my mind a thousand times with you as my date. Everyone was whispering about why I came to the dance alone. Roy said he could cheer me up with a couple a' beers from his trunk, and . . . I said yes. I know—poor judgment. But we'd just opened our second beer and I was feeling better when a group of girls came over to talk to us. Two *more* beers later and I was feeling dizzy, so I climbed into Roy's backseat to lie down a minute—afraid I might throw up in front of those girls. The backseat felt like a boat when I shut my eyes."

"Poor baby," Gayle interrupts with sarcasm. "Get to the point, mister."

"No, no, be nice and let him finish. Give him enough rope and he might just hang himself," Mary taunts.

Bobby's face flushes. "The next thing I knew, one of the girls climbed in the back with me to see if I was all right."

"I bet she did," scoffs Gayle.

"Enough! Shush!" Mary says to Gayle, wanting to get to the bottom of this seedy mess.

Bobby continues, "She started kissing me, and at first I thought I might be dreaming and imagined it was you . . . but how she was kissing me and where . . . it couldn't have been you." He watches Mary's discomfort with this information. "I told her to stop, to leave me alone, but she only got more aggressive, trying to unbutton my clothes. I pushed her out the way she came in. She tried one more time to come at me and that's when I saw her face. I pushed her away and I said something to her I'd rather not repeat and she spat on me. I lost it—I slapped her and told her to go home before her mother found out where she'd been."

"And?" both girls ask as Bobby falls short of full disclosure.

" 'And' what? That's everything. That's all that happened." Bobby looks down, tugging at his shirt.

"You left out, let's see . . . umm . . . only the biggest detail of the whole damn thing!" Gayle says, loud enough to draw attention.

"All right, calm down." Bobby hangs his head. "I . . . I can't tell you who she was. It would be devastating to her parents to find out through town gossip that their only daughter has loose morals."

"How am I supposed to believe that story?" Mary asks. "You've had three class periods to practice what to say and now you won't reveal this girl's identity? How convenient."

"If you don't believe me, you can ask Roy. He was there, saw the whole thing."

"If he was there the whole time, doesn't he know who she is?" Gayle asks.

"She isn't a senior, and it was dark—besides, he was drinking and had his own hands full . . . if you know what I mean," Bobby says, adding a cough for surreptitiousness' sake.

"So not a very good witness for you—or her, I'd say," Mary concludes.

"I guess not," Bobby admits. "It's the truth, though."

"Sorry to tell you, Bob," says Gayle, "but the truth won't matter to anyone once the majority has made up their own version—especially if the truth is boring."

Mary sits, arms folded, still deliberating. Bobby lays his heavy head on the table. Gayle mercifully rubs his back, wanting to believe him— and knowing she will ferret out the girl's identity by the last bell of the day.

"Girl fight!" a male student announces, waving excitedly at exiting students, including Mary, to witness the impromptu sporting event.

Mary groans. Not even five minutes after the last bell of the day, and Gayle has tracked down her quarry, now on the ground mid-interrogation.

"You have one second to tell the truth," Gayle growls, hovering over Veronica's face, teeth bared, firm grip on her shirt collar. Her left arm pins the liar's chest to the ground, and she holds an itchy right fist in the air above, waiting for the hussy to set the record straight for the crowd forming around the action.

"Oh, no," Mary says, running off to find Bobby before someone gets hurt.

"All right!" Veronica relents, shouting. "It wasn't Bobby's fault— but he *did* slap me!"

"Because you wouldn't leave him alone, right?" Gayle bears down on her. *"Right?"*

"Yes! It was my fault! I should have left him alone," Veronica cries.

"You see, people?" Gayle says to the crowd. "*That's* how you conduct an investigation. My work here is done." She releases her hold on Veronica and stands herself up triumphantly.

Veronica takes the opportunity to push Gayle and stands up with her fists cocked.

"Big mistake, you hussy skank bag!" Gayle shouts, launching an attack on Veronica and looking much like the Tasmanian Devil in Saturday morning cartoons.

Bobby arrives on the scene. The ineffective duty teacher is standing nearby, afraid to intervene, and Bobby is the only one brave enough to go near the tornado of limb-flying rage. He finds an angle and uses his football training to knock the girls over, placing himself in the line of fire. The sparring is over for now, but as the girls leave the scene, neither one looks like she is willing to let the animosity go. The duty teacher escorts Veronica to the office, where she will use her bloody face to bend the facts and have Gayle suspended from school for her angry outburst.

"Are you okay? Is anything broken?" Mary asks, inspecting for injury while dusting and straightening Gayle's clothes.

"That felt so good! Why the flying fuck did you stop me?" Gayle yells at Bobby, bent over, hands on her knees, still fuming.

Mary drags her hand away from her slack mouth to pet Gayle, trying to calm her down.

"Because I didn't want you to kill her," Bobby says, in all seriousness.

Gayle straightens, sobering up. "Thanks. You're right. I don't think I could have stopped."

"Let's get you some water," Mary says. She steers Gayle toward the school building, turning to mouth a *thank-you* to Bobby, who stays behind to make sure the crowd doesn't make up a whole new story about the situation.

Friday
October 31, 1958—Halloween

"How does my blood look?" Chick asks, grinning with his plastic fangs while Gayle applies more cherry pie filling, minus the cherries, to his face. He attempts to take a peek at himself in the bathroom mirror, but she forcibly pulls his face back into its original position facing her.

"If you don't hold still, I won't need to apply fake blood!" she says, shaking her fist at him. "It's my party and I want you to look super scary."

"Wasn't the lipstick enough?" he asks, careful not to move or cause her to make good on her word.

"The pie filling makes it look more real," Gayle says with agitation.

To Chick, she looks like a true artist at work. He studies Gayle's angelic face contorting as if it has some kind of mysterious connection with the movement of her hand.

"Gayle?" he says, and hesitates.

"What?"

"I love you, Gayle," he says softly, searching her face for reciprocation.

She takes a second to gauge how serious he is—the change is so all-of-a-sudden, it almost makes her suspicious and reconsider punching him anyway—before she responds.

"I love you, too, ya big goof. Now stop before we have to start all over," Gayle says, sniffing, then quickly changes the subject. "I still can't believe you got us all tickets for the cemetery tour. I'm so excited!" She puts the finishing touches on his sticky drips of gore. "Inviting my parents so we could stay overnight was priceless." Finished with her masterpiece, she carefully plants a kiss on Chick's mouth so not to mess up all of her intricate work. "There. All done." She stands back to admire her vampire creation.

"I vont to suck your blood," he says theatrically. As he leans in for another kiss, Gayle turns her head and Chick tastes the filling she has applied to her neck to make it look like she was a recent bite victim.

"Don't lick it off," she says, grabbing her supplies to reapply.

"Brings a whole new meaning to 'blood sugar,' " Chick says, trying to keep his plastic teeth straight.

"You're gonna need a transfusion when I get through with you," she says. "This is the only part that makes what I'm wearing a *costume*." She looks in the mirror to replace the missing goo on her red-streaked neck.

"It's not his fault you used your Halloween birthday party as an excuse to get a fancy party dress instead of a legitimate costume," Mary says playfully from the bathroom doorway.

Gayle squeals with delight at the sight of Mary in a home-made Dorothy costume. "You look adorable!"

Mary displays her blue-and-white gingham dress in a modest curtsy, her face managing only a partial smile.

"You said the same thing when I wore it last year," Mary says, feeling stupid for wearing the same costume two years in a row.

"But it fits much better this year," Gayle says, making hourglass curves in the air with her hands.

"You're right, it does, except for these shoes—they're a bit too small." Mary points to one of her red glitter-clad feet like a ballerina taking position. "By the end of the night, I might look as if Chick the vampire got a hold of them." She thinks about the stark contrast of the costumes, and the fact that the other half of her couple is still out-of-pocket. "It looks like I am going to be the odd man out, so to speak," she says.

Chick plays with his temporary dentures and says, "Didn't Gayle tell you?"

"Oops," Gayle says, "I was supposed to tell you that we invited Bobby to come tonight . . . and I'm pretty sure I gave him a hint about your costume." Gayle is nervously applying her lipstick, knowing that Mary is going to have a conniption at any moment. Upon hearing someone conversing with her mother in the kitchen, Gayle says, "That must be him now," and slides her lipstick back into its sheath, dodging the many daggers Mary's eyes are aiming at her.

"Don't worry, Mary. The boys and girls will be staying in separate rooms. Second thought—which room should we put Nancy-boy in?" Chick says, cracking himself up and preparing to accompany Gayle into the kitchen. "Victims first," he says, revealing the red satin lining of his cape as he offers for her to go ahead of him down the hall.

"I think I might need a minute," Mary says, her hand on the door.

"I'll meet you in Oz then," Chick says, pointing to the kitchen and leaving her alone in the bathroom.

Mary locks the door. She has to gather up a yard or two of material before she can pee. While she listens to the trickle of fluid leaving her body and echoing into the porcelain basin, she taps her feet on the tile floor, entertaining herself with the twinkle of her glittery red shoes, amazed by how much more comfortable they are when she is seated.

She stares at her reflection as she washes and dries her hands on the soft guest towel, she fondles her shiny pigtails, deep in thought.

How do I keep getting myself into this predicament?
If this keeps up, I'm bound to have a weak moment.
If Vinny loves me, how could he leave me for so long
without any word?

In a flash of anger, Mary picks up the red lipstick Gayle left on the counter and applies it to her quivering lips. She takes one last look at herself, like a challenge between the side of her that wants to remain faithful to Vinny and this new side that wants to conquer Bobby. Unable to resolve the conflict, she turns the light off and moves toward the laughter echoing from the kitchen.

Everyone is gathered around the kitchen table, helping Shirley disperse birthday candles as they wait for Mary. Shirley is dressed as an Indian squaw, wearing a headband with a single red feather standing up from behind her slickly parted hair, yarn braids resting on her shoulders. Gayle's father James is outfitted as a cowboy with a pair of cap guns, one on each hip. He looks like a blend of Howdy Doody and the Lone Ranger, since James has added a small black mask that only covers the area around his eyes.

"There she is! Now we can light the candles," Gayle says. She is ready to dig into the red velvet cupcakes with white cream cheese icing her mother baked—one for each year her baby girl has been alive, sixteen in all.

When Bobby turns to look at Mary, he is unable to tear his gaze away, watching her tongue follow the path of her freshly applied lipstick as she moistens her full red lips. He takes a seat of refuge, knees weak, all the blood leaving his head, realizing that he is staring at her with a rock-hard erection.

Mary looks at him in his scarecrow outfit complete with an old hat and real pieces of straw hanging out of his collar.

He is so completely adorable.

Upon wetting her lips, she tastes the lipstick, which reminds her what a dangerous game she is playing with his heart—amongst other parts. As she carefully moves across the room, not once do they take their eyes off of one another; she drops into the chair next to him.

After a healthy chorus of "Happy Birthday to You," Gayle breaks tradition by extinguishing only one candle with quick precision, peeling back the paper liner and sinking her teeth in. Following her example, each party guest devours a cupcake, creating a creepy cannibal scene with bits of red cake innards all over the plain white disposable plates. The cherry-flavored Kool-Aid doesn't help either, leaving everyone with bright red tongues.

"We better get the show on the road if we are going to make the tour on time," James says, looking at his watch, which seems out of place with his costume. He turns his eyes on Gayle. "Don't give me that look, young lady! Your mother and I will be following in our own vehicle. We need our peace and quiet," he says, knowing his dear daughter wouldn't want them infringing on her fun.

On the way to the car, Mary comes from behind and touches Bobby's hand. They both feel electricity as she wraps her hand around his index finger and he floats into the backseat of Chick's Impala.

Shirley catches the incident out of the corner of her eye before climbing into the idling sedan. "James dear, didn't Chick tell you that Bobby was of a . . . delicate persuasion?" she quizzes, not sure that she saw what she saw.

"That's the information I got. Chick even agreed to sleep on a cot in the room so they wouldn't have to share a bed," James answers, pulling out of the driveway and onto the road.

"Then I must be mistaken about what I just saw," she mentions, still puzzled. "I thought I just saw two kids that looked like . . . like . . ."

"Like what, dear?" he asks, not following her train of thought.

"Like I imagine we did the night we conceived Gayle," Shirley replies with a heat rising to her cheeks.

He lifts her hand to his lips and kisses her arm from wrist to elbow. She giggles like a teenager. He honks the horn and rolls down the window to get Chick's attention.

"Shirley forgot something in the house," James calls. "You go on ahead and we will catch up in a few." He pulls back into the driveway and bolts back into the house with Shirley.

"She must have left the oven on or something," Gayle says, watching her parents race back into the house looking like they need to put out a fire. "We are going to have so much fun tonight!" she continues, searching for a good song on the radio. She is hoping for something upbeat, but settles for "Sixteen Candles" sung by the Crests, since it fits the occasion.

Mary and Bobby are sitting silently, fighting the internal war of *shoulda*s, *coulda*s, and *woulda*s amidst a flurry of pheromones, sending signals to Bobby's brain, his body responding as their eyes accidentally meet, which both try to avoid for fear of losing control.

Mary reluctantly pulls her eyes to the blur of trees passing by her window. The dark is coming fast and it will be just the thing to allow some cover; poor Bobby can't seem to rid himself of the erection that now is beginning to throb and ache. He contemplates using a little friction to relieve himself since he is right on the edge, but he can't bring himself to do it in her presence, even if it is dim and she isn't looking.

"Look out!" Gayle shouts, pointing at something on the highway.

Chick swerves hard to avoid hitting a large armadillo that has wandered into the road, and the sudden movement throws Mary practically into Bobby's lap. He can't help but feel some of her curves brushing against him—and that is all it takes. Mary feels him shudder and whimper softly as she pulls away.

"Are you guys okay back there?" Chick asks after checking on his birthday girl.

"I think I may have hurt Bobby," Mary says, inspecting him with her hands and inadvertently extending his ecstasy.

"I'm all right," he manages, trying to keep her from encountering the wet spot in his lap.

"Are you sure?" she asks, worried that she has damaged him somehow.

"I'm fine . . . but I could use a restroom if we come across one," he says, feeling relieved and uncomfortable at the same time—that dueling sense of shame and satisfaction young men learn from such an act.

"There is a gas station up the road that has one," Chick says as he accelerates. "We need to stop anyway and give Gayle's folks a chance to catch up with us. I haven't seen them since we left the house."

"You guys have been awful quiet back there. This is supposed to be a party!" Gayle says, trying again to find a good song to get their spirits up. She turns up the volume when she comes across Jerry Lee Lewis banging on the piano and singing "Whole Lotta Shakin' Goin' On," followed by "All Shook Up" by Elvis Presley. Everyone is singing along as they pull into the gas station. Gayle leans over and whispers something to Chick as he gets out of the car to go inside, and Bobby jumps out as soon as he pinpoints the restroom sign.

Once the boys are gone, Gayle faces the backseat on her knees and says to Mary, "So is everything okay? Are you still mad at me for inviting Bobby? I just thought, you know, the more the merrier. Even numbers are always better."

"No, I'm over it. I'm just finding it harder and harder to be around Bobby now that Vinny has been gone so long," Mary replies. She looks toward the gas station distractedly, remembering the way Bobby's muscles felt when she touched him earlier.

"Chick told me he loves me," Gayle announced. "And I think he meant it."

Mary looks back at her friend, her own thoughts forgotten. "That's big! You're going to have to give me the details later. Did you say it back?"

"We almost cried, it was so emotional," she squeals, hopping up and down in the seat.

"Tell me you weren't . . ." Mary says worriedly, letting her voice trail away at the unmentionable.

"No! That's how I know it was real. We were in the bathroom putting on our makeup and he just said it out of the blue. We weren't even making out—in fact, he hasn't even tried to get me to go all the way yet." Now it's Gayle's turn to gaze off at the gas station. "I probably would if he asked."

"Please don't!" Mary tugs her friend's hands to get her attention. "I know it's difficult to wait, but the only way to know if he truly loves you is to see if he is willing to prove it by marrying you."

"I know! I just love him so much," Gayle says, looking out the window again. She sees Chick returning with a paper bag, and Bobby coming back to the car looking like he has had a fight with a hose.

"That clerk almost pulled a gun on me!" Chick says, climbing into the car and trying not to choke himself with his cape. "I forgot how scary I must look, and the poor guy forgot it was Halloween. I must have scared the piss out of him."

"Did he scare the piss out of you, too?" Gayle asks Bobby, who had settled in the back seat just in time to hear what happened to Chick.

"I had a little trouble at the sink—hey, Gayle, that must be your folks," Bobby says, pointing to the car that just passed, taking the heat off of his wet pants.

"That's them, all right. Let's hit the road," says Chick, handing the paper bag to Gayle.

Gayle turns a calculated grin to the backseat. "Mary, I know I told you not to get me a birthday present, but I do want you to do me a huge favor. I need you to loosen up tonight . . . so I had Chick score us some hooch."

"Some what?" Mary asks, unaware of what she is suggesting.

Gayle and Chick begin to recite phrases back and forth, sounding exactly like an Ernest & Julio Gallo commercial.

"What's the word? Thunderbird! What's the price? Thirty twice," they mimic, unveiling the cold bottle of high-octane wine, along with three bottles of soda to wash it down and a small bottle of Listerine mouthwash to cover the smell afterward. Lastly out of the large brown

bag comes a stack of Dixie cups that Chick managed to swipe from a dispenser in the convenience store.

Gayle pours a couple of ounces of the rotgut into one of the Dixie cups and hands it to Mary. As she accepts the offering, Mary looks to Bobby to be the voice of reason. He just shrugs and takes the next cup Gayle passes to the backseat. When Mary takes a whiff, the fumes alone nearly make her woozy. She looks at the contents, expecting to see the wax melting off her paper cup.

Repulsed by the smell, she says, "What's in this stuff—diesel fuel?"

"Please, Mary, you have to get it down while it's still cold! Hold your nose if you have to. It's barely enough to do anything, just enough to help you relax." With this sage advice imparted, Gayle knocks back her own cup of the noxious fluid. Doing so causes her to cough a little.

Mary looks to Bobby again. "Are you going to let me do this to myself?"

"I can't tell you what to do, Mary," he says. "But I can promise that you are with friends, and we wouldn't let any harm come to you. I won't drink mine unless you drink yours." He swishes the yellowish alcohol around in the cup, like airing it out might make it less toxic.

"On the count of three. One . . . two . . . *three*," Mary counts, and together she and Bobby succumb to Gayle's birthday wish.

"Down the hatch!" Gayle cheers them on as they throw the drink down their throats, hoping to bypass their taste buds.

No such luck. The taste is strong, reminiscent of paint thinner. The liquid burns going down, no doubt drying out the mucous lining of Mary's throat, causing her to choke, so she snatches the soda that Bobby has procured for himself before he can get a much-needed swig. The soda washes the Thunderbird down to her stomach, which becomes uncomfortably warm. Mary gives the soda back to Bobby, who appears to be experiencing the same affliction.

"You guys are a couple of lightweights," Chick laughs. He swirls the bottle's still-half-full contents as if taunting them.

"Where's your cup, hot shot?" Mary inquires. She is starting to feel a slight hum before the onslaught of a buzz, having only a single cupcake in her belly between her and the booze.

"I don't want to drink while I'm driving my precious cargo here," Chick replies, rubbing Gayle's knee. "I'll drink the leftovers once we get there."

Mary starts to feel like she is lighter, for once . . . free. Since this is her first experience with alcohol, she doesn't know what to expect. She likes the feeling enough to go for another sample, but only as much as the first one—a bit more than a shot glass. It does exactly what Gayle said it would. Mary is more relaxed, and the edge is gone.

In fact, everything around her seems to be a lot funnier and friendlier than it was before . . . the costumes, the music, Bobby's wet pants. Everybody is laughing and carrying on so much that they haven't noticed they are almost to their destination.

Bobby is having a great time with this side of Mary. He counts the times she has deliberately touched his arm, his shoulder, even his leg, pressing her palm to his thigh twice while she is telling a joke. He knows he promised to protect her, but the more he feels the alcohol in his blood, the more he finds his brain telling him to take any advantages afforded to him . . . even the ones he knows she wouldn't provide if she were sober.

Another side effect is that he starts to sweat, which causes the straw from his costume to become itchy. It sticks to the skin beneath his collar, feeling like a fresh haircut before the soothing talc powder.

As Chick parallel-parks the car outside the hotel, Gayle crows, "It's mouthwash time!" She, Mary, and Bobby all take a swish of Listerine and spit it into a Dixie cup. Mary clumsily exits the car and tosses the discards in a handy trashcan she finds ajar by the street, then totters back to the Impala.

Why didn't we just drink the Listerine, too? It tastes so similar.

Chick, careful not to ruin his artwork lest he upset his "precious cargo," chugs the last few ounces of wine straight from the bottle—less than he expected a group of initiates to leave for him—and follows it up with the mouthwash drill.

In the car they wait for Gayle's parents to check in for their room reservations. The hotel is a small collection of cottage-style cuteness, not grand in size, but it fits their needs with a quaint elegance.

Chick looks around to get his bearings. "Lafitte's isn't too far from here," he observes.

"Is that where we meet for the tour?" Gayle says with her *I'm-the-birthday-girl* excitement.

"Yeah, it's a bar a few blocks from here," Chick answers. He gets out of the car, stretching, and looks around in order to make a better guesstimation of whether or not his car will be safe parked on the street.

Following his lead, Gayle and Bobby pile out and take in the dank evening air together, sort of finding their legs, the ground unsteady as the deck of a ship.

"You guys need to be cool in front of the folks," Chick says, mindful that contributing to the delinquency of a minor is a class-one misdemeanor—added to whatever sentence Gayle's parents might impose. He locks the car and pulls the handles to make sure they are secure.

"Whatever you say, Chick-ster," Mary says, holding back a snicker.

Gayle smiles, giggles, and squeaks out, "Chick-let!"

"Like the gum!" Mary blurts, unable to contain the laughter, which has now spread to Bobby, who thinks of something funny to add, but the look he receives from Chick makes him rescind the idea.

Just then, Gayle's parents show up. "Are we missing the fun?" Shirley asks, hand-in-hand with James.

"It's just getting started," Gayle says, skipping across the street without remembering to look both ways.

"Let's move, ladies and germs! Don't want to lose anyone," James says, walking briskly along the sidewalk and checking his pockets one last time for wallet and keys. "Lafitte's Blacksmith Shop was built around 1772," he announces, reading from a brochure he picked up in the hotel lobby. "I have only known it as a tavern, but I suppose it wasn't always run as such."

As they approach, the building immediately captures Mary's curiosity, with its hip roof and dormers covered by a blanket of tattered weather-worn shingles, the frame made of wooden beams surrounded by brick and mortar, so aged that it seems to be drooping from exhaustion. Peeking inside, she sees that it is candlelit by glass globes scattered about the bar as if in the midst of a power outage. Mary puts her hand on the worn exterior, wanting to absorb some of its history . . . its wisdom. This building reminds her of her father: strong enough to endure the harsh passage of time, silent, watching and listening to all that goes on around it.

Perhaps waiting for all the people inside to leave, having
no more need of it,
before joining the ground below.

She frets, allowing a single tear to slip from her eye. Bobby, witness to her sudden digression, kindly fortifies her walk back to their group, rubbing the tear away with his thumb and putting it to his mouth, as if to kiss it away. This small act causes Mary to lead Bobby away from the group and into the shadows of a doorway of the dimly lit establishment. She then pulls him into her body and plants a kiss on him that makes their toes curl. At first he is overwhelmed with the firmness of her body, the softness of her lips, the sweet hint of some sugary hair lacquer . . . but then the medicinal taste of mouthwash brings him to his senses, and he pulls away.

She is shocked that he would do such a thing after his relentless pursuit of her, and Bobby sees this as clearly as if it were written across her face.

"I want this, I do . . . more than you could ever imagine. I just want it to be real, without all the guilt you will have tomorrow if I let you do this," Bobby says, his hands falling away from Mary just as Gayle approaches them with news.

"We just found out we accidentally signed up for the wrong tour. It will be just as good, though," Gayle says, flexible as a willow tree. "It's a haunted history Voodoo tour. Sounds spooky enough, right?" Gayle skips back to the street corner ahead to look at some interesting costumed pedestrians who have also just arrived for the walking tour.

Mary begins to sway a little. "Are you all right?" Bobby asks, bringing his hand back to her body to steady her.

"Yeah," she says. "I guess so." She touches her head as if she has just returned from an out-of-body experience.

As they return to their tour group, a modest dozen costumed revelers all waiting eagerly on the street corner, a young man clad in exotic, authentic-looking pirate garb introduces himself to the handful of ridiculously dressed tourists as the Master of Ceremonies. He literally wants to be referred to as "Mr. Master."

Bobby keeps his hand at the small of Mary's back to steady her as they listen to the guide tell the story of Jean Lafitte, Lafitte's life as a pirate, and all the intrigue surrounding every aspect of his life.

"Historians cannot agree about Lafitte's place of birth, the whereabouts of his treasures, or even where or how he died. All are shrouded in mystery. There have been many reports over the years of spooky occurrences on the premises of this bar. Some believe it is haunted by Lafitte's ghost." Mr. Master increases this description's hair-raising effect via a creepy flashlight glow beneath his face.

The group grows silent and riveted. They follow their guide on tenterhooks, plodding through the streets like hypnotized sycophants. Eager to hear more tales at each location, they hang on every word of Mr. Master's ghost stories rooted in documented bits of history, every one poignant in its own way.

The last stop on the tour is a small Voodoo shop. Mr. Master explains that Voodoo is a legitimate religion, and not all that different than the Catholic belief system. He tells of Voodoo history, drawing from ancient Africa and Haiti, and all the misconceptions surrounding its practitioners. Among the practitioners he mentions, one name drags both Mary and Gayle out of their spirit-seeking bliss.

Mary steps forward, raises her hand, and is acknowledged by the tour guide, who welcomes random questions from his guests with enthusiasm.

"Could you please repeat that last part? I think I missed something," Mary says, her eyes meeting Gayle's, which are just as wide and sober.

"Oh, sure. I was just speaking of Mambo Beulah Laveau. She was a descendant of the legendary Voodoo Queen Marie Laveau. Several women in their family line had a special gift of sight. Over the years, many people sought guidance from them to foretell events yet to pass. In fact," says Mr. Master, turning to the group as a whole, "we will be visiting both of their gravesites on tomorrow afternoon's cemetery tour. For those who want to participate, we will be meeting right here in front of this Voodoo shop. Purchase your tickets tonight and you will receive a discount! Now, last but not least for tonight, I will take you through the shop and explain about rituals and spells, which will include the ever-popular Voodoo doll." He leads them into the tourist trap, which is decked out in full festive Halloween décor and smells of black licorice and cloves.

Gayle tugs on Chick's shirt, signaling her desire to be signed up for tomorrow's excursion.

"I got it covered. Now you go listen closely and tell me which candle will bring us more money," he says sarcastically, and he goes to sign up and pay for tomorrow's tour.

Mary and Gayle push their way to the front of the group, afraid of missing any other details. When the tour is over, Gayle pulls Mary in a corner near a rack of Voodoo-related literature.

"I can't believe Mambo Beulah died since we saw her at the fair," Gayle whispers. She spies a familiar face on the cover of one of the books. "Hey, isn't this the crazy lady we saw at the tent that day?" She points out a picture of an older woman in a gypsy outfit. Her hand then flits to the next shelf, containing artisan bowls filled with an array of gris-gris bags promising to offer protection, prosperity, love, and whatever else a human's ego could possibly desire.

"Yep, that's the toothless wonder, all right," Mary confirms, picking up a copy of the paperback entitled *Journey into Tarot with Maiden Folse.* "You should get one of these gris-gris bags to keep

Veronica away," Mary suggests, dangling one that is supposed to ward off evil spirits.

Gayle considers the purchase, sniffing the small cloth sack, wondering what magic herbs could be inside. "Think it would work?"

Moving to better lighting, Mary verifies the image on the paperback book and flips through the pages, hoping it will tell her what happened to Beulah. It doesn't. Mary determines that the only information to be reaped from the book confirms her suspicion that Maiden Folse is a cheap sideshow version of Beulah. Each page contains an invitation to buy this, that, and the other, preying upon the reader's predicament. Her brow furrows increasingly with the turn of each page. Mary addresses her concerns by seeking out one of the shop's employees.

She spots a young woman who looks like a faithful follower of all that is strange and macabre—at least from what Mary can see from behind. She is crouched while stocking a shelf with herb-filled jars. "Excuse me . . . can you tell me who owns this place?" Mary asks.

Rising and turning all in one smooth motion, like a lipstick rising from its base, the painfully thin girl with sunken eyes and hollow cheeks embodies the description Mary has carried in her head of a legion of persecuted Jews ever since she studied the Holocaust in History class. In school, page after page of those nightmarish descriptions evoked a reaction similar to the one she's having now. Attempting to disguise her horror, Mary turns her head and coughs into a tightly closed fist, fighting the bile rising in her throat.

It could be the alcohol making me sick.

She swallows back the burning taste of sour half-digested cupcake commingled with cheap fire water.

"Can I help you find something?" the salesgirl asks, surprisingly enthusiastic for someone so malnourished.

Swallowing again, Mary says, "I was just wondering if you could tell me who owns this interesting boutique."

"Maiden Folse is the owner. She is performing Tarot card readings at a private party this evening. If you would like a reading, I would be happy to do one for you, or you can wait and make an appointment with Maiden Folse at a later date." The salesgirl's answer sounds as if it has been rehearsed a hundred times, possibly even programmed through some form of hypnotism.

"Thanks for the offer, but I really must get going." Seeing Bobby signal to her through the shop window, she adds, "My group is waiting outside."

"Are you going to buy that book?" the girl asks as Mary turns to leave. She hasn't realized she is still holding it open to page ten, with the explanation of the "true" meaning of Tarot's The Fool card.

"Oh, I don't think I have enough money with me," Mary apologizes, handing the book to the salesgirl before bolting for the door.

"But this one's on sale today only!" Mary hears her calling out just before she breaches the threshold into the night air.

It feels as if a cool front has come through in the few minutes she spent inside the store. Bobby, rid of his bothersome perspiration, is thankful for the comfortable change in temperature. He is waiting for Mary to catch up to the group. They are discussing the fastest way to get to the hotel from where they are, utilizing a complementary map provided with the tour package.

Bobby reaches out to yawn when a mourning dove lands on his arm.

"Some scarecrow you are," Mary says, shooing the pesky bird who re-lands on Bobby's hat and doesn't want to leave—at least not before making a healthy deposit on the old cloth hat. "I think the bird of happiness just pooped on your head, my sleepy friend. That can't be a good omen," she says, patting him on the back.

The patriarch James decides on a route, and they head back toward the bar on the corner of Bourbon and St. Phillip.

Gayle's stomach rumbles loud enough for everyone to hear. "I'm starving! Isn't anyone else hungry? This town is full of food and we haven't eaten any of it," she complains.

James stops to consult the map again. "There is a diner nearby called the Clover Grill," he says, "but we need to go this way to avoid bringing the girls along Bourbon."

Bourbon Street in New Orleans is synonymous with words like tawdry, steamy, and risqué. It has nothing to offer underage tourists except for twenty-four-hour provisions for the occasional late-night meal. They know they are close to Bourbon when they are accosted by a whiff of piss and booze as they ambulate down a dark side street of the French Quarter. Mary is glad to be part of a group, considering the street that they are on is eerie with inactivity and full of shadows.

One more turn of a corner and the diner is just ahead at the end of the block. Hanging there is a plain Coca Cola sign with green CLOVER GRILL letters against a generic white. Grateful for the beacon, the hungry crew quickens their pace.

"I wasn't expecting it to turn cold," Shirley says with chattering teeth. "We really should have brought sweaters or something. We are all liable to get sick."

Gayle and Mary would normally have been complaining, too, but the alcohol helps to warm their blood—even though the "fun" effects have worn off.

James had been to Bourbon Street back in his bachelor days, so he was slightly familiar with what took place on this particular stretch of cobblestone. "Stay close and keep your eyes forward at all times . . . all of you." He nudges his wife, who is peeking around the corner to spy on a beautiful woman, scandalously dressed, with a prominent Adam's apple.

The entrance of the eatery is two neatly painted, glass-paneled doors, with the word EGGS written at the top of each. Only the left-hand door is accessible; the right is locked in place.

Inside, the belly of the restaurant is long and narrow, only wide enough for counter seating and four small square tables aligned with the large picture windows. The tables are already occupied by a group of Marines. Judging by their macho mannerisms, freshly shaved heads, and matching USMC tattoos, they must be on leave shortly after boot camp. Just as Mary and the group enters, all but one table of soldiers clears out as if orders were given to do so.

The counter is long enough to accommodate eleven red stools, seven in a row of which are empty—plenty for their group of six. But the one empty stool isn't enough space between James and the fellow to his left, who smells like fresh, warm sewage. Unappetizing, to say the least. He doesn't look like a homeless man at first glance: his suit is worn, but no more than the average Joe with a few years in. After James takes a second look, he sees a deep impression around the ring finger on the man's left hand where a wedding band used to be—the mark of a married man gone astray, or at least one with a sad story to tell.

Everyone can almost hear Gayle salivating while they look at menus over the hiss of burgers being prepared under hubcaps on a nearby grill. "That's so incredibly cool! This is my kind of place," Gayle says, ecstatic about the finishing touches on her birthday extravaganza.

Shirley, however, seems repulsed. She voices her concern, saying, "Why must you cook them under a hubcap?"

"Seals in the flavor and keeps them good and juicy," the cook replies with intent to ease her fears. "I assure you, ma'am, these caps have never been used for any other purpose than on dis grill."

Unable to get past the quirky use of car parts, Shirley is the only one to order a chicken-fried steak and eggs. At the last minute, James changes his order to biscuits and gravy, feeling uneasy and unsure if he can stomach very much as long as the man nearby continues to sit anywhere within smelling distance.

As they wait for their orders, they catch a phrase or two of the Marines' comments on their costumes and the fact that the ladies out tonight are as savory as the food they just ate. One in particular has an eye for Gayle and her bare shoulders. Mary is glad to be wearing a more conservative outfit when she hears some of the choice words used in reference to Gayle and her attention-getting dress.

Once their food arrives, they focus on enjoying the meal and each other's company. It isn't until they get up to leave that a real problem becomes apparent.

It starts when Bobby heads to the bathroom to wash the bird droppings off his hat. He'd completely forgotten about the mess until one of the Marines asked if that was part of the costume.

"I'll meet you guys outside in a minute," Bobby says to Mary.

Gayle is next to get up. As she passes the table where her Marine admirer is sitting, he reaches out and grabs her by the arm.

"Hey, there, little doll," the soldier says, detaining her at his table. "How's about sharing your name with me and my buddies here?"

"Please take your hands off my future wife," Chick says, vibrating, not out of fear, but out of the rush of adrenaline he gets from placing his fingertips on the handle of a switchblade knife he keeps at the ready in his back pocket. Marine or not, this guy doesn't realize that Chick knows his way around a street fight—the kind they don't prepare you for in any boot camp.

Chick's loud proclamation doesn't just take the Marine and his buddies by surprise—Gayle's parents and everyone else in the diner are stunned into silence. Before the moment passes, Chick, still in the grips of his hormone-induced bravery, takes a knee.

"I haven't asked your parents' permission yet, and I don't have a ring," Chick tells Gayle, "but I have to know . . . if I came to you with both of those, would you consider becoming my wife?"

Before Gayle can take her hand away from her mouth to answer, everyone's attention is suddenly drawn to the stinky man at the counter, who loudly clears his throat, reaches into his pocket, and pulls out a beautiful matching his-and-hers set of diamond-clad wedding bands. He hands the rings to James, who is too bewildered to do anything except accept.

"She's been gone a year now from the cancer," the man mumbles. His words are slurred, and add to the stench in his vicinity. "I think it's time I let these go. I hope these rings will bring them the happy times that I shared with my Bernadette." Without another word, he stumbles out of the diner and into the street.

After a moment of awkward silence that stretches in the ring of the exit's bell, the room's attention is back on Gayle, who is searching her father's face for permission. James's eyes meet Shirley's. His face softens, and he hands the rings to Chick, who is patiently waiting, one knee still to the floor.

"Yes! The answer is yes!" Gayle announces, flinging her arms open and folding Chick into her embrace. She holds on as Chick rises to his feet and lifts her off the floor. Everyone is caught up in the moment, including the nervy Marine, who offers up a handshake to congratulate Chick on his engagement.

"We should celebrate!" shouts the cook through a round of applause. "Pie à la Mode on the house!"

As some diners cheer at this, James places his hand on the scruff of Chick's neck. "Son, I hope you didn't expect to get any sleep tonight, because you and I need to have a little chat."

"Yes, sir," Chick replies, swallowing hard enough to completely dry out his mouth.

Shirley, on the other hand, gives him a big hug. "I hope you know what you're getting yourself into!"

"Debt, I imagine," Chick replies without thinking.

"Exactly," Shirley says, a little too seriously.

"I wouldn't have believed it if I hadn't seen it with my own eyes!" Mary says, hugging Gayle so tightly that her eyes begin to bulge. "I'm so very happy for you!" She lets go just before Gayle runs out of air.

"Are you?" Gayle asks. "Or are you just saying that, but really thinking it's a mistake?"

Mary wilts. "I've always known you aren't interested in the same pursuits I am, but that doesn't make your path any less noble. You and Chick are good people, and I think together you have a chance at something very special. Look at your parents, for example—they got married fairly young and they're doing just fine." She directs Gayle's attention to Shirley and James, who are holding hands as they present their concerns to Chick.

Bobby returns with a freshly washed hat in his hands. "Did I miss something?"

Gayle rolls her eyes and joins her new fiancé, who looks like he could use her support.

"Have you been in the bathroom all this time?" Mary says in disbelief. "You only missed a pivotal moment in Gayle's life! It was the most incredible thing that I have ever witnessed. Chick asked her to marry him, right after he almost got into a fight with that tableful of Marines."

"And then what happened?" Bobby asks, intrigued.

"Just eat your pie and I'll tell you about it," Mary says, exasperated. Disgusted with him for missing such an exciting part of the evening over a silly hat, she hands him a skinny slice of apple pie with a melting scoop of vanilla on top,

Bobby sits quietly eating his pie and filling up on all the details of the few minutes he was missing in action. He revels in her excitement.

". . . and that's when the cook gave us the pie," Mary finishes, and takes a bite out of her own slice. "On her birthday, no less," she mumbles through the pie, causing a crumb to tumble onto her chin.

"Technically it's after midnight," says Bobby, trying to dilute the potency of the act.

In fact, Bobby had witnessed everything, starting with Chick reaching for his knife. Bobby was ready to come out and use his tackling skills to help Chick in the fight—until he saw Chick get on his knee to propose. It knocked the wind out of him—the look on Mary's face, and knowing there wasn't any way for him to possibly top this . . . ever. If there is one thing Bobby knows about females, it is how hard they are to impress. It is difficult to have Vinny as a rival, but this is an obstacle that can't be overcome. How is he supposed to sweep her off her feet when she will always be comparing his efforts to Chick's spontaneous proposal? He decides that if she thinks he hadn't seen it for himself, she can never accuse him of trying to replicate any part of it.

Mary's retelling of it is hurried, and in no way as romantic as it actually was. But it is getting late, and they all need to get their rest. As they walk past Lafitte's, they hear a piano playing inside, some old bluesy number, sparking a sing-a-long with several drunken voices working in dissonant unison, surprisingly melodious but otherwise unintelligible. James hums along and offers to give Shirley a twirl or two as they walk by. Chick and Gayle are directly behind them, arm-in-arm. Bobby takes the opportunity to hold Mary's hand.

She allows him to, but this time completely sober, coming off the high of the night and beginning to feel guilty and selfish for her actions—not only has she accepted his attention, but she actively sought it out, against her own good judgment. If she were to witness someone else acting in such a way, she would try and convict them of low moral fiber.

Out of the corner of her eye, she sees a large shadow looming near the bar beneath the streetlamp. When she turns to see what it is, it is gone.

Might be haunted by Lafitte's ghost after all.

She shrugs, and continues her stroll with Bobby.

As they approach the hotel, the guys visit the cars to retrieve all the overnight bags. Unfortunately, everyone is too tired to appreciate the peaceful courtyard as they breeze through. Yawns and the jingling of keys echo in the corridor, the air noticeably still and quiet. The silence is almost spine-tingling, considering the usual background cacophony of crickets, frogs, and other night-loving creatures. It is like they are somehow scared into silence. The couples are divided, heading to the separate rooms that James has made sure are a few doors apart, to deter any teenage shenanigans. In light of the engagement, James decides he will set the cot up in front of the door, and let the boys have the beds to themselves. It isn't only Chick that James doesn't trust—waiting for the promise of marriage is usually the only thing that prevents girls letting go of their virginity. James is determined that Chick will make good on that promise before his daughter let go of hers prematurely.

As soon as Shirley opens the door, the girls push their way into the room and slam the door shut, as if waiting one more second would have allowed an unseen force to overtake them. The French Quarter, like all old places, is known to have mystical entities that somehow lose their way to another plane and decide to dwell here amongst the living. It isn't until you experience something out of the ordinary—even if it's only a feeling—that you pay them any mind.

Gayle claims a bed to share with her mother and rushes to take off the smeared makeup she so painstakingly applied at the start of the adventure. For the first time in a long while, Mary collapses and goes to sleep to the sound of the faucet running, fully clothed and not having brushed her teeth. She does not even hear James knock to deliver the bags.

Saturday
November 1, 1958

"**G**ood morning!" Shirley sings, having already showered and dressed.

"Everything is bright ... *too* bright," Gayle complains after attempting to open her eyes.

"Loud ... too loud," Mary says in a whisper, holding her pounding head in her hands, looking quite similar to Gayle, who is now sitting at the edge of her bed begging for aspirin.

"If I didn't know any better, I would think you two had a hangover," Shirley says, searching in her cosmetic case and coming up empty. "I may have packed it in your father's bag. I'll go see if he has any in his shaving kit. Go ahead and start getting dressed for breakfast, or we'll be pressed for time." She opens the door, letting in rays of daylight that seem to burn the girls, as if they have become vampires overnight.

Feeling ebbing relief after Shirley shuts the door, Mary calls dibs on the bathroom in an attempt to cleanse away the grime from her teeth, her body, and her mind.

As the showerhead spits in her face, Mary reviews her participation in the previous night's affairs. Today is another chance to redeem herself—even though it will not absolve her of her shortcomings thus far. Before she and Gayle met the boys at the bus station, Mary had always considered Gayle the risk-taker and herself beyond reproach. These last two months—has it really only been two months?—have forced her to test those theories. The result? Gayle has emerged the victor.

Panic sets in, along with an onslaught of questions and doubts that line up to assault her.

Why have my body and my mind forsaken me?
Why am I suddenly so jealous?
I don't want to get married . . . do I?
What about school and all my plans?

Realizing that in all her confusion she has forgotten to breathe, Mary begins to gargle and choke on the water. She has long since finished showering but has simply been stalling to think in private. It doesn't take long for her to dry off, slip into her clothes, and throw her hair into a sleek ponytail. Taking one last look in the mirror, Mary feels like she wants to reach out and shake some sense into her reflection, to regain the sanity she knew before puberty and boys came along wreaking havoc in her life.

Shirley knocks on the bathroom door. "Mary, honey, I have some Alka-Seltzer for you out here. James went to the store. It seems the boys woke up with the same symptoms. I told you guys that hamburgers cooked with car parts was a bad idea, but of course no one listens to me."

Mary opens the door to find Shirley plopping two tablets into a glass of water, which she hands to Mary.

"Yeah, well, you sure got the last laugh this time, Mom," Gayle says, cracking a smile in Mary's direction as she drinks the fizzy concoction.

Mary can't help but laugh, getting the last of the Alka-Seltzer up her nose, where it burns like hell. But it's worth it, because it does wonders for her head and her sour stomach in just a matter of minutes—and clears her sinuses, too.

"Who said girls take longer than boys to get ready?" Gayle says, as they wander around the hotel surveying the layout.

Mary reads from a brochure she plucked from a wire stand when exploring the lobby. "I hadn't realized that this hotel is a grouping of Creole cottages from the eighteenth century."

Gayle rolls her eyes. "Thanks for the history lesson, Professor Poche."

"The boys are ready," Shirley says. "They're just having a bit of a discussion. As soon as they're done, we will have breakfast and check out with plenty of time to meet for the one o'clock tour . . . I hope," Shirley adds, looking to her watch for reference.

"So, you're saying we *won't* go blind if we do that . . . Are you sure?" Bobby asks after overhearing a conversation meant for Chick (accidentally on purpose) from the bathroom.

"Son, I believe that fornication is much worse than whatever insignificant damage you could possibly do by yourself. Besides, if that were the case, we would all be blind."

James wonders how he could have possibly gotten so off track as he continues to delicately explain how important it is to respect a woman's virtue, and how waiting until the wedding night will benefit both Chick and Gayle in countless ways.

"So, let me get this straight . . . If we wait until we're married, she's less likely to cheat on me because she won't know what she's missing?" Chick says in open contemplation, never having heard this theory before.

"Yes. If you don't wait, and something happens and you don't get married, then she will be stained. If you love her, you won't let that happen," James states, going back over the subject with cement.

"Sir, I love your daughter and I am willing to wait, if that's what you wish. One day I will be a dad myself, so I can understand where you're coming from." Chick hopes this eases his future father-in-law's mind—and puts an end to this uncomfortable torture.

"Thanks for that. Her mother and I will sleep much better now." James is jolted back to the present by glancing at the clock on the bedside table. "Oh geez, look at the time! The girls are waiting for us."

Gathering their few belongings, they file out the door and politely pass a maid there to clean the room.

"We should go back to the diner from last night," Gayle suggests to the group as the boys join them.

Shirley quickly shuts her down. "I don't think we have enough Alka-Seltzer to go around again!"

"I had forgotten about that already," Gayle says, disappointed, not wanting to admit they had been drinking. She comes up with a new plan post-haste. "Mary, what about the place that smelled so heavenly when we came here with Vinny? Isn't that somewhere nearby?"

"Oh, you're talking about the place with the beignets . . . Café Du Monde. It's near the river in the French Quarter. I bet I can find it on the map," she says, touching James on the shoulder so that he will allow her to take a look. Mary unfolds the map and finds the café's location easily. "Keep going straight, then hang a right on Decatur. It's quite a walk, but if we hurry, it can be done." She refolds the map and hands it back to James.

He is astounded that she is able to fold it back without any trouble. It had taken him twenty minutes just to fold it back to a rectangle, and even then, it wasn't in its original configuration.

"Last one there has to pay!" Gayle challenges, and starts running, trying to make up for the time they lost waiting on the guys while they had their "discussion." No one else runs, but they do pick up the pace quite a bit. When Gayle realizes that she has no real competition, she slows to a skip.

"Don't go too far!" Shirley calls after Gayle, who pays no attention. Shirley strains to see past the other pedestrians to make sure Gayle is still in sight, even putting herself in danger by stepping into the street to do so. This is born from an age-old misconception amongst mothers that as long as they can "lay eyes" on their offspring, no harm will befall them. Chick recognizes Shirley is sincerely distressed and decides to intervene. He fashions his hand to his mouth in some unusual configuration and lets out a piercing whistle loud enough to get everyone's attention—including Gayle, who stops in her tracks to see why he has summoned her. Shirley is both jealous and impressed with Chick's uncanny ability to easily do what she had always been unable to: control her daughter.

"Must be a mating call," Bobby whispers only loud enough for Mary's ears. She smiles at him and begins to skip to meet up with her friend. Bobby wishes not only that he could recreate Chick's whistle, but that it would also somehow have the same effect on Mary.

Walking at a brisk pace, they complete the six blocks in record pedestrian time, turning the corner at the French Market. The sweet aroma of fresh pastries and coffee lures them the rest of the way. Breakfast rush has just ended and the Café Du Monde actually has a couple of tables open and no line, so they snag a table near the front of the awning that gives them a good view of all the passers-by. Mary points out the mule-drawn carriages across the street waiting to take on passengers. During their conversation, pigeons happily dodge in and out of the outdoor seating area, extending their services by cleaning up any meal mishaps that occur.

The food wishes are fulfilled in a matter of minutes, as the server provides plates graced with beignets: piping hot golden-brown pillows of deep-fried dough squares, blanketed in mounds of confectioner's sugar. Although they agree on what to eat, not many have the same idea for a beverage, so their table is crowded with black coffees, café au lait, milk, water, and freshly squeezed orange juice. Every bite gets devoured, not even a crumb left for the birds, only wispy remnants of powdered sugar.

James signals the waiter for the check; after all, he was the last one to arrive on the premises.

"Honestly, if I had one more bite, I would pop," Shirley says, piling up the plates to make them ready for pickup.

"You're a lightweight, Mom," Gayle says. As if to prove her point, she licks her finger and takes a final swipe at the last of her sugar before the plate is taken away.

James pays the bill, and Chick contributes by tipping the server for his fast and genial service. A savvy street performer sets up to play his trumpet, sounding so jazzy and smooth, it is a shame they cannot stay any longer to listen. Chick throws several coins in the musician's case on the way out in appreciation for the added ambience.

Passing through Jackson Square is a delight. Artisans of all kinds turn out to flaunt their wares, some in the throes of creativity right in front of them. Continuing on their way to the Voodoo shop, they encounter a small group of Marines from last night, arms draping over one another, more inebriated than they had last seen them, singing a Dale Evans number.

"Happy trails to you, until we meet again," is all they manage before stopping to assist one of their buddies who has an unpleasant reaction to the song.

Mary, unable to look away, watches as he violently ejects bursts of clear liquid onto the sidewalk, thinking that she never wants to drink enough to have that experience. The incident is across the street, yet the fumes of alcohol and rancid bile travel far enough to assault her nose, igniting her gag reflex. Luckily, she enjoyed her breakfast way too much to let it go without a fight. She holds her nose until she is far enough away to safely inhale.

"That was a perfect example of what drinking can lead to. It's a shame when people do that to themselves," Shirley says, using the opportunity to teach the young and impressionable.

Just then they are startled by a high-pitched barking from a balcony up above. The small dog yaps at the potential trespassers passing beneath his porch.

"You better hurry, Bobby! You do have a recent history of the animal kingdom leaving their mark on you," Mary says, playfully pushing him forward.

"Hardy, har, har." Bobby musters a fake laugh at his own expense, but secretly he is glad to be out from under the remote possibility that it could have happened again.

When they arrive at the Voodoo shop, it seems less spooky in the light of day. Mr. Master, the leader of last night's tour, is dressed like a funeral director this morning, with a top hat in the crook of his arm; he is frowning down upon a clipboard full of paperwork. He looks up as they approach and his face brightens.

"There you are! Did you have a good night's sleep, birthday girl?" he asks, directing his attention to Gayle, who is at the forefront as always.

"Sleep wasn't the best thing that happened after we left. We got engaged last night!" she replies, wrapping her arms around Chick, who looks to her parents for a reaction; James and Shirley seem more comfortable with the idea than they were previously. Chick looks at Gayle's naked ring finger and remembers he had better remedy that soon.

"Congratulations! How fortunate for these lovebirds to have so much to celebrate—and to have me as your private personal guide today!" he says energetically.

"We didn't schedule a private tour, did we?" Chick asks, uneasily imagining the horrendous upcharge for the switch.

"It's to make up for the snafu. We found that the original reservation issue was our mistake, and we wanted to make it up to you somehow. Now, are we ready to check out the cities of the dead?" Mr. Master asks, happily leading the group to a Desert Sand 1955 station wagon.

Gayle is unimpressed with the body style of the vehicle, but when she hears that sexy Hemi spark up under the hood, she knows it has to be a DeSoto Firedome, earning her respect. Unfortunately, the drive to St. Louis Cemetery is fraught with too many turns and stop signs to pick up any real speed. "We never even opened her up," Gayle complains, walking away from the DeSoto.

Mary places her hand on one of the white columns that flank a decorative ironwork cemetery gate, examining the iron cross above it as she listens to the guide introduce them to the new location. "The dead often refuse to stay in the ground here," he remarks.

"The water table is too high," she utters, without meaning to ruin his punchline.

"That's correct. That is why we bury our dead in these above-ground structures," Mr. Master continues, explaining the history of St. Louis Cemetery No. 1, the first of three.

They meander through rows and rows of both plain and ornate crypts, forming a small community much like a living one. On one side, there is a healthy, well-kept vault, and on the other, a dilapidated tomb with crumbling corners. Mary notices brightly colored plastic flowers nested inside brass urn-ish vases on the nicer crypts, while many of the moldy vaults are lined with partially burned votive candles where visitors must gather often to commune with loss and memories. Faced with her swirling thoughts of mortality, Mary loses focus on the tour—until their guide speaks a familiar last name.

"The famous resting place of Marie Laveau," he announces, describing her life as a premier Voodoo priestess in the New Orleans area, and how she became the "Queen of Voodoo," and held that title long after she expired. During the intricate story, there is mention of a second Marie, rumored to be her illegitimate daughter. "That was how she appeared to have lived such an extraordinarily long time," Mr. Master explains. He reveals secret after secret of the eccentric woman and her controversial history. Once he completes his presentation, he urges everyone in the group to perform a wishing ritual. "You do not have to leave actual marks on the tomb for the wish to be granted," he says, making three simple X marks on the tomb with his finger and a bit of red brick dust.

Unfortunately, many people had not been made aware of this, judging by the indelible X marks blemishing the tomb's surface. Mary thoughtfully drags her finger through the brick dust and paints her own slow and deliberate set of red marks for her wish.

Mr. Master walks the group over to the next site, a single gray stone chamber less defiled than the others. "Now I will introduce you to another member of Marie's bloodline. This is the only one of her great-great-grandchildren who possessed the same psychic ability as the two wildly popular Maries—yet she did not necessarily enjoy having the gift. She occasionally complained of headaches and suffered distress at some of her visions. Uneasy about profiting from the gift, she often felt compelled to provide her services for little or no money to people who couldn't afford them. Those who knew her, loved her. Mambo Beulah was her title as a Voodoo priestess, but many called her Mama Beulah."

At the gravesite, Mary and Gayle stand in shock, staring unblinkingly at an oblong picture of Beulah—the same woman, down to the very clothing she wore the day of the fair. Below the picture are the beginning and ending dates of her life span.

IN BELOVED MEMORY OF

BEULAH LAVEAU

1898–1955

"Extra creepy with cheese," Gayle whispers slowly. They read the dates over and over—especially that last one, *1955*—as if it were an optical illusion.

Is that possible? She had been dead for three years?
I put my hands in her hands, I felt her skin, her energy.
I heard her speak, she touched my shoulder.
It was real . . . wasn't it?

Mary jumps when Gayle touches her shoulder.

"That date has to be wrong," Gayle tells Mr. Master. "Mary had a reading with Mambo Beulah at a fair just a couple months ago."

Eyebrows tightly knitted, the tour guide says, "Hate to contradict the newly-engaged birthday girl, but that's impossible. Everyone at the shop attended her funeral. Maiden Folse even bid on several of her belongings at auction, including her tarot deck." He pauses to study Mary's awestruck face as she desperately grasps for some logical explanation. "Unless . . ."

"Unless, *what?*" Gayle urges, losing patience with his mysterious showmanship.

"Tell me what happened in as much detail as you remember," Mr. Master replies eagerly. His interest is piqued, envisioning how he may be able to include the girls' story in his tour.

Mary unfolds every detail that she can recall surrounding the encounter, including the part about Maiden Folse being there later in the day. The only thing she leaves out is the actual reading, because she considers it too personal.

Mr. Master nods with perfect understanding, as if any of this could add up and become plausible. "Her spirit may still be attached to the cards. Her deck must have been at that fair. Whatever she told you was of strong importance, either to you or to her. The only thing I really don't get is how Gayle was able to experience it along with you. If nothing else, it's a great ghost story to tell people around a fire."

The sound of percussion and brass playing "Just a Closer Walk with Thee" draws near. The soulful song bellows as their group stands listening, eyes searching, when they spot a procession of people somberly walking into the cemetery carrying a coffin. A minute or two passes before the band enters.

Bobby, surprised by how rude and inconsiderate those people are being and unaware that ceremonies like this are common in the New Orleans culture, tries to impress Mary with his disdain for disrespectful behavior. "What's going on? Why would they make so much noise in a cemetery?"

Mr. Master jumps back into tour-guide mode. "That, my friend, is nearly a daily occurrence here. A prime example of a genuine jazz funeral, folks. They play somber music as they progress to the gravesite, and once they deliver the body and complete the service, they celebrate the person's ascent into Heaven with a joyful parade through the streets."

"Can we get a closer look?" Mary asks, curious about the process.

Bobby flinches, wishing he had kept his big mouth shut. Now he figures she must think of him as being intolerant.

"We have enough time to take a look at the last two statues and a family mausoleum. Then we can join the second line if you'd like," the guide replies, knowing that it is acceptable to join in the revelry behind the band and the family members.

As Mr. Master wraps up the last story of the tour beside the mausoleum of the famous architect Benjamin Latrobe, the music ramps up again, drawing their group's attention. Respectfully, they watch the mourners pass. The band performs a familiar hymn with a bit more bounce than before.

"Turn the body loose, Lawd!" one woman pleads with her hands up to her Savior. "Thank you, Jesus!"

The band transitions into a tune that would make anyone want to shake a leg. At the tail end of the gathering, several men begin dancing to the cheerful music, bouncing black feather-rimmed parasols in the air. Following for only two blocks, long enough to reach the DeSoto station wagon, wears the group out. On the ride back to the shop, Mary thinks about Mardi Gras. If a funeral can be that much fun, she can't even fathom what a party that day must be like.

Exiting the car, the tour guide offers Mary his business card.

MARK MASTERS

PARANORMAL TOUR GUIDE EXTRAORDINAIRE

NEW ORLEANS, LA

He writes his home number on the back, saying, "This is just in case you need to contact me for any more information with regards to your experience with Mambo Beulah."

Mary pockets his card, but decides that what she really wants is to forget the whole Beulah fiasco; it has done nothing but mess with her head, like being reminded of the time you got caught with toilet paper on your shoe.

Down the street on the next block, Chick spies a jewelry store sign and pulls James aside. "How about if we go get the cars," he suggests, "while the girls take a look at the jewelry store for her engagement ring?"

"Yeah, sure. We have a while with nowhere to be. We just need to be home in time to rest up for church."

Bobby, feeling weird about hanging out in a jewelry store with the girls all by himself, follows James and says, "I'll come with you guys if that's all right."

"What's going on over here? No keeping secrets!" Gayle fusses, thinking that she is being left out of something.

"I was arranging a surprise for you, but if you don't want it . . ." Chick trails off, knowing exactly how to make Gayle behave.

"Please, I'll be good." Gayle speaks quietly and childishly, with pretend shyness.

"We're going to pick up the cars," says Chick, "while you go with your mother and Mary to pick out a ring that goes with this one." He pulls out the smaller of the two rings so generously given to them at the diner the night before. "We'll meet you back here."

Gayle's face brightens. She snatches the ring from his hand and runs to her mother, who is waiting to escort the girls to the nearby jewelry store.

The bell on the door tinkles as they enter. The salesman acknowledges them with a smile and a wave as he attends to a svelte woman in an expensive-looking pale green skirt suit.

"I'll be with you shortly," he says to his new prospective customers, then disappears to the back of the store.

While Gayle studies the diamonds behind their glass cases, Mary searches for amethyst jewelry. She knows all there is to know about the purplish gemstone; after all, it *is* her birthstone. Out of all the books she read in the third grade, she most remembers the one on birthstones that told the history behind each month's gem.

Unfortunately, the woman in the suit is inconveniently leaning in front of what Mary is looking for, impeding her view. She attempts to snake around the woman to get a better view into the glass enclosure, when the memory pops into her head that "amethyst" derives from the Greek word *Amethystos*, meaning "not drunken," and that the stone is considered a powerful antidote against drunkenness.

Boy, I could have used one of those yesterday.

At this silly thought, she loses her balance and accidentally knocks into the woman.

"Are you all right?" the woman asks, slightly irritated but still helping Mary to get centered.

Mary knows her face at once. "Hi, Camille. Remember me?" she asks, surprised to see Vinny's friend away from her beauty salon.

Upon recognizing her, Camille becomes nervous, her slender neck craning in pursuit of Vinny. "What are you doing here? Is Vinny back?"

"No, but he does send a letter now and then," Mary fibs, not wanting to sound overly pathetic. "We came to the city to celebrate Gayle's birthday."

This distracts Camille. "She's getting a rock for her birthday?" Camille watches Gayle drool all over the diamond section.

"No, she just got engaged last night! Her fiancé Chick will be here shortly with the car," Mary blabs, to keep Camille from discussing Vinny.

The salesman reappears with a rolled-up paper bag and, without a word, unceremoniously places it on the counter in front of Camille. He removes a loop of keys from his pocket to find the one that will open the display case in front of Gayle.

"Clarence is getting married? That's stupendous," Camille's voice says, but her face is not equally enthused as she watches the man and his keys. She grabs the plain brown bag and shoves it beneath her arm like a clutch purse.

Where is her purse?

"I need to be going," Camille tells Mary, "or I'll be late for my next appointment. But first, show me what you were killing yourself to see." As she looks down at the merchandise, the paper bag makes a crinkly, cracking noise at being strangled in the tight grip of her armpit.

Mary pauses to find the exact one, then squats down low and says, "You see the amethyst set right there, the dainty one in the corner?" She points out a delicate, inexpensive amethyst necklace, ring, and bracelet set.

Camille scoffs at Mary's conservative nature. "Out of everything this store has to offer, you would choose that one?"

Mary shrugs, defending her choice. "Most jewelry seems unnecessary and vulgar to me."

"That may be, but you should at least think about having your ears pierced. It is all the rage right now. I've done three piercings just this week alone," Camille brags as they walk over to Gayle, who finally looks up from her diamond hunt and brightens with recognition at Camille.

Mary pinches her naked earlobe to test its sensitivity to being punctured, suddenly curious about the history behind the strange rite of passage.

Camille gives Gayle a brief, icy hug. "Congratulations, honey! Let me know when you set the date—maybe I can do your hair for the wedding. Now I really have to go or my client will think I forgot about her." Camille practically sprints out of the door as Chick drives up to the curb.

Mary is left feeling strange about Camille's behavior; something is . . . *off* . . . but she can't put her finger on what it is exactly. She stands at the window, curiously watching Camille cross the uneven pavement as fast as a woman in high heels can.

Gayle pulls her away. "I need your help to choose one of these diamond rings I picked out! They are both so beautiful!"

James and Bobby step into the jewelry store first. They spot a section of antique and modern timepieces to keep them occupied. Chick enters last; his attention had also been on the hurried woman in high heels. Mary's curiosity peaks as she tracks the invisible line between them.

How well do they know each other?

"Was that Camille?" Chick asks Mary as he joins the girls and Shirley at the counter.

Mary nods confirmation. She wants to quiz him on the subject, but is stuck trying to hear what Gayle is saying, since she already made her repeat it once.

"... and this one is a half-carat that sparkles like nobody's business," Gayle says, holding up a brilliant-cut solitaire engagement ring.

Mary looks at the two rings Gayle is holding, unable to tell them apart. She studies them like those hidden-object pictures they run in the Sunday paper.

"This one is *my* favorite," Shirley says, but she knows Gayle will not make a decision solely on her advice. In fact, she believes her opinion may sway her daughter in the other direction—that is simply what teenagers are hardwired to do.

"You know your mother is much better at this stuff than I am. Let me see each one of them on your finger next to the band," Mary prompts Gayle, who places one of the rings and then switches for the other. "The second one *is* a better match." Mary winks in Shirley's direction.

"What do *you* think?" Gayle asks, presenting her finger to Chick, who is having a financial discussion with the jeweler.

"Ohhh no! Don't put me in a position that may come back to haunt me later. Choose whichever one your pretty little heart desires— as long as we stay on *this* side of the case," he says, making sure Gayle sees the price-point within his reach.

"I guess I will go with this one," Gayle says, finally settling on one of the rings.

Mary checks Shirley's reaction to see that Gayle has chosen the one her mother prefers.

"I can go ahead and include the future fusing of the rings at no extra charge, if you want to go ahead and close this deal today," the jeweler says, in hopes that Chick will give in.

Chick sees that Gayle is completely mesmerized by the new ring. "Are you sure you'll be proud to show that thing off when you tell people you're going to be my wife?" he asks, picking up a pen to fill out the paperwork.

"Not as proud as I will be to *be* your wife," Gayle responds ardently.

Mary lowers her head, not sure if jealousy or blood sugar levels are causing her gag reflex to act up. To distract herself, she walks over to the window to investigate a street performer who has set up on the other side of the street, a young Negro boy, clearly younger than her, playing a drum—except it isn't. It is some kind of bucket that he cleverly makes sound as if it were a whole set of studio-quality drums. Mary feels Bobby's presence behind her; they both face the window, enjoying the little boy's impromptu performance. "Now how can they say that someone as ingenious as that little boy doesn't deserve the best education we have to offer because of his skin color? He could grow up to be . . ."

"Anything," Bobby says in agreement with her sentiment.

"I read an article about *Brown v. Board of Education*. Nothing has changed!" Mary says, sifting for an answer to the problem. " 'With all deliberate speed,' my foot. What do you think will become of him if he doesn't stay in school? You know they won't enforce mandatory schooling for kids like him."

"The street will eat him up and spit him out. And society will blame him every step of the way," Bobby replies—giving her an answer, but not the one she wants to hear.

"How are we supposed to believe that we can bring about change when *laws* can't even do it?" she says, delving into what is quickly becoming a full-blown funk.

"Why do you do this to yourself?" Bobby places his hands on her shoulders, gently shaking her from behind.

"Do what?"

"Take the world's issues and place them on your shoulders as if you were the cause of it all. It isn't your job to fix everything," he says, hoping to remove the burden.

"If not me, if not you—tell me who, then? Tell me how I'm supposed to be a part of the world and do nothing to make it better." Mary watches a mother instinctively slap the hand of a curly-headed toddler who is reaching for a piece of jagged glass on the sidewalk, resulting in a subsequent wail. The mother picks up her little girl and tries to make amends, patting her ruffle-covered bottom.

"You're going to make me depressed if you don't stop it," Bobby says, pretending to blow his brains out with a mimed finger-gun.

"You're smart, aren't you?" she says, wanting to engage him further.

"Yeah, I guess . . . ?"

"Do you ever wish you weren't? Wouldn't it be easier to not know any better? I'm intelligent, but all it's gotten me so far is a headache." She rakes her hands through her hair, removing her ponytail out of frustration.

"Boy, you are in some kinda mood today. What has gotten into you?" Bobby shakes his head, unable to grasp the enormity of the things soaring through her mind.

"Come on, you two! It's time to hit the road," says James, making them aware that their party is on the move. Gayle is already outside, presenting her bejeweled finger to anyone who looks her way.

"That might not be the safest thing to do, darlin," Chick says, ushering her into the car.

As Mary exits the shop and takes a step into the car, her eye is drawn to the last spot she saw Camille, when a thought hits her like a ton of bricks.

If she was going to work, why was she going the wrong way?

"I ordered no cheese with extra pickles, and he gave me this," Mary complains to Bobby. She notices that Chick is sitting alone at his table. Seeing her opportunity, she leaves with a tray full of food, letting Bobby stay at the counter to straighten out her order.

"How long have you known Camille?" she asks Chick, plopping the tray in front of him and sitting down.

Chick glances out the window at Gayle, who is busy outside in the Dairy Queen parking lot flaunting her wares to a group of ladies her parents happen to know; the ladies are headed back to Houma after a quilting seminar. Chick laughs at the women, who are acting like they have never seen a ring before.

"You can't know Vinny for very long without meeting Camille," Chick tells Mary. "She's like family . . . or something." He takes a huge bite of his hamburger.

"Did you ever date her? . . . Did Vinny?" She tries to keep her voice down as James passes on his way back from the restroom.

"No, not that I'm aware of. Vinny has never led me to believe that they've been anything more than close friends. He doesn't have any blood around, so he chooses his circle carefully. We are all he has. Why are you so worried about her, anyway?" He hefts the ketchup bottle, ready to drown his fries.

"I'm not sure yet." Mary bites her lip. "Something doesn't seem right about her. I have a feeling she's hiding something. She may be in some kind of trouble—or worse, maybe *Vinny* is in trouble."

"He would get word to us if that were true," Chick says, mopping up his chin with a paper napkin.

"I hope you're right."

Bobby arrives with a tray of the corrected food items. "Right about what?"

"Right about you not forgetting my extra pickles," she says, not wanting anyone else to know her business.

"Just as you ordered. I watched them make it," Bobby says, and takes a sip of his soda.

"We won't get home till midnight at this rate," says Chick. He gets up to retrieve Gayle from her small fan club outside.

Friday
November 21, 1958

It is their last violin practice before Thanksgiving break. Bobby looms behind Mary, pacing back and forth like a human metronome. She performs her warm-up scales with surprising accuracy. Unable to resist the vulnerable angle of her head, and overcome by the pheromones in the air, he stops his pacing and hungrily leans in to kiss her neck.

Mary pulls away, breaking off her final scale, startled by his unexpected advance. "What was that?" She finds herself both unnerved and excited by the attempt.

Bobby feels his cheeks grow hot. "I'm sorry . . . it's just that ever since you kissed me that night in New Orleans, I can't be in a room with you without thinking about it and wanting it to happen again . . . sober."

"That was my fault. I shouldn't have done that. I've tried to walk a line of friendship with you, but I mistakenly crossed it that night. Let's try to forget it, Bobby."

"Don't you like me—even just a little?"

"Of course I like you. Too much for my own good. In fact, I have found it to be increasingly harder to be around you lately." She holds on to her necklace out of guilt, the violin's neck still cradled in her other hand.

"Forget Vinny! If you like me, why don't you go out with me? Give me a chance to show you how I feel about you. You're too young to tie yourself down to one person—especially when that person isn't me."

Conflict claws at Mary's insides. "I don't know how to say that in a letter to Vinny and not be there to explain. I don't want to hurt him."

"Just let him know you need space and the opportunity to have choices. It's not like he asked you to marry him or anything," Bobby says, invoking the ultimate right of dibs: no ring, no thing.

"Actually . . . he did."

"Wh-when . . . what did you say?" Bobby stammers, suddenly sweating bullets in a perfectly cool room. He staggers a bit, falling onto the piano bench, his legs refusing to work.

"Not long after we met. I didn't really give him an answer. He's been very patient with me," Mary says, hearing absurdity in her own words.

"Well, I need to know where you stand. If you're in love with him, then stop giving me so much hope. The past few weeks I have fallen deeper than ever for you, Mary. This isn't just some infatuation. If I go much further and find out you don't want me, I think I'll . . . I'll . . . I don't know what."

Mary looks down. "I have to admit I feel conflicted. I'm not sure I know what love is. I know I care about Vinny . . . but I care for you, too."

"Define 'care.' " Bobby puts his head in his hands and mumbles, "Because I go to sleep with your name on my lips and I wake up missing you."

"Well . . . I can't imagine not having you in my life," Mary says, but she knows her answer is disproportionate.

"Do you really think he will stand for our friendship once he knows we're attracted to each other?"

This pokes holes in her bubble of denial. "No . . . I guess not."

"You have to tell him," Bobby says, even though he knows his demand may not land the way he wants it to.

"I'll tell him. But I can't just do it in a letter—it wouldn't be right. I'll tell him when he gets back around Christmas." Her throat tightens as she grows more upset at the thought.

"What do we do till then? I want you to wear my jacket. I want you to be my girl."

"I know . . . but you have to let me do this honorably or I'll never forgive myself." She brushes a tear away.

"I'd never leave your side the way he did—not unless you begged me to, and maybe not even then," Bobby says, opening and closing his fists.

Bobby's mom enters the room. "Begged you to do what?" she asks, putting down a tray of sandwiches.

"To play a duet, Mrs. Vicknair," Mary says quickly, then clears her throat.

Brenda clasps her hands together over her heart. "I think a duet is a marvelous idea!"

"Me, too," Bobby agrees. Still sitting at the piano, he places his fingers on its keys and plays the first few notes of "All I Have to Do Is Dream."

Thursday
November 27, 1958

"They must be in an awful bind to call for a plumber on Thanksgiving," Charlie says, basting the turkey, "and for Pa to need Mama's help! He's never done that before."

"Will you play us a song after we eat dinner?" Sarah asks Mary.

Mary is preoccupied, perturbed that her mother can't remember to store brown sugar with a marshmallow or two. Now she has to use a fork to stab the clumps of brown sugar needed to make the candied yams. At last, she looks up at her sister's question. "I guess. I do need the practice. I'm going to be playing a medley in the Christmas recital at school."

"There's something on the porch with your name on it, Mary!" Jason hollers from the front room, interrupting their conversation.

The mail doesn't run today, does it?

"Bring it to me, please," she calls back, continuing her task. "It's probably just the sewing patterns I ordered."

"I don't think so, Mary. You really need to come and see it first," Jason shouts insistently. "You'd better hurry, too!"

She drops the fork impatiently. "Oh, for crying out loud!" she says, washing her hands at the sink and drying them vigorously on her apron. "Charlie, can you finish gathering ingredients while I go see what's so important?" She hands him the recipe card and goes to see what Jason's fuss is all about.

When she gets to the front room, she sees a huge arrangement of autumn flowers—not unlike the one she admired in Bobby's foyer—peeking at her from the other side of the screen door.

"What in the world . . . ?" Mary utters. She slowly opens the door and looks around, as if it might be part of a trick, before reaching for the card that, sure enough, displays her name written in elegant calligraphy on the envelope. The message inside says *Go look on the back porch.* She turns the card over, looking for any clue of the sender. She hears running and giggles from inside the house and calls, "What's going on, you guys?" and takes one more look around before leaving the flowers and going through the house to the back porch, where she sees her dad's truck pulling up to the porch with a brand-new washing machine.

"What is going on? How did you get that?" Mary asks. She knows that her father saves all year long just to afford the essentials. Their old washer may be a pain to run, but it isn't dead yet.

Vivian steps out of the truck, excited and practically breathless. "It's a Kenmore Turbo-Matic. Must be a gift from Vinny. We got a call saying that the delivery guy caught a flat on the way to the house. Pa made the guy check the recipient three times to make sure there was no mistake. He didn't want to spoil the surprise for everyone, so he didn't even tell me until we left the house."

"Why did you put the flowers on the front porch?" Mary asks, confounded.

"What flowers? I don't know anything about any flowers," Vivian says, flipping through the new machine's owner's manual.

Margene tugs on Mary's apron. "I think you should get em inside before they get full of buggies."

"It's too big for the table! We won't have room to eat," Mary says, stepping back into the house, intending to find the perfect spot for the flower arrangement before retrieving it. "The console TV should be big enough to hold it. What do you think, Margene-the-jumping-bean?" she asks, ruffling the hair of the precocious four-year-old.

Margene looks up at Mary, licking the remnants of the milk mustache she had created moments before, and points at the screen door.

Mary's eyes follow the path of her sister's small finger to the porch where, while she was gone, her flower arrangement had grown a pair of legs—male legs.

"Who goes there? Show yourself or taste my lead!" Mary says apprehensively, having heard that line on some Western show the boys watch incessantly.

As she approaches, the screen door creaks slowly open. The flowers lower enough to reveal a mock-worried Vinny.

"Please holster your weapon before someone gets hurt," he says, setting the flowers down to pick her up and give her a proper hello—a kiss that makes Mary tingle to the tips of her toes.

"You don't know how happy I am to have you here!" she says, teary-eyed, not realizing how much she has missed him until now.

"You don't know how happy I am to be here—audience and all," says Vinny; the boys are ogling and making fun of them.

"You need to stop and give us a minute!" Mary yells at them, frustrated at the lack of privacy.

"We can continue later," Vinny whispers in her ear, sending tingles through her body again. "We have the rest of our lives."

Not knowing what to say to this, she leads him in the house where the whole family has gathered to welcome him back from his long absence.

It doesn't take long for Vinny to blend back in as if he never left. He helps Norman connect the new washing machine in place of the old one on the back porch, blowing Vivian's mind with his explanation of how this particular model washes and dries within the same unit. His sultry eyes find Mary at every opportunity.

"No more line drying?" Vivian asks in disbelief.

"Not unless you want to. Go get a load together so we can make sure it does what it says it does." He gives Norman a hearty handshake. "I want to thank you for coming to my aid on such short notice. I'll have that rental truck towed tomorrow."

"No thanks needed. Glad to do it. Now let's go have a drink on the front porch and have us a little pow-wow," Norman says with an undertone of seriousness, rubbing his neck with a handkerchief. He grabs a large glass jar filled with tea that has been steeping in the sun and carries it inside.

"Let me get that for you, Pa," Mary says, collecting two glasses from the kitchen cabinet. "Go relax. I'll bring it out to you."

"Daughter, these old bones thank you kindly." He sets the jar on the counter and heads for his favorite rocking chair on the front porch.

"You are so gorgeous . . ." Vinny says breathily on her neck. "You would look exactly like Liz if your hair was shorter." With that, he follows Norman outside.

Norman waits until he hears the screen door close behind Vinny before he begins to speak.

"I don't know a whole lot about you, boy . . . but I do know that my daughter has taken a liking to you. The thing I don't understand is why you're trying so hard." Norman speaks slow and thoughtful, hardly making eye contact as he leans forward to retrieve a pipe out of the pocket of his overalls. He begins packing it with a wad of tobacco from a worn zippered pouch.

Both men put the discussion on hold as Mary opens the screen door with her back and graciously presents them with large tinkling glasses of rich amber-colored refreshments. She can tell by the abrupt silence and the look on her father's face that he has something on his mind—he wants some time alone with Vinny. "I'll be in the kitchen finishing up if you two need anything," she says, touching Vinny's shoulder. Their eyes meet and Vinny gives her a wink to let her know he's got everything under control.

As soon as he thinks she is out of earshot, Vinny turns to Norman. "Sir, I don't know what I may have done to offend you, but I want you to know it was completely unintentional." With this said, he studies a small amount of undissolved sugar in the bottom of his glass.

"I'm only lettin you know that if you don't have anything to offer my daughter beyond your fancy gifts, then I'm afraid she will lose interest in a jiffy. I didn't raise my young 'uns to be distracted by shiny things, and I want to keep it that-a-way." Norman pauses, striking a match to light his loaded pipe. He puffs on it softly, hollowing his cheeks and filling the air with an unusual fruity aroma. "What I'm tryin to say is that if you're good people, ya don't need to be a show pony to be a part of this family. I want to see more of you and less of your money. It's the only way I'm gonna get a good look at ya."

"I wanted so much to help and show her what a good provider I could be," Vinny says in his own defense. He takes a sip of tea and clicks a piece of ice around on his teeth.

"I know, son, and you do a good job of that. I'm just tryin to give you a heads-up is all. I know my daughter better than you do, and I know that she's lookin past the wrapper. If you don't start showin you got substance, we'll all grow weary of you." He settles back in his chair to enjoy the decadent midday sun and the crystal blue sky with its ever-changing cloud arrangements.

Vinny pauses to chew his ice and measure his response. "I see your point and it has certainly opened my eyes, sir. I guess I've gone about this the wrong way. It's just that I've never had anyone like Mary in my life before. She doesn't ask me for anything and that makes me want to give her everything." He seems almost embarrassed by his honesty.

"We all struggle to find them so-called *real* things in life, son, and we become convinced that money will help us find those things—but in the end it blurs the line between what's real and what isn't. Most people who have money are left wondering if the folks around them are there out of love or if they were lured by the perks." Norman downs half his tea in one big gulp.

"Mary's not like that," Vinny says, slightly irritated and confused by where this conversation is going.

"There is a foolproof bait for every type of fish in the area, sittin in my toolbox. Some are smelly, some make noise, some wriggle, and some are bright and shiny. Every one is different, and every one is effective—if used on the right catch," Norman says, re-lighting his pipe that has gone out for lack of attention.

Vinny swallows, fighting back emotion to maintain his cool composure. "I know you're worried about her being young and impressionable. I just want you to know you did a good job raising her, because so far, instead of me changing her, she is changing me. I want to be whatever it is she needs me to be."

"I'm just thinkin she needs you to be strong," Norman says casually between puffs.

"I'm strong as an ox," Vinny says, muscles taut.

"Strong enough to wait?" Norman finally makes full eye contact, deflating Vinny's pose and humbling the young man to the point he has to look away.

"I'll try my best to do right by her," Vinny says with conviction.

"Even if it means letting her go? Because she will, you know."

"Will what?"

"Go. She'll go and she'll spread her wings. I love her enough to want that to happen. Do you?"

"If it comes to that," Vinny replies with a tinge of defiance.

"It will. We both know she is meant for bigger and better things than she can get around here. Until you and I see eye-to-eye on that point"–Norman says these next words powerfully, without raising his voice–"I can't give you permission to marry her."

Before Vinny has a chance to say anything further, Jenny bursts through the screen door. "Food's ready! Ma hid the paper . . . says you can't have it till after we eat," she tells her father with a sly smile–she knows he feels naked at the table without it.

Norman rises and faces Vinny. "I'm glad you're back with us today. Let's get some grub and we will talk more later." He claps Vinny on the back, reassuring him that the subject is not completely closed.

After dinner, Mary washes the dishes as she enjoys the antics of her younger sisters all vying for Vinny's attention, including the smallest of the clan.

"My, aren't you growing fast, little Barbara." Vinny lifts her into his lap as she begins giving him a lecture in a language only she understands, having mastered only two intelligible words, "mine" and "no."

Mary smiles at them, studying his apparent aptitude with children. She tickles herself remembering that Chick once told her that Vinny had a knack with females of all ages, a theory that so far has held strong.

At the conclusion of her task, she dries her hands and takes Barbara from Vinny.

"It's time for your nap, little lady," Mary says, kissing Barbara on the cheek. The toddler lets out a yawn.

"Meet me on the porch," Vinny says quietly, knowing that they will have it all to themselves, considering most of the house was taking advantage of Brandon and Barbara's naptime.

"Finally some time alone," Mary says a few minutes later. She takes a seat next to Vinny on the steps with two fresh glasses of tea, preparing to let him down easy.

He removes the glasses from her hands and quickly sets them down to pull her to him. Mary stiffens, not sure what to do. He inhales her natural fragrance as he holds her close.

"I don't have the words to tell you how much I've missed you," he says, his voice muffled in the thick strands of her hair.

A wave of guilt washes over her for even thinking that this man wasn't right for her. He certainly *feels* right. Her body relaxes into his embrace. With each soft kiss, wordlessly they melt together, there on the steps in the afternoon sun. Mary quickly forgets whatever it was she was supposed to say.

Later, startled by the creaking of the screen door, the two of them straighten themselves as Norman emerges for his early evening smoke.

"Can I go to New Orleans tomorrow with Vinny? I've really been thinking of having Camille cut my hair," she asks her father, holding the ends of her long locks.

Vinny shrugs at Norman to let him know he is clueless about this out-of-the-blue request.

"I suppose you are old enough to make those kinds of decisions on your own," Norman replies, knowing full well the pain he will endure watching his eldest daughter become a woman.

"You still gonna play me a song, Mary?" Sarah's small voice asks from behind the mesh of the screen door.

She looks to Vinny. "Do you mind?"

"I forgot you were learning to play the violin." Vinny helps her to her feet. "I would love to hear what you've learned."

"Hey, everybody, Mary's gonna play a song!" Jenny announces cheerfully.

Mary dashes to her room to find the sheet music and her violin case, experiencing the onslaught of a group of butterflies taking up residence in her belly.

How am I going to perform in front of the school
if I can't even hold it together in front of people who
like me?

"Will you hold my pages for me?" she asks Sarah, who proudly accepts the job of a makeshift music stand.

The children settle on the floor of the porch, near Vinny and Vivian on the swing and Norman in the rocking chair, all arranged for the special performance.

Mary nervously plucks the strings to ensure that they are in tune.

"I thought you were supposed to use the stick thing to play," fusses Jenny, who can't help critiquing the performance before it even starts.

"She's just warming up," Vinny says, giving Mary a comforting nod.

Her first note comes out a bit screechy. "Sorry, I'm a little nervous." She applies more rosin to her bow, clears her throat, and takes a cleansing breath. Starting again from the beginning, she plays a flawless rendition of "The Dreidel Song."

The trickled clapping makes her realize that no one on this porch knows the song and can't appreciate the performance for what it is worth. She decides to play another more familiar tune.

" 'Jingle Bells'!" Margene jumps up and announces before being shushed by Charlie, who sits her in his lap to keep her still. This time the last note is met with enthusiastic applause.

"Let's see if anyone can guess the newest song in my repertoire," Mary says, giving Sarah a new sheet to hold before preparing for her last piece.

After only a few notes, as if she's on the *Name That Tune* game show, Jenny shouts, "It's 'O Christmas Tree'!" She begins to sing along and soon everyone joins in the chorus.

When Mary finishes, she gently places the instrument down in its case and makes a reluctant curtsy in response to the acceptance.

"That was amazing!" Vinny says, never having had the gumption to learn a musical instrument himself. "You learned all that just since I've been gone?" He turns her hands over, looking at them in a whole new light.

"I know a few easier songs, but these are the ones I had to practice for my Christmas performance at school," she says modestly.

"If you play anything like you just did, I'm sure your music teacher will be as proud of you as I am." Vinny kisses her skilled appendages in appreciation of their newly discovered talent. "Oh, I just remembered—I have a gift for you!" He entices her into the front room beside the large flower arrangement, and pulls out a jewelry box too large for a ring.

Mary opens the box to reveal— "How on earth . . . ?" Mary says. Inside is the amethyst necklace and bracelet set from the New Orleans jewelry store where Gayle found her engagement ring.

"A little bird told me . . . but it didn't give me your ring size," says Vinny, turning her around to place the necklace. He unhooks the chain with the kitten pendant currently around her neck, allowing it to fall to the floor. "It's more adult than this one," he adds.

Mary scrambles to the floor after the pendant. "I can't believe you did that!" she cries, inspecting the condition of the discarded kitten. It bounced at least once, leaving a tiny dent in the soft golden hide. "I will treasure this always."

Vinny displays the newer, more expensive necklace ready for application, still smiling. "Out with the old and in with the new."

She gives him a deeply wounded glance before offering up her neck again, more slowly this time, twirling her silken hair up out of the way until he has the new bauble securely fastened. She lets her twist unwind, gently cascading over her shoulders, and rushes to see her gift in the nearest mirror.

"I have an idea . . . gimme the bracelet," Mary says. She removes the kitten from its chain, delighted to see the pendant slide on to its new home. "This will do just fine."

Friday
November 28, 1958

Camille combs her skilled fingers through Mary's silky mane. "Are you sure that's what you want?"

"Don't you think it will make me look . . . sophisticated?" Mary wonders aloud to her reflection, folding her hair up to the length that they are discussing.

"I just want to make sure this is your idea. I wouldn't want you to regret this as soon as I start. Once I start cutting, there is no turning back," Camille says as a final warning. She ushers Mary to the shampoo bowl.

"I take full responsibility for the decision," Mary says, laying back into the basin.

Camille massages Mary's long hair into a frothy helmet, preparing to lop off nearly nine inches. To reduce the chance of mid-cut meltdown, Camille averts Mary's eyes from her under-construction reflection.

When the haircut and loosely curled style is complete, Camille steps back to check her work and gasps at the glamorous creature her hands have created. Mary examines her stylist's face, but she can't tell if it's a good or bad reaction. To reveal the transformation, Camille slowly spins the chair around so Mary can see herself anew.

Mary gasps. "I love it! It's exactly what I envisioned. Vinny will be so impressed when he comes to pick me up." Mary continues to admire her changed reflection, now looking more like her movie star doppelgänger than ever before.

"Where is he, anyway?" Camille asks, her expert fingers still fussing with her masterpiece. "He barely said hello before he left."

"He's going to pick out a new outfit for me to go with my new look."

"You shouldn't let him treat you like some paper doll," says Camille. She removes the cutting cloth and drops her tease comb in a tall glass jar of blue disinfectant.

"He doesn't treat me like a doll. I like that he cares enough to put forth the effort. He just wants me to be happy."

"And are you happy?"

"I guess so. He tries so hard."

"No . . . I mean with your hair," Camille says. She lightly dusts Mary's face and neck with a fluffy brush sprinkled with fragrant talc.

"Oh—yes, thoroughly! I just hope I can recreate this at home," she adds, cupping the fresh edges of her do.

Camille begins to explain the process of home maintenance when Vinny walks in with a camera and garment bag, stopping in his tracks, unable to move, when he sees Mary.

Mary catches his frozen reflection in the mirror.

"Well, what do you think?" she asks him, tossing her short bouncy coiffure.

He doesn't respond, just stands there with a vacant stare.

Her eyes dart to Camille and begin to fill with tears.

"Tell the girl something . . . before she starts crying, you idiot!" Camille knocks him in the shoulder with her hand.

The motion wakes him from his daze. "You . . ." He swallows hard and tries again. "You are so beautiful."

"Really? Don't say it if you don't mean it. I can let it grow back," Mary says. She stands up and pulls on her hair, as if that would make it longer.

"No . . . I think it's wonderful," Vinny says dreamily. "Go try these outfits on and see if I got the sizing right." He holds out the garment bag.

Timidly, she takes it from his hand and scurries off down the hall to a massage room to complete her transformation.

"What's your problem? I've never seen you act so . . . so . . . uncool," Camille says with irritation. She swats the hair off the hydraulic chair with a towel, then wipes the blades of her shears.

"That girl has me in knots. Sometimes, when I look at her, I can't breathe . . . How am I supposed to let her go?" Vinny says, falling into the styling chair and spinning to face Camille, pretending to take her picture so he can hide his face with the camera.

"Go where?" she asks, retouching her lipstick in the mirror.

"Go off to some fancy college, with fancy college boys. Look at her—she's a living doll with an outstanding brain. Don't you think she's smart enough to figure out I'm not good enough for her?" He drops the camera to his lap, defeated.

"She cares about *you*—not about the money or the stuff you tend to throw at people to impress them. Yeah, she's a smart cookie all right—smart enough to see past all your shenanigans, down to who you really are." Camille busies herself cleaning and realigning her arsenal of products and equipment cleverly designed for the art of visual subterfuge.

"That's what I'm afraid of," Vinny admits. "It might send her running in the other direction."

"You're not as bad as you think. Sometimes I see glimpses of a guy who just wants a normal existence," Camille says, sweeping up the discarded locks of Mary's hair.

Vinny moves out of Camille's way as she threatens his shiny shoes with the broom. "She does that to me. She makes me want to be a better person," he says.

"Then treat her like a queen and she may not want to leave." Camille hands him the dustpan and Vinny takes it obediently, not even wrinkling his nose.

"Her father has told me I can't have permission to marry her until I agree to let her go off to college," Vinny reveals, crouching low to scoop up the nest of hair, then dumping it into a nearby bin.

Camille steps on the broom edge to remove some clingy strands. "Marriage? Moving a little fast, aren't you? You hardly know this girl!"

"All I know is that ever since I met her, everything inside me is different. I can't explain it," Vinny says, ready with the dustpan for the hair remnants. "I can't lose her to some college boy who just wants to add her to a trophy collection. You and I know how the world works, but she doesn't. She hasn't been used and abused. I want to protect her from that." He knocks the dustpan around the inside of the waste bin and sets it on the floor.

"You can't put her in a tower somewhere. Why don't you just go *with* her? You can do whatever and live anywhere."

"And constantly be compared to those young know-it-alls? No thanks!" Vinny says, holding his contaminated hands out away from his body.

Camille grins at his helplessness. "You can't keep her from growing up. That's a fact." She turns on the faucet and holds the shampoo nozzle for him to rinse his hands.

Vinny flicks a few harmless drops of water in Camille's face before drying his hands on the towel she tosses at him. "All I want to do is love her—and hope she learns to care for me, too," he says.

"I do."

Mary's voice startles Vinny and sends him wondering how much she has heard.

"I do care for you," she repeats, crossing the room to hold his hand.

Vinny is thoroughly charmed by all her wonderfully placed curves, enhanced by the form-fitting outfit he pictured her wearing in many tawdry dreams while he was away.

"You look lovely . . . very sophisticated," Camille says proudly.

"That's my Maggie," Vinny says, lifting his camera to snap a memory of this moment, and winding for a second shot from another angle. "Gorgeous!"

Humorless, Camille gives them a look of displeasure before glancing down at her watch. "You two need to get going—I made lunch reservations for you at Commander's Palace."

From the moment she walks into the restaurant, Mary feels self-conscious, crossing the room with strangers eyeballing her, like maybe she has left the tags on her outfit. During a trip to the restroom to check things out in the mirror, a stately older woman donning pearls comments on how lovely she looks. Having the Southern Belle's seal of approval sets Mary's mind at ease for the time being.

"I hope you don't mind that I ordered for us already," Vinny says, his wild eyes following Mary's every curvy move. "I told the waiter that whatever the chef's special is would do fine."

"How adventurous! I think I'm becoming more comfortable with all this experimentation." She takes a sip of ice water.

"Really, now?" Vinny rotates his own sweaty glass with intrigue. "Then you might want to save some room for dessert," he adds with a soft glance, his mouth revealing a salacious grin that makes Mary's temperature spike.

Throughout the meal, Vinny devours her with his eyes—more so than he does his own food—making Mary self-conscious again.

"Would you like another sip of my iced tea?" Vinny asks.

"No, it tastes funky to me. Long Island just can't beat good-ole Lipton."

Vinny lets out a quiet chuckle. "Yeah, you can't beat a sun-brewed tea like you make at home," he says, lifting Mary's hand to his smoothly shaven cheek.

Her thumb slowly caresses his face; she withdraws shyly when the waiter disturbs them to take their dessert order.

Alone once again, Vinny moves closer, drawn to her with an undeniable pull, one that both intrigues and threatens his core. Vinny has confessed love and adoration to many girls before, with all the pretty words that open doors, legs, and hearts, yet the words always fell hollow and deceptive. But this girl stirs inside him something foreign, something . . . *real.* All he knows is that this feeling is at the opposite end of the spectrum—far from his familiar rage, disdain, and indifference.

Mary becomes uncomfortable beneath the spotlight of his shameless visual pursuit.

"Is this okay? You can tell me to back off if I'm suffocating you," Vinny says. "Am I doing this all wrong?"

"You are doing everything right," she reassures him.

The waiter delivers two large ceramic mugs with creamy heads sprinkled with nutmeg quickly dissipating atop warm sweet java. Vinny nods at the waiter. Mary takes a sip, licking a decadent film of yumminess from her top lip.

"Please continue . . ." Vinny urges. "You were about to tell me all the secrets behind your gorgeous eyes."

She brings the cup to her mouth again. "This is simply delicious."

"You're not getting off the hook that easy! I need to know what you're thinking, what you're feeling," he says, and bats his mug handle back and forth with his fingers.

Mary digs around for an appropriate expression of her gratitude. "I don't know how to explain to you how different I feel right now. I don't think it's just the hair and the clothes, it's . . . *everything*. I just can't believe how much you have done for me and my family in such a very short time."

"That's nothing! Wait until you see what I have planned for Christmas." He pushes what is left of his coffee in her direction.

She looks in his cup, seeing that some of the creamy whipped topping is still there. "Please take whatever money you were going to spend on me and spend it on my family. There really isn't anything that I need other than to see them happy."

"I can afford to buy nice things for everyone," Vinny affirms.

"I know you can, but I don't want you to. Make it small and reasonable. My father saves all year to be able to afford presents, and I don't want him to feel like he has to compete with you. Promise me you won't buy me anything—and you won't go overboard."

"I think you're being ridiculous, but I promise." Vinny waves to the waiter.

Mary touches the waiter's arm when he arrives promptly. "What is this coffee called again? I *love* it."

"It's Irish coffee. Shall I bring you another?"

"Just the check, please," Vinny says, smiling at Mary. He's eager to get a quick kiss-and-cuddle in while she is feeling generous, before he has to drive her back home to friends and family who await, eager to see her new look.

Sunday

November 30, 1958

"**P**lease . . . please . . . *please*," Mary says, carefully removing the first wrap of the rag set that she and Gayle placed in her freshly washed hair right after church, under Shirley's warm-hearted tutelage. Mary stands staring at her reflection in their bathroom mirror.

Gayle offers words of encouragement and an extra pair of hands from behind Mary's worried reflection. "Remember, she said we can use juice cans next time if the curls are too tight."

Once all the cloth rag strips have been removed, Mary struggles to separate the curls the way Camille had done so effortlessly just two days before. "It doesn't look as polished as it did with the rollers . . . but it's not awful, is it?"

"It's still cute," Gayle says, uncertain, pulling on the curls. "It's so short and bouncy . . . maybe it takes a few minutes to relax. It should be fine for school in the morning. I wish everyone could have seen you on Friday. You looked like you stepped out of a magazine." Gayle wets her hands and runs them through Mary's hair again. "There, that should help." She bites her lip, rocking in place.

Mary makes a skeptical squeak in the back of her throat, hoping her friend is right.

Monday
December 1, 1958

Bobby, **late for** a morning rendezvous with his dream girl, winds up right behind her in the school hall without even realizing it—until he catches a hint of her ambrosial scent.

"Mary?" he asks, afraid that he isn't dreaming. "What have you done?" He walks around to face her, hoping to find the rest of her hair.

"Vinny brought me to the city for a haircut. Don't you like it?" Mary shakes her head softly, the relaxed curls cooperating.

"Was this *his* idea? How could you let him change you like that?"

"*Change* me? He didn't change me. I changed my hair—everything else is still the same," Mary says defensively, looking to Gayle for support.

"You were perfect the way you were!" Bobby says, unwittingly initiating a fight.

"Big mistake, pal," Gayle says, parting to take a seat in her homeroom.

"And now I suppose I'm flawed!" Mary tells Bobby angrily. "I'm glad I didn't break it off with Vinny to go out with you. I had no idea you just wanted to date my hair—if I had known, I would have saved the scraps for you!"

"That's not what I meant at all! Don't get mad—let me explain."

"I'll see you at music practice, but only because I have to." And with that, Mary walks away in a huff.

"Don't say anything unless it's about music," Mary says. She brushes past Bobby through his front door, violin case in hand. Reaching the front parlor room, she removes the instrument from its case and says, all business, "I'm having trouble with some of the transitions."

"As am I," he growls under his breath.

She rosins the bow and glowers in his direction.

"I just want to apologize for upsetting you this morning," he says, looking at the floor, pity-fishing.

"Music. Stick to the music." She plucks at the violin strings.

"What happened? I thought you were going to break up with him."

"He has been nothing but good to me. I couldn't hurt him for no good reason."

"I'm not a good enough reason?" Bobby says dejectedly.

"You know what I mean—"

"No, I don't know what you mean. First you say you feel the same as me, but then you pull away as soon as he's back in the picture. I think you like yanking my chain. More than just your hair has changed, because just a week ago you said you would give me a chance. What happened?" Bobby's teeth are gritted, his eyes accusing. "Did he spoil you, Mary?"

"I swear only my hair has changed!" She covers her hair as if it is suddenly shameful.

"Maybe you're not the good girl I thought you were! Maybe this new you is who you were all along, and I was a fool not to see it," Bobby says, blinded by his anger.

"I *am* a good girl!" Mary screams, running out of the house, leaving his lesson, instrument, and insinuations behind her.

Long gone is the exhausted sun, leaving Mary chilled and without a compass. In shadows, she finds herself unable to sleep, wandering the house and reaching for answers, settling for the light switch over the sink in the kitchen—where she is confronted with a messy counter.

The counter was never left like this when it was my job!

Mary seethes, disgusted by things that never bothered her before: the scratched, aging sink; the faded, mundane paint color haphazardly applied to the walls; having to pick up other people's slack. She hates herself for believing things could be different without—

"Change!" she cries aloud, staring at her altered reflection made grotesque by the overhead light in the darkened kitchen window.

Friday
December 19, 1958

Backstage at the Terrebonne High School Christmas recital, a tall girl with thick glasses stands patiently in the wings next to Mrs. Tisdale, waiting for Mary to complete her debut violin performance in the group medley.

After the last note is played, Mary scurries behind the theater curtain ahead of the group, forgetting to bow. Mary hugs the tall, bespectacled college girl whom Bobby recruited to help her in his stead, respecting both her anger and her boundaries. "Thank you, Rose. You have been such a big help this week."

"You were great! You didn't really need my help—Bobby prepared you well." Rose hands her an envelope. "He told me to give you this when your performance was over."

"Her performance isn't over yet, Rose," Mrs. Tisdale whispers as the caroling choir performs onstage. "Her solo is right after this song."

Mary pops the envelope seal and finds a plain piece of stationery— no greeting, no signature, no embellishments, just Bobby's words:

I'll always be here for you if you ever change your mind. I won't give up the hope that one day we will make music together.

No longer mad and actually missing his presence now, Mary feels the full impact of Bobby's words. It knocks her off kilter, along with her growing anxiety about having to perform alone.

"You all right?" Mrs. Tisdale asks, steering her into a nearby chair.

"I think I may be having stage fright."

"You don't have to do this," Mrs. Tisdale says, holding Mary's shoulders. "I can cover for you. No one even has to know."

"I would know," Mary asserts. "I can do this. I have to do this."

"Only if you are sure." Mrs. Tisdale waits for Mary's response as the choir leaves the stage to loud applause.

Mary looks at the empty stage and slowly nods.

Mrs. Tisdale walks out to the microphone. "Next, I would like to introduce you to a student who has been part of some of the wonderful music we have already enjoyed here this evening. She is new to the violin and has shown quite a gift for the instrument. Please welcome Mary Poche back to the stage with her rendition of 'Greensleeves' to conclude tonight's performance."

A smattering of polite applause accompanies Mary to stand alone in the middle of the stage. She hopes that no one can tell how scared she is to be there, and is desperately thankful she does not have to speak. She struggles to breathe, heart racing as she puts the instrument to her chin.

From the first note, Mary makes the cheap violin resonate in near-perfect intonation, her fingers aptly finding the strings. She loses herself in the haunting piece, eyes closed, gracefully arching and swaying with each gliding stroke of the bow.

When "Greensleeves" is over, Mary opens her eyes and everything is still. Just when she fears she has failed in her attempt to entertain, the crowd roars its approval, as if they'd been under a spell that has just broken. Mary takes a deep curtsy, then leaves the stage, filled with the joy of slaying the fear that tried to hold her back from the experience.

Mrs. Tisdale embraces Mary backstage. "You were magnificent! I'm so happy you chose to perform tonight. I was afraid you wouldn't after I heard about the falling out. I've never seen Bobby so distraught."

Mary averts her gaze, setting the violin back into its case. "I didn't want to let anyone down—especially my family. They have been looking forward to this. Now that the concert is over, I'm going to give this violin back to Bobby. I'm done with it."

"That violin isn't done with you," Bobby says, appearing out of the blue. Mrs. Tisdale fades into the wings. Bobby looks haggard, as if he has been stranded in some remote locale without access to proper nutrition. "You can't give it back. It belongs with you."

"I don't understand," Mary says.

"Sometimes an instrument chooses its owner. That violin doesn't sing for me the way it does for you. I wasn't positive until I heard you play tonight—you make that student instrument sound like a Stradivarius. I won't take it back."

"Really, I can't—" Mary says, latching the case closed.

"Consider it an apology. A Christmas present . . . or whatever will make you feel better about accepting it."

"I don't know what to say," Mary admits.

"Just say thank you, and don't keep your fans waiting any longer," says Vinny. He is standing on the staired entrance to the stage, irritation hiding just behind the corners of his smile.

"Oh . . . yes . . . have you two met?" Mary asks, swallowing nervously.

"I don't believe I've had the pleasure," Bobby says stiffly. "You must be Vinny. She mentions you often." He wipes the perspiration on his pant leg before offering up his hand.

"Does she now?" Vinny casts a foxy sideways glance at Mary while meeting Bobby's hand with his own in a brief but firm grip of male evaluation. "It's nice to finally meet the person who helped her develop such a remarkable talent. What was your name again?"

"Bobby. Bobby Vicknair. I was just about to tell Mary that I won't be able to give her any further lessons. I'm going to crack down on my studies, so I won't have the extra time anymore."

"That's a real shame. She has become so good at it." Vinny puts his arm around Mary, squeezing her rigid frame.

"Yes, she has. That's why I have arranged for a student from Nicholls to take over for me. Rose has a broader skill set than mine, anyway."

Blindsided, Mary says, "I don't think I can continue taking lessons."

"Of course you can," Bobby asserts. "Rose agreed to keep everything the same as it was, except you will be meeting in Mrs. Tisdale's room twice a week—which will probably be more convenient," he adds matter-of-factly.

"I guess it's all settled then. Shall we go?" Vinny looks at Bobby. "Thanks for getting her this far. I hope she wasn't any trouble." Vinny wants to shake the scene, looking to make a break from the nearest door.

"No trouble at all. In fact, I wanted to ask that you take real good care of her for me," Bobby says, his voice strong, sounding more like a threat than a request.

"Excuse me?" Vinny replies. His hands close into loose, itchy fists, anticipating an ill-fated response.

Bobby chooses his next words with care. "She ... I ..." He hesitates and stops to clear his throat, then starts again, rising up to his full height. "If properly nurtured, Mary has the potential to dazzle the world and make people fall madly in love with her," he says with intensity, a profound, almost haunted look in his eyes.

"Are we still talking about music?" Vinny says with relief, his hands going slack. "Don't worry, pal. We got it from here." He slaps Bobby on the shoulder, then leads Mary down the corridor and out to the parking lot.

Outside, Norman looks tired and defeated, standing with the rest of the Poche family gathered behind their not-so-reliable family ride.

"What's wrong with the truck?" Mary asks Gayle. Her friend is standing in front of the old red Ford, fists resting on her hips. Chick is under the hood, leaning on the engine and pondering what could possibly be keeping it from starting.

"I'm waiting for Chick to move out of the way so I can fix it," Gayle says, losing patience. "For the last time, it's not the battery!"

Chick pulls himself upright from under the hood and wipes his hands with a large red handkerchief. "She's all yours, princess. Work your magic."

"Finally!" Exasperated, Gayle pushes Chick to the side and tells him, "Now get behind the wheel and be ready to give her the gas, honey."

She climbs up on the truck and immerses the top half of her body in the mouth of the ornery machine. She fiddles with something. Two grunts later, she lifts up, jumps down, and slaps the front fender twice, giving the universal go-ahead signal.

Chick turns the key, presses his foot down, and—to the surprise of everyone except Mary—the engine springs to life.

"Better get in while the gettin's good!" Chick shouts, hopping out of the clunker to allow the cheering family to board.

Sunday
December 21, 1958

"**S**tar light, star bright," Mary sighs. She is finally relaxed, sitting next to Vinny on the porch edge, swinging her dangling feet to and fro like windshield wipers.

"What a good weekend we had," Vinny says. "It's a shame I have to leave for work soon." He leans back on his elbows, watching the stars reveal themselves one by one.

"But it's almost Christmas," Mary whines softly. She twists, reaching to hug his middle.

"I won't need to go far. I'll be back by Christmas. I promise." Vinny kisses the top of Mary's worried head. He slips the ribbon from her hair and puts it in his pocket. "I just have a few loose ends to wrap up before the holiday starts."

Monday
December 22, 1958

"What do I always say, Gator?" asks Carlos. He looks at Vinny expectantly. The two men are in Carlos's more relaxed office space at 1225 Airline Highway in Metairie.

Vinny walks through a beam of early afternoon light and around the office, investigating the surroundings for dust, additions, and information, much like nosy kids and cops tend to do.

"Which one? The thing about the hands?" Vinny replies like a true smartass, just to rile his boss.

"That's right," Carlos growls. "Never let your left hand know what your right hand's doin.'"

"And which hand am I?" Vinny asks, stone-faced.

"Neither. You are my bite—my wrath," Carlos declares adamantly, rising from his chair, almost out of respect.

Vinny doesn't respond, remaining disinterested in his boss's lust for retribution.

"At this juncture, I just need to make a point," Carlos admits through gritted teeth. He sits back down. "I'm not going soft, you see," he declares sharply. With a pinched face, Carlos leans back in his chair, adjusting and readjusting his laced fingers in frustration.

"Of course not. I don't think anyone would ever accuse you of that. I just don't want you to end a lifelong friendship over a 'maybe.' Do you have proof?"

Carlos catapults forward in his chair. "My stacks are short! What more proof do I need?" He's red-faced, banging his right fist on the desktop once to add punctuation.

"Calm down. You look like a heart attack waiting to happen," Vinny says dryly. "This guy has been with you a really long time. Are you sure he is the hole in your pocket?" Vinny picks up a meaningless merchant award Carlos received from some useless committee given to flatter him into an alliance of some kind.

"Get the proof, if it makes you feel better. I just want the job done."

"Did you have anything in particular in mind?"

"I don't care what pond you go fishing in as long as he gets wet. Capiche?"

"Have I ever let you down before?" Vinny needles.

"And you never will," Carlos warns.

Tuesday
December 23, 1958

"Where's Christmas?" Vinny asks Joe, who sits like a sentry on a flimsy retired bar stool by the entrance door of the pool hall.

Joe's strangely blue, sightless eyes brighten at the sound of the familiar voice. "Probably taking a dump in the lot down the street," he replies. His dark, leathery skin creases in a broad smile. "That dog you give me thinks she queena da block."

"Ole Black Joe, what's new?" Vinny asks, grabbing his old friend's extended hand.

"Hey, Vin, man, not too much new round here. Same ole shit," says Joe.

"Never shit where you eat—right, old man?" Vinny pats him on the back.

"Yes, suh," Joe laughs. "You sure been missed round here. What's been keepin you away so long?" He takes an inquiring sniff. "A woman, by the smell of it. A nice one, I bet." He takes another sniff. "Maybe even *the* one."

"What makes you say that?" Vinny asks, as if the man's blindness allows him to smell another person's soul.

"She don't smell like the others. Not like dried-up flowers. More like a spring cloud." The old man smiles and lifts his sightless eyes toward the sky. "Like a angel."

"Get outta here! What you know 'bout clouds, old man?" Vinny sniffs his own sleeve. "Probably just hotel soap."

"If it is, can you bring me a bar? I haven't had that scent round me since I was yo age."

"Would you like to take a ride to go and meet her?"

"We been friends a mighty long time. Why you wanna play me like dat, Car-lean-o?" Joe shakes his head, the smile leaving his face. "I know why you here. I'm going ta meet an angel, all right . . . but it ain't yours."

To be continued . . .

The story unfolds, questions are answered,
and fate will not be denied in . . .

THE GATOR
LEAVES NOTHING BEHIND

PART II

. . . Now Available!

Join the fun for our next release, **order a signed print copy***, and*
extras at

www.boleybooks.com.

Acknowledgments

As you may know, it takes more than one person to make a book come to life. I wanted to take a moment to thank the people who helped make this dream come true.

First and foremost, I would like to thank my daughter, **Kirstie Rae Schieffler**, and **James Boley**, for changing my life, and all the other wonderful miracles they perform (like having the compassion and patience to put up with me on my toughest days).

I also owe a debt of gratitude to the following:

Nicole Eva Fraser—For her expert guidance and steadfast belief in me, for being a dear friend and my biggest fan. I lay all my first draft work at her feet. I honestly could not have finished this or any book without the support of this lovely lady.

Spencer Hamilton—For getting my jokes, for understanding the soul of my stories, for smacking some words out of my hands even when I resisted, helping me dig for that one right word, for polishing my story to a high shine, and for all the hand holding.

Toni Palermo—For her kindness and willingness to share her honesty as a reader when combing through my clumsy first draft.

K.M. Weiland—For her friendship, allowing me to annoy her often and tap into her infinite genius. I appreciate all of her contributions to the writing world, including her podcasts, Helping Writers Become Authors.

Angela Ackerman / Becca Puglisi—For their collection of thesauri aiding authors in their descriptive writing efforts and online resource, Writers Helping Writers.

Tanya Faisal—For listening and sharing her honesty.

Terri Killingsworth—For connecting with me and bonding over all things bookish.

James Lewis—For being a loyal friend to me and for not laughing too hard at my ideas all those years ago.

Damonza—For a gorgeous book cover I can be proud of and a special thanks to Chrissy.

Sandeep Likhar—For formatting all of my prose and making it an enjoyable reading experience.

All the clients of Koncepts Salon & Spa in Prairieville, LA—For all of their support, patience, encouragement, and kind words.

The members of Tribe Writers, SPS, and other Indie authors that have reached out to assist me—For not letting me struggle alone.

My peeps that interact with me on Facebook, especially those that assist with difficult research issues.

. . . and last but not least, I THANK YOU!

Readers breathe life into a writer's words, so I wanted to take this opportunity to thank you for your purchase and for the support in making my dream of being an author a reality.

I am an Independent Author, a tiny voice in a big world. If you enjoyed this book, please leave a review, and help me spread the experience to others.

The next book is out now, so DON'T MISS IT! Please follow my writing journey at www.boleybooks.com.

About the Author

The author **Kami Boley** was born in Houma, Louisiana, in 1973. At

a young age, she discovered a deep passion for books and writing. As a young adult, she put that dream on hold to devote her time and energy to working as a cosmetologist so she could provide for a new love in her life, her daughter, Kirstie. Now that Kirstie is grown, Kami is ready to share her stories. Some stories will be for children, some will be for adults—but as she creates them, you will be able to find them all at www.boleybooks.com.